W9-AFN-584

HELPLESS

"Murphy, listen to me," Tom pleaded. "I can't leave Jill alone. She's not safe. I'm being set up. Somebody wants me out of the picture so they can get to Jill. I'm telling you, you've got to find Kip Lange. He's doing this to get me out of the way. Please! You're making a big mistake here."

Murphy crouched low so that Tom could see his face through the cruiser's open rear door.

"No, Tom," Murphy said. "Remember what I told you? Guys like you always screw up. The only mistake made here was you thinking you'd get away with it."

Tom closed his eyes and thought of Jill. In his mind, he saw her not as the teenager she was, but as the little girl she used to be. He remembered her in jeans and a plaid cowboy shirt. Her long hair tied in pigtails. A fourth grader with two missing teeth. Face full of freckles. Her knee skinned up badly and her bike a bent wreckage. Tears rolling down her cheeks. Back then, he could make it all better. He had cleaned up the cut. Put the bandage on it. Kissed the knee. Now he couldn't do anything to help her.

He couldn't protect her anymore.

He was helpless. . . .

Books by Daniel Palmer

DELIRIOUS

HELPLESS

STOLEN

DESPERATE

CONSTANT FEAR

FORGIVE ME

Published by Kensington Publishing Corp.

HELPLESS

DANIEL PALMER

PINNACLE BOOKS
Kensington Publishing Corp.
www.kensingtonbooks.com

PINNACLE BOOKS are published by

Kensington Publishing Corp.
119 West 40th Street
New York, NY 10018

Copyright © 2012 Daniel Palmer

All rights reserved. No part of this book may be reproduced in any form or by any means without the prior written consent of the publisher, excepting brief quotes used in reviews.

If you purchased this book without a cover, you should be aware that this book is stolen property. It was reported as "unsold and destroyed" to the publisher, and neither the author nor the publisher has received any payment for this "stripped book."

All Kensington titles, imprints, and distributed lines are available at special quantity discounts for bulk purchases for sales promotions, premiums, fund-raising, educational, or institutional use. Special book excerpts or customized printings can also be created to fit specific needs. For details, write or phone the office of the Kensington sales manager: Kensington Publishing Corp., 119 West 40th Street, New York, NY 10018, attn: Sales Department; phone 1-800-221-2647.

This book is a work of fiction. Names, characters, businesses, organizations, places, events, and incidents either are the product of the author's imagination or are used fictitiously. Any resemblance to actual persons, living or dead, events, or locales is entirely coincidental.

PINNACLE BOOKS and the Pinnacle logo are Reg. U.S. Pat. & TM Off.

ISBN-13: 978-0-7860-4458-0
ISBN-10: 0-7860-4458-6

First Kensington hardcover printing: February 2012
First Pinnacle mass market printing: April 2013

10 9 8 7 6 5 4 3 2

Printed in the United States of America

For Michael Palmer
Father, friend, and paragon.

CHAPTER 1

Shilo, New Hampshire, sometime in March

L ove can make you do surprising things. Lindsey
Wells flashed on that thought as she unbuttoned her
black sweater. Her racing heart knew she was crossing a
line she'd never crossed before. The hairs of her arms
stood on end, as though they, too, were anxious about
this unfamiliar but exciting experience. *Keep going,*
Lindsey urged herself. She smiled and released yet another button from its hole. There wasn't any little voice
inside her head screaming "No" or "Don't." So Lindsey
continued—undeterred, unashamed, and never in her fifteen years feeling more turned on.

Lindsey, known for her cheerfulness, enviable GPA,
and deft tackling skills on the soccer field, tilted her head
to the right, pinning her cell phone between her shoulder
blade and ear. Through the phone's compact receiver, Lindsey listened to Tanner Farnsworth's hard breathing. Her
body tingled with these strange feelings. She knew what
she was doing was a little bit crazy. On occasion, her
mind would flash a warning that something wasn't right
with this. Even so, she ignored those nagging worries be-

cause that was part of the fun. It was what made her feel so exhilarated.

"Tell me what you're doing now," Tanner whispered in her ear.

His voice. God, his voice alone was amazing. Deep timbred, not quite yet a man's, but not too far off, either. His voice resonated with confidence, and he made her feel desirable, beautiful even. The last time Lindsey had felt this beautiful, she was a nine-year-old girl, competing in local beauty pageants. Those events ended quickly as her body changed and her mother lost interest in shuttling her daughter from one losing effort to another. Soccer was what gave Lindsey confidence in her physical abilities, but it was Tanner who made her feel confident about her looks.

Lindsey unhinged the front clasp of her bra, brushing her fingers against the heart pendant of a gold necklace (or gold-plated, as Jill Hawkins joked) that Tanner had given her. That necklace made her somebody's girlfriend for the very first time. *Not just somebody, though,* Lindsey thought—Tanner Farnsworth, whose Taylor Lautner good looks, amazing body, and really sweet nature inspired jealous fits from her friends and teammates.

Normally, footballers and soccer players didn't mix at Shilo High School. Soccer players were accurately typecast as the studious ones. Football jocks ate their meals in C house like rowdy animals, while soccer players enjoyed a cerebral lunch in the F house cafeteria. Soccer players didn't take drugs, and most didn't even drink. Sandy Wellford, who'd had her stomach pumped clean of Jägermeister before getting booted off the team, inspired most players to abstain. The going rumor (which really wasn't a rumor, because Tanner told her it was true) had half the football team shooting steroids or popping some sort of speed. But not Tanner. Her boyfriend (*God, her boy-friend!*) didn't do any of that stuff.

Lindsey's body pulsed with energy. She felt ready to explode from the most scandalous act of her young life. Talking on the phone. Getting undressed. Sharing the details with him. It felt so wrong. It felt sexy. She felt powerful.

"Okay, my sweater is off," Lindsey cooed.

"Oh, you're killing me, Lin. Just killin' me."

She loved it when he called her Lin. It was just so sweet, the way he said it.

"Well, you asked for it."

"Yeah, but I didn't think you'd actually do it. I wanna see."

"What? Come over?" Lindsey cringed, fearing she sounded more panicked than she'd intended. Of course she wanted to see Tanner. She wanted to see him more than anything. But Lindsey was still a virgin, and Tanner wasn't. It had been a source of tension between the two early on, until Tanner assured her it was no big deal. He agreed to a compromise. Kissing. Touching. All fine. Now, add dirty talk to the mix. But *the deed?* No, it wasn't time for that yet. Maybe after the prom. Prom was only a few weeks away. If he could hold on until prom, then just maybe . . .

"Look, Lin, I think I should go."

No! she wanted to scream. *Don't hang up. Not yet.* Her mind raced with all sorts of imagined reasons for his ending the call with such abruptness. "He's going to dump me" topped her growing list of fears. She felt the pain of her heartbreak as though it had actually happened, and bit her lower lip to keep from saying too much.

"Why do you have to go?" Lindsey asked. Her voice had the force of a whisper.

"I don't know. I'm kind of bored, and you're just getting me frustrated."

Another wave of panic swept through her. *Oh no, he said the "B" word.* "I don't want you to hang up." Lindsey put her sweater back on but left the front open.

"Well, I thought this would be fun, but it's sort of lame. I mean, I can't see you. What's the point?"

Lindsey again pinned the cell phone between her shoulder and ear as she tied her straight brown hair back into its usual ponytail. The heat of the moment had vanished, and she regretted what she'd already done.

"Why do you have to see?"

"Because you're too sexy, that's why."

"My mom might come home."

That was a lie. Lindsey's mother had gone down the street to Ali's house, probably commiserating, again with too much wine, about their recent divorces. Mother would be home sometime after midnight, and snoring in her lonely drunken stupor a few minutes after that. And her dad had moved too far away to drop by unexpectedly.

"Like I said, it's no biggie. But I gotta run."

"I don't want you to go." *You're going to break up with me. I know you are.* Lindsey thought that but didn't voice it.

"Well, show me something to keep me sticking round."

"What do you mean?"

"You got a new phone for your birthday. I got one, too. Take a picture and send it to me. Like I said, I wanna see."

Lindsey's face reddened. She didn't debate him, though. Instead, while sitting centered on the green peace sign embroidered into her duvet, with her legs dangling over the side of her twin bed, Lindsey arched her back and took a picture of herself. Her bra was unhinged, though her sweater concealed her breasts. Still, she let the sweater hang open seductively. The top of her head got cut off in the picture, but at least she managed a smile. *He's going to think I'm ugly. He'll dump me before prom for sure now.* Even so, she text messaged him the picture.

Seconds were all it took for Tanner to get her digital snapshot, open it, and respond.

"You're amazing. I can't believe how hot you look, Lin. Forget Megan Fox. You've got the bod. I want more. I think I'm falling in love."

For Tanner to offer up a comparison to Megan Fox, the latest Hollywood "it" girl, gave Lindsey a fresh jolt of confidence. Not to mention, he said the "L" word (way better than the "B" word), and she could tell he meant it.

"You liked it?" Her voice still lacked certainty.

"More."

Lindsey knew what "more" really meant. *There's no way he'll break up with me now,* she thought. *Not when he sees this.* The sweater came off. One carefully placed arm across her chest to conceal her breasts.

Sent.

Received.

"Nice. How about more?"

"I don't think so, Tanner."

"No worries. Look, I'll call you tomorrow, if I can."

If! He said "if."

"Hold on," Lindsey said.

She kept her arm on the bed in the next picture. *Nothing left to the imagination this time,* she thought after sending it.

"Nice," Tanner said.

Lindsey frowned. He sounded less enthused. *My chest is too flat,* she lamented. She knew that her best features were her legs, long and toned, and her butt. She slipped out of her jeans. Next, off came her underwear. She wanted there to be no doubt. Lindsey stood in front of her full-length mirror. She turned her body sideways so Tanner would be able to see enough, but not everything.

Click.

Sent.

"Wow! Wow. I mean, whoa. You're so freakin' hot. Dammit, Lin. That's what I'm talking about. I'm totally in love with you. Do you know that? I'm the luckiest guy. Give me more!"

"Tanner, I'm not sure—"

"Prom's coming up," Tanner said.

She understood perfectly well his implied threat. It could be next week, or even prom day, that Tanner would suddenly decide not to go. But she wasn't going to let that happen. Lindsey went back over to her bed, lay down on it, and closed her eyes. With one hand she caressed her body; with the other she held the camera so that Tanner would see everything going on. Everything. Her breathing grew shallower. Her heart beat faster. She fantasized about kissing Tanner in the back of the limo. Pressing her body against his. She touched herself as she thought of him.

She sent him more pictures but deleted the ones she didn't like.

"This is for you, Tanner. Just you."

"No doubt. Can I tell you something?"

"Yes."

Lindsey slid under the duvet, hiding her nakedness from herself.

"This has been the most amazing night of my life."

"Really?"

"Really."

"Those pictures. Promise me you'll never show them to anybody. I'd die if you did. Promise me, Tanner."

"I promise, Lin. I promise."

CHAPTER 2

Shilo, New Hampshire, late August

"I've got ball!"

Jill Hawkins closed in to apply pressure on her opponent. It didn't matter that Jill played striker for the Shilo Wildcats girls' varsity soccer team. Being the player closest to the ball goal side made Jill her team's first defender. Jill's teammates, each of whom wore the same colored orange mesh practice jersey, sprinted into position to get compact behind the ball. The girls moved as a team and kept their opponent from pressing the ball forward.

Jill covered her gap at precisely the right time, and Lindsey Wells couldn't play the angled ball she had wanted. Lindsey faked left, but Jill wasn't fooled. Jill made a perfectly timed tackle and was dribbling the ball downfield before Lindsey even knew what had happened.

"That's how you attack the ball!" Jill's father, the girls' varsity soccer coach for the past ten years, shouted as he followed his daughter's progress down the sidelines. "Well played, Jill! Well played!"

Jill Hawkins lifted her head and flashed her father a bright smile. Tom stopped running and choked back his emotions. An outsider wouldn't have noticed anything unusual in the exchange between father and daughter. But Tom knew not to read too much into Jill's beaming face. Despite the warmth of her expression, he suspected their frigid relationship was no closer to thawing.

Battles.

Tom Hawkins understood from personal experience that soccer was a game of battles. He had been an all-American soccer player for the Shilo Wildcats boys' varsity soccer team. He also understood that soccer was a lot like life. Both were just a series of battles, each constrained by a time limit—a whistle to end one, and death the other.

At forty-three, despite a full head of dark hair, blue eyes that still reminded people of a husky, the same waist size from high school, and a muscular physique visible even through his Windbreaker, Tom Hawkins had essentially arrived at the halftime of his life. He had spent the last ten years teaching the girls to battle until the final whistle blew. He would do the same. It was why Tom had fought so hard to win back his daughter.

Tom blew his coach's whistle to signal it was time to practice set pieces. In soccer, corner kicks often decided who got the championship trophy. Coaches picked the drills, but it was the captains who ran them. Team captains Chloe Adamson and Megan McAndrews got the girls into action.

"Hey, orange, ball does not get past us!" Hawkins demanded of the girls with the pinnies on.

"Up, out, and far!" somebody yelled.

The girl's kick came at Tom low to the ground and did not travel nearly far enough.

"Nice try, Becky!" Lindsey Wells exclaimed.

"No, Lindsey," Tom scolded her. "It's not a nice try! That stunk, and you know it."

Tom's expression darkened. The girls nearest to him looked at the ground and kicked at the dirt with the toes of their cleats. They understood perfectly well why their coach had snapped at Lindsey the way he did. They had been taught to pound their teammates on the pitch. Outwork every player on the field. There were rules against Bobby Talk (talking about boys). Phrases like "Nice try" and "I'm sorry" were treated with the same disdain as curse words.

Tom had coached both boys and girls at the high school level, so he knew the inherent difference in their style of play. His first priority as coach for the Shilo girls' squad was not to accept those differences, but to change them. He began his coaching tenure by asking the girls as a group, "Why are you here?" Not a single player volunteered an answer. Tom prodded until at last one shaky hand rose and a girl meekly replied, "Because I have good foot skills." Just as Tom had expected, the other girls soon chimed in and offered supporting evidence of their teammate's brave claim.

"No, you have great foot skills!" one said, before then offering several examples.

Boys got their confidence from bravado. Girls seemed to get it from their teammates. Good, because it showed a respect for the team. Bad, because they tended to be less selfish players. They'd look to pass before they'd look to shoot.

"Play like you're six years old again," Tom often instructed. "Remember? My ball! Mine!"

Transforming his players into instinctive, selfish, smart winners depended on his ability to enhance their individual resourcefulness, while teaching them how to work effectively as a team. He applied many of the techniques he'd learned from his time with the Naval Special Warfare

Command. Tom often quoted one of his favorite SOCOM mottos: "Alone I am lethal. As a team I dominate."

Tom might have gone on to become a collegiate all-American soccer player if not for the career day event organized by the faculty of Shilo High School. At that event, a young Tom Hawkins had stopped by a metal folding table manned by a navy recruiter. A small television set on that table played a looped video depicting the physical demands and mental fortitude required to become a Navy SEAL. Two minutes into the three-minute production, Tom was hooked.

The recruiter never gave Tom the hard sell. He'd caught the excitement exploding like fireworks in Tom's eyes. Tom enlisted in the navy the day after he had his diploma in hand. College could wait, he explained to his somewhat surprised parents, but the youthful endurance and strength required to become a Navy SEAL could not.

Tom wasn't the only Shilo youth to forgo college for military service. Roland Boyd, Tom's childhood best friend and fellow soccer teammate, followed Tom's lead and enlisted on the very same day. While Tom had surprised his parents by deciding to serve his country, Boyd had enlisted to spite his father's wishes. But motivation didn't matter for shit once you signed on the dotted line. Tom was dead set on the navy, and Roland, who was somewhat prone to seasickness, decided to enlist in the army, same as their other military-bound classmate, Kelly Kavanagh.

Kelly and Tom had dated for most of their senior year in high school. Tom's decision to enlist might have influenced Kelly's choice as well, but not because she wanted to keep their relationship going. Unlike Roland, Kelly didn't come from money and claimed she needed the promised college financial assistance when she got out. Tom hadn't spoken with Kelly since graduation and assumed she'd followed her "go to college" plans. He certainly hadn't expected to see Kelly again when he arrived at a military base in Germany for training exercises with his SEAL platoon. He had no idea she'd re-upped for another six years with the army. It was a chance encounter for the two former sweethearts that altered both their lives profoundly and forever.

Their reunion in Germany might have been the first time Tom had laid eyes on Kelly since graduation, but his attraction to her had never waned. Less than a year after rekindling their romance, Kelly got her requested discharge, gave birth to a daughter, married the baby girl's father, and changed her last name to Hawkins.

The marriage lasted only six years.

The divorce turned uglier than any battle Tom ever fought with a gun.

Unable to get what she had wanted from Tom, Kelly took every opportunity to poison the father-daughter relationship and drive a permanent wedge between them. Kelly believed Tom would eventually cave in to her demands—even if it took years to accomplish her goal. From the age of six on, much of what Jill learned about her father were the lies her mother told.

"Is it true, Daddy?" Jill had cried into the phone one evening from her home in Shilo. "Did you beg Mommy to have an abortion?"

Jill took in every falsehood Kelly drummed up about him and believed it to be true. Every lie and slanderous insult became Jill's reality. On occasion, Jill would confront Tom about these stories.

"Did you do drugs?"

"No."

"Did you ever hit me?"

"No."

"Did you ever beat Mommy?"

"Never."

Tom could fend off whatever Jill sent his way. How successfully? Well, he couldn't know that for certain. But at least Jill cared enough to keep the questions coming. She had asked Tom, on many occasions, why her mother would say such terrible things about him if they weren't true.

"Sometimes people just do and say hurtful things because they're angry," Tom would often say.

Unable to reveal to Jill the secret of her parents' acrimony, Tom was forced to counterstrike Kelly's bitter campaign to discredit him in other ways. After the divorce, he moved to Westbrook, much farther north, but also affordable given his hefty alimony and child support payments. He kept his guidance counselor job with Shilo High School, despite offers for better-paying gigs with substantially shorter commutes. He wanted to maintain close ties with Shilo, where he had bought a house, and where Kelly decided to remain after the divorce. He did this to stay as connected as possible to Jill. He also wrote to Jill, letters and cards, almost every week. Tom never missed an opportunity to acknowledge a birthday, graduation, recital, or other milestone event in Jill's life. He had kept those letters coming, though they always went unanswered. In each he encouraged Jill to call him whenever she wanted, or needed. He reminded her that he'd be there for her—always.

His choice to invest the extra hours required to run a championship-caliber girls' soccer program was made with the hope that he'd one day get the chance to coach his daughter, convinced the experience would strengthen their tenuous bond. When Jill shunned soccer for field hockey her freshman year, the standout middle school soccer star had sent him a very clear message: *I won't play for the Wildcats if my father is the coach.* When Jill had shown up unexpectedly for soccer tryouts the summer before her sophomore year, Tom had turned his head so that other girls wouldn't see him tear up.

Tom couldn't explain his daughter's sudden change of heart. Perhaps she had become curious enough about him to try out for the team against her mother's well-verbalized wishes. Whatever Jill's reasoning, coaching his daughter proved to be a healing step forward, but not the leap Tom hoped it would be. Jill was now heading into her junior year, but to Tom's continued disappointment, their relationship still remained mostly stuck in the past.

Battles.

With the Wildcats' first game of the new season only two weeks away, time to prepare was in short supply. There were seventeen ponytails on the field, each chatting constantly with the ball in play. Tom listened to them talk. They sounded ready to win.

"Organize! Get to where the ball is going!"

"Crash the net!"

Tom blew his whistle and signaled the start of the day's last drill. The summer sun stood high in the sky as the captains worked quickly to get the players into position.

A few girls had turned their attention elsewhere, stopping to watch a police car as it turned onto the road beside the practice field. Tom looked too. The cruiser's lights were flashing, but the siren was silent. A pit formed in Tom's stomach.

Even after all these years, police cars still gave Tom a sinking feeling.

They know what I did, he'd think.

They're coming for me.

The secret is out.

CHAPTER 3

The black-and-white cruiser jumped the curb and pulled to an abrupt stop. To keep the narrow road clear, two of the cruiser's wheels were parked up on the sidewalk. Strobe lights and the late-day sun let Tom see only shadow. He could not make out the face of the single police officer seated inside the vehicle. Tom knew the police weren't here for what he feared most. They would have sent a lot more police cars. But his relief was fleeting.

Weighing at least 250 pounds and standing an imposing six feet six, Sergeant Brendan Murphy, dressed in a sports jacket and tie, made a graceless exit from his cruiser. Tom tried to keep his encounters with Murphy to a minimum. Back in the day, Tom's numerous accomplishments had earned him many admirers and one very vocal detractor: the standout high school linebacker, Brendan Murphy. Murphy the Mountain, who thought all soccer players were pussies. The Beast of the East, who couldn't stand that Tom's sports accomplishments eclipsed his own. The only kid who knew in grammar school that he'd grow up to be a cop on the Shilo PD, just like his old man.

The girls stopped moving simultaneously and watched

as Murphy approached the practice field. Murphy's gait often mimicked that of a horseless cowboy, but today he didn't have his usual swagger. Tom and Murphy crossed paths only occasionally—town meetings or student assemblies. Murphy had never looked so burdened.

"Captains, get the drill going!" Tom instructed. He glanced at assistant coach Vern Kalinowski, the middle-aged father of Flo and Irena, twins who were also the team's best defenders. Vern whistled using two fingers, a skill Tom lacked (to his own continued frustration), and got the girls moving again.

"Tom, we need to talk," Murphy said, without extending his hand.

"What's going on?" Tom asked. A tightness built in his chest. He read faces the way psychics purportedly could read minds.

Murphy lowered his mirrored shades until they rested on the bridge of his nose, and looked around until certain that he and Tom were out of earshot.

"There's no easy way to say this," he began, "so I'm just going to come out and say it."

Tom swallowed hard as he nodded. His stomach was in knots.

"Kelly's dead," Murphy said. "And we have reason to believe that her death wasn't entirely accidental."

The blue sky above Tom's head began to spin in quickening cycles. He felt his knees go slack, and his stomach sank. Tom looked behind him at Jill as she made a finely executed slide tackle. The pain he knew she'd soon be experiencing almost kept him from breathing.

Murphy took Tom by the arm and walked him over to the police cruiser.

"When? How?" Tom heard his own words as though they came from a great distance away. He kept himself upright by resting both his hands on the hood of Murphy's cruiser and battled back a jet of bile.

"A jogger found her in the ravine behind her house," Murphy said. "At first it looked like she fell and hit her head on a rock. But we found signs of struggle back in the house, and the ME noticed a bruise on her face that he believes was the result of blunt force trauma by a fist, not a rock. We think she may have walked in on a robbery."

"My . . . God . . . Jill."

"Tom, I've got a crisis counselor on her way over here right now," Murphy said. "We called Cathleen Wells, too. It's our understanding that Jill is best friends with Cathleen's daughter, Lindsey."

"Yes. Yes, that's right. Good," Tom said, his voice nothing but a distant echo in his ears.

"Is there anybody else you want me to call? Family? Neighbors? Clergy?"

Tom shook his head. "No. Not right now."

"I'm going to need someone to go the medical examiner's office to make the official identification of the body. Do you think Jill will want to go?"

Tom shook his head again. "No. No, I can't imagine she'll be able to handle that right now. But I'll ask her. Regardless, I'll go after I get Jill settled."

"You sure you want to break the news to Jill yourself? We can help there, too, if you need."

Tom's body had gone numb. He turned again and watched as Jill made a rocket of a shot on goal. His thoughts kept spinning like the ball she had kicked, but they were all focused on her.

My poor baby girl . . . I'm so sorry. . . . This is going to be so hard on you. . . . This is so unfair. . . .

Tom bit at his bottom lip. He said, "No, I'll tell her. She should hear it from her father."

"Okay. And, Tom . . ." Murphy's words brought Tom back into focus. "I'm going to want to speak with you down at the station," he said.

"What about?" Tom asked. He hoped his expression didn't betray his sudden concern. Had they found something inside Kelly's house? he wondered. *Something that would incriminate me?*

He studied Murphy and thought he picked up on something. Perhaps it was the way Murphy had shifted his eyes. Murphy's unease heightened Tom's concern.

"I need to start compiling some background information," Murphy said. "We're going to try and re-create as much of Kelly's past few days as possible. Nothing to be concerned about."

He doesn't know, Tom decided. *No, he'd be acting differently toward me if he suspected.*

But that didn't completely assuage Tom's worry. As a Navy SEAL, Tom had studied kinesics—the interpretation of body language, facial expressions and gestures. The skill was often used in the theater to ferret out friend from foe. With his folded arms, furrowed brow, and tightly pressed lips, Murphy conveyed that this was more than just a formality without his having to say it.

"You want to speak with me about Kelly's murder?" Tom asked.

"Her death hasn't been ruled a homicide—yet. It's really nothing. Routine type questions," Murphy said. "But just so you're not blindsided, I am going to want to know where you've been for the last twenty-four hours."

Tom did a double take. "Are you saying you want my alibi?" he asked, with evident irritation.

"I'm just saying that we need to talk."

Tom turned away.

He began his slow walk back to the practice field. Jill

saw him coming and must have sensed that something was wrong, because her arms fell limply to her sides. Tom's slow walk broke into a trot, then into a run. When he got to her, Tom put his arm around Jill and led her away from her teammates. He could feel her tiny body begin to shake.

"Jill, honey," Tom said, fighting to temper the panic swelling inside him. "I'm afraid I've just been given some very horrible news. Baby, I need you to brace yourself."

"What's wrong?" Jill asked, her dark, doelike eyes wide and fear filled. "What's going on?"

Tom broke from his daughter's gaze, readying himself. He caught a glimpse of Murphy eyeing him in the distance. Tom couldn't see Murphy's face clearly enough to read his expression, but the relaxed way Murphy sat on his police car, hands resting behind him on the hood, wasn't befitting a man hunting a killer.

He looked more like a guy who'd already found his prime suspect.

CHAPTER 4

Tom sat in the center of a neatly ordered row of black plastic chairs tucked inside the lobby of Shilo's single-story police station. He gazed absently through the Plexiglas window on the opposite wall at the dispatcher fielding a call. His body and mind both felt numb. He was here only to get this meeting over with, so that he could return his full attention to where it belonged—to Jill and her needs. The road she had to travel was going to be a difficult one, but Tom intended to be by her side every step of the way.

A loud buzzer sounded to Tom's right, drawing his attention. He saw Brendan Murphy, dressed in a jacket and tie, emerge from behind a large metal door.

"Thanks for coming down," Murphy said, his tone congenial enough. "Our interview room is this way."

Tom followed Murphy down a well-lit corridor with blue painted walls. Murphy passed one door marked BOOK-ING ROOM, and came to a stop in front of another closed door, this one labeled MEETING ROOM in stenciled black lettering. Murphy opened that door and went in.

Inside, Tom found a heavily scuffed table with a tape recorder and microphone. The table basically divided the closet-sized room in half. The concrete walls were bare, except for one that had a two-way glass window about the size of a fifty-gallon fish tank.

Tom took a seat on the red plastic chair facing the door. He was already thinking about leaving. Murphy sat opposite Tom and rested his interlocked fingers on the table. Tom disliked the coldness in Murphy's eyes.

"So," Murphy said as he pressed RECORD on the tape machine, "I'm sure you've heard of your Miranda rights."

"I have," said Tom.

"Well, I'm going to read those to you now," Murphy said. "It's the law, and this way we can keep the interview on file."

Tom looked stunned, but he had known this was coming. "You make it sound like you're arresting me."

Murphy laughed. "No. Just need to get the formality out of the way. But if you do become a suspect at a point in time, I can use this as evidence."

"That's very reassuring," Tom said.

"So, you know you have the right to remain silent and that anything you say can be used against you in a court of law. You have the right to have an attorney present now and during any future questioning."

Tom made sure Murphy could see his displeasure. "Sure. I give up the right."

"Good. Good. Thanks. Sorry about that. I know it's awkward."

"Yeah. It sort of is."

"So, tell me, how's Jill?"

The mere mention of Jill made Tom ache. He had pleaded with her to come and stay with him in West-brook, but Jill insisted that wouldn't be an option.

"I need to be with people who really know me and un-derstand me," she had said to him through her tears.

"She's doing as well as can be expected," Tom said to Murphy. "Right now she's staying with Cathleen Wells and Lindsey. They've put her up in the guest room. A doctor from the clinic came by to check on her, and he gave Jill a sedative to help her sleep. She was sleeping when I left there to come here."

"Were you able to make it over to the medical examiner's office to make the official identification?" Murphy asked.

"Yeah. That's all taken care of," Tom said, though his voice didn't reveal how much the experience had shaken him. He'd seen his fair share of dead bodies as a SEAL, but nothing could have prepared him for seeing the mother of his daughter lying lifeless on a steel table. His high school sweetheart dead, a thin green sheet hiding her nakedness.

Tom had seen the two wounds to her head: the one to her right temple, where police believed she had hit a rock, and the other, more suspicious one on the left side, where something else had struck her. Kelly's once lustrous blond hair was matted down and dark. Her lips were a disturbing shade of blue. The skin didn't look like it fit her bones anymore.

Death never looked pretty.

Murphy opened the file in front of him. "Well then," he began, "why don't we start with the last time you saw Kelly?"

Tom didn't have to think hard to answer that one. He almost never saw Kelly. She never came to any of Jill's practices or games and made it quite clear to his daughter that she stayed away intentionally to avoid seeing Tom.

"Two weeks ago," Tom said. "At Johnny Rockets."

"The place on one-forty?"

"Yeah. That's the place."

"What were you doing there?"

"Having my twice-a-month dinner with Jill. Kelly would drive her there, drop her off, and then come back forty minutes later to pick her up."

"Does Jill ever go to your place in Westbrook?" Murphy didn't bother referring to any notes. Troubling, thought Tom, that he was so well versed about his life.

"She hasn't been over to my house in about a year. There was some tension around that."

"Tension?"

"Jill didn't want to spend every other weekend with me, which was my court-ordered visitation right."

"You two don't get along?"

"I thought this was about Kelly," said Tom.

"Just compiling a complete picture here."

"It was interfering with her social life and extracurricular activities," Tom explained. "So I made a compromise, and we agreed to once-a-month sleepovers and twice-a-month dinners. That had worked fine up until last year. Kids get older. They get busier. Divorce sucks. What can I say?"

"Not married myself," Murphy said, "but I can imagine."

Not this you can't, Tom thought, but he didn't feel like going into Kelly's long-running campaign to discredit him in his daughter's eyes.

"So, the last time you saw Kelly was two weeks ago?"

"That's right."

"Do you know when Jill saw her last?"

"I'm guessing this morning," Tom said. "Jill's got a job this summer working at Lull Farm. She's there Monday through Friday, eight until four. Then she comes to soccer practice after that."

"First game of the season is coming up soon, huh?"

"Two weeks from today."

"Going for what? Your third state title in a row?"

"Fourth," Tom said. "But I don't think now is an appropriate time to be talking sports."

"No, of course not," Murphy agreed. "Perhaps it would be more appropriate to discuss some of the conversations I've had with Kelly's neighbors. They were pretty quick to point out to me that you two were not on the friendliest of terms."

Why were you talking about me at all? Tom wondered. "We had our differences."

"Would you characterize your relationship as hostile?"

"Are you trying to imply that I had something to do with Kelly's murder?"

"I'm not implying anything, Tom," Murphy said. "Just asking questions. But, since you've brought it up, where were you before soccer practice today?"

"I was home. Working on my deck."

"Anybody with you? Anybody who could verify your whereabouts?"

"No. I was alone."

"Girlfriend? Wife?"

"No to both."

"And you say you were at home all day?"

"No," Tom said. "I went to Home Depot for some supplies. I ran out of nails."

"Do you have a receipt?"

Tom didn't bother looking through his wallet. He never saved them. "No."

"How'd you pay?"

"Cash," Tom said.

Too bad for you, said Murphy's face. "Do you remember what you were wearing?"

"T-shirt and my Red Sox hat."

"Time?"

"Must have been around three in the afternoon. I drove right to practice from there."

"About how far a drive is it to that Home Depot, would you say? From your place first, and then from Home Depot to Shilo."

"Forty minutes from my place," Tom said. "Westbrook isn't close to any shopping. Then it's another hour and change to Shilo from there."

Tom could almost see Murphy running calculations in his head. "Did you and Kelly have any recent fights?" he asked.

"No."

Murphy grimaced a little. "No fights over alimony? Jill? Past resentment because of that nasty custody battle you had?"

"What does that have to do with anything?" Tom asked.

"Relax. I'm just getting a complete picture, like I said. I had your court records pulled, and I'm curious if there was any lingering tension between you and Kelly. Seemed like it was a pretty contentious custody battle after the divorce."

"Brendan, this isn't high school anymore," Tom said. "I hope you're not looking at me as a suspect because we didn't get along back then."

"That wouldn't be very professional of me," Murphy said. "Besides, I never said you were a suspect."

"That's because you didn't have to," Tom said. "But since you've brought up the past, I guess you should know that Kelly made a lot of unsubstantiated, unproven, and all untrue allegations about me. But that was a long time ago."

"Nine years," Murphy was quick to say. "Kelly called you a drug user. Said you cheated on her. Abusive. Prone to violent outbursts." Murphy had all that memorized as well.

"None of it was true."

"But you stopped fighting her in court and agreed to give Kelly full custody of Jill," Murphy said. "Why?"

Tom felt his anger beginning to rise. He calmed himself. Better to be cooperative than obstinate. "I thought it was hurting Jill," he said, coaxing his blood pressure back to normal. "I decided it was better to compromise for my daughter's sake. Anyway, I got the visitation rights I wanted."

"Have you been harboring a lot of anger over this?"

Tom reddened. "I'm starting to get angry now," he said.

"Do you know of anybody who might have wanted to hurt Kelly?"

"Kelly worked as a cocktail waitress and hostess at the Pinewood Ale House," Tom said. "Her friends weren't subscribing to *Good Housekeeping,* if you know what I mean. Maybe it was a customer. Someone she worked with."

"Was she dating somebody?"

"Kelly was always dating somebody, at least according to Jill. But I don't think she was involved in a serious relationship. Like I said, we didn't talk about our lives. In fact, we didn't really talk at all. Again, her choice, not mine."

"Because she hated you."

"Because she had issues with me," Tom said. "We had our differences."

"Why?"

Tom gave it some thought. "Well, I guess you could say that I didn't turn out to be the man she thought I was," he said.

"You guys began dating in high school, right?" Murphy asked.

"Sure," Tom said. "We went out."

"And then you were in the military with her?" Again, Murphy had brought up a fact about Tom's life without needing a reference.

Tom shook his head. "She was army. I was navy."

"But you two were stationed together, isn't that right?"

"We both enlisted after high school," Tom confirmed. "But I didn't see Kelly for years after I joined up. I trained to become a SEAL and got deployed to Kuwait for the First Gulf War."

"When's the next time you saw her after high school?"

Tom thought for a beat or two. "Kelly was about half-way through her second six-year, so almost ten years," he eventually said. "She was part of the First Armored Division Support Command assigned to the Wiesbaden Army Airfield in Germany. My SEAL unit was deployed to the same airfield for a series of training exercises."

"And that's where you two . . . reconnected? Germany?" Murphy said the word *reconnected* in a way that implied a sexual relationship.

"That's when she became pregnant with Jill, if that's what you're asking. What the hell does this have to do with Kelly's last twenty-four hours? I thought that's what I came here to discuss. I feel like I'm being interrogated."

"You can always leave," Murphy suggested. "Lawyer up." Murphy had just showed Tom his hand and didn't seem to mind.

"The only lawyer I'm going to need is one who will help me regain custody of my daughter."

"Is that why you broke into the house and attacked Kelly?"

"Hey, Murph. This interview is over," Tom said. He stood up and put on his jacket.

"Sure thing. Of course. But, Tom, before you go, I need you think about something."

"What's that?"

"I'd like you to look at this situation from where I'm sitting."

"And where's that?"

"I've got a woman who appears to be the victim of a homicide, an ex-husband with good reason to hold a grudge, and a weak alibi. The ME has put Kelly's time of death at between noon and three. Now, if you made that late-day Home Depot run like you said you did, well then, maybe even I would have a hard time pursuing you as a suspect. But if I were you, Tom, I'd be looking real hard for that receipt."

Tom left without saying another word.

CHAPTER 5

Tom leaned up against the doorjamb to Jill's bedroom and watched his daughter sift through a large box of photographs. In Tom's mind, he saw it as the room of a six-year-old girl. That was the last time he'd been inside the house. It was nighttime, but Tom could see the pink painted walls were now faded. The framed picture of colorful fish and the one of a lush green field with a smiling sun and rainbow on the horizon were replaced with posters of the U.S. women's national soccer team and half-dressed pop stars. The dollhouse he'd bought for Jill's fifth birthday was still in the same corner of the room, but now it was buried beneath an avalanche of her clothes.

Tall and long limbed, Jill looked like any teenager might, dressed in dark jeans, a low-cut white T-shirt underneath a partially zipped gray Abercrombie and Fitch hooded sweatshirt. Her long brown hair was pulled back into a tight ponytail, flattering her slender neck and showing off ears that were both studded with two sets of sparkling earrings. Tom figured the boys would call her cute, when what they really meant (but were not yet mature enough to say) was beautiful.

Jill closed one box of photographs and opened another.

Jill's eyes were red from crying, and Tom's stomach was in knots. She needed a picture to display on a table beside her mother's casket at the funeral and was having a hard time deciding.

Tom had taken care of most of the funeral arrangements himself. Kelly's parents were dead. Her friends, he knew, were bar rats and riffraff who might or might not bother to show and pay their respects.

"What about this one?" Jill held up the picture, which Tom took to be her way of inviting him into the room.

Tom sat on the edge of the bed. Jill handed Tom a picture of Kelly sitting on the living room couch. Sun pouring through the window behind lit Kelly's hair in an angelic way.

"When was that taken?" Tom asked, handing the picture back to Jill.

"A couple years ago at Easter," Jill said. "Mom liked the way she looked in that dress."

"Yeah, she looks great," Tom agreed. "The older you get, the more of her I see in you. You've got her eyes."

Jill gave him a pained expression and began to cry.

Every fiber of Tom's being wanted to hug his daughter. Pull her into his arms and hold her tight. But he was afraid of how she'd react. Instead, he bent down, reached into the box, and pulled out Jill's kindergarten class picture.

"Hey, I remember this," he said. "You lost your first tooth the morning this was taken."

"You remember that?"

"Of course I do," Tom said. "I even remember the tooth fairy gave you five dollars for that tooth."

Jill looked up at her father through reddened eyes. "You always get more for the first one," she said, quoting to him the same explanation he had given her for that windfall payment. Jill's lower lip quivered the way it always did whenever she fought back tears, but this was a battle she wasn't about to win.

"Do you think she's here?" Jill asked, looking about the room. "Watching us?"

Tom nodded and looked to an empty spot in the room where her spirit could be. "Yeah. I think she's watching us."

"I can't stop thinking about what happened," Jill said. "How scared she must have been."

Tom had anticipated it would be difficult for Jill to return home. She had been grieving for only thirty-six hours, a blink of time's eye. He had tried to undo any signs of struggle, clean up the disarray left in the wake of the police investigation. He put books back in their bookcase. Moved furniture that seemed out of place. Even fixed the screen door that Kelly had broken in her haste to get away. But he could feel Jill's panic as she entered. She moved from room to room, making several cautious glances over her shoulder, as though afraid whoever had attacked her mother was still lurking somewhere in the house.

"What do you think happened?" Jill asked.

Reflexively, Tom gripped the edge of the bed, bracing himself. "I think your mom walked in on a robbery," he said, hoping he sounded reassuring. "I think there was a struggle. Your mom managed to get away. She ran. What happened to her after that was a horrible accident. But I don't think she was targeted. I don't think whoever did this is coming back, if that's what you're thinking."

"Are you sure?"

"Yeah, honey. I'm sure." Tom paused. He'd been curious about something from the moment he'd set foot in the house. "I noticed there's some guy's stuff around," Tom said. "Clothes and such. Was your mother living with somebody?"

Jill shook her head. "No. Not really. But this guy Alfonso from the bar was basically using our home like his personal storage unit."

"Did your mom and Alfonso ever fight?" Tom asked. That was another way of asking whether Alfonso could be a suspect.

Again, Jill shook her head. "No. But I do know that Alfonso couldn't have been the one who broke in."

"Why?"

"Alfonso's in jail. He got busted for his third DWI, like, a month ago."

"Really?"

"Yeah. But we thought he was sober. He was going to AA and everything. He even got into mountain biking. His relapse really shook Mom up."

"I didn't know," Tom said.

A long silence followed. Then Jill said, "Do you think they'll catch whoever did this?"

"I hope so," Tom replied. "And I'll do everything I can to make sure they do."

Tom could see that his daughter was dwelling on the terrifying possibility that the crime would go unsolved. He searched his mind and found a change of subject. "I took care of ordering the flowers," he said. "Purple lilacs. Her favorite."

Jill looked surprised. "You know Mom's favorite flower?" she asked.

"There was a time," Tom said, "even though we were divorced, that I loved your mother very much. Honey, I wish I could bring her back for you. I really do. It hurts me more than I can say to see you in so much pain."

"I miss her."

Jill's tears came after that, whole body-shaking convulsions. It became hard for her to breathe.

Tom didn't hesitate. He got down on her bedroom floor and held her, and she let him. They embraced, kneeling on the blue carpet that he had laid down himself so many years ago.

The moment passed. Tom got a box of Kleenex from the bathroom. Jill's tears went from a river to a trickle. They returned their attention to the pictures. For a while, neither spoke. Jill left the room briefly and returned, carrying with her the laptop computer from the kitchen. She had some pictures in iPhoto to go through.

Odd the computer wasn't taken in the robbery, thought Tom.

"Any of these?" Tom asked as Jill switched from picture to picture, as if changing channels on the TV. There were pictures of Jill and Kelly on a hike, apple picking in the fall, skating in winter, swimming in summer. None of the pictures included Tom. It was like watching vignettes from a life that he could have lived.

"Some of them are okay," said Jill. "But if she doesn't have a cigarette in her hand, she's got a drink, or she's wearing something that isn't really appropriate." She grimaced and covered her mouth with her hands. "I can't believe I just said something bad about Mom."

Tom rested a hand on his daughter's shoulder and felt a lump in his throat. He fought back his own tears so that he could stay strong for her. "Honey, it's all right to say whatever you feel. Your mom wasn't perfect, but none of us are. Sure, I wish she didn't smoke, but I'm glad you don't. And I wish she didn't drink as much as she did, either, but never for a moment, not a single moment, did I think she wasn't taking good care of you. And as for her clothes, well, I think the picture on the couch looks great, if you like it, too."

Jill nodded. "That's the picture we'll use," she said. She got quiet, and Tom gave her the time she needed to speak again. "Did you know that Mom and I got into a huge fight last year, when I told her I was going to try out for the soccer team?"

Tom shook his head. "No. But I can imagine why."

"She didn't want me to have anything to do with you. She really hated you. I mean, I don't think I ever heard her say one nice thing about you. Not ever."

"So why did you try out?"

"I'll show you." Jill got up and went over to her closet. She came back holding a stack of colorful cards and letters. Of course, Tom recognized them; he had written them all. Jill dropped the stack on the floor, next to where Tom was kneeling.

"This is why," she said. "All these letters and cards you sent me. And I knew that everybody on the soccer team loved you. The players loved you. The parents loved you. I guess I finally got curious. It didn't make sense to me that the person who wrote these letters was the same person my mom couldn't stand."

Tom swallowed hard as his throat closed.

She had read them. He had reached her.

"And how do you feel about me now? We've got one season under our belts. Are you ready to trust me?"

Jill fixed her father with a cold stare. "You've really been there for me since . . . all this. I just don't get it. Why did Mom hate you so much?" she asked.

There it was again, the question Tom could never answer. "Sometimes people just turn against each other," he said. "I wish I could give you a better reason, but I can't."

"Did you hate her?"

Tom took in a sharp breath. "No."

"Would you ever hurt her?"

"No," Tom said again. He scooped up the stack of letters and cards and held them up for Jill to see. "Look, I know we haven't been close. I know your mom has said a lot of bad things about me over the years. But you've got to believe one thing. I would never—ever—hurt your mother. Ever."

Jill thought. Then she just nodded. Even though she didn't say anything, Tom could tell that she believed him. If anything, all those cards and letters had made her believe.

Tom glanced at the montage of digital pictures still showing on Jill's laptop. It was time, he decided, to become part of the photographs of her life. He could no longer wait for their relationship to heal itself. It was time to stop believing that being her coach was the closest he'd ever get to being her father.

They didn't speak for a long moment. All was quiet except for a dog's loud barking. The barking seemed to be coming from the neighbor's yard. Jill looked puzzled as she stood up, went to the bedroom window, and peered into the backyard.

"That's Rusty," she said, craning her neck sideways to get a better look outside.

"Haven't had the pleasure to meet him yet," said Tom.

"Rusty's about the quietest dog you could even imagine. Mr. McCaskey's always joking that he wanted a guard dog and got himself a big pussy cat instead."

Tom's body tensed, but thanks to his navy training, Jill couldn't possibly have noticed. "Bet it's a coyote or fox," he said, hoping he sounded certain. "We've had plenty of those animals around here lately."

"You think?"

Tom got quiet. He went over to her bedroom window, pushed the curtain aside, and peered out into the darkness.

A Navy SEAL was taught how to tune his night vision the way a bodybuilder learned how to put on muscle. Tom knew better than to discount the something he thought he saw out back as nothing. He saw movement in the woods.

"Yeah," said Tom. "I'm sure it's nothing. But I'll go check, anyway. Okay?" It was probably nothing, he reassured himself.

"Okay," Jill said, sounding tentative.

"Just stay here in your bedroom. I'll be right back." He didn't bother to tell Jill to lock the doors. Rather than frighten her for no good reason, Tom locked the back door himself. He checked the front door after closing it behind him. It was locked, too.

CHAPTER 6

Tom kept to the side of the house as he worked his way from the front yard to the back. He didn't want to reveal himself just yet.

Just in case.

Just to be careful.

His breathing stayed even, pulse rate steady, nothing elevated. His SEAL training never left him. It was ingrained. He was, and would forever be, a warrior.

The dark vinyl siding of the house provided excellent cover, while the roof overhang kept him out of the moonlight. To keep noise to a minimum, Tom put all his weight on one foot, while stepping with the other. He used short steps. That helped him maintain his balance. Tom reached the far edge of the house, and there he waited, listening. Rusty's barks continued unabated. The noise made it impossible to hear any movement in the woods at the edge of the wide, flat backyard.

"Shoot, move, or communicate and do it with violence of action." That sacred maxim was a SEAL's response to any threat. It was what made the enemy fear the SEAL above all others. They were the men who ran to, not from, the sound of gunfire. But SEALs weren't reckless in their bravery, and the saying "The more you train in peacetime, the less you bleed in war" had served Tom and his fellow combatants well.

Tom visualized what he could not see. The dog was barking from the McCaskeys' back porch. The porch was elevated about twenty feet off the ground. He remembered having seen lawn signs for the McCaskeys' electric fence. Rusty could get down into the yard if he wanted. Why didn't he? Maybe Rusty couldn't see what was bothering him from the yard, thought Tom.

Tom listened some more. Perhaps Rusty was using the porch like a hunter's observational tree stand. From the McCaskeys' yard, Rusty's keen eyes could scour the woods directly in front of Tom but would not be able to see what Tom had observed from Jill's bedroom. Whatever was troubling Rusty was probably near the spot where Tom had spied something rustling in the woods.

Good doggy, thought Tom. He knew the path to take where he couldn't be seen.

Tom waited for a thin stretch of clouds to scud overhead. With the moonlight obscured, he crouched low to the ground and made a quick dash for a tall oak tree about halfway to the woods. He waited for more cloud covering before he moved again. He darted from tree to tree until he cleared the backyard entirely, then sank into the vast woodlands behind the house.

Rusty's barks camouflaged Tom's footsteps. He walked just inside the perimeter of the woods. He stopped. In a few more yards he'd be directly across from Jill's bedroom window. The threat, if there was any, could be lurking anywhere from this point on. Tom had plenty of tree cover to conceal his location. He peered out from behind an ancient hemlock and saw movement some twenty yards ahead. He didn't need good night vision to make the sighting. The moonlight helped.

Tom saw a shadow flicker when the moonlight turned even more revealing. He crawled forward on his belly, keeping his legs open, consciously using the insides of his knees to maintain contact with the ground. His elbows, fixed at ninety-degree angles, pulled him over dirt and rocks. Tom got to within a few yards of the shadow before he saw it in full view.

It wasn't a fox or coyote.

It was a man.

The prowler had a muscular build, visible beneath his tight-fitting clothes. He was dressed all in black and wore a ski mask to conceal his face. He used binoculars to survey the rear of the house. He looked to be watching Jill, who was at her bedroom window, probably searching for Tom. The binoculars were night vision capable, had to be— but not army issued, something store-bought, costing below a grand. The man was crouched on one knee, making it hard for Tom to estimate his height and weight. But he was broad shouldered, so Tom put him at about six foot two, and somewhere between a buck ninety and two-ten.

Shouldn't be hard.

Tom tossed a small stone into the woods, ten or so feet behind the prowler and to his left. The stone landed with a thud on a bed of fallen leaves. The man lowered his binoculars and craned his head to look over his left shoulder.

Tom sprung to his feet and charged. Two steps, and he was within striking distance. His first blow would need to be a decisive one. Tom smashed his elbow crosswise into the side of the man's head, which was turning from the direction where the stone had fallen, toward the new noise coming from his right. Should have been the end of it, but

the prowler had surprisingly quick reflexes and pulled
back, so Tom merely delivered a glancing blow.

The prowler executed a flawless shoulder roll on the
uneven ground and was back on his feet in seconds, with
some distance between himself and Tom. The move looked
effortless. *Training,* thought Tom. The prowler retreated
into the woods.

Tom took five long strides before he launched himself
into the air. With his body still in flight, and parallel to the
ground, Tom made a diving tackle, wrapping his arms
around the man's waist as he spun right. He used the
prowler's body to cushion his fall.

Tom got off two quick punches, one to the man's solar
plexus, and the other connecting hard to the same spot his
elbow had only brushed. The air rushed out of the man's
lungs, and Tom heard a satisfying grunt. Tom ripped the
ski mask off the man's head, but it was too dark to see his
face.

"Who are you?" Tom shouted. "What do you want?"
Tom took hold of the man's black wool sweater and pulled
him close to his face. "Answer me!" Tom shook him by
the sweater.

No answer. Tom freed one of his hands and used it to
snap off two quick blows just beneath the right orbital
socket. *Damn the missing moonlight,* he thought. What
more could he tell in the dark? *White male? Yes. Hair color?
Brown. Eye color? Unknown. Distinguishing marks? Unknown.*

The moonlight returned. It illuminated the man's face.

An icy chill streaked down Tom's back. *It's impossible.
It can't be him. He's in prison.*

The last time Tom had seen the man's picture was fifteen years ago.

It couldn't be him—but the face was too distinctive to

be mistaken. He had the same aquiline nose Tom remembered. A jaw that was much more narrow than his cheekbones. The eyes were set deeply and stuck in a permanent squint. His lips were neither thick nor thin. His eyebrows were straight as the horizon.

"Lange?" he asked. "Is that you?"

From behind, Tom heard a panicked cry. "Dad! Dad, are you all right? Dad! What's going on?"

Tom turned to look. He looked only because it was his daughter calling him. In that split second his focus was no longer locked on his target. The very next instant, Tom felt a heavy blow crash into the side of his skull.

The binoculars.

Tom fell to the ground.

"What's happening!" Jill shouted into the dark woods.

Tom staggered to his feet, and took two uneven steps. Blood pounded inside his head. He could see the prowler running away. He started to give chase, but his vision went dark. He took two more steps, tripped over a root, and fell. Off in the distance, Tom heard the sound of fast-falling footsteps breaking branches and crunching leaves.

Lying facedown in the dirt, Tom reached forward, searching out a root, a branch, anything to give him leverage to stand. He listened to the prowler's footfalls as he made an escape into the darkness of the woods. In a few hundred yards the intruder would reach the same ravine where Kelly had died. Tom searched the ground around him for the black ski mask, but like the prowler, it was gone.

"Dad! Dad!" Jill screamed, breaking branches as she rushed to his side. "Are you all right?"

Tom sat on the ground and rubbed his throbbing head. "Yeah, I'm fine," he said, breathing hard.

"Who was that?" Jill asked, her voice nearing a frantic

pitch. She knelt on the ground beside Tom and clutched his shoulder with her hand. Her fingers dug painfully into Tom's skin.

"I think it might have been somebody your mom and I once knew," Tom said, still struggling to catch his breath. "We knew him from a long, long time ago," he continued. "When you were just a baby. A guy from the military named Kip Lange."

"Do you think he's the one who broke into our house?"

"Maybe," said Tom. "I don't know. I'm not even sure it was him. It just looked like him."

"I don't understand. If Mom knew him, why would she have run?" asked Jill. "Why would he have come back?"

Tom locked eyes with his panicked daughter. Her face had a ghostly white pallor, the same color as the moon. "I don't know," he said.

He did know.

But he couldn't say.

CHAPTER 7

The receptionist jumped a little as Tom Hawkins neared her desk. "Attorney Pressman is waiting for you in his office," she said, pointing to Marvin's closed office door.

He took off his Red Sox baseball hat, damp from an August rain, and thanked her. The woman, not yet thirty, did not reply.

I'm the ex-husband of a woman who was murdered three days ago, Tom told himself. *People aren't going to know how to act around me.*

Jill shuffled along behind her father. He hadn't let her out of his sight since the incident in the woods. She had spent the night with him at his house in Westbrook. What she didn't know, but soon would find out, was that she'd be spending every night there.

Tom paused at the door to Marvin's office. "I haven't seen Marvin since high school," he said. "We're going to need a few minutes to play catch-up. Then we'll get down to business."

Jill had her head bowed and her mouth in a frown. "Whatever," was all she said.

"Everything is going to be all right, Jill," Tom said. "I'm not going to let anything happen to you." Tom gave

Jill a hug, but his daughter turned her head sideways, leaving her arms hanging limply by her side.

Persistence and patience, Tom reminded himself. *Persistence and patience.* The two Ps formed the foundation of Tom's well-proven coaching philosophy. Showing frustration with a struggling player was the surest way for that player to lose interest in the game. Tom had made huge strides in repairing their damaged relationship. But he understood that he still had a long way to go. If his daughter sensed his own frustration with her, she could easily lose interest in him.

Tom knocked on the door to Marvin's office, heard a muffled "Come in," and went inside.

Marvin was standing behind an expansive desk, reading a document he held in both hands. Back in high school, Marvin had been a good-natured kid with a tangle of unkempt, curly hair. Tom remembered him struggling through several failed bids to make the soccer team. But his former classmate had gone from skinny to heavyset, and his thinning hair looked to be losing the battle.

Sifting through Kelly's papers, Tom had discovered that she had recently hired Marvin to help her negotiate a settlement for her mounting credit card debt. Tom had called Marvin and confirmed for himself that he was the right man for the job.

"Tom Hawkins," Marvin said, coming out from behind his desk and walking toward him with lumbering steps. His voice was a deep, pleasing baritone, befitting his large frame. He shook Tom's outstretched hand with vigor. "It's great to see you. Though I'm terribly sorry about the circumstances."

Marvin quickly turned his attention to Jill. "Hi there," he said, shaking Tom's daughter's hand as though she were his peer. "I want you to know how truly sorry I am for your loss. I knew your mother well. This is all just a terrible, terrible tragedy. You have my deepest sympathy."

"Thanks," Jill said in a quiet voice.

"Honey, if you want to take a seat on the couch over there," Tom said, pointing. "Marvin and I have some catching up to do."

Jill slipped buds into each ear and sat on the couch without verbally acknowledging Tom's request. Even from across the room, Tom could hear snippets from whatever music was permanently damaging her hearing. Jill took out her cell phone, and Tom could tell that she was texting.

"How's she holding up?" Marvin asked, motioning with his head toward Jill, who seemed oblivious.

"She's doing okay. As well as can be expected."

"The funeral is next Wednesday, right?"

"That's right," Tom confirmed.

"Any break in the case?"

"No, nothing new," Tom said.

"Any theories?"

"Only that she walked in on a robbery in progress, but that's still speculation. All we know is that somebody was definitely in the house with her. There's evidence of a struggle and assault. The police think at some point she broke away and ran out the back door, slipped and fell down the ravine, hit her head on a rock, and died instantly. But they don't know who broke into the house."

"Any suspects?" asked Marvin.

Tom pointed to the red welt on the side of his head where he'd been hit with the binoculars. "I caught, or almost caught, somebody out back of Jill's house, surveying the property with binoculars."

"You think it's him?"

"Maybe. I told Brendan Murphy about it. Gave him a

name, because I thought I recognized the guy. He said he's looking into it. That's all I've heard."

"Sounds like progress."

"I'm not sure about that," Tom said in a low voice. "I think Murphy is still convinced that I had something to do with what happened to Kelly."

"What makes you say that?"

Tom glanced over at Jill, still seated on the leather couch, relieved her attention was fully engaged in electronics. "I went to the police station voluntarily, and he did everything but name me as an official suspect. Apparently, he visited Westbrook and interviewed some of my neighbors to see if any of them witnessed me leaving my house when I said I did."

"Did any of them see you?"

"No idea," Tom said. "But Murphy paid a visit to my next-door neighbor. She felt bad telling me that she didn't see me leave."

Marvin scoffed. "Murphy's always had a pole up his ass about you," he said. "But . . . now, I'm just being curious, mind you. . . . Do you have an alibi?"

"Well, I was at the Home Depot near where I live, buying a box of nails when it happened, only I didn't save the receipt and I paid in cash."

"That's a drag," Marvin said.

"Figures my car was parked where the mall security cameras couldn't see it, and I was wearing a hat, so it was impossible to make a positive ID from the surveillance inside the store."

"Did you save the box?"

"Why would I do that?"

"The box should have a SKU number on it," Marvin said. "That SKU number can be matched up with Home

Depot's store records and can confirm you were shopping when you said you were."

"I may still have it. I'll look."

"You know, I do handle criminal defense cases, not just estate planning and family law."

"Well, let's plan on my *not* needing those particular services of yours."

Marvin studied Tom and seemed to take notice of his physical conditioning. "Thinking I might waive my usual fee in exchange for some personal training," Marvin said, patting his ample midsection. Marvin's rumpled suit suggested that he might have slept in it, an assessment confirmed by the attorney's bleary eyes.

"Coaching high school soccer has made me fret off the pounds," said Tom.

"State champs three years in a row now. Pretty impressive."

"Thanks. The girls put in a huge effort."

"Well, Jill's been a rising star for the Wildcats, from what I've read in the *Journal*. Guess I know where she got the talent from." Marvin pointed to a photograph on his office wall, which was covered with dozens of framed pictures of great moments in sports history. The specific photograph was one Tom remembered well: Marvin himself had taken the picture of a young Tom Hawkins making a bicycle kick shot against onetime New Hampshire powerhouse Wiltshire.

"That's a great shot, Marvin."

"Yours or mine?" Marvin said with a slight laugh.

"We lost that game, if I remember," Tom said, thinking of the hours he'd spent in the coach's room, watching game tape and going over every mistake he'd made on the pitch.

"We did, but as I recall, both teams were pretty evenly matched," Marvin said. "Did you know that if two teams are equally matched, seventy-two percent of the time it's randomness that makes one of them lose, not real skill difference? So that loss wasn't your fault. It was just a random outcome."

Tom shrugged. "Doesn't make me feel any better. Though I admit, that's one soccer stat I've never heard before," he said.

Marvin gestured to other sports pictures that adorned his office walls. "Well, I was never a great athlete," he said, "but I am a freak for sports stats. I can tell you the stat that goes with every picture on my wall."

"You weren't that bad an athlete, Marvin," Tom said.

"That's kind of you to say, but completely untrue," Marvin corrected him. "I got cut every year I tried out for the soccer team."

"But at least you tried."

"And you were one of maybe three other guys who didn't laugh at me whenever I did. Besides, there are approximately seventeen thousand professional athletes in the United States. That gave me a point zero zero five percent chance of becoming one myself. The law seemed a far more surefire way to financial security."

"By the looks of it, you're doing well," Tom said.

By all appearances, it was true. The cozy office inside the well-kept Victorian home was smartly furnished with several dark bookcases stocked with legal tomes. A richly colored Oriental rug lay over a pale wide-plank hardwood floor. The meeting area within Marvin's high-ceilinged office had an unmarked whiteboard, similar to the type Tom used to map out soccer plays; a large black-lacquered conference table; and a set of six plush leather chairs.

"Business keeps growing," Marvin said. "I might not be scoring goals, but I am helping people, and that feels good. So, you ready to get started?"

Tom tapped Jill on the shoulder. She pulled the buds from her ears and followed Tom over to the meeting area. Tom sat first, and Jill sat on his side of the table, but two seats away. Marvin sat across from them.

Marvin began by addressing Jill. "So, Jill, we're here today to talk about your future."

"Okay," she said.

"I spoke with your dad, and he told me to be very candid during this session," he said. "As the attorney for your mother's estate, I'm most familiar with her affairs. I'm afraid the news about your mother's finances isn't good."

"What's 'not good' mean?" Jill asked Marvin, her sweet voice edged with concern.

"Your mother had no savings. No life insurance. Really, no provisions at all for your care. On top of that, your house has two mortgages, which she was already behind on, and the bank is threatening to take it to foreclosure."

"What does that mean?" Jill asked.

"It means we need to talk about where you're going to live," Tom said.

"I'll live with Lindsey," Jill said, refusing even to glance at her father. "They already offered."

"Jill, I'm not going to allow that. Not with what happened last night."

"But it's my life!"

Tom cleared his throat. "I believe I have custody now."

Marvin nodded. "That's correct," he said. "Until Jill is an adult, you become the custodial parent."

"What are you saying?"

"I'm saying to come and live with me in Westbrook."

"What? No! My life is here in Shilo. I don't want to

just leave it behind. Especially now. I need my friends more than ever."

"Jill, you were there. You saw what happened. It's not safe, and I'm not going to take any chances."

"I can take care of myself," Jill snapped. "You think Mom was looking out for me? She could barely look out for herself."

"Look, I'm not going to trust your friends to keep you safe."

Marvin cleared his throat, his way of clearing the air. He said, "Well, you're within your parental rights to have Jill come live with you, Tom. Westbrook is a nice town, Jill. Great schools, from what I hear."

"Don't do this to me," Jill pleaded. "If you love me, like you say you do, then just let me live with Lindsey. Let me stay here. Please."

Tom thought. Then he asked, "Marvin, what if I moved to Shilo? Took over Kelly's mortgage?"

"Remember, the bank is coming after the house," Marvin warned. "But all the bank is interested in is money. If we can get the mortgage caught up and show proof that you can continue making payments, I'm sure they would be satisfied."

"I've got my job with the Shilo public schools, and I can sell my place in Westbrook," Tom said. "Whatever it takes to make this work, I'll do it." He felt absolutely confident about a plan he'd spent all of ten seconds concocting.

"You would do that?" Jill stammered. "You'd move here so I could stay?"

Tom nodded. "I'm your father, Jill," he said. "I'm going to do what's best for you."

Jill's downcast face brightened. Tom smiled too.

The next hour passed in a blur. Papers needed to be

signed. Forms to be filled out. Each completed check-box item made Tom feel one step closer to his goal: to be thought of as Jill's father again.

But he had other concerns that needed resolution.

Who was the man in the woods?

Where was Kip Lange?

Could Tom realistically keep them both safe?

When they were finished for the afternoon, Tom escorted Jill back into the waiting room. "Hang here a second, kiddo," he said. "There's something I forgot to ask Marvin."

Jill's iPod earbuds went back into place before Tom reopened Marvin's office door.

"Forget something?" Marvin asked.

"Marvin, do you do any investigative work?" Tom asked, keeping the door slightly ajar so that he could keep an eye on Jill. "You seem pretty good at digging up esoteric sports stats. I'm guessing you're good at finding out a lot of things."

Marvin's eyes narrowed on Tom. "Is this about Kelly's killer? Because I don't do PI work."

"If the guy I fought in the woods is who I think it was, then his name is Kip Lange."

"Go on."

"Almost sixteen years ago Lange was stationed at the same military base in Germany as Kelly and I. He was arrested for the attempted murder of a U.S. Army officer. He's supposed to still be in prison."

"Yeah? What do you need to know?"

"I don't trust Murphy to investigate this properly. He's too focused on me. So if Lange's not still locked up, I need to know where he is."

"Do you think Lange had something to do with what happened to Kelly?"

"It's possible," Tom said. "But unlikely. Like I said, he should still be in prison."

"Tom, I'll do what I can to help you find him, but you have to level with me. What's the real story here? I don't like to operate in the dark. You've got to give me something."

"We have attorney-client privilege working here?"

Marvin nodded. "We do."

"Then I can tell you that it has something to do with a gun and millions of dollars' worth of smuggled heroin."

CHAPTER 8

The work never got easier.

Her superiors had assured FBI special agent Loraine "Rainy" Miles that she'd eventually grow numb to it. She had joined the Innocent Images National Initiative, part of the cyber crimes against children investigative squad, five years ago. In all those years, Rainy had yet to feel a tingle of that promised numbness.

Not once.

The computer jocks assigned to the cyber squad were members of the FBI's Computer Analysis Response Team, or CART for short. Rainy handled procedural duties and was the person most responsible for gathering evidence for the U.S. Attorney's office (USAO). CART made it possible for Rainy to get that evidence, and thanks to them, Rainy had enough material to put James Mann away for a very, very long time.

From start to finish, Mann's arrest in his suburban Boston home had taken only a few hours. But the events leading up to it had been several months in the making, and it had all started because of that tip. Tips, Rainy had come to learn, were the lifeblood of the squad. If it weren't for them, her team would have a hard time finding a child porn ring, let alone breaching one to shut it down. Whoever had jump-started the Mann investigation apparently knew how to stay in the shadows. Mann, a pharmaceutical executive and fa-ther of two, fortunately did not.

CART had created the mirror images of Mann's com-puters with their typical thoroughness. Procedurally, Rainy couldn't begin to gather evidence until she had a bit-by-bit re-creation of Mann's physical hardware to work from. She hadn't seen much of the sun since Mann's arrest, as she'd spent almost every working hour cramped inside the windowless confines of the Lair, the pet name given to CART's forensic lab. In her world of justice, James Mann couldn't do enough time, but the law had different standards for punishment.

Rainy, and others who thought like her, were appalled that the legal language in cases like Mann's didn't imply a crime and a victim. Rainy didn't think much of the de-fense attorneys who decried the lengthy sentences handed down for federal child porn cases. Rainy was part of a growing movement pushing to change the term "child pornography" to "child sex abuse images," "exploitation of children," or better still, "crime scene images."

She believed this issue was less a moral failing of the general public than a need for better education and infor-mation. To that end, she urged any of the defense attor-neys or rights activists who disagreed with her to come to a trial and listen to victim impact statements. Then they'd know a real crime had occurred. They'd know these im-ages would haunt the children long past their youth. They'd agree that predators like James Mann were no different from sex offenders and should pay justly for their crimes.

Ten years, Rainy thought. Mann would do ten years knowing he had no chance for early parole. But Mann's lawyers would soon be crawling over their casebooks, sniffing for the smallest infraction of the USAO investigative guidelines that they could use to spring their client. Every move the cyber squad made involved careful orchestration, painstaking detail work, and for Rainy specifically, the horrific task of forensic categorization.

Forensic categorization was by far the toughest part of her job, but in many ways the most important. Rainy had to sift through every image personally, watch every video from Mann's collection, and count them up. Sentencing for convicted child pornographers was based partially on the number of images in their possession. Six hundred images (each video counted as seventy-five images for her tally) was the maximum number considered by the courts at sentencing time. The fewer images they had, the less time they did. Simple as that.

But even if James Mann exceeded the six hundred image count, Rainy looked for other enhancements that could add years to Mann's sentence. Pictures of sadomasochism, masturbation, and oral and anal sex, or those that featured prepubescent youth, were all justifiable cause for a sentencing enhancement. The USAO left it up to Rainy's best judgment to decide which images were sexually explicit, child erotica, or simply nude pictures that were not sexually suggestive.

She'd look at each image, examine every frame of video for close-up shots of genitalia, or something that made the depictions lewd and lascivious. Some of the images counted for multiple categories, so Rainy was responsible for keeping track of that as well. She did this work, even though it tore her up inside to see such horror inflicted on innocent children. She did it, even though sometimes she had to drink herself to sleep.

"So where are we at, Carter?" Rainy asked.

CART team member and special agent Carter Dumas,

whose first name's resemblance to the team name was a running joke, was Rainy's favorite forensic analyst. They'd worked several cases together over the years, forging a sibling-like camaraderie. Rainy stood up from her seat to ask her question. She didn't have to; the Lair was small enough that Carter could have heard a whisper.

Carter had boyish looks, thanks to his curly blond hair and an almost creaseless face. He was also exceptionally pale because, as he pointed out, computer monitors glowed but did not tan. Rainy threw Carter a Snickers bar, one of several snacks she kept tucked away for times of low blood sugar.

Carter ripped open the wrapper with his teeth and took a hearty bite. "Well, I've finished scanning the hard drive, and I'm about to run a timeline report. We'll need a few binders for this guy, though. Seems like he worked OT to build up his library."

"Any exculpatory evidence?" Rainy doubted it, but there had been cases of viruses turning a home computer into a porn server.

Carter shook his head. "Nope. We've got plenty of emails from Mr. Mann demonstrating his undeterred commitment to secure the goods." Rainy bent forward to stretch her stiffening leg. "You staying late again?" Carter asked.

"No, I've got a hot date tonight." Carter held her gaze, then grinned. Rainy laughed in return. "Actually, I was thinking about busting out early."

"You almost had me that time. Rainy on a date would warrant a front-page bulletin on our intranet."

"What are you implying, Carter? That I'm undesirable?" Rainy leaned over her favorite tech and gave him her best menacing glare. She got enough looks from the men she worked with to know they found her attractive—

compact, petite, shoulder-length brown hair, hazel eyes, and photogenic smile. But it had been years since she'd had a boyfriend. Her work schedule made it a challenge, and the work itself stuck with her long after she left the office.

"I think any news of you having a date would break a hundred hearts here, that's what I think," Carter said.

"Well, let's just say I have yet to find a man who can restore my faith in men. You being the exception, of course. The married exception, that is."

"There's always women."

"There's always keep your fantasies to yourself. Especially while we're doing this."

"Yeah, right on." Carter finished the Snickers with two more bites and focused again on his computer monitors.

Rainy watched him work. Her boss, supervisory senior resident agent Walter Tomlinson, had pursued Rainy for the cyber crimes against children investigative squad not because of her technical acumen, but for her dogged procedural and investigative skills.

All the geek speak Rainy had picked up along the way, she attributed to osmosis. Just by observing Carter's monitors, Rainy could tell he had several searches running in parallel. Keyword parsers in action. Registry key analyzers kicking at full speed. Recovery tools burning up RAM to restore any deleted files. Rainy couldn't understand how any of these perps she arrested thought that what they did in the privacy of their home was really private. Technology, she had quickly discovered, could turn anybody's door into a window.

"Did we get any CVIP hits yet?" Carter asked.

"The report was still printing last I checked. I'll go look." Rainy walked over to the printer and removed the report from the National Center for Missing and Exploited Children pertaining specifically to the Mann investigation.

Earlier, Rainy had sent a batch of images from Mann's computer to the NCMEC for comparison against the CVIP database of known images. The NCMEC maintained a vast catalog of child pornography on its highly secure database. The NCMEC was operationally in charge of the Child Victim Identification Program, or the CVIP for short.

The CVIP was a national clearinghouse for all child pornography. Every image or video file obtained by law enforcement—state, local, or federal—got processed through the CVIP and assigned a hash value, a nonpictorial, alphanumeric identification that was unique to each computer file. Because of this uniqueness, hash values functioned a lot like digital fingerprints, and Rainy used them for matching purposes. When image evidence Rainy submitted to the CVIP matched an image already on file, she called it a "hit."

Rainy wanted to get as many hits as possible from her CVIP analysis, and for good reason. A "hit" meant the child in question was already known to the system, that presumably the child was no longer in any danger because they'd been identified by authorities. Sadly, Rainy had come to learn that "out of danger" often meant deceased or dead inside.

When the CVIP didn't return a hit, Rainy's work became a lot more intense. A no hit image meant that a child might be in immediate danger and must be identified as quickly as possible. Sometimes hash values didn't match up because the image Rainy fed into the CVIP had been altered from the original file in some way.

"Image A is already logged in the CVIP," Carter had once explained to help Rainy grasp the concept. "Let's say it's a picture of a teenaged girl with a fifty-year-old man. The CVIP assigns Image A a hash value. Done. Later we feed Image B into the CVIP. Image B is the exact same picture as Image A, only someone cropped out the old man. The CVIP will catalog Image B by its own hash value. It doesn't know the old man has been removed. The CVIP will think Image B is a new image, and we'll have ourselves a no hit to investigate."

Rainy's job was tough to stomach, but a CVIP analyst had it worse. The CVIP team further classified images into series—images of the same person, setting, or type that should be grouped together. They had to visually inspect every image without a hash value match to see if they could match it on their own. CVIP analysts knew, just based on their vast experience, that certain bathtubs or wallpaper patterns, for instance, came from images they'd seen before. These images could be assigned to a known series even though the hash values didn't match.

"So far we've got all matching hash values and known image series here," Rainy said to Carter, flipping through the pages of the CVIP report she had printed from her e-mail.

Many of the images taken off Mann's computer had victim impact statements on file, too. Those statements would need to be read aloud by either the victim or a witness coordinator at Mann's sentencing if he got convicted.

When he gets convicted, Rainy assured herself.

Some of the images in Mann's collection had been in circulation a long time, even dating as far back as the early 1980s.

"Rainy, I've got some more lovelies to send your way if you want to go through them," Carter said. "Sorry."

Perhaps Carter had apologized because he saw the look

in Rainy's eye that said she really didn't want to look any-more.

"That's okay, Cart. I'll check them out."

Carter electronically transferred a batch of encrypted files to the password-protected external hard drive, where Rainy conducted her forensic categorization.

She settled back into her workstation chair and opened one picture after another. She categorized each image for the USAO's report. She captured the image properties they'd need for trial. She verified the images with the CVIP. So far, every image sent to the CVIP came back with a hit.

Very good news indeed.

"A little over three hundred left to go," Rainy said to Carter.

Rainy opened the next image in the batch. During her five years on the squad, she thought she'd seen it all. Every vile and disgusting act she could imagine. Compared to those images, the one she opened next wasn't graphic at all. It wasn't very sexually explicit, either. It was just a picture of a girl, a teenager perhaps, lying partially undressed on a bed. She didn't think much of it as she opened the next bunch of images in the batch that Carter had sent.

She kept looking. What seemed only a curious departure from Mann's more explicit image collection suddenly became a lot more interesting.

"Carter," Rainy said, her voice breathy from a pulse of adrenaline. "Stay close by. I may need you. Just want to check these out with the CVIP first."

Rainy sent the images over to the CVIP for processing. It would take some time for the CVIP results to return, but Rainy had seen enough images to have a gut feeling about the report she'd receive back.

Of the 325 images Rainy sent to the CVIP, there wouldn't be a single hit in the batch.

Not a one.

CHAPTER 9

Carter inched his chair over to where he could see Rainy's computer screen better. Rainy had lined up a twelve-picture display, each a shot of a different girl. "Tell me what you notice about these," she said.

Carter leaned forward to get an even closer look.

"Young girls," he said.

"How young?" Rainy asked.

"Between fourteen and eighteen, I'm thinking."

"Most of Mann's other shots were of girls younger than that. What else do you notice?"

"Well, it looks like they're in their bedrooms."

"Exactly. These weren't taken in some low-rent studio, dingy basement, or roadside motel."

The rooms were remarkably similar. Colorful bedspreads. Lots of clothes in various heaps on the floor and on dressers. Closet doors mostly concealed by an array of hanging clothes. Posters of current pop stars and cultural icons adorning the walls. Small desks with vanity mirrors. Bright colors throughout.

"Look here." Rainy pointed to a picture of a girl kneeling on the floor, wearing only her underwear. Her back was arched. Her arm folded across her ample chest concealed her breasts. Her plump lips were puckered and inviting. "These posters on the wall behind her, a corkboard with a bunch of photos tacked to it, the floral-patterned bedspread, this is a girl's bedroom. Her bedroom, I'm betting." Rainy tapped her finger against the girl's digital face.

"I get it. And he has a bunch of these pictures?"

"Three hundred twenty-five, by my count. Forty different girls. Each girl is in a different bedroom setting. There is no way these were staged. These pictures are personal. Not forced or faked. Taken willingly by the girls themselves."

"You think these girls took the shots themselves with their cell phones or something?"

Rainy nodded her head. "Yup. Look at the angles of the shots, too. In each one, the girls have one hand just outside the frame. The hand not visible is the one holding their cell phone, I'm willing to bet."

"Uh-huh. Yeah, I see what you're talking about. The quality too. Some are really pixelated."

"Suggesting a low-quality camera. Some phones are better than others at taking pictures. And there's another thing troubling me. Look at their eyes." Rainy opened up several similar crime-image pictures. "These girls have a proud look to them, Carter. It's as if they're bragging about their bodies."

"You think they're being flirtatious?"

"That's exactly what I think. Girls that age are almost begging for attention. And these pictures scream, 'Look at me and how sexy I am.' They don't say, 'Help me.' They don't say, 'Get me out of here.' These girls wanted to be seen."

"By James Mann?"

"Oh, I doubt any of them thought a creep like James Mann would be looking at their naked selves. I'm betting they sent these pictures to their boyfriends or someone they trusted. Maybe they texted the images to them. A sext, you know? And somehow, Mann got hold of them."

Rainy studied the crop of images with rapt focus. Some of the girls were partially dressed, but what they wore fit tight, like an extra layer of skin. They were posed. Backs arched. Legs raised. Hips swiveled. Eyes playful—taking (it seemed) much delight in showing the undersides of their thighs. Hands touching their fawnlike bodies in all the wrong places for James Mann to see.

"Well, I'm hoping our forensic analysis will show us how he got the pictures."

"Sure. But even if you manage to do that, we're still going to need to get the subpoenas. And that's going to take a long time."

"Hail to the Queen of Paperwork!"

"Thanks for the vote of confidence," Rainy sighed. "But I'm thinking, what if we could work from a source?"

"What, like one of the girls themselves? I checked, and there's no GeoTagging or other metadata information on any of these images. We have no way of knowing who they are," Carter said. "How do you figure on finding that out?"

Rainy didn't need to think about her answer. Identifying girls from a bunch of poorly focused digital snapshots required an expert in imaging technology. Somebody who understood everything to do with image verification, enhancement, facial recognition, and analysis.

"Clarence Stern," she said.

Carter just laughed. "The Bureau's Rembrandt of imaging? Good luck getting Tomlinson to authorize his time."

"But you believe he could do it."

"Yeah. Maybe. I don't know."

"Well, I just emailed Tomlinson, and he said he'll come down and take a look. Let's see if he'll throw us a bone."

"Get ready to lick your chops."

CHAPTER 10

Tom didn't pass a single car in his ten-minute drive to Roland Boyd's cul-de-sac, which real estate agents had dubbed "desirable south Shilo."

Jill was seated beside him. She was texting. Thumbs of fury, he called her.

Tom had never been to Roland's new house, but he knew the area well. The stone and brick mansions, spaced acres apart, belied the town's rural character and farming heritage. Tom and Roland had once lived in the same neighborhood, in what Shilo youths had always called the tree streets. Oak. Pine. Elm. Maple. If Shilo had a wrong side of the tracks, it was among the tree streets. Tom had hoped to move his family out of the tree streets, but his divorce from Kelly had tapped out the necessary funds to turn that plan into a reality.

Roland had found his way out of the tree streets. Just as he'd always said he would.

"Good thing you caught me on my work-from-home day," Roland had said on the phone. "I'm tied up in a conference call for a bit, but Adriana's around. She can keep you company while I finish up."

Even though Tom worked in the same town where

Roland lived, the once close friends hadn't seen each other since the funeral for Roland's firstborn child. Divorce had destroyed not only the marriage, but also many of the friendships built around it.

The first time Tom met Roland's wife, Adriana, the young couple was living together on the Wiesbaden Army Airfield in Germany. Their son, Stephen, was only one at the time, but they were talking about having another. It was a mini high school reunion in Europe, of all places. A week after Tom's arrival, he and Kelly had rekindled their high school romance, and soon the quartet, comprising three Shilo grads plus Adriana, became fast friends.

Tom was sad when his SEAL training exercises ended and it came time for him to leave Germany, Kelly, Roland, and the new bond he had formed with Adriana. As it turned out, Tom had carried a little part of that German military base back home with him—in something that Kelly had secretly packed inside a crate of gifts and knickknacks she'd given Tom to bring back to Shilo. It was the same part that Tom had hidden and eventually promised Kelly he'd never destroy.

Tom drove his Taurus past a sea of green, well-manicured lawns and down Roland's long and winding driveway. Judging by the appearance of Boyd's new house, the largest McMansion in a neighborhood of McMansions, Boyd Capital was doing a spit better than the days when it was a father-and-son operation.

Tom parked, and he and Jill exited the car.

"Do you know Mitchell Boyd well?" Tom asked his daughter.

"I know who he is," Jill said, "but we don't hang out, if that's what you're asking."

Tom nodded, but inwardly he breathed a sigh of relief. Young. Good looking. Rich. Mitchell Boyd, Roland

and Adriana's youngest and now only child, had a reputation around Shilo High School for viewing girls as conquests, not companions. Every teacher, it seemed, held a poor opinion of him. And every teacher with a high-school-aged daughter was glad it wasn't their kid dating him.

They walked single file along the stone walkway with inground floodlights on either side, and past landscaping with the beauty of a Japanese garden. They came to a large and ornate wood-carved front door. Tom rang the front doorbell and listened to the eight-note chime.

When Adriana Boyd opened the door, she greeted Tom with a sad little smile and a welcoming embrace. She held on to Tom a beat or two longer than felt comfortable.

"Tom . . . goodness . . . how are you holding up?" Adriana placed a delicate hand on Tom's shoulder and gave a look as if to say, "Don't even think about lying to me."

"I'm doing okay, Adriana," he said. "Thanks for asking."

Adriana said to Jill, "Honey, I'm so very sorry for your loss."

"Thank you," Jill said.

"Please. Come in. I put out some drinks and food for us in the living room until Roland is through with his call. We'll chat and play catch-up."

Adriana took Tom by the hand and led him into the house. She was decked out with plenty of expensive-looking jewelry and wore a slim gray pantsuit, with just the hint of a white silk T-shirt showing. It was impossible to ignore Adriana's beauty—porcelain skin, with light blond hair, wavy and past her shoulders. She was fit, too: older than Roland by four years, she still looked thirty.

The heels of Adriana's black shoes clicked loudly on the marble floor of the majestic foyer. Tom thought the living room, with its antiques and oversized oil paintings, could have been cordoned off by ropes like a museum exhibit. Framed pictures stood on tables and shelves throughout, which helped to give the cavernous space a more homey feel. They were simple snapshots of the family's life together. The pictures were of happy and pleasant times—vacations to the Caribbean, skiing in the White Mountains, graduations, and birthday parties and such. But many of the pictures Tom saw evoked a deep sadness. Those were the pictures of Stephen, who had died of a drug overdose five years earlier.

"What would you like to drink?"

"Just water," Tom said.

"For you, Jill?"

"Water's fine."

A boy entered through the open archway. He had short hair with gelled spikes, a silver cross earring in his right ear, and wore faded jeans that were frayed at the bottom. The tight-fitting blue shirt he wore underneath his light jacket revealed a wiry but muscular frame. Tom had once advised Mitchell about colleges and had talked to him about Stephen after his brother's death. Other than that, the two didn't have much interaction around school.

"Mom, I'm going out," said the boy.

"Mitchell, please. Come here. Mr. Hawkins has come over to see Dad. And I asked you to stay and keep Jill company until they go."

"It's okay," Jill said with a shrug. "I can just wait."

"Nonsense," Adriana said. "Mitchell is a wonderful host, and I'm sure he'll be delighted to delay his plans to be a supportive friend."

"Come on, Mom. She said she's fine," Mitchell said. "I'll be back later."

Kid is all heart, thought Tom.

"Tanner can wait. The Hawkins are going through a difficult period, and they need our support."

Mitchell's protest receded like the tide, and his demeanor shifted from emboldened to sheepish. "Sure thing," he said.

"That's better. Why don't you give her a tour of the house? I don't believe Jill's ever been over here before."

"Come on," Mitchell said to Jill. "I'll show you around. Then we can chill out in the basement if you want. You play air hockey?"

"Yeah, I'm pretty good at it," Jill said.

"That's more like it," Adriana said.

Mitchell nodded with his head for Jill to follow. Tom watched them leave through the same archway where Mitchell earlier had appeared. He noticed Mitchell had a tattoo on the back of his neck—a yin and yang symbol in the shape of a skull.

Yikes and yikes, thought Tom, relieved again that Mitchell and Jill ran in different circles.

Adriana went over to the cart with drinks on it. She squeezed Tom's arm as she passed.

"It's four o'clock, and I'm going to have a glass of wine. Sure you won't join me?" she said, pouring herself a near full glass of white wine from a bottle on ice.

"Thanks for the offer, but no. Water's fine."

Adriana sat down on the couch and sighed. "Sorry you had to witness that unpleasant exchange. Little kids, little problems. Big kids, big problems," she said before taking a healthy sip of her wine.

"He seems like a good kid," Tom said.

"Trust me, he's a handful. How are things with Jill?"

"Little kids, little problems. Big kids, big problems," Tom repeated.

Adriana nodded knowingly. "It must be hard on you both," she said. "Any break in the case? I've heard that the police think it was a robbery."

Tom took a seat on the couch beside her, following Adriana's prompt.

"There were some items missing from the house," Tom confirmed. "And signs of a struggle. But so far, no suspects. No arrests."

"I heard about what happened in the woods," Adriana said, touching the spot on his head where he'd been hit. Tom flinched. Adriana seemed oblivious to his reaction. "Do the police think it's connected with what happened to Kelly?"

"If they do, they're not saying."

Adriana flashed Tom a frown, and though she didn't say it, Tom could tell there had been some talk about him within her circle of friends.

"I play bridge with Cathleen Wells, and she told me that you're moving back to Shilo. Is that true?"

Tom nodded. "I need to do it for Jill. She doesn't want to leave town to come live with me, and I don't blame her. All her friends are here. Her life is here, and she won't be able to go to Shilo High School unless she's living in Shilo. We're going to try and make it work, but I'm not going to kid myself into thinking it's going to be easy. We've had a pretty tough go of it, even before her mother's death."

Adriana gave Tom a knowing glance. "I used to see Kelly occasionally after you two divorced," she said, "but we did talk from time to time. She took every opportunity to put you down, I'm sorry to say. I'm sure that's had an effect on Jill."

"It's made for an extra big challenge," said Tom.

A glaze of tears filled Adriana's eyes, and she dabbed

them away with her fingers. She excused herself and returned with a box of Kleenex. She laughed, but in a slightly embarrassed way.

"I'm sorry," she said. "When I think about children not getting along with their parents, it just breaks my heart. They don't understand how precious life is, how fragile."

Tom swallowed hard. He understood Adriana's pain. "I can't imagine how hard it is for you, still. I'm sure this is bringing up painful memories."

Adriana bit her lower lip and nodded. "When your child dies, it leaves a hole that can never be filled," she said, her voice shaking. "I've never forgiven myself for what happened to Stephen."

Tom's chest felt heavy with sorrow. "It wasn't your fault," he said. "You did everything you could to get Stephen the help that he needed. I remember."

"I could have done more."

Tom didn't know what to say. Stephen Boyd had been a troubled kid early on. He never went to Shilo High School, because either he was in rehab or he was being schooled at home. Even more tragic, Adriana had been the one to find Stephen's body. He was locked inside her car. He still had a needle sticking out of his arm. Tourniquet tied tight. He'd been dead for more than six hours.

"There isn't a day that goes by that I don't think about him," Adriana said. "I can't help wondering what Stevie would look like today. What would he be doing?"

Tom's throat went dry just thinking about Adriana's loss, and he needed a sip of water before he could again speak.

"I'm so very sorry for your loss. Anytime I try to get philosophical with Jill, she just gives me a blank stare," Tom said. "We haven't had any real bonding opportunities, so I'm just not sure how I'm going to reach her."

"You just have to be patient with her," Adriana said. "And stay persistent, too."

Tom smiled.

"What?" she asked, her voice rising with a squeak of interest.

"Nothing," Tom said, with a slight laugh. "It's just that my personal mantra is 'Persistence and patience.' The two Ps."

"Well, I think you've got a fabulous mantra. Don't let her go, Tom."

"I won't," Tom said. "I'll never give up on Jill."

Adriana surprised Tom by giving him a hug. She put her warm lips close to his ear and whispered, "I know."

Roland cleared his throat. "*Ahem!* I hope I'm not interrupting anything."

Adriana quickly pulled away. She stood and smoothed out the fabric of her pantsuit. Tom stood as well.

"Darling, you surprised me," Adriana said.

"And by the looks of it, just in the nick of time," Roland said.

CHAPTER 11

Roland crossed the room with a cool smile on his face. Tom understood why. Shortly after Stephen's death, Tom had overheard gossip about Adriana's affair with Doug Henderson in the teachers' lounge. Adriana's paramour had been the father of a Millis teenager who had died in a car accident. They met at a support group for grieving parents—a group that Roland had refused to attend. She'd been unfaithful to Roland before. Judging by the look Roland flashed Tom, he evidently believed she could be unfaithful again.

Tom had picked up other details about Roland and Adriana's troubled marriage from teacher lounge gossip. Roland hadn't thought Stephen's drug problems were as serious as Adriana believed them to be. Against Adriana's wishes, Roland insisted Stephen remain in school, not return to rehab, after another of his many relapses. Six months later, Stephen was dead.

Boyd wore a creaseless light blue polo shirt, dark khaki cargo shorts, and wire-rimmed reading glasses. His short military crop was now a healthy head of dark hair with distinguished gray patches at the temples, which he slicked back with a glossy gel. Boyd's thin face didn't have a sprig of facial hair on it, and his youthful appearance was strikingly similar to that of his son Mitchell.

"Tom's moving back to Shilo," Adriana said, with excitement in her voice. "Isn't that wonderful news?"

"Yes, it certainly is," Roland said.

"I'm moving back into the Oak Street house," Tom said. "So Jill doesn't have to leave."

"Well, let me know if there's anything I can do to help."

"If you'll excuse me," Adriana said, "I've got a lot of planning work to do for the party." Adriana's face lit up in a bright smile, as though she'd been struck by a fantastic idea. "Oh, Roland," she said. "Have you invited Tom? It think it would be good for him to make some new connections now that he's moving back into town."

Roland nodded. "Sure. That's a great idea."

"What is?" asked Tom.

"My annual client appreciation party at the club. You really should be there. Adriana's right. It's a good way for you to meet some of your new neighbors. Or old neighbors, as the case may be."

"I'll make sure you get an invitation before you leave," Adriana said.

"That would be great," said Tom as he exchanged air kisses with Adriana.

Roland turned to watch his wife leave the room. "I'm a lucky man," he said, but only after her footsteps could no longer be heard. "How are you holding up, Tom?"

"Doing okay. Thanks for asking."

"And Jill?"

"She's doing all right."

"I'm trying to rearrange my schedule so I can come to the funeral," Roland said.

"Thanks," said Tom.

"Look, Tom, I'm happy if you just want to hang out and chat, play catchup, but on the phone you sounded like you had something pretty important to talk about. No need to beat around the bush with me. Just saying."

Tom nodded. He always appreciated Roland's style. "Do you remember a guy named Kip Lange?" Tom asked.

Roland pursed his lips. "No. Is he from Shilo?"

"Not Shilo," Tom said. "Wiesbaden."

Tom could see the recollection come to Roland's face. "Lange . . . Isn't that the guy who shot Stan Greeley?"

Tom nodded. "About sixteen years ago. You, me, and Kelly, we were all stationed there at the time."

"Right. But if my memory serves, I think I was in Denmark when that went down. Who knows? Feels like a lifetime ago. Why? What's up with Lange? You don't think he had something to do with what happened to Kelly, do you?"

"I don't know," Tom said. "But I was wondering if you might have seen him around town."

"Isn't he still in prison?"

"He got out on appeal, sixteen years into his twenty-five-year sentence," Tom said, quoting facts that Marvin had uncovered.

"The guy shoots an officer and wins his appeal? Explain that one to me."

Marvin had unearthed the answer to that question as well. "I guess two of the ballistics experts and the MP who was first on the scene after the shooting gave their testimony via two-way video technology. Lange's defense argued that their testimony violated his constitutional right of confrontation and should have been inadmissible during trial. It took sixteen years, but the CAAF got some new judges appointed, and well, they agreed with the defense. The evidence was thrown out, as was Lange's conviction."

"So when did Lange get out?" asked Roland.

"Apparently, just a few days before somebody broke into Kelly's house," Tom said. Tom told Roland about his scuffle in the woods behind Jill's house—his house now.

"No idea where Lange's at now?"

Tom shook his head. This was where Marvin's efforts had come up short. Marvin was able to tell Tom when Lange got out and why, but he was unable to provide that most vital piece of information.

Roland looked dismayed. "I don't get it. Wasn't Lange busted for attempted murder? Why did he even get such a short sentence?"

"It wasn't a slam dunk case, if you remember," Tom said. The story was fresh in Tom's mind because he'd been studying up on Lange. "Greeley was shot in the head but didn't die. The wound left him badly brain damaged. Poor guy could barely speak after and couldn't even remember what happened to him that night. Lange played innocent the whole way. According to ballistics, Greeley had shot him in the leg and stomach. Lange said that he heard a scuffle in the lieutenant's home and came in to help Greeley. Greeley shot Lange by mistake, or so he claimed. But Lange couldn't explain to the MPs what had happened to his gun. That was a big problem for the JAG lawyers. Without it, they weren't able to match the ballistics. But they still went ahead and tried him for assault with a deadly weapon and got a twenty-five-year conviction. Lange shouldn't have even been up for parole for another ten years."

Roland shook his head in disbelief. "But he's out."

"He's out," Tom said.

Roland gave Tom a puzzled stare. "And you think

Lange is the one who broke into Kelly's house and assaulted her?"

"I'd like to be sure that he didn't."

"Have you gone to the police?" Roland asked. "I mean, if you think this guy had something to do with Kelly's death."

Tom nodded, but his face showed some frustration. "Yeah. I told them. But Murphy is heading up the investigation, and he thinks I may have had something to do with what happened to Kelly. I told him, but his expression didn't scream 'We'll get right on it, right away,' if you know what I mean."

Roland nodded. "So what makes you think Lange would have had anything to do with what happened to Kelly? I mean, why would he go see her after he got out of prison?"

Tom had rehearsed what he was going to say, knowing that Roland was going to ask the question.

"I guess Kelly and Lange were seeing each other romantically on the base," Tom said.

"Yeah? I didn't know that," Roland said. "Then again, there were twelve thousand people on that base, and I was traveling a lot of the time. She could have hung out with him, but I don't remember ever seeing them together."

"Kelly broke it off with Lange right after she and I got back together. I guess he became pretty jealous, started sending her threatening letters and such. He even sent her some from prison."

"Makes sense that you'd be concerned," Roland agreed. "Look, if you really need to know where this Lange character is, I'd be happy to make some inquiries on your behalf. A lot of my former military contacts are clients with Boyd Capital. High-ranking people, too. I've got connections to people who can help track him down."

"Thanks, Roland. I really appreciate that."

"You know, Tom—and don't take this the wrong way, because I know you can handle yourself—but with Jill and all, and that guy prowling in the woods, if you wanted to alarm the house, just to play it safe, one of my clients does all the local installs for APS Security. I'm sure I can get you a deal on a really good system."

Tom smiled. "You're not offending me at all," he said. "In fact I'm glad you mentioned it, because after speaking with you, alarming the house was the next item on my to-do list."

Roland shook his head in disbelief. "So you think Lange might still be harboring a jealous rage all these years later, huh?"

"It's a possibility," Tom said.

Nothing suggested to Tom that Roland had picked up on his lie. If it was Lange who had broken into the house, then he'd come looking for his share of the heroin Kelly had stolen from Stan Greeley. The drugs that Tom had unwittingly smuggled out of Germany.

Either that, thought Tom, or he'd come looking for his cut of the profits.

CHAPTER 12

Hours after Rainy sent her e-mail, supervisory senior resident agent (SSRA) Walt Tomlinson entered the Lair with an air of urgency. Tomlinson had three grown daughters, so Rainy figured he'd give her a fair chance to make her case for Stern.

Tomlinson's eyes looked troubled. Rainy read the deep creases defining Tomlinson's sagging face like a palmist predicting a bleak outcome.

"Show me what you got, Agent Miles."

Rainy showed Tomlinson several dozen of what she determined to be sexts culled from Mann's computer.

"What do you make of these, Carter?" Tomlinson asked.

"No idea where they came from. We don't think we're going to get any CVIP hits on these."

"What about our own database?" Tomlinson asked.

The FBI maintained a collection of their own hash values, non-official, of course, which came out of the Bureau's national center.

Even a partial match would have generated a KFF, or Known File Filter alert. The KFF alert flags files identifiable from the FBI's less extensive library of known images—most of which are depictions of child pornography.

"I checked and we got zilch," Rainy said. "Whoever supplied Mann with these pictures is probably a new source to us."

"So what's next?" Tomlinson asked.

Rainy started to answer, but Tomlinson pointed a finger to forestall her.

"We're going to continue with our forensic analysis here," Carter said. "The log file data is useless to us until we can get valid IP and MAC address information."

"And you can't?" said Tomlinson.

"Mann's basically encrypted all the header data on the file transfers. He used a new computer program that makes it easy to stay anonymous on the Internet."

"What program is that?" Tomlinson asked.

"It's called Leterg. We've busted a few kiddie porn collectors trying it out."

Rainy made a face. The software name sounded nonsensical.

"It's 'Gretel' spelled backward," Carter explained. "Basically, if you think of Hansel and Gretel's breadcrumb trick as an unencrypted data header that would allow us to follow a trail, Leterg makes it impossible for anybody to navigate a single path back to a source."

"I'm not sure I'm following," Tomlinson said.

Rainy followed perfectly well, but Tomlinson had several other squads under his command, including terrorism. He was a busy man with little time to absorb the nuanced details from the constant influx of new technologies.

Carter was more than happy to explain; he enjoyed talking technology. "If you laid down bread crumbs on your way home from work," he began, "I could easily tell what route you took home."

"Assuming the birds didn't eat the bread crumbs, yes." Tomlinson was always on the lookout for a hole in an explanation.

"Well, if every ten feet that single bread-crumb path split, went off in different directions, and stopped at different houses, could I ever tell where you started, or where you went?"

"No," Tomlinson answered.

"Well, that's exactly what Leterg does. Mann was communicating with somebody who was also running Leterg. Everything they sent went through that program, so we have no way of tracing it to a specific Internet hosting provider, let alone to a specific IP address."

"That sounds pretty sophisticated," Tomlinson said, rubbing at his temples as though the concept physically hurt.

"Actually, it's pretty damn easy for somebody who knows what they're doing," Carter said. "And it's a great way to cover your tracks. No evidence left to connect the criminal to the crime."

"How did we catch on to Mann?" Tomlinson asked Rainy.

"We got a tip. Fed him some of our stock images and he bit. Got a warrant. Made the bust."

"So how do we figure out Mann's suppliers?"

Carter sighed. "Leterg requires that both the sender and receiver use the software to block our traffic analysis. Multiple people can use the same software, but every supplier has a unique key. If we had the computer of one of Mann's suppliers, we could crack the encryption code, and you'd have the kind of evidence that makes the USAO tap-dance."

"Did Mann use a single source or multiples?"

"We think multiples. But everyone who supplied him was running Leterg. He probably installed the software and then went looking for suppliers who used the same CYA technology."

"CYA?" Tomlinson asked.

"Cover your ass," Carter explained.

Tomlinson nodded slowly and did not appear amused. "So do we know who these victims are?"

Rainy's face brightened. Tomlinson had touched upon an important point.

"It's my opinion that these images are of the same type, but not from a single source," Rainy said. "I think they're different girls—forty of them, by my count—taking pictures of themselves with their cell phone cameras."

"And they sent their pictures to James Mann using Leterg?"

"I don't believe that's true."

"Do we know how Mann got hold of these images?"

"No, sir," Rainy said. "And it will stay that way unless we can crack the Leterg encryption codes."

Carter held up his hand to indicate caution. "Remember," he said. "If Mann had forty suppliers, we'll need to crack forty codes. That's a pretty unlikely outcome."

Tomlinson thought. "A bit of a chicken-and-the-egg conundrum, it seems."

Carter hoisted his hands skyward in a show of defeat. "Hence we come to a dead end. At least we can still get Mann for all the porn he downloaded."

Rainy nodded in silent agreement. Thanks to the Adam Walsh act, James Mann met the interstate nexus requirement. The FBI could charge him with federal crimes simply because he had used the Internet to download pornography. As far as the law was concerned, Internet equaled interstate.

"Sounds good to me. Agent Miles, what's the issue here?"

"The issue is these teenage girls who are sexting are stupid and haven't a clue what they're getting themselves into," Rainy wanted to say. But she thought better of it. "Mann possessed a very large quantity of these unknown images—over three hundred. I think it's important we confirm these images did in fact originate as part of a text message the girls themselves sent," she said.

"Good. Then eventually you'll get to that conclusion if the evidence takes you there."

"We could speed things up, maybe even figure out Mann's supplier if we could ID one of these girls. But there isn't enough detail in these pictures for me to make one."

"In your opinion, are any of these girls in immediate danger?" Tomlinson asked.

Rainy knew better than to lie. "No, sir," Rainy said. "The images are consistent with other sexts that we've seen. But I'm wondering if somebody is hacking cell phones. If I could get some of Clarence Stern's time, maybe put together a bigger task force, we could—"

"Out of the question," Tomlinson barked. "Stern is fully booked investigating what may be a terrorist sleeper cell in Somerville. I can't spare him."

"But he's the best at image manipulation."

"Which is why he's working terrorism."

Rainy bit her lip. After 9/11, the FBI had rocketed right to the top of Washington's most important agency list. Budgets ballooned as a result, but most of the money and resources went toward combating terrorism. Meanwhile, drugs, child porn, organized crime, mainstay assignments of the FBI for years, continued to skyrocket. Rainy couldn't complain. It was well known that terrorism was job one at the FBI.

"Well, what do you suggest I do, Walt?"

"What I suggest you do is your job, Agent Miles."

"Sir, if one of the girls finds out that her naked pictures are being passed around the Internet, it could end in tragedy. It could be another Melanie Smyth."

Melanie Smyth was a fifteen-year-old girl from Newton who'd hung herself in the bedroom closet after her boyfriend posted the naked pictures she texted him to Facebook.

"Stern is booked. End of conversation. After you alert the major carriers about a potential hack, I suggest you talk with Mr. James Mann and figure out how we crack those Leterg codes."

"He's not going to know. Suppliers using Leterg do it to keep themselves anonymous."

"Then it looks like you've got your work cut out for you," Tomlinson said, and left.

Rainy picked up the CVIP report and read it again. Tomlinson was wrong about this one. These girls might have taken their pictures willingly, but that didn't mean they weren't in any danger.

CHAPTER 13

Tom watched the Wildcats soccer scrimmage from the sidelines. It felt good to be coaching again. He needed the distraction.

"How are we looking out there, Coach?" Lindsey asked.

"We're looking a little sloppy," Tom said. "But I'm sure we'll pull it together."

"Yeah. I'm sure. Do you think I'll get more playing time?"

"I'm not sure, Lindsey," Tom said. "You know my position. You've got to work harder out there. You've got the talent. Now you've got to show me you have the desire."

"I need to play more. I'll get better. But I'm not going to get any colleges interested in me with the minutes I got last year. Please, Coach."

Tom nodded. "I'm not saying no," he said. "Okay? I'll sub you in for Ashley in a minute."

"Thanks, Coach."

Jill was at practice, but not dressed to play. She wasn't feeling ready yet. Tom understood completely, but he needed to get back to coaching the team and couldn't let Jill out of his sight. Not with Kip Lange still on the loose.

The first game of the season was just a week away.

Tom noticed something in the distance. A police car was again coming down the road abutting the practice field. The cruiser parked where it had before, and Brendan Murphy climbed out with his signature lack of grace.

"Vern, keep the girls working hard," Tom said to his assistant coach as he crossed the field. Tom didn't notice the metal storage clipboard tucked under Murphy's arm until the two met up on the other sideline.

"Good afternoon, Tom," Murphy said, without extending his hand.

"Long time, Brendan," Tom said, making no attempt to hide the sarcasm in his voice. "How've you been?"

Murphy removed his mirrored shades. Tom found the gleam in the cop's eyes most unsettling.

"Well, okay, Tom. I've been okay."

"What brings you to practice today?"

"We've got ourselves a situation, I guess that's what."

"Is this about Kelly's homicide investigation?"

"No," Murphy said. "Looks like we've got ourselves a new situation."

Murphy peered over Tom's shoulder and waved to somebody approaching from behind. Tom turned and spotted the school's athletic director, Craig Powers, waving and walking toward the pair. Tom and Craig Powers had worked together for years and were fond of each other. Powers approached from the direction of Shilo High School, a redbrick building that, according to the school committee, had too many students and too few cafeterias.

Tom turned back and looked at Murphy. "Is somebody hurt, Brendan? One of the kids' parents, I mean."

Murphy responded with a grunt but stayed quiet. He apparently wanted Powers to hear whatever had to be said. Powers, thin, balding, looked unsteady on his spindly, long legs. He moved in an unathletic way for an athletic director, Tom thought. But something about this impromptu gathering seemed wrong. Tom had a dreadful feeling that made him forget all about Kip Lange.

Tom noticed how Murphy extended a hand toward Powers. The men shook the way poker buddies might.

"Thanks for making the time, Craig."

"Does Tom know yet?" Powers asked.

"Not yet. I was waiting for you," Murphy answered.

"Know what?" Tom asked.

"Heck on a high stick," Powers said. "I'll tell him, then."

Powers loved inventing phrases—without the expletives, of course. Tom often found those folksy colloquialisms not only novel, but situation appropriate as well. Heck on a high stick, indeed! Again Tom called up his kinesics training from his Navy SEAL days and could see Powers's concern as clearly as he could read an opponent's defensive scheme.

"Tell me what, Craig?" Tom asked.

"We got an anonymous tip about a Web blog that somebody started," Powers said. "And it involved you." He said this in a tone that was more annoyed than alarmed.

"Me?"

"Yeah, that's right. I got an email from somebody—I don't know who," Powers continued. "The message said simply that I should check out this link and that it pertained to you. So I clicked on it and opened this Web site called Tumblr.com. Ever hear of it?"

"No," Tom said.

"It's for blogging," Murphy said. "You can post text, photos, quotes, links, that sort of thing."

"Well, this wasn't protected at all," Powers said. "Anybody who had the link could have read it. Whoever created the page was looking for attention and wanted people to see it, if you ask me. That's my guess."

"Yeah? An attention-seeking mystery blog," Tom said. "Well, what was on this blog that's got the attention of the police?"

Powers cleared his throat as if he were about make an important announcement. He didn't get the chance. Murphy answered for him.

"It said that you've been having sex with one of the girls on your team." Murphy looked smug, as if to say, "I may not get you for Kelly's murder, but I'll nail you for something else."

"You don't really think I'm sleeping with a player?" Tom said. "Come on. Are you joking?"

Powers and Murphy each held a blank stare.

Tom frowned. "By the looks on your faces, I'm guessing no. You're not joking."

Murphy opened his storage clipboard and took out five sheets of paper, which he handed to Tom.

Tom leafed through the pages. As he did, his skin began to crawl. Murphy put his sunglasses back on. *Perhaps,* Tom thought, *to hide the glee in his eyes.*

"I think the first post called you a better sex teacher than a coach," Murphy said. "By the fifth one, well, let's just say that stuff would make a stripper blush."

Tom's first thought was that some twisted kid was preying on Jill's tragedy. Teens engaged in cyber bullying all the time. One of them must be out to humiliate Jill by attacking her father. Tom crumpled the pages Murphy had given him into a tight ball.

"Ah, shucks, Tom. That's evidence," Murphy said, but with a mock dismay. "No worries, though. I brought more copies. To show the girls."

"To what!" Tom exclaimed, loudly enough for some of the girls to stop running, and for Vern to whistle to get them moving again. "What did you just say?" Tom asked.

"Tom, Sergeant Murphy and I believe this might be some sort of prank," Powers said. "Sergeant Murphy suggested the best way to ferret out a prankster is to confront him or her head-on."

"Well, that's just insane," Tom said in a disgusted tone. "Craig, please tell me that you don't really think this is a good idea! Just the rumor of my being involved with a player will have devastating consequences for the team. You know that's true—"

"Nonsense," Murphy broke in. The sergeant patted Tom on the shoulder. The taps felt like blows from a sledgehammer, each one driving Tom deeper into the ground. "Best way to get the prankster to come forward is to get these girls talking as a group," he continued. "In my experience with this sort of thing, once the group gets talking, they end up pressuring whoever pulled the stunt to delete the account. Or at least get one of them to come forward with some useful information."

"And how much experience have you had with this sort of thing, Murph?"

"Are you questioning my judgment here, Coach?"

"Damn straight I am! We both know what this is really about. Don't we?"

Powers looked first at Murphy, then at Tom with a degree of confusion. "What's going on?"

"Murphy thinks I had something to do with what happened to Kelly," Tom said. "Craig, he's making a spectacle out of this anonymous blog because he knows what it'll do to me in the aftermath. He's only doing this to put the screws to me."

Powers looked over to Murphy. "Brendan, is this true?" he asked.

"Not at all," Murphy said. "One thing doesn't have anything to do with the other. We agree Tom's reputation is under attack and we think it's a prank. Now we'll find out who did this. I've already issued a preservation request with Tumblr. That way the data is safe and I can try to remedy the situation by interviews without having to go through the mountain of paperwork to obtain a search warrant."

"My concern isn't that you keep the data safe," Tom said. "My concern is that you want to bring it to my team's attention."

"You worried about something else coming to light, Coach Hawkins?" Murphy asked. His tone was knowing, like a hunter setting his trap. Allow the interview because you're innocent, and you end up screwed. Refuse to cooperate because you're innocent, then you look guilty *and* you're screwed.

"What I'm worried about, Sergeant Murphy, Craig, is the repercussions of false allegations."

"If it's a prank, Tom, we need to get to the bottom of it fast," Powers said. "I'm here to reinforce the fact that we're viewing this as a prank and only that. I'm here to protect you, Tom."

Tom shook his head. "If you want to protect me and this team, you'll put a stop to this right now."

"You're making a way bigger deal out of this than you should, Coach Hawkins," Murphy said. "We won't show the girls anything they shouldn't see. The copies of the notes I brought have everything racy blacked out. Well, to be honest, the page is mostly black, but there's still some stuff they might see that will help us ID the account creator."

"Why don't you just look at who made the damn account?"

"Gee, Coach, you're a bit out of the know on how this technology stuff works," Murphy said. Tom hadn't been spoken to in that way since boot camp. "These kids make secret profiles all the time so they can bully each other online. Bogus email addresses. Fake profile pictures. Bottom line is we don't know who made this Tumblr account. But we will soon enough."

Tom clenched his hands. Murphy looked down and saw Tom's tightly balled fists. He looked Tom in the eye and gave him a smile, as if to say, "Go ahead. Take your best shot."

"I can't tell you how much I'm against this, Craig."

"Your objection is noted, Tom. But I'm following police advice here, and it's not your authority to dictate how I run my athletic department. Sergeant Murphy has assured me this is the best way forward."

"Forward into hell," Tom wanted to say.

"Okay, call them together," Murphy ordered.

Tom bowed his head, sighed, and blew his coach's whistle.

The girls didn't need another blast. They all came running.

CHAPTER 14

Vern Kalinowski got the girls into a row, their toes touching the white line that marked the playing field's boundaries. Sergeant Murphy stood beside Powers. Murphy had his hands on his hips and watched the girls as they lined up. He looked like a dog licking his chops in anticipation of a juicy bone. *His* juicy bones.

Tom marched over to where Powers stood. He believed he still had time to prevent the coming disaster. He wasn't worried about himself as much as about Jill.

"You're a minute away from making me an outcast in this town."

Powers gave Tom his best "come on, now" look, which Tom wanted to rub off with his knuckles. "Let's not blow this out of proportion, Coach. We have every confidence that we'll find the prankster within this group here."

"And if you don't?"

"If we don't, then we'll keep digging."

"And how do you expect me to coach these girls after this, Craig?"

"The same way you always do," Powers said. "You stand strong. Once we figure out who's responsible, the whole incident will blow over. Trust me on this."

"And what about my daughter?" Tom lowered his voice and asked the question through clenched teeth.

"We thought about that, too," Powers replied, also in a low, secretive voice. "We know you two haven't had the easiest time adjusting, what with her mother's death, the circumstances, and you moving back to Shilo and all. I don't want to imply anything here, Tom, but, well . . ."

A thick vein on Tom's neck, usually visible only when he was working out, began to pulse for another reason. Every muscle in his body felt tense—on fire. "Say it," he demanded.

"It's just one theory, but . . ."

"You think my daughter is behind this?"

Powers looked around, worried that someone might have overheard. "Consider the timing."

The thought churned Tom's stomach. His chest tightened while his mind explored the unfathomable. Could Jill have done it? No! That was impossible to believe, but . . . but what if she had somebody do it for her? But why? Revenge for all his perceived wrongdoings?

Is it possible she thinks I had something to do with her mother's death? he wondered.

Tom rubbed his hands back and forth through his hair. He glanced over at Jill, who stood in line, stone-faced and still. Unlike him, not a bead of sweat glistened.

Powers called for the girls' attention. Tom considered leaving the practice field altogether in protest but decided to stay. Murphy had it all figured out from the start—Tom Hawkins, stay or go, was about to be branded guilty of something.

"Hello, girls," Powers began. "So, I bet you're wondering why the gathering."

There were murmurs. Some said, "Sure." Most stayed silent.

"Okay, so here's the deal. Somebody sent me a link to a Web blog on Tumblr.com," Powers explained. "The page contains some very graphic content, with serious allegations pertaining to Coach Hawkins and one of you players. Now, we don't believe these posts are authentic. If we did, Coach Hawkins would not be standing here with us while we confronted you all."

The girls weren't ignorant. They knew "graphic content" meant sex.

Tom looked up and down the line, studying his team carefully. He didn't doubt that somebody had taken the trouble to create the salacious posts. The question on his mind—Powers's and Murphy's, too—was who and why.

Tom's ability to read body language wasn't helping at all. The girls were openly and obviously nervous: fidgeting with their shorts, bouncing on their heels, looking at the grass. If they were in on it as a group, perhaps they feared they'd all been busted. More likely, they were feeling anxious because some plus-sized cop was parading in front of them, wearing mirrored shades and doing his best O.K. Corral strut.

Tom caught Jill's eye. She held her father's gaze for a beat. A pained expression washed over her face seconds before she looked away, and that hurt Tom more than any prank ever could. The SEALs had taught him how to maintain control over his emotions. But it took every bit of his training to keep from shouting out to her, "Baby, don't you believe it. Don't you believe for one second I would ever do that!"

He mouthed the words to her, though.

"This is not a joke," Powers continued. "Some of you may know Sergeant Murphy here from the D.A.R.E. program. Sergeant Murphy and I have discussed this situation in detail over the past several days, and we are in agreement that one or more of you girls know who created the account and wrote these posts."

Murphy took that as his cue. "I've brought handouts with me," he said. "Printouts from the blog. I'm going to pass them out to you, then collect them before we break. Anything inappropriate, we've blacked out with marker. Now, the reason I'm showing you this is because we want you to come forward with information about who created these posts. If you recognize something about the writing that can help us identify that person, well, great. That's what we want to know. But as a team, you should be very aware that there are serious consequences for this sort of behavior. It can cost you a lot more than some embarrassment."

Murphy walked the line and, as he did, handed each girl a piece of paper. The girls didn't hesitate to read what they could. Widening eyes and dropping jaws made it clear to Tom that their imaginations were filling in what the black marks had taken out.

Vern moved in close to stand a whisper's distance from Tom. His assistant coach made little effort to conceal his deep concern. "What the hell is going on?" he asked.

"Vern, have you heard any of the girls talking about me?"

"Talking? About what?"

"Any of them angry? Did I offend one of them? Are any of them upset about something I did or said?"

"Nothing I heard about. Why? What's this all about?"

"Either somebody is going to step forward now, or I think you're about to witness the end of my coaching career at Shilo."

Tom's mind raced to ID a suspect. He'd been tough on Lindsey Wells for sure, but he didn't think he'd crossed any lines with her. She was upset about her playing time, but not enough to make him a target. McAndrews? Grass?

Vern's twins? It could have been any of them, but Tom doubted it. What were they after? A new coach? They had a record number of wins. State championships. Was he too hard? Too demanding? The feedback at team meetings had only been positive. The girls made it a point to tell him what a good job he'd been doing. All of them, except for Jill.

"I realize you girls have already been through a lot these past couple of days. But Sergeant Murphy is right about consequences," Powers said. "This sort of thing is not only illegal, but it can very well cost you the season. It's an embarrassment to Coach Hawkins as well as to your school. I don't know if one of you is angry with Coach about playing time, coaching style, or the drinks he gives you at halftime. No matter what it is that led to these posts, they are way—and I mean *way*—out of line. It won't be tolerated. Now, I've worked out a deal with Coach Hawkins and Sergeant Murphy intended to save your season."

Vern nudged Tom, but Tom hadn't a clue about any deal. Murphy walked the line and collected the handouts. The girls seemed relieved to give them back.

"As long as the girl who created the account comes forward, or one of you anonymously tells us who did it, and we can verify it's true, there won't be any repercussions at all. Not for the person who wrote it or the rest of the team. If this sounds like I'm pressuring you to rat out your friend, well, damn straight I am. This is a very serious matter that I intend to take very seriously."

Silence. All Tom heard was their silence. *Come forward, dammit! End this now.* Soon, he knew the girls would be back home with their parents. Parents would be calling parents, and the news would spread. Emails about him would clog up Shilo's notoriously spotty Internet service.

The superintendent would demand a meeting. Powers seemed oblivious. Murphy seemed to be gloating.

"Coach, do you have anything to add?" Powers asked.

Tom glared at the athletic director. "No, Craig. I think you've done quite enough already."

"So, is anybody ready to come forward and take ownership?"

Not a single hand rose. Not a single girl spoke or took a step forward, until Jill's cheeks flushed a bright shade of red. Without saying a word, she took off across the practice field, running faster than Tom had ever seen her run before.

Murphy went to his car and came back holding a clipboard with a paper attached. He handed the clipboard to Tom.

"Coach, we're going to want to take a look at your laptop computer."

"My school-issued computer?"

"That's the one," Murphy said.

"What's this?" Tom asked.

"A consent form. You're agreeing to let me take possession of your work computer."

Tom didn't say anything. He just started filling out the form.

CHAPTER 15

Tom paced around the kitchen. It was almost seven o'clock. Jill should have been home hours ago.

He texted her again.

Again she texted back: Green.

Where are you? I want your location, not status.

No answer.

He texted her again.

This time she responded.

Green!!!

At least he knew she wasn't in any danger. Kip Lange hadn't gotten to her. Jill was following their established communication plan in case they ever got separated. Tom would text her the question, "How are you doing?" If she was fine, her required response back to him was the word *green*. Any other reply, or no reply at all, and Tom would know something was wrong. Jill's responding only with the word *green* was also her way of saying, "Leave me alone."

Tom wanted to know where his daughter was and, more important, who she was with. He called every player on the team to ask if they'd seen or heard from Jill since practice. Shilo had two proper ways to exist: married with kids or retired with visiting grandchildren. Tom didn't fit the Shilo mold. With news of the blog post spreading like a virus around town, Tom not only broke the mold, but he'd taken a bat and damn well shattered it.

Somewhat to Tom's surprise, many of the girls and their parents hadn't turned against him. At least for the moment, they were willing to believe Tom wasn't a sexual predator. That he was innocent of any wrongdoing. Unfortunately, cooperative as some of them were, nobody could help him locate Jill.

Tom's anxiousness increased to the point of making him physically ill. Headache. Upset stomach. His only relief came when Jill responded to his last three text messages.

Green.

Green.

Green.

Nine o'clock came and went. Tom put his jacket on. He had his car keys in hand, ready to drive the streets of Shilo, when a fire red Mustang pulled up to the curb and Jill jumped out of the passenger-side door. Tom watched Jill through the front-door sidelight windows. She bounced her way along the brick walkway, as though her world was void of worry. Tom retreated up the short carpeted staircase, and he stood in the kitchen entranceway, his arms folded tight across his chest.

Jill closed the front door quietly behind her.

"Where have you been?" Tom asked. Jill marched up the front stairs, passing within a foot of Tom without acknowledging his presence, let alone answering his question.

"Jill, I asked you a question. Please answer me. I've been worried sick. Where have you been?"

Jill took off her jacket as she walked the carpeted corridor toward her bedroom door, which was the first room on the right. She closed the door to her room quickly, barely giving Tom a glimpse inside. Pressing his body up against the pinewood, he understood perfectly well that the door wasn't the real barrier between them. Tom silently cursed Craig Powers and Sergeant Brendan Murphy.

We were getting closer. I know we were, he thought.

"Jilly-bean, please talk to me. Who was that who drove you home?" Tom used her nickname, though he hadn't done so in years. It came out because she would always be his Jilly-bean.

"I don't want to talk right now," came a muffled reply.

"Well, that isn't really an option. I'm your father, Jill. I have a right to know where you were. You didn't answer my calls, and I want to know who drove you home."

Again no answer.

Tom continued, undeterred. "Look, I know today was really rough on you. I'm beyond angry about how it was handled, and I plan on speaking with Mr. Powers about it first thing tomorrow. I know it was embarrassing for you, too."

Nothing.

"Dammit, Jill, I'll stand here all night and talk to this door until I get an answer. Do you hear me?"

Tom pressed his open palm against her door. He heard the doorknob turn and felt the door open just a crack.

Jill placed her bright and beautiful moon-shaped face into the opening. "Did you do it?"

"No, sweetie, I didn't do anything like that. They thought peer pressure would get the person who made up that stuff to come forward."

"I talked to a bunch of the girls afterward. Nobody wrote it. They think it's true."

"Jilly, come out. Let's talk about this."

Jill opened the door. Whipped it open would be more accurate.

"What are you trying to do to me?" she shouted. "Ruin my life? Because that's what you're doing!" In that instant his daughter, who had been simmering with anger, broke into a boil.

"I moved here so you didn't have to move away. I did this for you."

"Well, next time don't do me any favors, okay!" Jill tried to slam the door shut, but Tom's foot got in the way. "Move your foot. I'm tired and I want to go to bed."

"Not until you talk to me. Who drove you home tonight?"

Jill slammed the door against her father's foot again and again, hard as her momentum would allow. Sharp jolts of pain shot up Tom's leg each time the door slammed into his foot, but his face didn't show the hurt.

Jill opened her bedroom door with an exasperated sigh and slipped past Tom before he could stop her. She went straight into her mother's bedroom, where she once again closed the door behind her. Jill slept in her mother's bed some nights, but Tom never let on that he knew. If she wanted to open up about her feelings, he figured she'd do so in her own time.

Tom knocked. "I'm not giving up until you talk to me."

When Jill didn't respond, Tom pressed his ear against the door and could hear the shower running. Tom trotted downstairs. With a few turns of a knob, he shut off the hot water. It took a few minutes for the water in the pipes to go completely cold. Once it did, Tom heard Jill shriek, curse, and finally open the bedroom door. She had on her mother's green terry-cloth bathrobe, the one Tom had bought for Kelly a year before the divorce. Jill's hair looked a tangled, wet mess, with soapy remains throughout.

"That's not fair."

"Neither is ignoring me."

"Turn the hot water back on." Jill tried to pass him, but this time, Tom blocked her way. Jill sighed loudly. "Fine," she said. "What is it you want to know?"

"Where were you and who drove you home?"

"At a friend's house and a friend. There. Happy?"

"No. Which friend's house, and who's the guy with the Mustang? I sure as heck hope he's young enough to still have a curfew."

"Why? You afraid of another old guy competing with you for all the young girls?" Jill saw the hurt in his eyes and gave a slight smile of victory.

"Craig Powers thought you might have started all this," Tom said.

Jill's face turned a bright shade of red before her color drained. Tom hadn't meant to say it, but Jill made it impossible not to become confrontational. Tom watched as she shook with rage.

"That's disgusting! Why did he even say that?"

"He was thinking you did it to get me in trouble. I told them they were wrong. You'd never do anything like that. Even if you hate me."

"I do hate you," Jill said, but quietly, without much emotion.

"I don't believe that's true," Tom replied. "But I need your help, Jill. I'm going to go on the offensive and find out who posted that garbage. But you have to believe me. I would never do such a thing, and I would never do anything to hurt you. I love you more than anything in the world. You are my world." If Tom could have one dying wish, at that moment it would be for Jill to let him embrace her. He knew better than to ask. He lifted her chin.

"Mitchell Boyd," Jill said, pulling her chin away.

"What?"

"You asked where I was and who drove me home. I was with Mitchell Boyd."

"Roland Boyd's son?" Tom wanted desperately for it to be another Mitchell Boyd from another town, though that was more than unlikely.

"Yeah. But we're just friends, so don't worry."

Tom was worried. Very worried, in fact. Mitchell's reputation made it impossible for a father not to worry. He cursed himself, because he was the one who had brought Jill to Boyd's house. "I don't approve."

"I don't care," Jill said.

An hour later, Tom and Jill had come to a truce of sorts. After their big blowout, he'd gone to the basement and returned carrying a large whiteboard that he used to map out different plays for the team. On that whiteboard, Tom had drawn a soccer goal. In front of the goal he drew a large square, creating an obstacle in the way of two stick figures that he'd also drawn. Tom drew a bow behind the head of the smaller of the two stick figures.

Jill realized that bow was meant to signify her. "I'm not a ten-year-old girl," she said, but not angrily.

"Humor me for a second. When we can't figure out something going wrong on the pitch, we always draw it out. It helps us to visualize the challenge and search out solutions."

"So you want to draw out our issues?" Jill asked.

Tom nodded. "And together we'll look for ways to get around them."

Jill went silent.

Tom smiled, undeterred. "I think trust is our number one challenge." He wrote the word *trust* in the center of the square. "On the field you've got to trust your teammates. You've got to believe that they'll be in position to receive your pass. If you don't have trust, you don't have a team. What's it going to take to get you to trust me, Jill?"

Jill thought awhile before answering. "Time," she said.

Tom nodded and wrote the word *time* on the whiteboard. He drew an arrow from the word to the stick figure representing himself. "That's on me, Jill," he said. "Over time I've got to earn your trust. I accept that. But you also have to earn mine. I didn't know where you were. I didn't know if you were hurt. Or worse. I had no idea who you were with. To make this work, we need to trust each other. So I'm just asking, what could you have done that would have helped me?"

"Call, I guess," Jill said. "I should have told you where I was. But I was upset."

Tom wrote *call* under Jill's stick figure.

With his hand, he erased a small corner of the square with the word *trust* in it. "Even if you're upset, we're still on the same team. Shutting me out won't change that fact. We've got a long way to go to get past this obstacle." Tom dotted the square with the point of his dry-erase marker to emphasize his point. "But I think this is a start."

"Tell me again you had nothing to do with what happened to Mom."

"Honey, I had nothing to do with it," Tom said. "And I need you to trust me on that." He tapped the marker against the written word *trust* on the whiteboard and forced a hug out of her. It was a brief, strained embrace, but it lasted long enough to give him hope.

CHAPTER 16

Rainy felt whole-body tired. Lately, she'd been working way too much OT. She'd put a bug in Clarence Stern's ear about needing help with some imaging work. She didn't mention the images were from a series Tomlinson told her not to bother Stern about.

"No can help," Stern had said during one of their passing hallway conversations. "These days I've got to schedule time to take a piss."

Rainy remained convinced that one or more of these images would eventually leave the closed circles of the child porn trade for wider distribution across the Internet. It was only a matter of time before there was another Melanie Smyth, she had warned Tomlinson. But Tomlinson didn't share her sense of urgency. If the pictures had been of a bomb, no doubt her boss would have made Stern pee in a cup until he tracked down the source.

But this was terrorism of a different kind.

When Rainy's cell phone rang, she answered it without checking the number or thinking about who might be calling.

"Rainy, it's Clarence. I've got a trade to offer."

Rainy's heart skipped a beat.

"Talk," she said.

"Do you have any plans tonight?"

"No," Rainy lied. She had a blind date that would need to be canceled.

"Then come up to my office, and let's make a deal."

Stern's office was a spacious, refurbished conference room on the sixth floor of their new building. The agency might have preached fiscal responsibility, but such frugality was not on display in Stern's world. The Lair looked like an Atari 2600 to Stern's Xbox 360. Stern sat on his swivel chair with his back to Rainy. His head bobbed to whatever beat thumped in his headphones. The array of computer monitors cast his body's heavyset outline in a bright blue glow.

In Stern's case, Rainy figured the Bureau decided to ignore their physical fitness requirement in exchange for his boundless talent. The man's round physique suggested he would struggle to pull a cumulative score above a six on the physical fitness test. Rainy's last score of thirty, by contrast, was reported to be among the highest of all female agents.

Rainy tapped Stern on the shoulder. Stern slowly pulled the headphones off his head. Even though he'd invited her up, Stern looked irritated by her intrusion, but he looked irritated by just about everything.

"What's the trade?" Rainy asked.

"I've got four arms' worth of work here and two arms to do it all."

"You want my arms?" Rainy asked.

Stern nodded. "Not in a physical sense. Do you know how to log surveillance video?"

"It's not rocket science," said Rainy.

"It's six hours of tape."

Rainy groaned. "Six hours? That's torture."

"You do six hours of logging for me, and I'll ID as many of the girls in that new series you found."

"You're that tired of my bugging you?"

"I'm that tired of logging surveillance video," Stern replied.

"Deal," said Rainy.

Rainy returned to Stern's office twenty minutes later and handed him a thumb drive. The Lair offered a protective environment for safeguarding her evidence. She preferred not to take evidence out of the Lair, but saw no alternative. If she wanted Stern's help, she had to take the risk.

"Okay, you start logging. I'll work my magic. Take a seat."

Rainy pulled up a chair beside Stern and set about the arduous task of logging.

"Note the time each person enters and exits the apartment building. Here are snaps of our delightful suspects. Match them to the people coming and going, and write your findings in the logbook here. Simple enough."

"Don't you have somebody to do this for you?" Rainy asked with a sigh of desperation.

"Normally, yes. This week, no."

Over the next four hours, Stern would groan, pout, shake his head, and grunt, all presumably signals that he had failed to find anything useful. Meanwhile, Rainy kept logging while Stern kept searching. Only once did Rainy see Stern stand up to stretch. On more than one occasion, Stern threw a pencil at his computer monitor, never failing to connect with the eraser end. He kept muttering to himself, "No, not that one," and then he'd start working with another picture in the batch Rainy had provided.

"What are you looking for?" Rainy asked him after Stern again switched to a new image.

"Something useful," he said.

Rainy just nodded and resumed her logging duties.

Three hours into his promised six, Stern exclaimed, "I've got it!"

Rainy had drifted into a zone of tape logging, and Stern had to repeat himself before she got excited. "You did? Who is she?"

"Well, I don't know."

"I thought you said you got it."

"I got how we can do it. I've run twenty girls through every sophisticated facial reorganization application we have. I even did some aging analysis in case the picture is an old one."

Rainy felt a sudden disappointment. She hadn't thought of that. These girls could be in their twenties by now.

"But you got nothing."

"Nada. Zilch. Then I figured out what I've been doing wrong. I spent so much time focusing on the faces, I've been ignoring the setting. Their rooms."

"Carter and I looked. But we didn't see anything useful."

"Well, you can't enhance pixels the way I can. I'm going to work off this picture. She took it standing in front of her mirror, so I've got a lot of the room to work with visible in the reflection. Keep logging. This may take another hour."

What Stern could do in an hour, Rainy knew, would take normal programmers five times as long to complete. When he announced success, Rainy understood that he'd basically churned out two days' worth of product in less

than half a day's effort. Rainy positioned her chair closer
to Stern so she could get a better look at his screen.

Stern manipulated the image on his monitor to show
Rainy an enhanced view of the girl's bedroom.

"First thing I'm going to do is crop out everything but
what's visible in the mirror," Stern said. "Then I'm going
to flip the image around so that it doesn't look like a reflection."

He did both in less than two seconds.

Next, he used his computer mouse to highlight a corner of the room, and the picture zoomed in closer. All
Rainy could see were the fuzzy, pixelated outlines of a
dresser, mirror, and chair. On the chair she could make
out a blue Windbreaker, but it, too, was barely recognizable at the current magnification level.

"I'm not seeing anything," Rainy said.

"Watch. I'm going to run my script."

Stern hit a button, and the entire image went black,
save for the chair with the Windbreaker on it. Then image
magnified tenfold, until Rainy saw what she took to be a
design of some sort.

"Is that a logo on the Windbreaker?" she asked with
growing excitement.

"Watch," Stern said.

Stern's program began to twist, wrap, and stretch the
image, while adding new pixels to the design. The transformation took what had been a blurry, shapeless form
and rendered it anew. It was now clear and easy to inter-
pret.

"This is how we'll figure out who this girl is," Stern
said. "You see, the jacket was folded over the chair. What
my program just did was to take the pixels that were invisible to us and hypothesize what the lettering would be
if the jacket were to be unfolded. It's a lot of vector analy-

sis, but this is the best match I got. The proportions aren't right, because the Windbreaker was folded, but at least the lettering is legible."

Rainy read the words Stern's program had generated.

"Shilo Wildcats Soccer."

"Now to Google," Stern said. He did a few Web searches before finding a picture he thought might be useful.

"What's that?" Rainy asked.

"A team picture of last year's girls' varsity soccer team. Assuming, of course, that 'Shilo' is Shilo, New Hampshire. But they are the Wildcats, so . . ."

Rainy studied the team photo. She didn't need to look at the girl's picture again. Her face was burned into Rainy's memory. And there she was. Back row. Second to last on the left. Rainy scanned the names of the girls listed in the photograph.

"Her," Rainy said, tapping a finger on Stern's spotless monitor. "That's her! You're a miracle worker, Clarence, you know that?"

"Nah. I just can't stand logging video." Stern leaned in close to read the name for himself. "Yup, that's her, all right. Lindsey Wells, of Shilo, New Hampshire."

CHAPTER 17

The Woonsocket Country Club boasted a membership so wealthy, it was the target of every community fund-raiser from Shilo to North Coventry. The reception room at the exclusive Harold Ross Grill, perched proudly on the nineteenth hole, advertised an ambience both elegant and casual. Surfaces were made of stone or oak, and the dining room blended family-style dining with a more upscale interior design.

Tom felt woefully underdressed. His thrown-together outfit (ancient tweed jacket, chino slacks, somewhat wrinkled collared shirt, no tie) might as well have been procured from a Goodwill reject bin.

Tom took out his cell phone and sent a text message to Jill.

How are you doing? he typed.

Jill's reply came seconds after his message was sent.

Green.

He'd dropped Jill off at Lindsey's with a promise that she'd stay there until he came to pick her up.

Most of the dinner guests were standing, milling about, when Tom entered the main dining hall. He recognized many of Roland Boyd's clients. Several were parents of players on this year's team or teams from the past. The host of the Harold Ross Grill escorted Tom past men who chatted in close clusters. Their attractive wives, many in low-cut black dresses, talked in tight circles of their own.

Every few steps somebody would reach out and grab Tom by the arm. They'd express their condolences, ask about Jill, and wish him luck on the upcoming season. But he also heard whisperings about the blog-post scandal. From what little Tom picked up, the opinions on the matter varied widely.

At least the superintendent of Shilo schools, Angie Didomenico, was on his side. She had given Powers a formal reprimand for not informing her of his plans to question his team about the Tumblr blog and had filed a complaint with the Shilo Police Department to protest their handling of the investigation.

Thank you, Angie.

Tom was glad Jill was at Lindsey's house and not on display here. The funeral had been a hard enough stage, though he had marveled at his daughter's courage in eulogizing her mother.

Tom spied Adriana seated at one of oval tables, with Mitchell beside her. Adriana's face lit up, and she stood as Tom neared. She clutched Tom's arm in her tight grip.

"Well, hello there," she said in a husky voice that resembled Demi Moore's. "I'm so glad you decided to come. I know this can't be easy for you."

Adriana looked breathtakingly beautiful, shimmering inside a sequined blouse and slim-fitting black slacks. She kept hold of Tom's arm and wouldn't let go even when he shifted his weight to slip his hands inside his pants pockets.

"Well, Jill wanted to go over to Lindsey's, and I didn't really feel like hanging out alone in my old house. I'm glad I had a place to go, which I guess is a roundabout way of saying thanks for inviting me."

"How are things going with Jill?"

"Persistence and patience," Tom said, with a slight smile. Adriana smiled, too, and gave Tom's arm another squeeze.

"I know you two will do great together," Adriana said, and added, "Come sit with me and Mitchell a moment."

But before Tom could oblige, Roland appeared and took hold of Tom's other arm. A mini tug-of-war ensued before Adriana finally let go.

"Sorry, darling," Roland said with a wry grin, "but no sitting until Tom here has had something to drink. We'll be right back."

Roland led Tom to the bar, dodging caterers, who roamed the floor like heat-seeking missiles. Roland was dressed in a pin-striped linen suit, with a pocket square, straight as a ruler's edge, tucked into his jacket pocket. His shirt was a light blue oxford; the tie a pattern of pink and blue hues, like those of a sunset. But even in a fancy suit, Tom still saw echoes of Roland's younger self. The kid who sometimes brought a flask of whiskey to school, which he was always willing to share. The guy who favored buzz cuts and gray hooded sweatshirts in any weather. A townie kid from Shilo, New Hampshire, with big plans for big living, but no real road map to get there.

Well, it looks like you found your way, thought Tom.

Roland patted Tom's hand as the two reached the bar, his skin cool to the touch, despite the room's warmth.

"Glad you could make it out," Roland said.

"Nice club," Tom said. "You've been a member long?"

"Long enough." Roland's trademark grin hadn't changed any over the years. It held a hint of playful mischievousness, a sly suggestion that he could still be the same troublemaker that many parents had believed him to be in their high school days.

"How's your game?" asked Tom.

"Seven handicap. Yours?"

"I have a hard time getting through the windmill and the whale's mouth, but I'm getting better."

Roland chuckled. "Buddy, we don't play *that* kind of golf here. Drink?"

"Coke."

"Right, with a lime," Roland said, remembering.

"With a lime," repeated Tom.

"What's this I'm hearing about you hooking up with one of your players?" Roland said. "I hope for your sake that it's all a bunch of bull."

"I guess these days you can put anything on the Internet and people will believe it. Yeah, it's all bull."

"Good to know," Roland said.

Though the bar was packed with thirsty patrons, the bartender took Roland's drink order first. Roland's clients were loud and chatty, which Tom attributed to the open bar.

"Tom, let me introduce you to a friend of mine," Roland said, placing one of his well-manicured hands on the shoulder of a heavyset man seated on the bar stool next to him. The man had the thick neck of a former football player, greasy dark hair, and a round tough-guy face that suggested he, like Roland, had led a very different lifestyle before becoming country club elite. "Frank Dee, I'd like you to meet an old friend of mine from high school and fellow vet, Thomas Hawkins. Tom just moved back to town . . . under difficult circumstances."

Dee nodded in a knowing way. "Good to meet you," he said in a voice that sounded like gravel was lodged someplace deep inside his throat. The two shook hands. Dee's breath smelled of alcohol. The man's grip felt like a vise squeezing Tom's hand. Tom noticed a thick band of whiter skin just below the knuckle of Dee's ring finger and wondered if he'd recently divorced.

Dee said, "I'm sorry about your ex-wife. Tragic. It's really rocked this town. Any breaks in the case, if you don't mind my asking?"

Tom shook his head. "No. It's still very much an active investigation."

"Well, I hope they catch the scumbag who did it and hang 'em by the balls," Dee said.

Tom was glad their drinks showed up, because it gave him something to do besides respond.

"You two served together, huh?" Dee asked.

"I was navy. Roland was army," Tom clarified.

"Navy SEAL," Roland added.

Dee's eyes widened. "That's badass. Very badass."

"It's also very much in the past," Tom said.

Dee just laughed.

"Frank's in the restaurant business, owns a bunch of different franchises in southern New Hampshire," Roland said, keeping one hand on Dee's massive shoulder. To Tom, Roland jokingly whispered, loud enough for Dee to overhear, "I got sick on one of his burgers last week."

Another man came over to their perch at the bar. He was rugged looking, about Tom and Roland's age, with a strong jawline and tanned skin that accented his bright white teeth. He reminded Tom of the guys who advertised Just For Men hair coloring products on TV.

"Hey, Simon. Glad you made it."

"Have I ever missed one of your client parties?"

"Not to my knowledge," Roland agreed. Turning to Tom, he said, "Tom, I'd like you to meet Simon Cortland.

He runs a PR firm in Boston that does a lot of work for clients of mine."

"Nice to meet you," Tom said, giving Cortland's strong hand a firm shake.

"Likewise," Cortland said with a pleasant smile and another flash of teeth. He turned his attention back to Roland. "You still up for the boat on Saturday?"

"You know it," Roland said.

The bartender appeared with two drinks. "Gentlemen, if you'll excuse me, the host's lovely wife has asked me to bring her a drink," Cortland said.

"Best not to keep the lady waiting," Roland said.

"Tom, nice to meet you." There was no handshake this time, as both of Cortland's hands were occupied with beverages.

Roland watched as Cortland crossed the room and went over to Adriana. Tom thought he seemed slightly bothered. Roland's gaze shifted left, and his new expression revealed an even harsher edge. "Oh, good," he said, his eyes narrowing.

Tom turned to look but observed nothing unusual. He half expected to see Kip Lange come sauntering toward them. "What? What is it?" asked Tom.

"I need you to do me a favor," Roland said. "Frank, if you'll excuse us."

"Of course," Dee said. "Do your thing."

Roland took Tom by the arm and led him back into the crowd.

"Is this about Lange?" Tom asked, his voice betraying some concern.

"Lange? No," Roland answered quickly. "I told you, I've had all my best sources checking on him. That guy's off the map. Vanished. No, this is a personal matter that could use your assistance."

Roland pointed to a set of nearby French doors. "Look, buddy, head out to the patio and wait for me there. I'll be out in a few minutes. We're going to have ourselves a little bit of fun. Just like the old days."

CHAPTER 18

Tom waited for Roland on a wide stone patio, accessible only through a set of double doors located toward the rear of the club's dining room. The doors and windows were blanketed by heavy curtains, so Tom couldn't see in, and those inside couldn't see out.

He texted Jill again.

She responded seconds after he hit SEND.

Green.

The evening air took on a slight chill that felt refreshing to breathe. It wasn't long before the closed patio doors opened and a distinguished-looking man, fit, trim, and in his fifties, stepped outside. Roland followed closely behind.

"Shut the doors, Tom," Roland said to Tom as he passed. Tom remained curious, but calm. "And don't let anybody come out here," Roland added.

Tom went from relaxed to tense in a breath. He took another, much closer look at the man Roland had escorted outside, and saw a fearful look in his eyes.

"Roland . . . please . . . this is all just a misunderstanding," said the man. The man's hands were trembling, and his voice carried a slight waver, which Tom suspected wasn't natural.

"A misunderstanding?" Roland repeated. "Really? That's what you call it, Bob?" Roland's face scrunched up to convey a profound incredulousness. "You made a pass at my wife, and in my house, too. That's no misunderstanding at all."

Bob's face reddened. "It wasn't like that, Roland," he stammered. "We were just talking."

"On the couch? Resting your hand on her knee? Drinking my best vodka?"

"She poured us the drinks," Bob explained. "I was just showing her brochures for vacation property on Waban Lake. That was all."

"You sure about that, Bob? You sure that's all?"

Tom stepped away from the door and took a few tentative steps toward Roland. He didn't like the dark tone in Roland's voice. It definitely sounded menacing. Bob might be fit for his age, but he'd be no match for Roland if this confrontation turned physical.

"Please, Roland. I got confused."

"You tried to kiss her, didn't you?"

"No . . . I didn't."

"Don't lie to me, Bob. Tell the truth. You tried to kiss her." Roland got right up into Bob's face, and the older man took a few cowering steps in retreat.

"No."

"No? I saw you," Roland said, looking like a poker player who'd just showed his winning hand. "I saw you," Roland repeated, this time in a much softer voice.

Bob's face went slack. "You were there?"

Roland just grinned—the same one that Tom knew so well. "Ever hear of a nanny cam, Bob?"

Bob looked as though he might faint. "Roland, nothing happened between us. I swear."

"You swear, huh? I have video evidence contradicting that claim."

"What do you want me to do?" asked Bob.

"You've got to take your punishment," Roland said.

"My what?"

"I've got to hurt you, Bob. Physically. Right here, right now. And you've got to take it like a man."

"Roland, please. Let's be rational about this!"

"This is going to hurt you a lot more than it is me, Bob." Roland cocked a fist backward and let it fly—a hook punch aimed squarely at Bob's head.

Tom sprang forward, putting himself between the two men. With one hand, he pushed Bob backward, out of Roland's range. With his other hand, Tom caught Roland's fist in midair. "Roland, don't do this," he said. He kept putting up resistance until Roland eventually relaxed. Even then Tom held on to Roland's fist a few seconds longer, until he felt it was safe to let go.

Taking advantage of the lull, Bob took several quick steps in retreat. Roland danced past Tom with a little spin move he had perfected on the soccer pitch, and seized Bob by the lapels of his suit jacket.

"Not so fast, Bob," Roland said. "We still have an issue to deal with."

"What do you want me to do?"

"I want you to go home. Mull over what you did wrong. Call me later to apologize. Sound like a deal?"

"I'm not going to just forget about what you did to me tonight," Bob said. "You'll be hearing from my attorney."

"Not if you want to stay married, I won't," Roland said. "Remember the nanny cam? I'm sure Veronica would be highly disappointed to see what I could show her."

"You wouldn't dare."

"Don't test me. And, Bob . . . don't ever talk to my wife again."

Bob straightened out his suit jacket and gave Tom a quiet look of thanks. If Bob had recognized Tom from news reports of Kelly's death, it didn't register on his face. Bob left the patio through the French doors.

Tom waited outside with Roland. "What the hell was that about?" he asked.

"The guy tried to make it with my wife," Roland said. "What more do you need to know?"

"Why'd you invite him to your party if you knew what he had done?"

Roland scoffed. "Tom, I'd have thought you, of all people, would understand the advantage of a surprise attack. Bob showed up here with his guard down, and I just scared the absolute crap out of him. That's why I invited him."

Tom recalled the look Roland had flashed Adriana the afternoon he stopped by their house to ask about Kip Lange. Ironic, thought Tom, that he had lied about Lange's jealous streak to a man who really had one.

"You weren't really going to hit that guy, were you?" asked Tom.

Roland just laughed. "Nah, I was going to pull back. But I must say, you still got your speed, Tom. Haven't lost a step."

Tom grunted. "For a second there, I thought you were going to really pummel him."

Roland chuckled again. "I don't get mixed up in any physical altercations," he said. "It's bad for business."

"Good to know," Tom said, feeling only a modicum of relief. Roland might be loosely wired, but at least he wasn't dangerous.

"I just said I wouldn't hit him. I never said he wouldn't get hurt."

"Oh, you have guys who do that for you?" Tom asked with a slight laugh, believing Roland had to be kidding.

"Keep flirting with Adriana and maybe you'll find out for yourself." Roland kept a serious expression, then cracked a broad smile, laughed loudly, and slapped Tom hard on the back, but in a playful way.

Tom returned a smile of his own, but it didn't last long. It didn't matter that he and Roland hadn't spoken much in the past several years. Tom knew when his friend was serious.

CHAPTER 19

Rainy drove the fifty-six miles from Boston to Shilo without the aid of her car stereo or air-conditioning. Both were on the fritz. She wondered how long it would take the Bureau's notoriously cumbersome bureaucracy to fix her work-issued sedan.

Wendy Toman, a kind-eyed woman of forty-eight and one of the best victim-witness coordinators Rainy had ever worked with, read through Mann's case file during the trip. Wendy was an "all business, all the time" kind of gal, which Rainy greatly appreciated on these long drives. There was never any talk about Wendy's three kids or doting husband, which meant Rainy didn't have to reproach herself about not even making time for a date.

In truth, Rainy wasn't *all* that concerned about her anemic social life. Thirty was the new twenty, or so she often told herself. Rainy's mother, however, believed that thirty was the same damn old thirty, and worried that her daughter was destined to become a lonely cat person. Rainy continued to assure her she didn't even have a cat. *Not yet, you don't,* her mother would counter. For now, the job was Rainy's life, and she was committed to making it the best life possible.

Rainy's mission in Shilo was a straightforward one: to make an official identification of the girl in the photograph. Rainy hadn't had any luck figuring out how Mann got Lindsey's naked pictures. Rainy had contacted all the major cell phone providers, but their on-staff security experts assured her they had no foreign code on their servers, nothing that could give someone access to private text messages. Even if a hacker managed to gain access, it didn't explain how they'd know which messages contained pictures of naked teens.

Had Mann obtained Lindsey's image solely through the file-sharing feature of Leterg? Rainy wondered. Had Lindsey been coerced by Mann into sending those pictures? If so, she could charge Mann with production—a fifteen-year mandatory minimum.

He can't do enough time, Rainy thought.

Rainy worried about Lindsey's reaction. The girl was about to learn that the FBI had found her naked pictures on the computer of a suspected child pornographer. Wendy had come along to guide Lindsey through the tumultuous aftershocks of finding out her revealing images had been made public. She'd work quickly to establish a trusting relationship. Lindsey would have a safe place to share her feelings and express her sorrow. Victims who grieved openly and freely were less likely to turn against themselves.

Lindsey Wells's home was a stately custom colonial on a quiet street, tucked inside a pleasant, tree-lined neighborhood. Rainy rang the doorbell. Nice chimes. She doubted she'd ever have a doorbell of her own. She assumed she'd always be a buzzer girl, just like her fellow apartment dwellers in Cambridge.

Lindsey opened the door without hesitating. No reason for caution when there was no reason to fear.

"Can I help you?" The girl sounded nervous when she saw the two women.

"Lindsey Wells?" Rainy asked.

"Yes?"

Rainy took out her badge and flashed it to Lindsey. "I'm Special Agent Loraine Miles with the Boston FBI. This is my colleague, Wendy Toman."

"Hello, Lindsey," Wendy said in a soothing voice. "We'd like to speak with you about something."

"About what?" the girl stammered.

"Are your parents home?" Rainy asked.

"My mom's here. She's with her bridge club."

"Maybe it's better if we talk together," Wendy said.

Lindsey opened the door wider and motioned for the agents to follow. They passed through a bright foyer and into a high-ceiling kitchen with dark cabinets and even darker granite countertops. Fruit magnets on the stainless steel refrigerator held pictures of Lindsey, Lindsey and her friends, and Lindsey and her mother.

Where's Dad? Rainy wondered.

The kitchen opened up into a large family room, with a television big enough to watch while cooking. A group of four women sat around a foldout table, playing cards.

A woman who looked like Lindsey would in thirty years stood and approached. "Hello. Can I help you?"

"Mom, they're with the FBI," Lindsey said.

Rainy noticed how the girl's legs were trembling. The mother's coloring went from summer kissed to pale. Her fingers touched her lips as her eyes grew wide. She came into the kitchen with quick, hurried steps.

"Is everything all right?"

"We're here to speak with your daughter about something that should be discussed in private," Rainy said. "Is there a place we can talk?"

The woman introduced herself as Cathleen Wells, glanced at the agent's identification, and led the women into a first-floor office. Once there, they stood in a close cluster.

Wendy spoke first. "I want to start by saying we're not here to arrest anybody. Nobody is in trouble with the law. We're here to help."

Wendy tried to sound reassuring, but Lindsey didn't look convinced. Her coloring hovered near translucent. Rainy continued by explaining her role with the FBI's cyber crimes squad and, more specifically, crimes against children.

Lindsey's eyes betrayed her, making a connection. "So what does this have to do with me?"

Cathleen Wells nodded vigorously. "Yes, what does all this have to do with my daughter?"

Rainy opened her case file, took out an envelope, and handed it to Lindsey. In that envelope were the pictures she believed were of Lindsey. The images were sanitized, so they didn't show anything revealing. Lindsey flipped through the short stack of photo printouts.

"We found these pictures on the computer of a suspected child pornographer."

Lindsey put her hand to her mouth, perhaps even stifling a cry. "H-h-how . . . ?"

"Well, that's what I was hoping you could tell me. Did you send these pictures to anybody?"

Lindsey shook her head vigorously, giving her most emphatic "No way" nonverbal response. Rainy called that the "liar's reaction." She'd seen it dozens of times, whenever suspects were confronted with their actions. Perhaps they believed the extra exuberance would miraculously negate the truth.

"Do you know a James Mann? Is that name familiar to you?" Rainy asked.

Again a shake no, but this time with far less conviction. Rainy believed that answer to be true.

"You're not in trouble for this, Lindsey, if that's your concern," Wendy said. "But we need to know some things if you can help us."

"Like . . . like what?"

"Like when you took these pictures," Wendy said. "And where."

"I was just playing around with my cell phone," Lindsey said, tears filling her eyes. "It was a bunch of months ago."

"From here?" Rainy asked.

Lindsey nodded. "Yeah, why?"

"It just helps us," said Rainy.

Lindsey sucked in her lower lip, pushed it out, and sucked it in again. *A nervous habit,* Rainy thought.

"Wendy will help you through this, Lindsey. Okay? You don't have anything to worry about."

"Are these on the Internet? Can my friends see them?" Lindsey asked.

"I can't answer that at this time," Rainy replied. "Once your images are out there, there's nothing we can do to get them back. You have to prepare yourself. They might show up again one day. You have to be ready for that possibility. We don't know everybody who has downloaded these pictures, and I can't promise that we'll ever find out."

Lindsey nodded slowly, as though she was inching her way into this new reality.

"I'm going to help you through this," Wendy said, setting a comforting hand on Lindsey's shoulder. "I promise everything is going to be okay."

Thank God for Wendy Toman, Rainy thought.

Cathleen's expression showed pure disgust as she looked through the pictures of Lindsey. "We are going to have a long talk about this, young lady," she snapped.

A woman from the bridge club made a trepid entrance into the office. Cathleen introduced her as Adriana Boyd. *Attractive,* Rainy thought. *In a* Desperate Housewives *kind of way.*

"Is everything all right?" Adriana asked.

Cathleen flashed Adriana an upset look. "No," Cathleen said. "I'd say things are not all right. Not in the least. Just be glad you have a son and not a daughter." Lindsey grimaced as though in pain.

"What's going on?" Adriana asked.

"These people are with the FBI," Cathleen said to Adriana. "Apparently, they found pictures of Lindsey . . . compromising pictures . . . during some child porn bust."

Rainy was surprised and a little dismayed by Cathleen's candor. Cathleen perhaps sensed she'd crossed a line, because she said to Rainy, "Oh, don't worry. Adriana is one of my closest friends. She's like family to us. Especially since my divorce."

"Is Lindsey in any trouble?" Adriana asked in a way that a concerned aunt might speak.

Rainy assured her that she was not, then went on to explain the situation and her role with the FBI.

When Rainy had finished, Adriana appeared as distraught as Cathleen and Lindsey. "Oh my," she said. "What happens next?"

Rainy's lips tightened as she tried to temper her officiousness with a softer tone. She wasn't a mother herself, but she could certainly empathize with a mother's concern. "Well, I have other images from our investigation, but for reasons of privacy, I'll show them only to the school superintendent. We'll try to make other victim identifications. Wendy's here to help Lindsey through the witness process. If Lindsey wants, she can make a victim impact statement. It'll be read aloud in court if the accused is found guilty of the crime."

"Then what?" Cathleen asked.

"Then we're going to try to figure out how the guy we arrested came to possess pictures of your daughter. We're going to track down his source, or sources, and try to shut them down."

"Can you do that?" Cathleen asked.

"Well, it would speed things along if Lindsey would be honest about who she sent these pictures to."

"Mom, I swear I didn't send them to anybody! I swear. Somebody either got my cell phone or hacked into my account or something."

Cathleen frowned at her daughter.

"What happens to the person who did this?" Adriana asked. "The person who sent these around, I mean."

"He'll be charged with interstate trafficking of child pornography."

"What does that mean?" Cathleen asked.

"It means whoever did this will spend a long, long time in jail."

CHAPTER 20

Rebecca Bartholomew had been Tom's favorite neighbor on Oak Street. Rebecca was the first to greet Tom after he moved back into his former home. Tom wasn't surprised that days later she again stopped by unannounced.

"Want some pie?" she asked, flashing him some berry-rich homemade delight.

"If you don't mind a mess, I'd love the company," Tom said.

The pie, he knew, was an excuse for her to check up on them. It was just Rebecca being Rebecca.

The bulk of Tom's belongings remained packed inside boxes and milk crates. The boxes and crates were strewn about the living room and upper hallway of the split-level home.

"Is this all you own?" Rebecca asked, evidently surprised by Tom's lack of possessions.

"One day and a rented van was all it took to move me here," Tom said with a degree of pride. "That's why I'm a big fan of my milk crate storage system. Just flip 'em over and, voilà, you're moving."

Jill had been quite helpful with the move. They talked

some on the trip up and back, but not very much. She'd been quiet in the days since her mother's death.

At Marvin's suggestion, Tom and Jill began seeing a social worker to help facilitate the transition to her new custodial parent. Tom found it reassuring to know that Jill's quiet demeanor was normal for this stage of the grieving process, according to Maggie, the social worker.

Rebecca followed Tom into the kitchen. She stepped over an open toolbox, then navigated a field of corroded parts that Tom had removed from the newly disassembled kitchen sink. Rebecca made it safely to the refrigerator without tripping and seemed well aware of the accomplishment.

"We've been getting a lot of takeout," Tom said to Rebecca, who looked inscrutably at the sink and about the kitchen mess.

"I was going to make us a cup of tea," she said, as if to imply that was no longer an option.

"We have bottled water in the fridge," Tom said.

Rebecca nodded, got the water out of the refrigerator, and retrieved an electric kettle from one of the kitchen cabinets. She didn't have to ask Tom where to get it. In another life, Tom, Kelly, and Rebecca had been friends, so it was no surprise that she knew where to find the kettle and Kelly's substantial collection of teas.

Rebecca had an apple-shaped figure, an unruly nest of dark, wavy hair, and a pretty face, which Tom could not recall ever looking so concerned.

"Does it feel strange to move back into your old home?" Rebecca asked as she filled the kettle with bottled water.

"Everything about this feels strange," Tom said. "Ten years ago I got divorced and moved out. Jill was just six. Now she's fifteen, and I'm sleeping in the basement of the house Kelly and I bought together."

"The basement?"

"Jill's not ready to touch her mother's things, and I can't blame her for that. But I keep on finding things I bought as gifts, or shopped for with Kelly, in just about every room of the house."

From the living room, Tom heard the familiar whistle of the wall-mounted cuckoo clock announcing the top of the hour with seven quick tweets. Tom had first laid eyes on that wooden cuckoo clock from the Black Forest region of Germany when he opened the crate of knick-knacks Kelly had asked him to bring home for her from Wiesbaden.

"Make sure you unpack everything as soon as you get to your folks' house," Kelly had said before his troop transport plane departed. "I don't want any of my mementos getting squished."

But Kelly had had another reason she wanted Tom to unpack that crate. Tom had been staying at his parents' house in Shilo for a little R & R. They weren't at home when he pried open the box, but it wouldn't have mattered if they were. They'd never seen pure heroin.

"Listen, Tom," Kelly had said when he had called in a fury. "Before you get too angry with me, I need to tell you something."

"What?" Tom had said, his voice bordering on rage.

"I'm pregnant," she had said. "And you're the father. Now, if you don't want your child born in prison, you're going to have to do something to help me out."

Rebecca poured milk into her tea and offered to do the same for Tom, but he declined. She cut two good-sized pieces of pie, which she served on paper plates.

"Where's Jill?" asked Rebecca, her pie knife ready to cut a third piece.

"In her room, studying," Tom said. "She thinks I'm a prison warden because I haven't let her out of my sight for more than a couple hours."

"Well, it was pretty scary, what happened to Kelly. And then the whole incident in the woods. Did the police ever catch the guy?"

"No," Tom said, his voice revealing his disappointment. Even more dismaying, neither he, Roland, nor Marvin could find Lange anywhere, despite all three having made considerable efforts. It appeared that the former private had vanished from earth like the morning fog.

"That must be very unsettling," Rebecca said.

"We're taking precautions," Tom said. "The house is now fully alarmed. And thanks to my 'friend of Roland Boyd' discount, we've got ourselves an outdoor-lighting perimeter detection system, too."

"What's that?"

"Sensors in the woods that trigger outdoor floodlights if any of them get tripped."

"Wow, sounds impressive."

Tom laughed a little. "So far we've scared away a bunch of deer."

"Well, between your close watch over Jill and the alarm systems, what else can you do?"

"I could have forced her to leave Shilo and move to Westbrook," Tom said.

"And have a sullen, furious daughter to look after? No, I think you were right to move here."

"Thanks for the vote of confidence."

Rebecca took a sip of her tea and looked at Tom in a sorrowful way. "Tom, are you really up for this?" she asked.

"For what?" answered Tom, though he knew what she was asking.

"Raising a daughter," said Rebecca. "Not to mention one who doesn't seem very open to the reunion, if you don't mind my saying so."

"Well, we both know that Kelly never had many nice things to say about me."

Rebecca puckered her face. "Forgive me for speaking ill of the dead, but we both know that Kelly was full of s-h-i-t. And I told Jill on any number of occasions to give you a chance."

Tom returned an appreciative smile. "I figured one day my free plumbing and tree removal services would pay dividends."

"Well, I'm just saying, if you need anything, anything at all, don't you hesitate to ask. Now then, back to Jill and raising a daughter. I'll help out as much as I can. Cooking, carpool, what have you. But this is a lot to take on, Tom. What about your dad? Can he help out in any way?"

"Dad hasn't been right since my mom died. He's living in Florida these days and his health isn't very good, and I don't think he could make the trip back to New Hampshire anytime soon."

"Not even for Jill?"

"Kelly kept Jill out of his life, same as she did mine. No, I wouldn't put that on him."

Tom heard loud knocking on the door. Four quick, hard bangs. He gave Rebecca a curious look.

"Are you expecting anybody?" Rebecca asked.

Tom shook his head. He left the kitchen, trotted down the carpeted front stairs.

Through the sidelight windows Tom saw Brendan Murphy and Rich Fox lit up by the yellowish glow of the two outside front lights. Murphy was dressed in a tweed sports jacket and tie. Fox wore his police uniform.

Jill! Tom thought. Had she snuck out of the house without his knowing? Was she in danger?

Tom opened the door in a hurry, and Murphy more or less pushed himself inside, flashing a piece of paper clutched in his hand.

"I've got a signed warrant to search these premises," Murphy said, slipping on rubber gloves as he marched up the front stairs. "Officer Fox will be assisting me as a witness, ensuring that I've conducted the search to the specifications of the warrant. Oh, and we'll be removing all your home computers, too."

Tom felt an icy chill. He didn't think the police had been all that thorough investigating the house after Kelly's death. It was just a robbery gone bad, or so they believed. But a search warrant was an entirely different matter. Tom wasn't worried about Murphy finding evidence that would incriminate him in Kelly's homicide.

But he did worry Murphy might dig up something else.

Something Kelly might have hidden.

Something Tom wouldn't want anybody to find.

CHAPTER 21

Tom held the door open for Fox.

"Tom," Fox said, taking off his hat and tipping his head toward Tom in a quick salute. He trailed Murphy into the house.

"Hang on, Brendan," Tom shouted, bounding up the stairs behind Fox and Murphy. "Let me see that piece of paper."

"Suit yourself," Murphy said.

Tom read the warrant over while Murphy and Fox got to work searching the living room. They both wore gloves and had plastic bags and markers for evidence gathering. Pink anti-static bags for computer stuff, clear plastic bags for other evidence.

Rebecca emerged from the kitchen and surveyed the disruption with a stunned expression. "Brendan, what's going on here?" she asked.

Murphy didn't answer. He was opening the drawers of a living room desk and rifling through the contents.

Fox walked over to where Rebecca stood, and Tom joined them. "Hi there, Rebecca," Fox said to her. "We won't be too long. A couple hours at most. Sorry about this."

Rebecca looked at Tom for confirmation. "The search warrant is official. I've got to let them do it," Tom said.

"Well, what are you looking for?" Rebecca wanted to know.

"That's police business," Murphy replied.

Tom didn't like Murphy's tone. "Were you waiting for me to move my stuff here before you got a warrant?" he asked. "Was that your plan?"

"Whatever you want to think," said Murphy.

"Were you thinking I'd crack because of the pressure your little team interrogation put me under?" asked Tom.

"Do you have something you want to confess?" asked Murphy. A brief two-man stare down ensued. "I didn't think so," Murphy eventually said.

Fox looked sheepishly at Tom. "Listen, Tom, I'm sorry about this," he said. "I know this is awkward."

"Well, considering I have to coach your daughter, I'd say 'awkward' is a bit of an understatement," Tom replied.

"If it's any consolation, Abbey loves playing for you," Fox said. "She's not going to know we were here."

Tom gave a strained smile. He knew that wasn't true.

Jill had come out of her room. "What's going on?" she asked, her arms folded across her chest in a defensive posture.

Tom stood beside his daughter. "Honey, they have a search warrant for the house," he said. "We have to let them do this."

Jill's expression became one of total disgust. "Why? What are they looking for?"

"I think they're trying to decide if I'm a suspect in your mother's death," Tom said.

"What! You're kidding! Don't they know that I saw the

guy spying on us in the woods? That's who did it! That's who broke into the house. Why aren't they looking for him?"

"We're following all leads," Murphy said, "including the name your father gave us."

"Kip Lange," Tom said to Jill, so she'd know what he told them. Tom didn't worry about tipping the police off to Lange. Lange could give up Kelly's role in the drug theft, for all he cared. The link to Tom had died with his ex-wife in that ravine.

Unless Kelly told Lange something before she ran . . .

Jill was what mattered to Tom now—her safety and as a result, his peace of mind. Tom would sleep better at night knowing Lange had been either ruled out as a suspect or arrested for Kelly's homicide. But if Roland and Marvin couldn't locate Lange, Tom doubted Murphy would fare much better. Especially given how Murphy's sights seemed firmly locked on Tom.

"This is so unfair," Jill said. "Do they have to search my room, too?"

"Every room," Murphy said.

"Well, do you guys want some tea while you're digging through their stuff?" Rebecca asked.

"Yeah, that'd be great," Fox said.

Murphy shot his partner a disapproving stare that could have melted steel.

"Actually, we're fine, but thanks," Fox corrected himself.

"Well, we'll be in the kitchen if you need anything," Tom said, guiding Jill to follow him. Tom stopped in the entranceway and looked back at Murphy. "Murphy, I sure hope you're doing what you said and looking for other suspects, because this is a big waste of your time."

Murphy didn't respond.

Tom wished he hadn't thrown out the box of nails from Home Depot with the SKU number on it.

Tom didn't watch the search. It was bad enough just listening to it from the kitchen, where he, Jill, and Rebecca now sat. Nobody was in the mood for pie.

"I can't believe you're just going to let them do this," Jill said, with more venom in her voice than Tom had ever heard.

Tom shrugged it off. "Maybe they'll find something that will help with the investigation," he said. "What they won't find is anything connecting me to what happened to your mom, because there is nothing. Look, Rebecca, why don't you go home? This could take a while."

"I'm not leaving until they leave," said Rebecca.

"Okay."

Tom and Rebecca chatted only in spurts. Jill, for the most part, kept silent.

"I'm not telling anybody at school about this," Jill said. "I'll never be able to show my face in school."

"It's going to be okay, honey," Tom said. "I promise."

The noises continued.

Drawers opened and closed. Closets searched. Boxes ripped open. Computers bagged and tagged. Papers shuffled and scattered. The three sat at the kitchen table, drinking tea—the same table Tom and Kelly had bought when they first moved to the Oak Street home. Tom had made the decision to move back to Shilo the day after Kelly told him she was pregnant with Jill.

She'd put in for a 529, the military separation code for pregnancy. It would take a few months for the paperwork to process and clear, she had said. But their conversations that week weren't focused on their future together. It was all about the crate, and what Kelly had packed inside.

"Please. Hide the drugs," she had begged. "Please do

it for me. For your baby. Give us a chance. I'll explain everything when I get back to the States. Please, Tom. Do it for us."

Tom had done as she asked. He hid the drugs where nobody would ever, ever find them.

On his drive back to his parents' house, he took a shortcut down Oak Street, where he had seen the rusted FOR SALE sign tapped lopsided into a lawn that was more brown than green.

"This is where we'll live," Tom had said to himself. He had a mortgage three months before he had a daughter. Despite all Kelly had done, Tom still loved her deeply and wanted to give them a fighting chance to live together as a family.

The cuckoo clock chirped ten times. Jill had gone back to her bedroom an hour before, presumably to sleep. Murphy popped his head into the kitchen.

"We're all set," he said, ripping off his rubber gloves and bagging them. "Thanks for your time."

Tom finally let himself relax. His secret was safe, at least for now.

"Find anything?" Rebecca called without looking back or even getting up.

"Have a good night," was all Murphy said. "We'll see ourselves to the door."

"I can't believe Brendan Murphy thinks you had anything to do with Kelly's death," Rebecca said with disgust.

"He's just doing his job," said Tom.

"Yeah? Well, his job stinks," said Rebecca.

Tom stood from the table, left the kitchen, and caught up with Murphy at the front door. "Brendan, I hope you're satisfied."

"Like I said, we're all set."

"Thanks, Tom," Fox called out from the front walk. "Sorry again about the intrusion. I'll see you at the game."

"Yeah, see you at the game," Tom said, hoping Fox realized how ludicrous he sounded trying to put things back to normal. "I'm assuming you didn't find anything helpful here," Tom said to Murphy.

Murphy didn't respond, but he couldn't hide his disappointment, either.

"Well, I hope now you'll really start investigating elsewhere," said Tom.

Murphy's eyes narrowed, and he put his face close to Tom's. "Guys like you always screw up," Murphy said in a low tone. "That's been my experience. I want you to know that I'll be waiting for you to slip, Tom. And when you do, I'll be right there to slap the cuffs on."

"Have yourself a good night, Brendan," Tom said, closing the door behind him.

Rebecca bounded down the stairs just as Tom was coming back up.

"Heading home?" he asked.

Rebecca nodded her head in the direction of Jill's bedroom. "I think you and Jill could use some alone time," Rebecca said, buttoning her coat.

"She's not asleep, is she?" Tom said.

Rebecca shook her head no, kissed Tom on one cheek, and patted him playfully on the other. "You're a good man, Tom Hawkins," she said. "A very good man."

"I try."

Tom closed the front door and watched through the sidelight window as Rebecca traversed the walkway. He kept watching until she disappeared into the dark of night.

He breathed out the last bits of tension still coiled up inside him.

On his way back up the stairs, Tom's cell phone buzzed.

Strange, because the only person who texted him was Jill. Tom looked at his cell phone's display screen and saw the familiar text message icon, but an unfamiliar phone number.

Tom clicked the envelope icon and realized a picture was attached to the message. The picture began filling his phone's display screen, painting rows of colored pixels, like a magician's curtain being raised to reveal whatever magic lay behind.

Tom's eyes widened in surprise when the image finished downloading. His heart kicked into overdrive, and his mouth went dry. He read the text message with an open mouth.

I hope you enjoy these!!! XOXO :) UR Eyes Only!

It was a picture of a teenage girl. She was lying naked on a bed. The girl's back was arched. Her legs were open slightly. One of the girl's hands was hidden between her knees. The other she extended beyond range of the camera's lens. The girl's breasts were showing. Her nipples were erect. Her lips were puckered in a pouty and seductive kiss.

He didn't know this girl. He'd never seen her before.

Tom's phone buzzed again.

He looked.

It was another text message. With another picture attached.

CHAPTER 22

Seated at her conference table inside her crammed and cramped office, Superintendent Didomenico looked defeated and worn.

"What were these girls doing?" she asked Rainy.

"I believe they were sending text messages with their pictures," Rainy said. "But there is no way for me to prove it."

Didomenico, a meticulous woman in her fifties, wore her wavy hair short. The coloring, Rainy observed, was a mix of blond, brown, and—not unexpectedly—a lot of gray. The white piping of her black sweater tastefully matched the single strand of pearls around her neck. Judging by the numerous staff interruptions for which Didomenico had to apologize, the job evidently pulled in more directions than the superintendent had limbs. Yet her face didn't show the strain, and her eyes remained patient and kind.

The superintendent sifted through dozens of computer printouts of the images Rainy had brought with her. All the images were sanitized in some way, to conceal anything revealing, except for the girls' faces. That was what she had come to see Didomenico about.

Rainy was convinced that Lindsey's image belonged to a fetish series, previously unknown to authorities, that was actively being sold to child porn rings on the Web. Teen girls sexting—that was what Rainy believed the multimedia format images to be.

Defense attorneys liked it when their clients were found in possession of only known series. It was easier for them to argue that the evidence had been planted on their clients' computers. Known images and series were widely available on the Internet and therefore more easily obtained. But a single unknown image put some doubt into that defense. Hundreds of unknown images made that strategy almost laughable.

It was hard to get one's hands on an unknown series. It took work. It took effort. It took real commitment. Rainy knew how men viewed images like the ones of Lindsey Wells. They were hot, sexy, and alluring. The girls were no longer prepubescent. They were in their late teens, with bodies that were well developed. They could turn on most any man. They certainly did James Mann. It didn't surprise her in the least that a market existed for these images.

Of the forty girls in what Rainy dubbed James Mann's Text Image Collection, ten of them (according to the superintendent) attended, or had recently graduated from, Shilo High School. Each girl had taken an image of herself in some stage of undress. And somehow, those images ended up on James Mann's home computer.

Ten of forty.

"This is very troubling news, Agent Miles," Didomenico said as she flipped through the picture archive again. "What do we do from here?"

"Well, I'm going to want to speak with the girls individually. I need to know when the pictures were taken. What their ages were at the time. And more importantly, why they took the pictures."

"You'd question all the girls?" Didomenico said with alarm.

"It's the only way for me to track down the path these images took. Of course, they could have been emailed. Uploaded to a Web site. They might have even been taken using a Web camera on a site like Chatroulette or Omegle. Hard to tell. I think they were sent by cell phone. But that's just my theory."

"Well, in that case, why not just check with the cell phone providers?" Didomenico said.

"Would if I could," Rainy replied. "But the only cell phone provider that stores that sort of information beyond thirty days is BlackBerry. So even if we did obtain a search warrant for their cell phones, we'd never be able to see the content of the messages the girls sent."

"I hate the idea of your questioning all these girls. News of that would spread quite quickly, I'm afraid. It could even become a national story, with lasting implications for the girls. What good will come of this, Agent Miles? If you don't mind my asking."

That question had given Rainy pause. *What good would come of it?* The Feds had their case. Mann possessed well over a thousand illegal images, enough content to warrant federal prosecution. Add to that interstate trafficking charges, coupled with Lindsey's official ID, and the USAO had more than enough evidence to proceed with a federal case. But Rainy had a job to do. She would be discreet, of course, but the crime needed to be investigated properly and the girls had a legal right to make their victim impact statements.

It was the law. It was just the way things were done.

"I promise to keep as low a profile as possible. But what if I spoke to the school as a whole?" Rainy asked.

Didomenico looked perplexed. "That sounds worse."

"It may prevent future incidents," Rainy suggested. "I can talk to them about the dangers of certain behaviors on the Internet. Perhaps then some of the girls I need to question would actually come to me. That way I wouldn't have to do as much digging around."

Didomenico's expression brightened. "That's a wonderful idea," she said.

Rainy left Didomenico's office with plans to present to the student body her well-traveled talk about cyber safety and the dangers of sexting. She made clear her post-assembly plans to Didomenico. Either the girls involved in the Mann investigation would come to see Rainy, or she'd go to see them.

CHAPTER 23

Jill was back in uniform. Tom couldn't have been more proud of her.

Lindsey Wells took a perfect centering pass from Lauren Grass. She pushed the ball down the right wing and centered it into the middle of the penalty box. Jill Hawkins was in the right place at the right time.

Instincts.

Jill unleashed a rocket of a shot that landed in the back of the net.

"Nicely done, Jill! Very nicely done!" Tom called out.

Jill did her best to smile at the compliment, but Tom could see his daughter's heart wasn't in the game. How could it be?

With the social worker's help, Tom had learned about the eight stages of grief. Shock, stage one, had allowed Jill to function physically in the days immediately following her mother's death—which was now officially ruled a homicide. She succumbed to tears mixed with anger as she stumbled through the emotional release stage. She suffered frequent headaches and a seemingly endless upset stomach—the physical expression of distress. Now it was guilt's turn to eat his poor daughter alive. He knew she felt guilty about playing soccer again. She felt guilty that she'd returned to school. She felt guilty trying to live her life. But nothing compared to the guilt she felt about letting her teammates down.

"I'll dedicate the season to Mom's memory," Jill had said to Tom. "But I'm not going to quit the team."

"You can come back to the squad anytime," he had tried to reassure her. "There's no reason to rush."

Jill shook her head. "Shilo hasn't been beaten in three seasons," she said. "That's tied for the state record."

"I don't care about records," Tom had said. "I care about you."

"Well, the team cares," answered Jill. "And I don't need that kind of guilt on me as well. We barely beat Dover last week. We've got Riverside coming up this week. I'm going to be on the field for that game. And we're gonna win."

My daughter's a fighter, Tom thought, and he had never felt more proud. But hers was proving a hard battle to fight. Throughout the scrimmage, Jill ambled down the field without much urgency. Even at half effectiveness, however, she was still one of the best players on the field. Tom knew she was right about Riverside. Without Jill on the pitch, the much-hyped Shilo unbeaten streak was destined to end.

The girls were just starting to play with real intensity again. This was the best scrimmage Tom had seen since Powers and Murphy tag teamed Tom and nearly destroyed his team's morale over some misguided prank.

It was Angie who had stepped in and pulled the team out of a tailspin. During a closed-door meeting, Angie gave both the varsity and JV squads a lengthy lecture about cyber bullying. A long period of silence followed the lecture. Afterward, Angie changed her tune and told Tom's players to go out and win another state championship for Shilo. The cheers had lasted a good two minutes.

You can't keep a good team down, Tom had thought.

This practice was proving his assessment to be true.

Lindsey Wells put one hand on her knee and raised the other high in the air—a signal to the coaches that she needed a rest. Vern Kalinowski blew his whistle and subbed in Jenny Fielder for Lindsey. Lindsey passed through a gauntlet of high fives before trotting over to where her head coach stood on the sidelines. She was all smiles, and her brown skin glistened with sweat from the warm September sun. Lindsey put her hands on her hips, still breathing hard from the workout.

She lay down on the ground and began to stretch. She formed a bridge with her body, feet flat on the grass, chest pressing skyward. Tom had seen Lindsey do this stretch a thousand times. But for Tom, it was no longer an innocuous way for a player to keep loose. The stretch, Tom realized, was strikingly similar to a pose made by a naked teenage girl in a picture somebody had sent him.

He had called the sender's number, only to get a messaging service provider called TxtyChat.com. According to the TxtyChat Web site, the service was used to send text and images to mobile phones from a dedicated bank of phone numbers. Untraceable—that was one of TxtyChat's featured selling points, as documented on the Web site.

Untraceable.

Tom had spent some of the previous day researching the legal and ethical issues around his thorny situation. He knew that what he'd received was a sext—digitally transmitted, sexually suggestive, nude or nearly nude photos.

What he didn't know was whether he could be charged with any crime for simply receiving an unsolicited image.

The blog posts had already cast suspicion on him. Complicating matters, the legal landscape of digital laws was in a near molten stage, changing and reforming as new precedents and cases cropped up. He concluded only that his receipt was unsolicited and therefore didn't violate any sexual harassment or child pornography laws.

But the question still remained: what should he do about it?

The first thing Tom did was to delete the pictures from his phone. A girls' soccer coach's possessing naked pictures of a female minor was like walking around with a stick of dynamite in his pocket. Bringing it to the attention of any of the school staff would launch a formal inquiry. Lots of questions would get asked. The blog posts might not seem like a prank anymore. The additional attention wouldn't do his already struggling daughter any good, either.

Tom decided to leave it alone.

He hadn't received any more pictures. Perhaps the pictures and the blog post were unrelated coincidences. Maybe this mystery teenage girl had intended those pictures to be seen by somebody else. Maybe that person's phone number was close to his own. If so, with luck she had realized her mistake and wouldn't make it again.

Tom contemplated calling Marvin for legal advice.

Not yet, he decided.

Marvin might insist Tom make his concerns public. Document them in an official statement. There'd be a formal inquiry for sure if he went that route. And Jill would be caught in the middle.

No, for now, the best thing for Tom to do was wait and see.

Coincidence or attack?

Prank or something else?

He'd find out for certain before deciding his next move.

Another question still bothered Tom. Was Jill doing the same thing as the girl who texted him?

Tom couldn't get his thoughts around that one. He'd gone from being the occasional father of a distant and disinterested daughter, to a full-time parent of a beautiful teenage girl with a stew of cooking hormones. How could he keep an eye on what she was doing without her feeling that he was intruding on her privacy?

Kelly had allowed Jill to keep a computer in her bedroom. Tom knew that wasn't a wise decision. It made it harder to keep her safe from online predators. He hadn't planned on battling Jill to establish new and far stricter limits. She had enough on her plate to deal with. But after seeing those images, Tom's concerns intensified.

How could he know what his daughter was doing behind closed doors?

Tom blew his whistle to signal practice was over. The girls, as usual, dashed for their gym bags stacked on the sidelines. They didn't go for water bottles or snacks; they went for the first thing they always went for when practice ended.

They took out their cell phones.

Tom was gathering his belongings when he heard a loud shriek. He looked and saw some of the girls huddled together, talking anxiously. He saw more girls being drawn toward the huddle. They were all looking at Lauren Grass's cell phone.

He saw them pass her phone around. The chatter become more fevered. The girls made a sudden break, collected their bags, and took off for the locker room. Jill came over to Tom, panic on her face.

"Dad, what is going on?" she asked.

"What do you mean?"

"Do you know what that was all about?"

"No," Tom said. "But I assume you're going to tell me."

Jill tilted her head back and looked up at the sky. Tom could tell she was trying to keep from crying. "Lauren said she friended somebody she didn't know last night," Jill said, her voice shaky.

"Friended, as in school?"

"No, friended as in Facebook."

"Oh."

Jill continued, "The friend request said, 'Do you want to know a secret?' She was curious. Normally, she doesn't accept friend requests from people she doesn't know."

"And what was this secret?"

"They posted it on her wall during practice."

"Wall?"

"Her Facebook wall," Jill said with exasperation.

"Oh? And what did they post?"

Now the tears came. "That they know for a fact you're sleeping with somebody on the team," Jill sobbed. "And they know who it is, too."

CHAPTER 24

"**D**o you want to know a secret?"

That was the message delivered in a mysterious friend request from somebody who called themselves Fidelius Charm.

Rebecca was good friends with Ellen Grass, Lauren's mother. Lauren's sister, Julie, and their father, David, were at home when Tom and Jill came over to get a look at the Facebook posts that had ignited a firestorm of controversy. Judging by the way David Grass glared at Tom upon opening the door to his house, he thought it doubtful the Grasses would have been so accommodating without Rebecca having smoothed the way. In contrast to David, Ellen Grass, dark haired, slim, and pretty, gave Tom a strained smile and a compassionate look more befitting a wake. The Grass family represented a microcosm of the opinions about Tom spreading around town.

"What kind of name is Fidelius Charm?" Tom asked Rebecca.

Rebecca did a quick Google search.

"Fidelius Charm," Rebecca said, reading from Wikipedia, "is a spell from the Harry Potter books. It's a charm used to keep secret information hidden. This information stays hidden until the Secret-Keeper chooses to reveal it."

"Great," Tom said with an exasperated sigh. "So we're looking for someone who's a Harry Potter fan. That should narrow down our list of suspects."

"How many people do you think have seen the posts?" Rebecca asked Lauren.

Lauren took the mouse from Rebecca and, leaning over her shoulder, opened up her Facebook page.

"Fidelius Charm sent a friend request to every girl on the varsity soccer team with a Facebook account," Lauren said. "Ten of my friends are also friends with Fidelius."

"So how many saw the wall post?" asked Tom.

"The privacy setting on the content was set to 'Friends of Friends,' " Lauren explained. "So any of my friends who aren't friends with Fidelius Charm can see it."

"How many friends do you have?" Rebecca asked.

"Eight hundred and fifty-five," Lauren said.

"That's pretty normal," Jill said.

"Who has eight hundred and fifty-five friends?" Tom asked Jill.

Jill and Lauren looked at each other and shrugged.

"Tom, some of these kids are Facebook friends with their teachers."

"As if the blog post wasn't bad enough," Tom said.

"There's no easy way for us to know how many people saw the wall post," Rebecca said.

In a small town like Shilo, a few could mean a lot.

Looking over Rebecca's shoulder, Tom reread the wall post on Lauren's Facebook page, doing his best to temper his anger and frustration.

Coach Hawkins is sleeping with a player. And I know who it is.

"Can I see Fidelius Charm's Facebook page?" Tom asked.

Lauren pulled it up. The page contained only the default Facebook settings, no pictures, nothing personalized, no way to know who had created the profile.

"Kids make bogus online profiles all the time," Lauren said. "They bully other kids with them all the time. They've gotten pretty good at not getting caught, but don't ask me how they do it."

Jill looked at Tom with wide, panic-filled eyes. "Dad, what are you going to do?"

Tom thought. "I'm going to call Angie Didomenico right now," he said. "And then I'm going to call the police."

Angie scheduled an emergency meeting at her office for the next morning. Attending that meeting were Angie, Tom, Craig Powers, Principal Lester Osborne, and Officer Richard Fox. Tom was glad the Shilo police captain had granted his request to have any officer other than Sergeant Murphy assigned to investigate. Tom had expressed concern that Murphy would be biased, given his ongoing involvement with Kelly's homicide investigation.

Tom started the meeting with a confession. He told the gathering about the text messages he had received the night before.

"And do you have pictures of this mystery girl?" Fox asked after hearing Tom's account.

"No. I deleted them," Tom said. "I would have saved them if I'd known about this next wave of attacks."

"Mind if we check out your phone?"

"Of course not," Tom said. "Mind if I get my work computer back?"

"It's still with the state computer forensic guys."

"Great. What about my home computer?"

"It's with them as well."

"No reason you shouldn't have my phone, too," Tom said, making no effort to conceal his displeasure.

"Thanks," Fox said.

"I haven't made any solicitation attempts," Tom said. "It's not like I've been chatting online with a teenage girl who's really a cop. Guys, somebody is trying to destroy my reputation. That's what's going on here."

"We're doing everything we can to sort this out," Fox said. "Just stay patient. We've already made some progress."

That got Tom's attention. "Such as?"

"We know that the Facebook profile was made at a Panera Bread in Millis. They have free Wi-Fi. The friend requests and wall postings were sent from there as well. Facebook helped us with the IPs."

"Surveillance tape?" Tom asked.

Fox shook his head. "Nothing for us to match the time the profile was created to any customers in the store. And it was a busy day, too. Lots of customers. Lots of laptops. Lots of lattes. We asked."

"Tom, there's no hard evidence that you've done anything wrong," Angie said. "And kids texting inappropriate pictures of themselves is an epidemic in this country. We have a problem with that very same thing here in Shilo."

"We do?" said Tom.

"Yes, and we're investigating," Angie added, with an end-of-discussion finality.

"You haven't tried to download any illegal images,"

Fox chimed in, "or, like you said, tried to meet up with an underage girl."

"Right now, we're treating these incidents as just rumors," Angie said. "Vicious and very damaging rumors."

"And the pictures? What about those?" Tom asked.

"A coincidence," Powers suggested.

Shrugs and blank stares from around the table suggested that nobody could come up with a better explanation. Tom's concern only intensified.

He couldn't come up with a better explanation, either.

CHAPTER 25

Empty containers of Chinese food were strewn about the Lair. Half that number of discarded cans of Diet Coke had been tossed into the recycle bin. Rainy used chopsticks to nibble at the remnants from a sixth container, a spicy chicken and oyster sauce dish, which she ate simply for want of something to do. Carter typed with one hand as he slurped out the last drops of his soda. Even one-handed, Rainy figured Carter was doubling her productivity.

Rainy had just finished a quick phone conversation with Angie Didomenico that left her feeling charged up, but puzzled.

"I thought you should know," Didomenico had said, "that there have been some new developments pertaining to our longtime girls' soccer coach, Tom Hawkins."

"Developments?"

"There have been some escalating allegations that he's been sexually involved with one of his players."

Rainy's ears perked up, and she asked Didomenico for an explanation. Rainy jotted down Tom Hawkins's name in her notebook as Didomenico filled in the background information. It was certainly an interesting development.

Perhaps more so if the Shilo police were able to ID who-ever wrote the blog posts and created the Facebook account.

Most interesting to Rainy, Tom Hawkins himself had mentioned having received a sexually explicit text message from an unknown teenage girl.

"Now, I should say that the school board is fully back-ing Tom Hawkins," Didomenico went on. "He's been a standout coach and guidance counselor for our school system for years. We have tremendous confidence that this will all be sorted out, but in light of your investiga-tion, I thought you should at least be aware of what's going on here."

"Is there any evidence that clears the coach?"

"Unsure," Didomenico said. "But Coach Hawkins has an impeccable reputation. The students love him. His ex-wife recently died. Police believe she walked in on a robbery, and things escalated from there. But Coach Hawk-ins's relationship with his ex was less than cordial, and there's been talk. He came in to speak with me about all this just a while ago. He's convinced somebody is out to destroy his reputation, but no one has any idea why. He's won the state championship for the past several years. Perhaps it's someone from a rival program, jealous of his success."

If Rainy's FBI training had taught her anything, it was never to overlook a coincidence. Mann had downloaded a large collection of sexts from an unknown source. Hawk-ins came forward about receiving a sext, but only after he'd been accused online of sleeping with a player on his team.

Did Hawkins come clean about the images he received because he knew the walls were closing in?

Was there a connection between James Mann and the high school coach?

A little bit of background checking should give her an answer.

Rainy had access to classified databases. Many of them contained the sort of information privacy advocates feared the U.S. government collected on its citizens. *Thank you, Patriot Act.* Tom Hawkins, Rainy soon learned, served his country, had a daughter, and as Didomenico said, used to have an ex-wife. He had never been arrested and, aside from his divorce, had never been to court.

Mann had a similar history of walking on the right side of the law. Married his college sweetheart. A respectable businessman. His only courtroom appearances had been for jury duty. Rainy made a fan of the photographs from James Mann's Text Image Collection on the surface of her workstation. She studied the images with a steady focus. She looked for connections that didn't seem to exist.

The two men hadn't attended any school together. Their paths had never crossed at work or in the service (Mann had never served). From what Rainy could gather, these two were no more connected than motorists passing on the highway. Rainy could ask James Mann these questions herself but doubted his lawyer would allow it.

Plenty of investigative work remained to be done, even without Mann's help. Rainy reached for a yellow legal pad. She jotted down the facts as she knew them.

Ten girls from Shilo H.S. took pictures of themselves.

Who did they send them to? Where did they post them?

Four of the girls had graduated but were students when Hawkins was coach.

Six were still students.

Hawkins coached Lindsey Wells!!

Rainy circled that statement several times.

There were forty different girls in James Mann's Text Image Collection.

All the other images on Mann's computer were from known series per the CVIP.

Very unusual!

None of the images in the Text Image Collection were known.

Did the girls text the images? Did they post them online? They texted them.

Rainy circled that statement several times as well and next to it wrote in parentheses:

(Conclusion, not fact, that's my guess!)

Beneath that she wrote in all capital letters—*HOW DID MANN GET THESE PICTURES?* She drew a large question mark beside it.

Did he have people working for him? Online recruiting?? Did he know these girls?

She let out a heavy breath and sat quietly. She didn't want to force herself into any more conclusions. If she opened herself up to possibilities, flexed her mind enough, a workable theory would come to her. At least, it sometimes did.

Instead, her phone rang.

"This is Agent Miles," she said.

"Agent Miles, my name is Sergeant Brendan Murphy with the Shilo Police Department. I called the New Hampshire FBI office, and they directed me to you."

Rainy felt her pulse accelerate. "What can I do for you, Sergeant?"

"We've been conducting an investigation into some suspicious activity involving a student and a teacher in our high school. A coach, specifically."

"Go on," Rainy said. She wanted Murphy to talk first. She'd tell him what she was investigating if it seemed connected.

"Well, our forensics guys have come back with some pretty interesting stuff."

"What sort of interesting stuff?"

"Have you ever heard of a program called Leterg?"

Rainy's whole body tensed. "I have," she said.

"Look, normally we like to do our own homework," Murphy said. "But we've had to pull in computer forensic help from the state police. They've taken a couple cracks at figuring out what this guy was up to, and we've hit a couple of roadblocks."

"What are you asking?"

"Wondering if you might be able to spare some of your computer expert's time to help us gather the evidence."

"Who's the coach?" Rainy asked, though she already knew the answer. Her head was spinning with possibilities. Connections were beginning to appear.

"The guy's name is Hawkins. Tom Hawkins."

"When do you need us?"

"Soon as possible. We want to move on this thing."

"Hold on a second," Rainy said. She covered the phone's receiver with her hand and looked over at Carter.

"Do you have any plans tonight?" she asked.

"Yeah. I'm taking Gigi out to dinner and a movie. Why?"

"Cancel them, send your wife flowers, and grab your coat," Rainy said. "We're taking a drive north to Shilo."

CHAPTER 26

In just over an hour, Tom would coach his first soccer game since the Facebook scandal broke. Tom tried his best to stay focused on the upcoming match. He anticipated this game would be a brutal and physical battle of wills. But the last practice had been a disaster, and his team was in shambles.

The Riverside bus arrived thirty minutes before game time. The Riverside girls were dressed in red jerseys and spread out across their half of the field, already doing stretches. Some kicked the ball around for warm-ups. Soon after, Vern showed up, and so did the kid with the video recorder.

Tom saw Mitchell Boyd and a bunch of his friends loitering on the hilly rise on the opposite side of the field. Mitchell had never come to a Wildcats home game before. Then again, Jill had never before been dropped off at her house by Mitchell Boyd—and hours past her normal curfew. Tom wasn't a math whiz, but he could quickly solve this equation and didn't much like the answer.

His daughter was potentially Mitchell Boyd's next conquest.

Tom pushed Mitchell Boyd out of his thoughts, in the

same way Boyd and his horsing-around pals were shoving each other. He returned his focus to the game at hand. The team. The win. The forty-ninth straight victory of his tenure. It was a great accomplishment, but one the girls deserved all the credit for achieving. He was just a guide. A map for them to follow. They had to walk the long and difficult trail to each "W" themselves.

Tom's Wildcats began arriving. They were dressed in their Wildcat whites and looked ready to play. Jill led a group of girls onto the field. He noticed Jill stop and wave to Mitchell. Tom didn't detect much oomph in Jill's greeting to Mitchell. She didn't look happy or the least bit enthused. Tom noticed Mitchell give a slight thumbs-up salute in return.

Cool kid, thought Tom.

Tom flipped to the attendance sheet on his clipboard and checked the players in with a pencil mark next to their names. Vern's girls . . . Lauren Grass . . . McAndrews . . . Adamson . . . Wells . . .

He counted them. Seven in total.

Where's the rest of the team? Tom wondered.

He had a nagging suspicion but refused to believe it could be true. Jill came trotting over to him. Tom patted her on the shoulder. "You going to bring it to them, Jill?" Tom asked.

"Can we talk?" Jill said.

Tom's insides went cold.

Seven players had taken the field.

"What's going on here, Jill? Where's the rest of the team?"

"They're not coming," she said. "Either they're quitting the team or their parents won't let them be on it anymore."

"Why?"

"You know why. They all think the Facebook thing is true."

"Okay. Okay," Tom said. He was thinking. His mind started to race. But the jumble of emotions and concerns narrowed down real quick when he thought about what mattered to him most.

"Jill, honey," he said. "You trust me on this. Right? You know it isn't true. In your heart, you know it. Right?"

"Yeah," she said, though it was obvious she was down-trodden. "I know it."

Tom nodded, acknowledging to himself what he had to do next. The referees took the field. Riverside was running a commonly used shooting drill as part of their warm-ups.

"What are we going to do?" Jill asked.

Tom looked over at the glum group of Wildcats, each with a disquieted expression on her face. A referee blew a whistle to signal ten minutes until game time.

"I've coached a lot of matches, Jill," Tom said. "I've won a bunch and lost a bunch, too. But this is the first time I've ever had to forfeit."

"I'm sorry," Jill said.

Tom put an arm around his daughter. "Not as sorry as I am, kiddo," he replied. "Not as sorry as I am."

CHAPTER 27

Tom drove Jill to Lindsey's house.

Jill was too busy texting to talk. Tom asked who was sending her so many text messages.

"Mitchell," Jill said, using her third spoken word of the drive.

Tom remained deeply troubled by his daughter's new "friendship" with Roland Boyd's son. He didn't know any details about their burgeoning romance. It wouldn't be an easy topic of conversation even if he and Jill were closer. Tom had felt his relationship with Jill was progressing like some of his favorite Bruce Springsteen lyrics—the song about taking one step up and two more back. One step up, five hundred steps back, it seemed.

"Persistence and patience" had become a difficult motto to follow with his reputation under heavy attack.

But the Jill-Mitchell tandem was only one check-box item on Tom's growing list of concerns. Kip Lange had yet to be found. Kelly's homicide investigation remained active. The police had made no progress identifying the mysterious girl who texted him her naked pictures. And they still didn't know who had created the blog or bogus

Facebook posts that razed ten years of his good works in a single swoop.

Tom pulled into the Shilo Middle School parking lot ten minutes before the school board meeting was scheduled to start. That was part of his plan. He figured the corridor outside the gymnasium would be mostly deserted by now. He knew, as did everybody else, that Millie Rubenstein's home-baked cookies would be gone. Since Millie started baking cookies for these school board meetings, people had stopped showing up late and most had begun to come early. Better to miss out on the cookies, he decided, than be forced into chitchat with people who might consider him a rapist. Tom parked his Taurus as close to the entrance as possible. That way he could make a quick escape if need be.

It had been two days since new rumors about him spread. *Thank you, Facebook*. Two days for a town to rush to judgment. Two days for parents to pull their kids from the soccer team. Two days to bring a three-year winning streak to an abrupt and sad end.

Superintendent Angie Didomenico had called Tom after he forfeited the Riverside game to warn him of a potentially chilly reception at tonight's meeting, not knowing that he planned to resign from the school board. Angie disagreed with his decision and went on to say that despite the unfortunate circumstances, she felt it imperative he not resign. Tom was one of the two teacher representatives on the board. His absence would be viewed with suspicion, an admission of guilt. Angie feared it would add fuel to an already fast-spinning rumor mill.

Tom had thanked Angie for her support in what both referred to as a difficult time, though he well understood the subtext of their conversation. She'd better not be making a mistake by throwing her support behind him.

Tom traded a warm summer breeze for the cool air-conditioned corridor of Shilo's only middle school. As he expected, no people were milling about, and all that remained of Millie's cookies was a scattering of crumbs on the long foldout table. Before Tom could make a stealthy entrance into the gymnasium, he felt a gentle tap on his shoulder. Surprised anybody could sneak up on him, Tom whirled around to see the porcelain-smooth face of Adriana Boyd smiling at him. Roland's wife, adorned in gold jewelry, dressed in an elegant all-black pantsuit, had a Styrofoam cup of coffee in one hand and a napkin blanketing a cookie in the other.

"Good to see you, Tom," Adriana said. She shrugged her shoulders because she could not shake Tom's hand. She didn't offer Tom her cookie, and he couldn't blame her.

"Nice to see you, too, Adriana. What brings you here tonight?"

"I'm going to give feedback to the board about our PLC initiative."

Tom nodded. PLCs (professional learning communities) were in vogue with many educators and parents these days. The big idea behind PLCs was that students should not just be taught, but rather that they needed to learn. It was a simple shift in thinking that carried profound implications. School systems with an effective PLC policy developed action plans based on intervention, not remediation, and provided systematic guidance that required that struggling students receive additional support until they mastered the concepts being taught. Opponents of PLCs feared that the policy would lead to a diminishment of teacher effectiveness and that all its benefits would accrue to a small minority of students.

Of all the PLC champions in Shilo, Adriana was the most vocal and determined advocate for change. Mitchell Boyd, along with a handful of other struggling Shilo High School students, took part in a PLC pilot program developed by Adriana herself and approved by the board only after several contentious debates.

"How did the public sessions go?" asked Tom. He knew a lot about the subject, because PLCs had been the talk of the teacher lounge.

"Very well. Thanks for asking," Adriana said. "Mitchell should be proof enough that the PLC effort can work."

"He's doing better?" Tom asked.

"From a two-point-two to a three-point-four in one semester," Adriana said, pride in her voice.

"Well, that's all credit to you, your vision, and your perseverance," Tom said.

"They don't call me Black Hawk for nothing," said Adriana.

Tom gave her a puzzled look. "Black Hawk?" he asked, because he'd never heard her called that before.

Adriana grinned. "You've heard of helicopter parents," she said.

Tom nodded. "Sure. Of course."

"Apparently, some people in town think my style of parenting is a bit . . . well, extreme. I guess they think my helicopter is state of the art, fully armed, and combat ready."

Tom laughed for what felt like the first time in days. "They're just afraid of a good fight, that's all," he said.

"Maybe they don't know the fight I've already had."

In that instant, all levity was pushed aside, and Tom looked down at his feet, unsure how best to respond. "Nobody should know that kind of pain," he said in a soft voice.

"But you understand," Adriana said. "I can see it in the way you fight for your daughter. I can feel how much you love her. If there's one good thing to come from what happened to Kelly, it's that Jill will finally get the chance to know the man you really are."

Tom felt his fears about Jill and Mitchell's burgeoning romance lessen. The force of Adriana's convictions made him believe Mitchell Boyd could be more than the promise of his reputation.

"We should get inside," Tom said. "I'd hate to miss the opening gavel." Tom gave Adriana a wry grin, nodded toward the gymnasium double doors, and took two steps in that direction.

Adriana reached out and took hold of Tom's arm, pulling him back toward her. "Listen, Tom, I've been meaning to call you," she said. "I heard about what happened at soccer practice and the game against Riverside. Everybody has by now. I want you to know that there are a lot of us who don't believe it's true."

"A lot?"

"Well, some," Adriana amended. "The Internet can be a dangerous place. We all know that."

"You don't have to remind me."

"Just the other day, Roland told me about one of his employees who sent an email to his entire address book with a link to a gay porn site. He claimed he'd never been to any of those sites. Turns out it was a computer virus that sent the emails without his knowledge."

"That's a nasty virus."

"Trust me, I saw the site. Very nasty."

The two shared another quick laugh. Having Adriana in his corner felt significant. Tom needed every friend he could get.

Merle Gornick, an eleventh-grade chemistry teacher, a late arriver herself, walked past the pair and fixed Tom with a hard stare. Adriana definitely noticed.

"Around school I only get that look about half the time," Tom said with a forced smile.

"Well, people talk, and I know there is plenty of support out there for you," said Adriana. "Just not everybody. No matter what happens to you, you'll come out on top. I sense that about you."

Adriana expressed so much empathy, Tom believed it genuinely hurt her to see him suffer.

"I appreciate all your support, Adriana. I really do."

"Roland believes in you, too. He's traveling on business but wanted me to tell you that we've got your back."

Tom laughed. "That sounds like Roland," he said.

I'd hate to be on his bad side, thought Tom, remembering the confrontation with Bob at the club.

Now it was Adriana who nodded toward the gymnasium doors. Tom followed, walking beside her. Inside, a dozen or so rows of small gray plastic chairs were set up. Most of the people were seated, but some noticed Tom and Adriana enter. Tom didn't hear anybody gasp over the echoed din of voices, but he saw expressions change. Soon others began to notice him. Some stared. Some whispered. Dale Rivers, the father of one of the girls he coached, looked ready for a fight.

"Not feeling the support right now, Adriana," Tom said under his breath.

"It's there for you," said Adriana. "Just not everybody."

The two made their way to the front of the room, where school board appointees and representatives sat. Tom felt their eyes on him all the way to his seat. He understood that these people didn't need any evidence to convict him. All they needed to hear were the words *sex* and *coach* in the same sentence for it to be true. Understanding their reaction didn't make it easier to endure.

Angie Didomenico approached Tom, while Adriana found her seat a few rows behind his.

"Thanks for being here," Angie said, giving Tom's right arm a strong squeeze.

"As long as everybody left their torches at home, I should be fine."

"I know you will be."

Angie brought the meeting to order. Things seemed to settle down after that. The board agreed to add kitchen staff to better clean pots and pans for kids with nut allergies. Adriana presented her PLC report crisply and without much discussion. They debated longer and more intensely over several ways to ease parking lot congestion at the high school. Tom kept silent throughout the meeting.

At ten till ten, Angie slammed her gavel and the meeting concluded. Tom felt a modicum of relief that his quick escape plan had proved an unnecessary precaution. He texted Jill.

Green.

He texted her again. Pick you up in ten.

She texted back. Green.

Very funny, Tom typed.

Tom opened his car door, and the darkness around him ignited into a bright frenzy of red and blue strobe lights. Two police cruisers from the Shilo PD pulled up, boxing in his car. Brendan Murphy emerged from one of the police cars. Officer Rich Fox was with him, as well as two other uniformed police officers, whom Tom didn't know or recognize.

Tom's eyes scanned in all directions for an escape. It was instinct, his navy training kicking in.

Distract and evade.

But no retreat was available. Not without inflicting casualties.

Murphy approached, and Tom observed his hand on the butt of a weapon. People from the board meeting heading for their cars stopped to watch the spectacle unfold.

"Turn around! Hands on the hood of your car! Feet spread wide!" Murphy shouted at Tom.

Tom did as he was told.

Murphy took hold of Tom's arms and pulled them behind his back. Tom knew better than to resist.

"Tom Hawkins," Murphy said, "you're under arrest."

Murphy recited Tom's Miranda rights.

Again.

Tom felt handcuffs secured around his wrists, locked tight. Amidst the flashing lights, Tom spotted Adriana standing close by, watching. Her face was frozen in a horrified expression, and she appeared to be crying.

Tom glanced over his shoulder, back at Murphy. "What are the charges?" he asked.

"Possession and trafficking of child pornography," Murphy said.

"What the . . . What are you talking about?"

"Let's go," Murphy said.

Murphy grabbed hold of one of Tom's arms, while Fox took the other. Together they escorted him to a waiting police cruiser. Tom could almost feel Murphy's pleasure as he shoved him into the back of the cruiser.

Tom's thoughts quickly turned to panic. Not for himself, but for Jill. He finally understood what this was all about.

"Murphy, listen to me," Tom pleaded. "I can't leave Jill alone. She's not safe. I'm being set up. Somebody wants me out of the picture so they can get to Jill. I'm telling you, you've got to find Kip Lange. He's doing this to get me out of the way. Please! Brendan, you're making a big mistake here."

Murphy crouched low so that Tom could see his face through the cruiser's open rear door.

Tom could see he was smiling.

"No, Tom," Murphy said. "Remember what I told you? Guys like you always screw up. The only mistake made here was you thinking you'd get away with it."

Tom closed his eyes and thought of Jill. In his mind, he saw her not as the teenager she was, but as the little girl she used to be. He remembered her in jeans and a plaid cowboy shirt. Her long hair tied in pigtails. A fourth grader with two missing teeth. Face full of freckles. Her knee skinned up badly and her bike a bent wreckage. Tears rolling down her eyes. Back then, he could make it all better. He had cleaned up the cut. Put the bandage on it. Kissed the knee. Now he couldn't do anything to help her.

He couldn't protect her anymore.

He was helpless.

CHAPTER 28

Rainy met Sergeant Brendan Murphy in his office. Murphy was going to bring her to Tom Hawkins, who'd been processed and transported to one of the interrogation rooms.

From the start of Rainy's interactions with Murphy, the oversized police sergeant had given her the creeps. He stood too close to her, almost hovering. He would touch her when he talked. A tap on the shoulder. A pat on the arm. She didn't like the way he kept looking at her, either. But the man had provided her with one incredibly useful service. Thanks to Murphy, she had one possible answer to her ongoing investigation into James Mann. Hawkins, she now believed, had sold Mann the images she'd categorized as sexts. But Murphy's usefulness had just about run out, so one more touch, another lecherous stare, and he'd come to regret those octopus arms.

"We've moved Hawkins from our holding cell to the meeting room."

"Thanks for making it possible."

"Hey, a favor for a favor. Your man Carter is really quite the wizard. He unlocked the whole shebang."

"I'm assuming you'll want to be present when I question him."

"Nah. We'll be watching through the two-way. You do your thing, Agent Miles."

He tapped her on the shoulder, then touched her on the arm.

"Sergeant Murphy, do you have a problem keeping your hands to yourself?" Murphy stammered but could not speak. "I didn't think so," said Rainy.

Rainy followed behind a silent and stoop-shouldered Murphy as he led her down a well-lit corridor with blue-painted walls. They stopped in front of a closed door marked MEETING ROOM in stenciled black lettering.

Murphy opened the door. His sullen mood fell away, and he returned to his former cocky self, albeit without the touches. "Crap this guy was into, don't feel you need to go easy on him," he said. "I know we've got cameras and two-way glass and whatnot, but we can shut those off and turn our backs. You just give the word."

"Thanks. But this won't take long. Close the door on your way out," Rainy said.

Tom Hawkins rested his handcuffed hands upon a heavily gouged table dividing the small concrete room. Light from powerful fluorescents danced off the two-way mirror. The room behind it, Rainy knew, was kept intentionally dark to allow the officers inside proper viewing. Murphy wanted to record the interview for the New Hampshire DA's office, but Rainy had denied the request. It was against department procedure to record any interrogation without the approval or presence of someone from the US attorney's office.

Hawkins would probably be tried by the state, not the Feds. FBI resources were under constant strain. With the type of images and the quantity found on Hawkins's computer, it was doubtful Tomlinson would allow Rainy to bring him up on federal charges. He'd much prefer to let the state take the resource hit in prosecuting the crimes. But she was here to see if Hawkins could help her with her James Mann investigation. It would be good to get to him before he lawyered up. It never failed to amaze her how much information perps revealed when given a chance.

She tried to make an assessment of him based on behavior. It surprised her that Hawkins had no trouble making eye contact. In fact, his eyes followed her into the room and watched her take the seat across from his. They were cold, though, with touches of gray that reminded her of a wolf.

Training told her to steer clear of on-the-spot reading. Evidence trumped gut instinct every time. But the way he looked at her was not typical. Usually, the men Rainy interrogated gave her the shivers, as if they were broadcasting their sickness on an FM frequency she picked up in stereo. But for the life of her, Rainy couldn't recall a single instance where she found one of these men attractive. That was, until she met Tom Hawkins. Hawkins was ruggedly handsome, and easy on the eyes.

Stop it, Miles, Rainy silently berated herself. *Look beyond his looks.*

Rainy returned her focus to the mission. She was here to obtain information. She hoped Hawkins wanted to share his side of the story. With luck, he would talk. Rainy reached into the pocket of her suit blazer for her badge, making no conscious effort to conceal the holstered weapon she carried. "I'm Special Agent Loraine Miles, from the FBI," she said.

"Where's my daughter?" asked Tom.

Rainy handed Tom a cell phone. This was part of the

deal she'd agreed to so that Tom would talk. She watched Tom key in a number. The handcuffs didn't get in his way. He put the phone to his ear. He waited. She listened.

"Hiya, Jilly-bean. It's Dad. . . . No, I'm fine. . . . Don't worry. . . . Everything is going to be all right. . . . Yeah, yeah, stay with Lindsey. That's fine. . . . No, the police car is outside because I asked them to keep an eye on you. . . . Right, the guy in the woods . . . No, I don't think you have anything to worry about, but I'm not taking any chances. . . . You stay strong, okay? . . . I'll see you real soon."

Tom handed the phone back to Rainy. His eyes were burning with rage.

Now she got the shivers.

"Is your daughter all right?" Rainy asked.

"She's scared."

"You can help," said Rainy.

"How?"

"Talk to me."

"What's this got to do with the FBI, anyway?" Tom said.

"Well, I was hoping you could tell me that," Rainy said.

"I'm not playing games. Get specific, Agent Miles."

"I want you to tell me how you came to know James Mann, and how you got the images the police found on your computer."

"I don't know a James Mann. And I don't know what images anybody found."

"Don't make this harder than it needs to be, Tom," Rainy said. "You know as well as I do that cooperation will be taken into consideration at sentencing."

"I won't be convicted. I'm not guilty of anything."

"We have the images, Tom. Forty girls. Hundreds of

images. Were the pictures taken with cell phone cameras?"

"I'm only speaking to my attorney."

"We've got the computer logs that show a lot of cash payments. Did you get paid for sending these images?"

"Are you my attorney?"

"Did you coerce the girls into giving you these pictures? Were you having a relationship with all of them or just the one?"

"I'm only speaking to my attorney," Tom repeated.

"How did you recruit the others in your ring? Craigslist? Some other message board? How many people do you have working for you?"

Tom said nothing. He'd gone statue on her.

Rainy sighed, pushed her chair back, and stood up from the table.

"Suit yourself. Last chance from me. Judges like it when a felon cooperates with the Feds. Doesn't do you much good to put up walls, Tom. Why not just tell me the truth? I can't promise you'll do less time, but I'll put in the good word. Tom, think about your daughter."

Tom was looking down at his hands. He picked his head back up.

"She's all I think about," Tom said. "Look at me. I'm just a father desperately worried about my daughter's safety. I'd cut a deal with you in a heartbeat if I could."

A twinge of sadness, sudden and unexpected, overcame Rainy.

She had come to Shilo ready to extort Tom's cooperation but was leaving with a new question.

Could this seemingly genuine and decent man really be so evil?

CHAPTER 29

"Your lawyer's here. Let's go."

Tom rose from a small cot pushed flush against the concrete wall of his eight-by-twelve jail cell. He rubbed his eyes, because somehow he had fallen asleep. He still wore his street clothes, but they'd taken his shoelaces and belt.

Two uniformed police officers stood guard outside Tom's cell, while two others entered with shackles and handcuffs jangling from their hands. The officer putting cuffs on Tom's wrists looked only a few years older than the kids in Jill's class. The guy who secured his ankles was Rich Fox, the father of a girl he coached.

"What time is it?" Tom croaked.

"Eighty thirty in the morning," Fox said.

"How long are you going to keep me here?"

"Hell, Coach, you're gonna be here all weekend. Can't get you an arraignment until Monday."

"I have a daughter. She can't be left alone all weekend."

The shackles closed about his ankles with tiny clicks.

"Child services has been contacted. She'll be fine. Worry about yourself right now, is my advice."

Four officers escorted Tom out of his cell and down a long corridor.

Memories of his arrest lingered. The smell in the backseat of the police cruiser, skunk beer and cigarettes masked poorly by a pine tree air freshener, stood out above all others. What was it Murphy said between cackles from the police radio? *Not only are soccer players pussies, but they're stupid pussies, too.* Tom said nothing in reply. He just stared blankly out the front window, through the grime on the Plexiglas divider, which made Murphy feel safe to taunt him.

They brought him to a room that looked similar to the one where the FBI agent had tried to pry a confession out of him. Only this room didn't have a two-way mirror and wall-mounted cameras. At least here his conversations would be private. Here he still had some basic rights.

Tom took a seat and rested his handcuffed hands on the wood table. His lawyer would occupy the only other chair. Tom locked his fingers together and waited. He hadn't hesitated about whom to call for representation.

Tom let out a relieved breath when Marvin Pressman stepped into the room. As before, the man's rumpled suit appeared to have been slept in. Marvin hoisted his lawyer's briefcase onto the table and took his seat across from Tom.

"Heck of a pickle you've got yourself in, Tom," he said. "Did you speak with anybody?"

"Police tried to get me to sign a confession, told me I could go home if I did."

"And?"

"And I didn't sign it."

"Good."

"An agent from the FBI came to see me as well."

"And?"

"And she was cute."

"And."

"And I didn't say anything. Just that I'd speak only with my attorney."

"Good man."

"Tell me about Jill."

"The social worker you've been working with is going to make a huge difference here," Marvin said. "They're not going to force her into state custody. She's going to let her stay with Cathleen Wells until after your arraignment."

"Good."

"Maybe."

"What's that supposed to mean?"

"We'll get to that in moment," Marvin said.

"Is Murphy keeping his word?"

Marvin nodded. "They've had patrol cars pass by the Wellses' house at random intervals, like he said he would. He's taking your concern about her safety very seriously. I spoke with Jill, as well. She told me she's staying indoors and won't be alone for a second."

Tom leaned back in his chair until the two front legs were elevated off the floor. "You're looking good, Marvin," he said. "Have you been doing the exercises I sent you?"

"That workout is pretty intense. But the results seem to be worth it." Marvin patted his belly, which was still ample, but visibly less so.

"And the salt? Have you dropped the salt from your diet?"

"Gone. Well, mostly gone."

"More potassium, less sodium. Remember that. And keep checking the labels. Amazing how much sodium they cram in there."

"I think we should worry less about me and focus more on you. Deal?"

Tom wasn't ready to take any deal. "Have you worked up the nerve to ask out Rebecca Bartholomew? I'm telling you, she's a real catch." This was stalling, but the pleasant chitchat was helping Tom relax.

Marvin smiled and seemed to understand Tom's motivation. "No, but she did come up on my Match.com suggested matches," he said. "I didn't go through with it, though. Too nervous, I guess. Maybe in another ten pounds."

"I'll get you that ten. No problem."

"Let's win your case first, and then we can figure out my social life."

Tom inhaled deeply, then exhaled slowly. It was time to get down to business. "I'm being set up," he said.

"That's our working premise."

"It's got to be Kip Lange."

Marvin's expression darkened. "Tom, I'm advising you not to implicate yourself in another crime. I don't want to know any more about Lange. You've alerted the police to your concerns. That's enough for now."

"What about Murphy? The guy has been gunning for me from day one. Could he have planted the evidence just to make an arrest?"

"Anything is possible."

"I don't think it was a player. But I can't be sure. A rival coach, maybe?"

"We've got a long road ahead of us, Tom. This is going to take time, and I'm not going to tell you that it's going to be easy."

"Marvin, can you tell me that you're good at this sort of thing?"

"I'm good."

"Tell me how we're going to beat this," said Tom.

"Do you remember the controversy around your state scoring title?"

"Sure. You found out that the state's official statistician didn't record all my goals."

"Not only did he not record all your goals, but it was his kid who was nearest to you for the most scored in state history. And lo and behold, it was his kid who ended up with the title."

"I'm liking the memory-lane trip, Marvin, but can you tell me what that's got to do with my case?"

"Ask yourself, what is it about Marvin Pressman that made him start digging into that scoring record in the first place?"

"You thought it was bullshit," Tom said.

"More than bullshit. I knew it was an outlier."

"Outlier?" Tom said.

"You know, something that deviates from the norm. You being beat out by that kid, in my mind, was simply impossible. I knew it right away. He wasn't even a senior. So I went back and watched all your games on tape and documented the date, time, and minute when you scored each goal. That's how I figured out his daddy was cooking the official books so that his kid came out on top."

"All very interesting, but how does this help me?"

"Why did Bjorn Borg generate more topspin with his backhand than any other player on tour?"

"Marvin, does it matter?"

"Because his backhand was almost like a hockey slap shot. It was that loose style that gave the ball its unique spin. Why can Rory Delap execute a longer throw-in that is more accurate than most corner kicks?"

"Why?" Tom said, going along with this thought train.

"It's all in the way he throws the ball. Low, flat trajectory, tons of backspin, which counters gravity, even though his release is at a low angle."

"And what does this have to do with my case, Marvin? Help me out here. I'm putting my life on the line with you."

"What it means is that even though I've never tried a case exactly like yours, I'm really good at finding explanations for unusual events. I'm good at picking up insights that will make a jury nod their heads and say, 'Hey, that does present us with some reasonable doubt here.' I think it's that wiring that gives my clients the edge. So the first rule of working with me is that you've got to trust me. Second rule . . . See rule one. *Comprende?*"

Tom nodded. "Okay. So what do you know?" he asked.

Marvin reached behind him to close the door. "I'd like some privacy with my client," Marvin said to the police officer standing guard. The door closed with a soft click. "Why don't we start by you telling me what you know?"

Tom scoffed. "I have no idea. Somebody created these bogus blog posts claiming they were having sex with me. Supposedly, one of my players. The police turned it into a public spectacle by questioning my players about the post as a group. Nothing came of it. Then I gave Sergeant Murphy my school-issued laptop computer—"

"Gave it to him?"

"He asked for it, and I had nothing to hide. So yeah, I gave it to him. Then some girl sent me text messages with pictures attached. Naked pictures. Obviously, that's part of the setup. I know that now. But at the time I thought it wasn't related. I didn't want to shine an even brighter spotlight on me, and subsequently on Jill. In hindsight, that was probably a mistake, because the next day someone used Facebook to say that they knew which player I was sleeping with. I got the police involved then, school officials, too. Now, why would I have done that if I was guilty? Doesn't make sense."

"Maybe you knew the jig was up. Maybe the police think you were trying to make it look like it was a setup."

"I don't know what they're thinking," Tom said. "All I know is that a few days after somebody sent me that picture, I got arrested, booked, and questioned by the FBI about my connection to somebody named James Mann."

Marvin nodded. "They've booked you on numerous counts of possession and trafficking of child pornography. Did she say why she wanted to talk to you?"

"She thinks I'm involved with a case she's investigating. But that's insane. I didn't do any of what she said I did. It sickens me to even think about it."

Marvin took off his glasses and stared through the lenses. He polished away some grime. "That'll be the last time you tell me you're innocent. Deal?" Marvin put his glasses back on.

"But—"

"I'm here. I'm your lawyer. I'm going to defend you."

Tom had to close his eyes to keep from saying anything more.

Marvin continued, "Now, usually when I conduct my first interview, I don't know much about the evidence, and the cops generally aren't too forthcoming. But . . ."

"But what?"

"But on my way in, Murphy said to me, 'Don't waste your time on this one, Pressman. The case is a slam dunk.' So I say, 'Why's that?' And he starts blabbing about things he probably shouldn't be blabbing about."

"Such as?"

"Such as the consent search you gave them for the laptop. And the evidence they found linking you to a sexual relationship with Lindsey Wells."

"Lindsey Wells?"

"Apparently, they found a number of pictures of naked girls from Shilo on your computer, Tom. Including pictures of the girl you described to Rich Fox at that meeting. Murphy said ten are from Shilo and about thirty they couldn't ID. He was being sarcastic when he said he'd ask your help with that."

"Which I can't do," Tom said.

"Of course you can't. But they think you recruited other people, kids probably, to help you obtain these images, which you then allegedly sold on the Internet."

"And they found all this on my school-issued laptop?"

"Well, according to the forensic report—and again this is what Murphy told me—there is no sign of any tampering with the machine. No viruses. Nothing. It's clean."

"What about my home PC? They searched that, too."

"I don't know," Marvin said. "But they also found alleged correspondences between you and Lindsey Wells. They got a search warrant, and a computer forensic team is over at Lindsey's house right now, working on her machine."

"But you told me Jill is staying there."

"That's why I said it might not be so good that Jill's staying there. Murphy also showed me a printout of a Facebook message spreading around. Apparently, a Facebook user calling himself Fidelius Charm made a new profile after the company deactivated his old one. This person sent out a bunch of new friend requests and more messages after your arrest."

"What did the message say?" Tom asked glumly.

"The secret is out," Marvin said, reciting what he had read. "Coach Hawkins is sleeping with Lindsey Wells."

Tom groaned and rubbed his manacled hands vigorously through his hair.

"My guess is the police are going to find out that it was Lindsey who made the initial blog posts about you. It's one way to link you to the naked images of hers they found on your school computer. Don't ask me how they'll try and link you to the images of the other girls."

"If Lindsey says anything to the police about our having a relationship, she's lying. What does Jill know?"

"Tom, I haven't spoken to Jill about it," Marvin said. "But what I do know is that at your arraignment on Monday, you're going to plead not guilty."

"That won't be a problem. Can I get out of here now?"

Marvin appeared glum. "The bail commissioner came down. Murphy sent him away. Bail commissioners almost never go against a police officer if they recommend you be detained until your arraignment."

"What happens at my arraignment?"

"You'll hear the charges against you. Bail will be set. You are presumed innocent. The judge should give you personal recognizance bail. They're not supposed to bootstrap the current charges to your bail condition."

"That sounds positive," Tom said.

"But these are very serious charges," Marvin said, "and just because a judge isn't supposed to bootstrap current charges to bail conditions doesn't mean they don't. The prosecutor is probably going to argue that you're a flight risk given your extensive military contacts and training. Bail could be high."

"How high?"

"Fifty thousand," Marvin said. "Maybe even a hundred."

Tom's mouth fell open. "I don't have that kind of money. What happens if I can't post bail?"

"You'll sit in jail until your trial."

"How long will that be?"

"Your case could come up for trial a year from now. Even longer."

CHAPTER 30

Woonsocket County was home to five district courthouses. The morning of Tom's arraignment, a team of three officers entered his tiny cell to secure their prisoner for transport to the closest courthouse, in the bordering town of Millis. Sergeant Brendan Murphy oversaw the transport effort, with an expression, Tom thought, more appropriate for a big-game hunter than a police officer. Then again, Tom Hawkins was the biggest game in town, as evident from the hordes of media types, from Boston to southern Maine, closing around the disgraced coach as soon as he exited police headquarters. They shouted their questions and blinded Tom with camera lights, which they used despite the bright, cloudless morning.

Tom decided not to conceal his face from the onslaught of photographers and TV news crews documenting his every step. Whenever he'd seen people hiding their faces under hoods or jackets, Tom always thought they looked guilty of something.

On the short walk to the waiting police car, Tom's thoughts drifted back to Kip Lange and what he had done to protect Kelly and Jill almost sixteen years ago.

Had Kelly told Lange that he'd been the one to hide the drugs?

Tom felt certain the man in the woods that night was Kip Lange. But that certainty left him with two vital questions he couldn't answer. What did Lange want? And what did Lange know?

Marvin had some friends, former cops who did investigative work for him from time to time. To help ease Tom's worry about Jill, Marvin had coordinated a 24/7 watch over his daughter until after his arraignment. No way would Tom be able to afford to keep up that watch if he didn't make bail. According to Marvin's report, the PIs hadn't seen anybody lurking around Cathleen Wells's house. They'd been watching it nonstop for the last forty-eight hours. No prowlers. No strange cars. Nothing. If Lange was going to make a move on Jill, it would have been while Tom was locked up. Soon he'd be out on bail, ending what would have been Lange's best opportunity to get to his daughter.

Why didn't Lange take a shot?

Tom could think of only one answer to that question. Lange's plan wasn't to kidnap Jill.

He was going to blackmail Tom.

Tom's police escort drove to the back of the Millis District Courthouse. The parking lot was unusually full, even for a Monday morning. If the police didn't have designated spots for cruisers, they might not have had a place to park. Tom didn't know the type of car Marvin Pressman drove, but felt certain that his lawyer was among the early arrivals.

Murphy and another police officer took hold of Tom's arms and together hoisted him out of the patrol car. After checking the handcuffs on Tom's wrists, they ushered him inside, through the security checkpoint, and into a locked room. They pushed Tom down by his shoulders until he sat on the only chair in the otherwise empty waiting room.

"What's next?" Tom asked. Murphy pretended not to hear Tom's question. "I said, what's next?" Tom repeated.

Murphy grunted and pointed to another door on the opposite wall. "Your name gets called by the state. You walk through that door. You sit. You get arraigned."

"Sounds simple enough."

"Yeah, simple."

They waited. Two police officers, one prisoner, silent as could be. Body heat and poor circulation turned the air inside the room thick and oppressive. The longer Tom waited, the more his nerves fired. Sweat dotted his forehead.

In those anxious moments, Tom pondered his fate. *Will the judge set bail? Will it be as high as Pressman warned?*

A wellspring of emotion flooded through Tom. If he went to jail, he would lose everything. He would lose his freedom. He would lose his good name. Certainly, above all else, he would lose his daughter forever. Marvin had advised him to suppress his emotions during the arraignment. Cool and calm demeanor, the lawyer had recommended. But Marvin's life wasn't the one on the line.

Tom tried patterned breathing to slow his pulse but couldn't suppress the toxic mix of anxiety and rage boiling within. Tom's muscles tightened to the point where he thought they might snap. His expression morphed from stony to snarled. Thick veins on the side of his neck pulsed angrily.

"Whoa, this guy looks like he's ready to pop off," a police officer said.

"Take it easy, Coach Hawkins," Murphy said. "I wouldn't want to cause a scene before your big day."

Before Tom could respond, probably in a way he'd regret, the PA speaker mounted flush to the wall crackled with static.

"Docket CR-thirteen-s-sixteen-fifty-seven, *State of New Hampshire versus Thomas Hawkins.*"

The moment they called his docket number, Murphy opened the door leading into the courtroom and escorted Tom through.

Marvin had done his best to explain where Tom would be seated during the proceedings, but the reality was far worse than his lawyer had described. Tom found himself standing inside a box that looked out into the courtroom. One wall of the box was made from concrete brick, but the other three walls were built using floor-to-ceiling Plexiglas. Through the plastic walls Tom could see crowds of people jammed inside the tiny courtroom. He recognized many of the faces.

Marvin Pressman stood behind a long table that was barren, save for a single manila folder. One end of the table was pressed nearly flush against Tom's holding cell wall. The Plexiglas had holes in it so that Tom could speak to his attorney. Marvin wore a well-pressed, nicely tailored suit. It was the first confidence booster of the day.

He's dressed like a man ready to get me out on bail.

The dearth of documents displayed on the defense counsel's table, however, didn't engender much confidence.

Marvin moved his chair closer so he could speak to Tom through the cell's tiny puncture holes. "Are you ready for this? You look good."

Tom spoke in a low voice. "I look like crap and you know it. I haven't bathed or shaved in days. My clothes stink, and I feel like a freak show on display in here."

"Well, naturally you're keyed up. Try to calm down.

We have only one dog in this fight today. Bail. You got that?" Pressman gestured to the table across from his, pointing to a female attorney, actively organizing her stacks of folders, files, and case evidence.

"She looks more prepared," said Tom.

"She's not. Trust me. It's all show. But she's a mother who is very active in the community, her name's Gina Glantz, and this judge likes her a lot. We'll do what we can, but I need you to focus, and above all else, remain calm. Promise me that."

"Yeah, I promise," Tom said.

Tom allowed himself to think about Jill. He conjured up an image of Jill in better days, and that helped calm him. He'd come back to Shilo for her. Everything would eventually turn out all right.

Next, Tom cast a sweeping glance at all the spectators gathered inside the courtroom. He couldn't see everybody in the sizable crowd, but he did happen to catch Rebecca's eye. He didn't wave to her, though she motioned to him. Tom saw Vern seated behind the front row of benches. His assistant coach gave Tom an encouraging thumbs-up sign. At least some had come to show their support.

The judge, midfifties, with a full head of dark hair, wearing wire-rimmed glasses, was seated at his bench. With a bang of the gavel, the courtroom chatter fell into silence.

The proceedings began. The charges against Tom were read aloud. A dozen counts of felonious sexual assault, along with the possession and distribution of more than three hundred images deemed to be lewd and lascivious depictions of minors.

"Do you understand the charges against you?" the judge said, directing his question to Tom. For somebody with "judge" in his job title, Tom felt the man had already passed sentence, just by the way he looked at him.

"Tell him you do," Marvin whispered.

"I do."

"And how do you plead?"

"Tell him not guilty," Marvin said.

"Not guilty."

The judge wrote something down. In answering the judge's questions, Tom's throat felt dry and his own voice rang weak and defeated in his ears.

The judge spoke again. "Is there a question of bail?"

"There is, Your Honor." The D.A.'s prosecutor, Gina Glantz, rose from her seat.

"Proceed."

"Your Honor, these are very serious charges levied against Mr. Hawkins. I would like to remind the court that before Mr. Hawkins's recent move, he had not been a resident of the town for nine years."

Marvin pounced. "Your Honor, I believe that's irrelevant to the question of bail."

"I think it's quite relevant. It demonstrates the potential for a flight risk, no real ties to the community, especially given the gravity of the charges Mr. Hawkins is facing."

"Your Honor, my client is an upstanding citizen. He's a military veteran, a Navy SEAL at that, with no criminal history and strong ties to the community as both a guidance counselor and a soccer coach."

"Which is precisely why the state is recommending that he be held without bail. Mr. Hawkins very well may be a threat to children. No bail, Your Honor, is the best way to ensure the public's safety, especially given the preponderance of evidence against the accused."

Held without bail. Tom let the words tumble about his head and rattle away all other worries.

Held without bail.

"This isn't his trial, Gina," Marvin countered. "There is precedent here for reasonable bail. The defense has yet to be provided with any of the evidence against my client. Bail should be based solely on risk or danger or flight and not any assumptions about my client's guilt. He's returned to Shilo to look after his daughter, of whom he now has full custody. I'd say he has strong ties to the community."

The judge gave both attorneys a stern look.

"Picking up the defense's argument, Your Honor, Mr. Hawkins also has many contacts throughout the world from his days in the military, justifying my flight risk concern. The defendant is trained to disappear. He has the skills and the resources to do just that."

"I'm inclined to agree with the prosecution here," the judge said.

Marvin rose to his feet. "Your Honor, in *Dunlap v. the State of New Hampshire*, a town-purchased computer was used by the accused to view child pornography. The bail for that case was set at twenty-five thousand dollars. I believe this sets a precedent for bail, given that both Dunlap and Mr. Hawkins are accused of similar crimes."

"Mr. Dunlap was never charged with felonious sexual assault," Glantz countered. "If Mr. Pressman requires adherence to this precedent, then the state recommends bail be set at two hundred thousand dollars."

Somebody attending the proceedings clapped loudly.

The judge slammed down his gavel. "There will be no disrespect in my court!" he shouted. The room became uncomfortably silent.

"Your Honor, my client would execute a waiver of extradition to assure the court of his commitment to this trial," Marvin said.

"Bail will be set at one hundred thousand dollars," the judge decided. He banged the gavel again.

Tom gave Marvin a panicked look. "I can't afford that, Marvin. Not even if I mortgaged the house. You know that," he said. "Do something."

"Tom, I'm sorry. The judge sets the bail. At least we have bail. You'll have time to rally your supporters and raise the funds. Then we'll have our day in court."

"I'm going to lose Jill, Marvin. I need to be free so I can fight to clear my name."

"Attorney Pressman, is your client in a position to post bail with the clerk's office?"

"No, Your Honor. The bail set is too high."

"In that case, I'm ordering Mr. Hawkins be remanded to state custody in the house of corrections for a period of—"

"Your Honor! Your Honor! Please . . ."

"Is somebody addressing the court?"

Tom turned around to see who had spoken. Everybody else inside the courtroom did the same. Adriana Boyd, dressed in a sharply tailored navy suit, with a glittering emerald brooch on the lapel, rose from her seat at the back of the courtroom.

"I will post bail for Mr. Hawkins."

The room exploded in chatter, and the judge had to bang his gavel several times to regain order. "You understand you'll be taking on the financial risk here?"

"I understand, Your Honor."

"Okay. Mr. Hawkins, you'll be escorted to the clerk's office once your bail has been posted. A probable cause hearing will be scheduled for October the fifteenth."

Tom turned again to search out Adriana to thank her. But she was already gone.

CHAPTER 31

A ngie Didomenico repeated her demand. "I'm asking you to resign, Tom, effective immediately."

Tom sat back in his chair. He had anticipated this, but it stung to hear it aloud. They were alone, seated across from one another in Angie's cramped office. In the aftermath of his arraignment hearing, Angie had hastily scheduled an emergency meeting with Tom, Craig Powers (who was apparently back in her good graces), and Shilo High School principal Lester Osborne. Angie, it seemed, wanted some time alone with Tom and requested that he show up fifteen minutes before the others were scheduled to arrive. Twenty-four hours spent as a free man, and already Tom felt persecuted again.

Marvin had spent an hour on the phone prepping Tom for this meeting. He'd painted a bleak picture of Tom's finances. Tom had enough saved to keep up with the mortgage payments. But he'd be hard pressed now to land another job, with all the negative publicity surrounding him. And without the teaching and coaching income, his ability to make the mortgage payment was once again in jeopardy.

Marvin warned him it was unrealistic, but Tom had

hoped to hold on to both positions, at least until his trial. With one swift demand, Angie had all but crushed that possibility.

Resign.

"I'm not guilty of any crime, Angie." Tom assessed Angie's stern, unyielding expression and tried, but failed, to read any agreement on her face.

"It doesn't matter, Tom. The battle for public perception has already been fought and lost. The risks here are substantial if you don't resign."

"Tell me. How could this get any worse?"

"If you ever want to teach again, it can certainly get much worse. Resignations are protected under employment laws and maintain better confidentiality. Firing you will make it a public record."

"Are you firing me?"

"Not yet," Angie said. Her expression now betrayed a feeling of sadness and remorse. "But you don't have to be convicted of this crime to get fired. We can look at the evidence and make our own assessment. That's within our rights."

"The union wouldn't like that move, I bet."

"True. They probably wouldn't," Angie said. "They could agitate the situation, try to overwhelm us with paperwork, but they can't change the eventual outcome here. Look, Tom, I don't want to fire you."

"Then don't."

"It's not that easy. I'm getting a lot of pressure. Calls are flooding our office from concerned parents demanding you be kept away from their kids."

"This is no better than a witch hunt, and you know it," Tom said. "I haven't done anything wrong here. I have no idea how that junk got put on my laptop. But I do know that I haven't been convicted of any crime. The only crime here is my arrest. Whatever evidence the police have against me is bogus, and we both know it."

Angie held her stony gaze. She was less convinced of Tom's innocence than he'd first assumed.

"Do what's right, Tom, and make this go away."

"No, you do what's right, Angie. I love teaching. I love coaching. I love helping these kids. And I'm not going to go quietly. My daughter is still here. And I won't stop fighting to clear my name and provide for her."

"Just what sort of future can you provide if you can't work, Tom? Think about it."

Though she'd just pricked at one of his biggest concerns, outwardly Tom did his best to seem unfazed. "I'll work a dozen different jobs if that's what it takes," he said. "But if I've read my union guidelines correctly, you can't officially fire me without documenting your case to the union's satisfaction. So if I don't resign, you'll first have to place me on paid administrative leave. Isn't that right?"

Angie's brow furrowed. "Yes, that's right," she said.

"Well then, that should quiet down the tribe. I'll take that option and go from there."

"You're going to be fired," Angie said, her face now reddening from anger. "You're making a mistake, Tom."

"No, Angie, you are," Tom said.

The office door swung open. Craig Powers and Lester Osborne entered. Tom stood. Without saying a word to either man, he left.

CHAPTER 32

Jill couldn't look her father in the eye. She knew only vague details about the charges against him. She knew that her best friend, Lindsey Wells, was suspected of having a relationship with her father. She knew the police had found illegal images on his laptop computer, that her father had been charged with possession and distribution of child pornography, but she did not know the specifics.

Because of privacy laws specific to crimes involving minors, and Angie's concerns for the students' well-being, everybody involved with Tom's case had agreed not to reveal any information to the public. Nobody knew the identities, ages, or nature of the images Tom had been accused of distributing. Jill was unaware that her father allegedly possessed lewd and lascivious pictures of her classmates, her best friend's images among them. Or that he would be accused of masterminding a distribution ring that deployed online recruiting to scout victims to procure new product.

Jill's already shaky world seemed shattered beyond repair. First her mother, and now this. Tom didn't want to further test her ability to cope.

"It's not fair, kiddo," he kept saying to her. "It's just not fair to you."

They sat together at the kitchen table, but neither spoke for quite some time. On a usual school-day morning Jill would have her backpack ready for the day. But today she had her army green duffel bag at her side. And the bag was stuffed full of her clothes.

"Don't give up on me, Jill," Tom said. "Did you look at any of the articles I gave you?"

"I read them."

"And?"

"And what do you want me to say?"

"I want you to say that you'll give me some time," Tom said. "You'll give me a chance to clear my name."

Jill looked past him, out the kitchen window and into a backyard that was green and lush and peaceful.

With Marvin's help, Tom had found dozens of cases of computers being used to falsify evidence of statutory rape. Men wrongly accused on the Internet of having a sexual relationship with a minor. Even the sensationalized TV show *A Predator Among Us* was found guilty of entrapment. Apparently, one overly zealous producer had goaded a man with whom he'd been quarreling into meeting a girl presumed to be twenty-one years old. But when the guy showed up, the producer had changed the transcript of his "chat" and lowered the age to thirteen. The poor guy was arrested but later acquitted. The producer lost his job. Not surprisingly, the other guy's company found cause to fire him as well.

Marvin found even more instances of pornographic images that were maliciously transferred to an otherwise clean computer. The motive for planting evidence was often revenge—a disgruntled employee or jealous lover. It happened frequently enough to give rise to a cottage industry of attorneys who specialized in proving that exact defense. Marvin didn't count himself among those self-proclaimed experts, but Tom remained confident that his attorney was better.

Marvin had printed out more than a hundred pages from the different cases that had similarities to his own. Tom had put them in a folder, which he gave to Jill.

"Read through this," he had said. "I just want you to see that it's possible that I'm being framed."

Tom was glad to know Jill had read them. At least she was willing to sit with him at the kitchen table. On the day of his release, that hadn't even been a possibility.

"I know you want me to believe you," Jill said. "But what am I supposed to do in the meantime? Stay here? I don't think I can do that."

"No, honey. I'm not asking you to stay here. I understand that this is hard for you."

His worry about Kip Lange was now barely a pulse. There had been no sightings. No outside perimeter alarms had been set off. No blackmail attempts. Nothing from Lange at all. In some ways, Tom wished that it was Lange behind this nightmare. At least then he'd know why somebody was out to destroy him.

"Did you do this? Did you do what they're saying?"

"Of course not, honey. But I am going to find out who did."

"I don't know what to believe about you anymore. I'm going to talk to Lindsey. I'm going to find out for myself." Jill's attitude seemed to change. For a moment, she was no longer distant. Tom saw a fresh surge of anger, and an aura of newfound determination.

"This will work itself out. I promise."

"So we're all clear, right?" Jill said. "You know what I'm doing."

"You'll be staying at the Kalinowskis'."

"Flo and Irena have cleaned up the guest bedroom for me."

Jill might have been placed into the foster care system if it weren't for the social worker's intervention. She had petitioned the state to let Jill legally reside with the Kalinowski family.

"I have the number. But the same rules apply. You don't go anywhere alone. You tell an adult where you're going, and check in when you get there. We talk at least once a day. Just briefly, if that's all you can manage. Just to let me know that you're all right."

"Okay, I guess," Jill said.

"Do you have everything you need?"

"If not, I can come back and get it."

"You can come back anytime," Tom said. "This is your home."

"I just need to do this for now, okay?" Jill stood up from the table and disappeared through the doorway. She came back, holding Teddy.

Tom saw the raggedy bear tucked under her arm and his whole face brightened. "Hey, I didn't know you still had him," he said.

Teddy was missing one eye. His gray fur was nappy in places, missing in others. Jill was only four when Tom had brought home the bear she'd been eyeing at the toy store. It took only one night of bonding for her to need Teddy to fall asleep every night thereafter.

"Whatever," Jill said, stuffing Teddy into her duffel bag. She could zip it only part way because the bag was already crammed full. Teddy's arm was sticking out the top as if the bear were crying out for help. Tom heard three quick beeps from a car that had pulled up and parked out front.

"That's my ride," Jill said. She put her backpack on, then slung her duffel bag over her shoulder.

"Once a night. A quick call. Agreed?"

Jill kept her back to Tom. No embrace. No kiss good-bye. "Okay," she said reluctantly.

Tom waved to Vern from the door. Vern got out of his Subaru sedan just as Jill was getting in. Tom could see his daughter through the windshield, talking to Vern's kids and already more animated.

Vern hurried over to Tom. The two men shook hands.

"Hey, Tom. How you holding up?"

"As well as can be expected," Tom said.

Vern nodded. "I just wanted you to know that I've got your back here, buddy," Vern said. "You're going to get through this."

"Thanks, Vern. That means a lot to me. Promise you'll be good to my girl."

"You know I will. Heck, Sylvia's got a week's worth of gourmet meals planned. Trust me, she'll be well looked after. And she'll be coming home soon, too. This is all a setup. I know it is."

"I appreciate the faith, Vern. I really do."

The men shook again. Vern returned to his car, and Tom watched him drive away. He waved to Jill, but she didn't wave back.

With a heavy sigh, he turned and walked back up the stairs to the top floor of the split-level home. He glanced to his right and saw the whiteboard perched up against the rolltop desk in the living room, where he'd last left it. He looked at the whiteboard and noticed something about it was different. Hadn't he erased a corner of the square representing their trust obstacle? *Of course I did,* he thought to himself. He had wanted to illustrate some initial progress made in getting past their mutual distrust. But the square didn't look the way he had left it. No, the partially erased square was once again complete. He didn't know when she'd done it, but she had.

Jill had drawn that missing corner back in.

CHAPTER 33

It wasn't easy for Jill to send Lindsey a text message. She contemplated not doing it at all. Jill worried about what she'd say if they got together, and didn't know how she'd feel or react. But the uncertainty was killing her. It made it impossible to think about anything else.

Once, when she was seven, her father had taught her ways to spot a lie. The lesson followed a confrontation over five dollars missing from her father's wallet. He had told Jill not to lie to him, because he could always tell when she did. And that was when he showed her how—and pointed out that she flared her nostrils, never made eye contact, and rubbed her hands together. Convinced that she couldn't get away with it, Jill returned the five dollars she'd taken. In exchange for telling the truth, her father had bought her the bracelet she intended to buy with the money.

Jill remembered how her father's techniques seemed to work on Lindsey, because she'd witnessed Lindsey lie to her mother on more than one occasion. And whenever she lied, Lindsey would flick her hair back right after she did. But was it every time? Jill wasn't quite sure. If they met in person, Jill believed that her gut would know.

Jill gazed at her phone and read through past text messages they'd sent each other. Each message she read made her feel worse, not better. They reminded her of a friendship that might be ruined forever.

After several minutes of internal debate, Jill decided that it had to be done. She sent Lindsey a message, which read simply: we need to talk! Lindsey responded almost immediately. Where are U??? she wrote back. A quick exchange followed. Jill agreed to meet Lindsey in front of the Kalinowskis' house in twenty minutes.

Jill was waiting outside when Lindsey drove up. Lindsey had only her learner's permit, so her mother was sitting in the car with her. But her mother didn't get out when Lindsey did.

Lindsey took several quick, purposeful steps over to Jill. For a moment, the two friends stood face-to-face, silently staring at each other. Jill's hands found the pockets of her hooded sweatshirt.

"Hi," Lindsey said.

"Hi," said Jill.

"So," said Lindsey.

"So," answered Jill.

"Well, this sucks," Lindsey said, with a nervous laugh.

"Yeah, I'll say."

"I didn't do it," Lindsey said. "I never would."

Jill studied her friend closely. She watched for that telling hair flick. But Lindsey kept her hands to her sides. Even without that tell, Jill remained unconvinced. This wasn't just about Lindsey getting it on with some teacher. This was her *dad*. The thought of it was enough to churn her stomach.

"Okay," was all Jill managed to say. Her voice came out soft as the breeze. But Jill couldn't look Lindsey in the eyes anymore. Everything felt wrong to her. Worse than wrong, it felt so terribly sad. Jill felt the pang of a hollow pit form in her stomach. It wasn't as bad a feeling as the days and weeks following her mother's death, but it was enough to remind Jill of that loss.

"What can I do to convince you?" Lindsey asked in a voice that pleaded for understanding.

Jill turned her gaze back to Lindsey. Her vision was blurred by gathering tears, which she wiped away with the back of her hand. "I thought if I saw you, I'd know," Jill said. "I thought you could tell me that you didn't do it and I'd believe you."

"And do you?" Lindsey asked. "Do you believe me?" Lindsey's voice came out sounding shaky like Jill's.

"Yes!" Jill wanted to say. "Yes, I believe you!" But Jill only thought those words; she didn't voice them. Instead, Jill stared at her friend and hoped to be convinced.

"Do you believe me?" Lindsey asked again.

This time, however, Lindsey's right hand gently brushed her long hair back behind her ears.

Jill's eyes went wide, and she quickly turned her head.

"I'm sorry, Lin," Jill said as she studied the ground. "I don't know what to believe anymore."

"What are you saying?"

Jill looked up and said, "I don't think we should talk for a while."

"Why?" Lindsey appeared to be on the verge of tears.

Jill thought about Lindsey's right hand brushing back her hair. Was that her tell? Did Lindsey just announce her lie?

"I don't know what to think," Jill eventually said. "I don't know how I feel. And until that changes, I'm not sure we can still be friends."

CHAPTER 34

Tom sat in his car, alone, keeping watch over room number 32. He'd been waiting in the Motel 6 parking lot for a little over an hour. He'd wait all night if needed. The motel was just off the highway in Framingham, Massachusetts. Tom had had no trouble finding out where his target resided. His contacts from the navy hadn't vanished when he left the service.

Tom knew better than to bring a gun. His only weapon, a penknife, fit inside the palm of his hand and didn't violate any bail conditions. It would work just fine on an untrained adversary.

At seven o'clock he saw his target's car pull into the lot. None of the other motel guests, he presumed, drove a new black Infiniti M. Tom's target passed in front of his Taurus. The man's gaze was fixed, directed on the concrete path that ran along the front of the motel rooms. He took quick and purposeful steps.

Tom opened his car door. The man didn't even look in his direction.

The man swiped his access card through the access card slot in the door's locking mechanism. Tom timed his approach perfectly and stood directly behind his target when the lock light turned green. Tom's target pulled down the door handle to enter the room. The door opened up just a crack.

Tom turned and shoved the man hard from behind. The man grunted loudly, then stumbled into the dark room, falling to the floor as he did. Tom stepped into the room. He closed the door behind him and locked it with the dead bolt and chain. Then Tom turned on the light.

His target, a gaunt man with sunken eyes marred by dark rings and a thick beard that dipped below his chin, cowered on the floor next to the queen-size bed. The target blinked rapidly to adjust his eyesight to the sudden change in light.

Child pornographer or not, Tom hated to see a grown man look so afraid.

"Who . . . who are you . . . ? What are you doing here? What do you want?"

"James Mann?" Tom asked.

"Yes . . ."

"If you try to run, I'll hurt you," Tom said. "If you make any noise, I'll hurt you worse. Understood?"

James Mann just nodded.

"Take a seat," Tom said, pointing to the bed.

"What do you want?" Mann asked, sitting as instructed.

"I want to know why the FBI thinks I sold you pictures of naked teenage girls."

"What?"

"I've been arrested for distribution of child pornography in New Hampshire," Tom said. "My name is Tom Hawkins. You can look it up if you want. The FBI came to see me."

"Who? Who at the FBI?"

"Special Agent Loraine Miles," Tom said. "She asked me about you. Do you know me?"

"No," Mann said.

"Do you know her?"

"Yes," Mann said. "She was one of the people who arrested me."

"Okay. All right. That's good. I think we're getting somewhere now," Tom said. "Have you ever seen me before?"

"No. No, never. Look . . . look, I'm being framed, too. Somebody set me up. I'm not a child pornographer. I'm a family man."

Tom looked around the room. "Could use a woman's touch, if you ask me."

"I've lost my wife," Mann said. "I haven't seen my kids since my arrest. I've been fired from my job. I've been completely destroyed. Even my friends and family don't want me living with them. That's how I ended up here. I swear it's all true."

"Talk," Tom said. "What happened to you? I want to know everything."

"I live in Medfield, Massachusetts," Mann said. A pained expression overtook his face. "I mean, I did, before I got arrested."

"Go on."

"A few weeks ago, I came home really excited. I had big news to share. I could finally tell my family about my promotion. You see . . . I used to work for PrimaMed."

"The pharmaceutical company?" Tom knew all of this already. His information source didn't miss.

"Yeah, that's the one. Paul Rutledge, PrimaMed's president, was retiring, and I'd been tapped by the CEO to become—"

Tom interrupted before Mann could finish. "The new president and chief operating officer," he said.

"You know?"

"I know a lot of things about you."

"Such as?"

"Such as you've only ever worked for PrimaMed. You started your career in sales, until your first big promotion into major accounts twenty years ago," Tom said. "You were asked to lead a profitable business unit after only two years as a top performer. You held your current position as vice president of sales longer than any of your predecessors. You were a corporate superstar. Life had been good. Until PrimaMed's rock steady stock tanked. Three consecutive quarters of missed Wall Street estimates. Tough luck. I'm guessing you didn't receive a bonus like last year's."

"How . . . how did you?"

"What happened with your promotion?" Tom asked. "I obviously don't know everything."

"Four months ago I was called into a closed door meeting with the CEO," Mann said. "I found out the FDA was close to approving our new drug application for diabetes. Internal projections predicted hundreds of millions in new revenue."

"Interesting. Keep going," Tom said.

"We came up with a public relations plan to announce my appointment to president and COO on the same day we announced the FDA's approval. That way Wall Street wouldn't think Paul was leaving because of the company's health."

"Sounds like a good plan. What happened?"

"The night before the press release was scheduled to drop, I got a call from our CFO, Sue Rossnick. She was in a panic. Said that message boards all over the Web were lighting up. Word was spreading that something big was going down. Somebody leaked news about the NDA. Our stock was moving in after-hours trading."

"Was that a problem?"

"Not really," Mann said. "It was close enough to the drop. But one of the guys contributing to the chatter on-line ran an influential message board. A lot of the after-hours traders follow it. He posted something about me. He wrote that he had a reliable source in the FBI who told him that I was going to be arrested for distribution of child pornography."

"Really?"

"Really."

"I guess you were arrested," Tom said.

"You'd guess right."

"And what did they find on your computers?"

"A lot of child pornography."

"Including the stuff I allegedly sold to you?"

"I wouldn't know."

"Who knew about the NDA?" asked Tom.

"A handful of people in the company," Mann said. "The CEO, of course. Paul. Folks at the FDA. Some of our clinical trial vendors. It was endgame. Like I said, we had all the press releases ready to go. Word was getting around."

"Why would somebody want to make it look like you were a child pornographer?"

"I don't know," Mann said, sitting straighter on the bed, perhaps trying to convey to Tom that he still had some dignity remaining. "Listen, you've got to believe me. I'm in this like you are. I haven't done anything wrong. I'm being framed. Just like you."

He's not lying to me, Tom assessed.

"How far would you be willing to go to clear your name?" Tom asked.

"As far as I had to go."

Tom nodded. "Okay, here's what's going to happen," Tom said. "We've got to find who's the real supplier of these pictures I had. You're apparently a client of this supplier. You're going to work backward until you find the real distributor."

"But I told you I didn't download any child pornography. I'm innocent. Just like you."

"I don't know if that's true," Tom said. "As far as I'm concerned, you do know how to find the dealers. If you don't, you're going to learn so I don't have to."

"That doesn't seem fair to make me take all the risk," Mann said.

"Life isn't fair, James. But I am giving you a chance. I supply the names of the girls. You find the distributor. If you succeed, we both win. I'd say it's a pretty fair trade."

"What if I refuse?"

"You'll probably end up a convicted child pornographer, and I'll probably clear my name."

Mann thought, then nodded.

CHAPTER 35

As Tom pulled into the parking lot of the Plenty Market, he noticed one peculiar thing. The parking lot was empty. The supermarket store lights were off as well. Tom checked his watch. It was quarter past nine at night, and according to the sign taped to the inside window, the market had closed over an hour ago.

Where was Boyd? Tom wanted to know.

Tom heard a loud whistle. The supermarket's back door opened, expelling a thin shaft of yellow light that illuminated a narrow column of dark asphalt. A silhouetted figure emerged from the doorway. It was Roland. He held open the back door and motioned for Tom to come inside.

Tom didn't realize there was additional parking by the loading zone, and now observed two cars taking up four available spaces. One of the cars, the Mercedes, he knew belonged to Roland. Tom entered a dimly lit stockroom, noticing Roland had on a neatly pressed dark suit. The stockroom was a cavernous, dry space with stacks of corrugated boxes sitting atop wooden pallets. A small office fronted by a large plate-glass window stood to Tom's right. Tom saw a heavyset man seated at a desk inside that office.

The other car had to be his.

For a moment Tom thought it could have been Lange's.

"Shopping after hours?" Tom asked Roland.

Roland didn't respond. Instead, his eyes did the talking, and they didn't appear pleased. Roland closed the door. Tom thought he heard it lock.

Roland walked past Tom and went to the back of the stockroom. Tom took a quick look behind him as he followed. The guy in the office stayed put.

Roland stopped, then turned to face Tom. He kept his arms at his sides.

"Where's Lange?" Tom asked. "Is he here?"

"I didn't find Lange," Roland said. "I lied."

"Why would you do that?"

"Because I needed to get you down here, and I knew if I told you I'd found Lange, you'd come. I don't like to leave things to chance."

"What are we doing here, Roland?" asked Tom. "I'm not a big fan of being lied to."

"We need to talk."

"About?"

"Adriana. Why'd she post your bail?"

"I don't know," Tom said. "I'm guessing she felt sorry for me. She hasn't returned any of my calls. Why don't we call her now and get this straightened out?"

"I told her not to call you back," Roland said. "She already gave me her story."

"And?"

"And she said she felt sorry for you."

"Well, there you have it."

"I don't believe her."

"Oh."

"This is really tough for me," Roland said. "I consider you a friend. One of my best. So I'm going to keep this as simple and straightforward as possible. Are you sleeping with my wife?"

Tom glanced behind him. The big man was still safely tucked inside his office. Tom didn't know where this was headed, but every instinct told him it wouldn't be someplace he wanted to go. Roland kept his expression about as revealing as the cardboard boxes behind him.

"Roland, this is crazy. You're dead wrong if you think I'm sleeping with your wife. Let's stop this right now, before it escalates."

Roland stayed calm, calmer even than the night he confronted Bob at the club with the same accusation.

"I'm going to ask you again," Roland said. "Are you sleeping with my wife?"

"No. I'm not."

Tom kept his arms at his sides. Roland's folded across his chest. Neither man spoke. The only sound Tom heard was a constant humming from the large walk-in cooler to his right.

"I don't think I believe you," Roland eventually said. "Last chance to convince me. Why did my wife put a hundred-thousand-dollar bet on you?"

"Roland, I'm just as curious as you are."

Roland's face slipped into a snarl. "Are you fucking my wife?" he shouted.

"If I were, don't you think that'd be a stupid way to hide an affair?"

At that, Roland unhinged his folded his arms and let out a deep sigh. He studied Tom a long while. "Didn't the SEALs train you in how to lie without being detected?"

"They trained me to do a lot of things," Tom said.

"I bet."

"I think now would be a good time for both of us to

cool off," Tom said. "Let's have a sit-down. Me, you, and Adriana. We'll talk tomorrow, with clearer heads."

Tom moved to leave, but Roland grabbed him by the arm.

Tom spun around and locked eyes with Roland. "You don't want to fight me," he said. He kept his voice calm. "Bad odds. A lot worse than your wife's bet on me."

"I told you, I don't fight."

"Have a good night, Roland. We'll talk." Tom took two steps toward the rear door.

From behind, Tom heard Roland whistle loudly.

Damn, how he wished he could do that whistle.

The man seated inside the office emerged. Heavy jowled, with an oil slick of dark hair, he waddled over to Tom and blocked the way out. He wore a short-sleeved yellow shirt and a poorly knotted red knit tie that arched over his considerable belly. His name tag, pinned to his shirt, identified him as both Gill Sullivan and the general manager of the Plenty Market.

Tom eyed Sullivan with suspicion. "I'm guessing he's not here to offer me a special on ribs," Tom said, turning around to look at Roland.

Sullivan stood grinning, his arms folded and resting upon his massive midsection.

"Do you want to spend all your pretrial time locked up?" Roland asked.

"That's not your call to make, Roland. Thanks to Adriana—who I'm not sleeping with, by the way—I'm a free man until my trial."

"Not if you violate the conditions of your bail."

"Well, I'm not going to do that."

"Here's my proposition to you, Tom. Admit to me that you're having an affair with Adriana, or spend the night in the walk-in refrigerator here." Roland pointed to the large refrigerator, coated in steel on all surfaces, big enough to park a VW Bug.

"What?" Tom squinted his eyes, unsure that he'd heard the man correctly.

"Admit it to me, right here, right now, or spend the night in the cooler," Roland repeated.

"I'm not even going to dignify that with a response," Tom said.

"Admit it."

"I'd be lying. That's not fair to your wife."

"There's no other reason she'd have bailed you out!"

"She likes me. We bonded over what happened to Stephen and my struggles with Jill."

"Bullshit! I've seen the way she looks at you. She can't keep her hands off you."

"It's the truth."

"If you insist on lying to me, then you've got to spend the night in deep freeze," Roland said.

"You can't make me do that."

"Yes. I can." Roland turned to Sullivan and nodded.

Sullivan stepped around Tom, cocked his arm back, and thrust it forward with surprising speed. The general manager hit Roland in the face with a closed fist, hard enough to make a popping sound.

Roland staggered backward, then tumbled over a box of paper goods stacked knee high on a pallet behind him. When Roland got back on his feet, Tom saw a giant welt, red and rising, on his right cheek. Roland was breathing hard. He touched his hand gently to the injury.

"What the hell are you doing?" Tom cried out.

"What am I doing?" Roland said with disgust. "What are *you* doing? is the better question. Gilly, did you just see Mr. Hawkins here assault me?"

"That's what I just saw," Sullivan said.

"And you'd be willing to make that statement to the police?"

"Of course I would, Mr. Boyd. That man just attacked you."

"What? What are you two trying to do?"

"Assault and battery are serious charges, Tom. I don't think the judge is going to put up a bail number that Adriana, or anybody else, for that matter, could afford to post. Now, get in the refrigerator, Tom."

"I'm not sleeping with your wife."

"Get inside. Sleep on it. Maybe when you come out, you'll be ready to confess."

Tom tensed. Moving faster than Roland or Sullivan could react, he lunged forward and seized his former teammate by his suit jacket lapels.

Roland just grinned. "Touch me and I won't give you the option of not going to jail."

Tom let go of Roland's suit jacket. He flashed on the hundred different ways he could snap the man's neck. Sullivan maneuvered himself behind Tom and opened the door to the walk-in refrigerator.

Tom closed his eyes and balled his fists. He could level these men with two punches. But he knew what outcome that would bring.

Prison. Jill would give up on him. He'd never convince a jury that he'd been framed.

One thing Tom had learned from his time in the navy was that everything with a way in also had a way out. Ducking to pass underneath the low-framed metal doorway, Tom stepped inside the chilling space. The door closed with a quiet click. And Tom plunged into total darkness.

CHAPTER 36

Tom stood still. Soon his eyes began to adjust, until he could make out various shapes within. Shelving units, boxes stacked on the floor. His skin began to chill.

The best way to survive in an extreme cold situation was to have the will to live. Despite the efforts of his BUD/S instructors, will wasn't something that could be taught. When it came to will, Tom was well aware that some had it more than others. Even the best-equipped individual thrust into a do-or-die situation could perish if he lacked will. Fortunately, Tom had that will in spades.

Most of the blood circulation ran just under the surface of the head. That would be the first place he'd need to protect. Tom slipped off his Windbreaker and forged a makeshift hat from the pliable fabric. He'd scavenge for other warming options in a moment. But first, he wanted to listen.

Through the insulated wall panel Tom could hear Roland and Sullivan talking but could not make out what they were saying.

Tom had taken a visual measurement of the refrigerator door frame just before he stepped inside, and guessed the walls to be about four inches thick. With a couple of well-placed kicks, he could punch holes in the polyurethane insulation. But the only way he knew to get through the stainless steel outer wall required an angle grinder with a steel cutting disc. He doubted he'd find one of those nestled within the Butterball turkeys.

Roland and Sullivan spoke indistinctly for five minutes at most. Then all went silent, save for the constant humming of cooling fans.

Tom had no intention of spending the night locked up, but he didn't feel like confronting Roland again, either. When Tom felt certain that Roland had left, he searched the walls with his fingertips for an inside light switch. He stumbled upon it, gave the switch a flick, but nothing happened.

Assholes probably took the bulb.

He shuffled back over to the door. His body did what it could to combat the cold. Hairs on his arms and neck stood erect on goose-bumped flesh, trapping in air, which formed a layer of protective insulation. Helpful, but by no means all that warming. What would really help, Tom thought, would be to find the inside release handle. He figured there had to be some type of mandatory safety latch to keep employees from accidentally locking themselves inside.

What he found was a rough steel mounting, secured to the inside wall by three five-millimeter screws. What he didn't find was the steel rod and flange he could push to trigger the latch and open the door.

A pulse of anger swept over him and gave a brief, but pleasant, rush of warmth. He wondered if Roland had used this cooler as a torture chamber before. *It would explain the missing safety release,* Tom thought. It made sense they pulled this stunt after hours so that no Plenty

Market employees would discover him slowly freezing to death inside their refrigerator. A bunch of yelling and banging would only cost him precious degrees of body heat. Any moves he made to escape would have to be well thought through.

Tom closed his eyes, despite the darkness within, and allowed his body to shiver. Shivering, he knew, would cause the body to produce heat. He was aware it could also produce fatigue, which in turn would lower his body temperature. Still, the air movement from shivering warmed him some and allowed him precious time to think clearly.

Again moving toward the shut door, Tom felt around the sabotaged inside release handle. The hole where the steel rod should have been was smaller than the tip of his pinkie finger.

Tom smiled.

He worked his way over to the shelving unit closest to him and felt three levels of wire shelving fastened to a freestanding structure. Tom removed all food items, making sure he kept the path to the door clear. He removed the top two levels of shelving, leaving the bottom shelf in place. He gripped the sides of the shelf unit and tested its sturdiness.

Good.

Settling into position, he set his foot down atop the bottom shelf. He had enough maneuverability with the other shelves removed to generate significant force with a downward thrust of his leg. They had measured how much force his kick generated in the navy, and it exceeded a thousand pounds of pressure, more than the equal of a good martial artist.

Tom hoisted his foot knee high and brought it down with as much power as he could generate. His body shook from the impact, but he felt the steel rods of the shelf begin to loosen. Again and again he slammed his foot into the shelf, until at last he heard a pleasing snap. Tom removed the broken shelf from the structure holding it in place and felt around the edges for where a rod had separated from the frame. Then he bent that rod back even farther with his hands. He had no doubt the rod he bent would fit inside the hole, but would it be long enough to engage the latch?

His shivering hands made it difficult to manipulate the unwieldy shelf with its broken wire rod into the tiny hole at the center of the release handle mount. Before long, though, he had the rod inserted and the trigger mechanism engaged.

Tom emerged from the darkness of the cooler, wearing his Windbreaker on his head. He blinked his eyes to adjust them to the light.

"Thirteen minutes," Roland said. "Not bad, Tom. Not bad at all."

Tom turned.

Roland Boyd kept his distance from Tom and held a stopwatch in his hand. Even from twenty paces, Tom could see the welt on Roland's face—it was red but had subsided some already. Cold air from the open cooler door continued to chill Tom's skin. Sullivan was there, too, diagonal to Tom.

Smart move.

With the three of them forming a ragged triangle, Tom could go after either Sullivan or Roland, but definitely not both. Sullivan now had a suit jacket on, and Roland still wore his. Tom had to believe both men were armed, though neither brandished any weapon.

Tom shivered as he spoke. "What the hell game are you playing, Roland?"

"Sorry, Tom," Roland replied. "But you're not as easy to frighten as Bob."

"You could have just asked me to stay away from your wife."

"Not good enough. I needed to be sure."

Sullivan shifted his weight, right to left. Tom kept his eyes fixed on Roland, but he was ready to evade Sullivan if the need should arise.

"Hope you're satisfied," Tom said.

Tom battled back the urge to take down Roland. Sullivan aside, having his bail revoked proved to be a powerful deterrent.

"Look, Tom," Roland said. "This whole thing is really unfortunate. I considered you a friend. And I still do."

"Can't say the feeling is mutual," Tom replied.

"What choice did I have? You're a friggin' Navy SEAL. Guys like you don't frighten that easy."

"Well, I'm not scared now."

"But at least you know how far I'm willing to go," Roland said. "You know if I want to put you back in jail, I can do just that. I hope we're clear about this."

"Crystal."

"Keep away from my wife, Tom."

"Like I said, you could have just asked."

Roland's smile looked more like a grimace. "Maybe when the dust settles, you and I can go out for drinks, have a little laugh about this. Okay?"

"That's not going to happen," Tom said.

"Never say never," Roland replied. "Look, I regret it had to come to this, Tom. But a man's got to protect his castle."

Roland opened the stockroom's rear door, then retreated to his prior position. Sullivan didn't move. Tom walked between the two men with his gaze fixed forward, but stopped just short of the open door. Tom looked first at Sullivan, then at Roland.

He walked outside and stood between the yellow painted lines of the loading zone. He took a few steps forward, then stopped. He kept his back to the open door, arms hanging loosely by his sides. He waited there, with his eyes fixed on a shapeless patch of unlit woods before him. He kept perfectly still. Didn't flinch. Not even when Roland's shadow appeared within the narrow shaft of light cast outward from the open door behind him, not even when Roland closed that door with a slam.

Tom had delivered a message of his own: he was not afraid.

CHAPTER 37

"**Y**ou've got to tell us where she is."

Irena Kalinowski sat at her kitchen table, looking sheepish and defeated. Vern Kalinowski sat across from his daughter, glaring. Tom tried to keep his composure but found it challenging under these circumstances. Jill, who should have been upstairs in the Kalinowskis' guest bedroom, was gone.

Earlier, Tom had called Vern from the Plenty Market parking lot. Vern's home phone rang several times before his former assistant coach finally answered it. Tom had told Vern he needed to speak with Jill, and that it was urgent. While Vern went to get her, Tom sat in his car and watched Roland and Sullivan drive away.

He commended his own restraint.

The purpose of Tom's phone call to Jill was simple—he needed to tell her that Mitchell Boyd, effective immediately, was officially off-limits.

Tom's stomach sank when Vern picked up the phone again. "She's not there," he said. "She must have snuck out the window, or something."

Tom sent Jill a text message.

She replied: Green.

The tightness in Tom's chest released some. Where are you? he texted her.

In bed, she sent back.

You're lying.

No response.

He texted her again: Where are you?

Still no response.

Now it was up to Irena, Vern's oldest by twelve minutes, to tell Tom what he needed to know.

"Honey, this is a very serious situation," Vern said to Irena. "You'll be in big, big trouble if you lie to me. Where did Jill go?"

Irena let out a loud sigh. Her gaze sank to the table. Tom could see her trembling. "She went to this place called the Spot," Irena said in a quiet voice.

Tom and Vern looked at each other.

"When?" Vern said.

"About an hour ago."

"Who'd she go with?" asked Tom.

Irena paused. She looked at her dad, then to Tom.

"Mitchell Boyd," Irena said in an even softer voice. "She's there with Mitchell Boyd."

Tom heard the music long before he saw any of the kids. It was an unseasonably warm September night, which made the Spot the ideal place for a weekend hangout. The moon stood high and bright in the cloudless sky. Almost full, Tom observed, and from its position, he could tell it was closing in on midnight.

Tom knew this place well, almost by memory. Each step brought him deeper into his past. The trail markers—yellow triangles painted on trees—were the same as he remembered from his high school days. But Tom didn't need any markings to guide him back to the Spot. His soul was connected to this place like the deep, flowing roots of the forest trees surrounding him.

The Spot was nothing more than a large clearing of land tucked inside Willards Woods. Willards Woods occupied hundreds of acres of undeveloped land in Shilo, vigorously protected by conservationists and taxpayer dollars. The Spot had been a favored teen hangout long before Tom's high school years, and from his work as both a coach and guidance counselor, he knew it remained in vogue to this day. Kids from Shilo and neighboring towns came to the Spot to do what Tom and Roland had done back in their heyday.

Listen to tunes.

Drink beers.

Swim in the cold quarry water.

Tom emerged from the overgrown trail and into the clearing. When he did, the chatter of teens abruptly stopped, like a hunting tiger silencing the noises of a teaming jungle. A fire burning bright in the stone fire pit cast a flickering yellow light across Tom's face.

Teenagers, long and lanky, some with short hair, some not, some fully dressed, some soaking wet, some smoking cigarettes, some smoking something else, turned in the direction of Tom's bright shining flashlight.

Somebody shut off the music.

Tom heard a loud splash.

Somebody yelled, "Cops!"

Tom heard another loud splash.

The frantic scramble to escape capture was in full effect. The teens packed up their illegal pleasures in backpacks and cardboard boxes and made for the woods with great haste. Tom heard branches breaking, leaves crunching. There were panicky voices shouting from within the darkness: "This way!" and "Over here!"

A flashlight cut through the dark and shone directly on Tom's face. Somebody yelled, "It's Coach Hawkins! It's not the cops. It's not the cops!"

Soon, more flashlights were shining in Tom's eyes, blinding him. He continued to hear the sounds of kids scattering, but no longer could he see them. Movement to Tom's right pulled his head in that direction. He stepped out of the beams of light and into the path of two boys trying to make their escape. Tom grabbed hold of one boy's jacket, pulling him to an abrupt stop.

The other kid kept on running.

It was every man for himself, same now as it was back in his day.

Tom recognized the boy—a senior at Shilo High School named Matthew. Matthew was holding a can of beer in his hand.

"Where's Jill?" Tom asked.

Matthew said nothing, probably too scared to speak.

"Where's my daughter?" Tom asked again. Tom turned his flashlight to shine it on his own face. He wanted Matthew to see the seriousness of his expression.

"She was hanging out at the ledge," Matthew said, with each word wavering.

"Are you driving?"

"No."

"Good," Tom said, ripping the beer can from Matthew's hand before crushing it.

Tom walked toward the ledge. He heard several more loud splashes. In the moonlight, he saw a silhouetted figure standing near to the quarry's edge, facing him. As he approached, Tom knew it was his daughter.

"What are you doing?" Jill shouted.

Tom shone his flashlight on Jill's face, fixed in a hateful sneer. She was wearing jeans and a sweatshirt. She didn't look wet.

She hadn't been swimming.

He got close enough to smell her breath. He didn't believe she'd been drinking, either.

Tom shone his flashlight into the impenetrably dark water below. The kids down there were easy to spot. Their white skin glowed brighter than the moon. They were treading water, hoping to avoid detection.

"Get out of the water and get home!" Tom shouted. He followed their movement with his flashlight beam, knowing they were swimming for the water's only exit. It was safest to jump from the place where they did—the water here was the deepest, no jutting or shallow rocks, either. Sunken railroad ties represented the only real danger here. A good leap outward ensured any jumper that they'd safely clear the lethal obstacle below. But the twenty-five-foot quarry wall was too sheer to climb back up. With luck, these kids were smart enough to keep towels and dry clothes where they'd be getting out. Tom doubted any of them would return to the Spot to dry off.

"You are totally embarrassing me," Jill said. "Please go away. Now!"

"You need to come with me," Tom said, keeping his voice calm, but determined. "Now." Tom put his hand on Jill's shoulder, but his daughter shrugged it off with a quick and violent jerk.

"Get your hands off me," Jill snapped at him. "Leave me alone."

"That's not an option."

"You can't make me come with you."

"I'm still your father."

"Yeah, well, I don't live with you anymore. Remember?"

"Where is Mitchell?" asked Tom.

Jill sighed in disgust. "I don't know," she said. "He probably took off when you scared everybody away."

"Listen, from now on Mitchell Boyd is off-limits to you. His father's dangerous, and I don't want you anywhere near that family."

"You can't make that decision for me," Jill said, shaking her head. "You can't."

"You have to trust me on this, Jill. It's not safe for you to be with him."

"Why should I trust you?" Jill said in a voice steeped with exasperation. "I don't even know you. For all I know, you did have something to do with what happened to Mom. And you know what else? I think you are sleeping with Lindsey. I can't trust you and won't. Ever!"

Tom's thoughts flashed on the whiteboard still in the Oak Street house living room—more specifically on the square around the word *trust,* which Jill had redrawn.

It was time, he decided. It was time.

The Spot was now completely deserted. A symphony of nighttime forest creatures buzzed in a cacophony of sound. Off in the distance, Tom could still hear the sound of kids swimming to get away. Sparks crackled and burst skyward from the fire.

"You're right, Jill," Tom said, nodding his head while biting on his lower lip. "I haven't given you enough reason to trust me. But if you come with me right now, I'll tell you why your mother hated me so much, why she tried to come between us."

That got her attention. Jill looked as though she might burst into tears.

"What are you talking about?" she asked.

"I need you to trust me," Tom said, resting his hand on his daughter's shoulder. This time, she didn't shrug it away. "For your safety, you've got to believe me when I tell you to keep away from Mitchell Boyd. I have good reason."

"What are you talking about?" she asked.

"I've been keeping a secret from you, Jill. A secret your mother and I never wanted you to know. It will explain everything. Why Kip Lange was in the woods that night. Why your mother hated me so much. And probably why somebody is out to destroy my reputation."

CHAPTER 38

Tom pulled the faded yellow armchair in front of the couch where Jill was seated. His stomach spun a few nerve-rattled cartwheels. He knew what had to be done, but that didn't make it any easier. To keep Jill safe, she had to learn to trust him.

"What I'm about to tell you is going to shock you. I'm not proud of what I did. But I had my reasons. I'm not expecting you to understand completely. But I need you to listen with an open mind. Deal?"

"Deal," Jill said.

His daughter's eyes were owl-like, wide, and intently probing.

"Even though your mother and I never officially broke up after high school, I didn't see or hear from her for ten years. I was focused on becoming a Navy SEAL, and that's all that mattered to me. Then my unit was sent to Germany to conduct a series of training exercises. It was a few years before September eleventh, and our combat deployments were few and far between. Your mother was living on that base. We reconnected and fell back in love, or so I thought."

"What is that supposed to mean?" Jill asked.

"A shooting took place while I was living on that base. One of the lieutenants, a guy named Stan Greeley, was attacked in his home and shot several times. The military police found Kip Lange inside Greeley's home. Lange had been shot twice in the leg and once in the shoulder and couldn't walk or even crawl away. They arrested him on the spot. But the MPs never recovered his gun."

"I don't understand. What does this have to do with Mom?" Jill asked.

"Be patient. You need to know all this. Lange was deported back to the States, where he was going to face court-martial. Greeley had been gravely injured and was in a drug-induced coma. I had only a few days left before I was scheduled to fly home with my unit, so your mother and I tried to make the most of what little time we had left. On the day I was to leave, your mother showed up at the airport with a crate in the back of a truck she had borrowed. She asked me to bring the crate home for her."

"Why?"

"She had a limit to how much stuff she could bring back, and I didn't. With rank comes privilege. She opened the top of the crate and showed me a couple bottles of a German beer we both liked, and told me to call her when I got home so we could have a toast together. The rest of the crate was really densely packed, but I caught a glimpse of some of the other things inside—dishes and souvenirs and . . ."

Tom pointed to the cuckoo clock mounted on the living room wall.

"Ugh! I hate that clock," Jill said.

"But that wasn't all she had packed in that crate. Security and customs, even for military transport, weren't like they are today. The guys working customs knew me. We joked around together. So when my team was getting the plane ready to fly home, they made only a cursory inspection of what we were bringing home with us. Like I said, with rank comes privilege."

Jill's eyes were unblinking, deeply focused on Tom.

"I had a few weeks of leave, so I drove to Shilo to stay with your grandparents. I remembered the beer bottles your mother had packed in the crate, and our plan to toast together. I got the bottles out and decided to unpack the rest of the crate to see what your mom had me bring home for her.

"That's when I found it. Ten objects, wrapped in black plastic and shaped to look like the insoles of shoes. They were buried underneath several layers of shredded newspaper and packaging peanuts. There was also a gun."

"What was wrapped in plastic?" Jill's expression said she didn't really want to know.

"Heroin," Tom replied. "Seventeen pounds or thereabouts."

"Is that a lot?"

"I'm glad you don't know," Tom said. "I didn't know myself, but I later found out it was ninety percent pure, enough for over half a million doses. It had a street value of about ten million dollars."

Jill's hand went to her mouth. She gasped.

"That's when I called your mom. I was incensed. I couldn't believe what she had done. But she was crying hysterically. She told me she was in very big trouble. That men had threatened to kill her if she didn't get me to smuggle the drugs out of the country and be their mule."

"What's a mule?"

"A drug smuggler," Tom said. "Glad you didn't know that, either."

"Who was threatening her? Kip Lange?"

"She wouldn't tell me. She just begged me to hide the

drugs. I told her I didn't think I could do that. This was a very serious crime that could destroy both our lives. I asked her whose gun she'd packed. She said she didn't know, that the same men gave her the gun when they gave her the heroin. Then she told me something else." Tom paused.

"She told you she was pregnant with me," Jill said. "That's what she said, isn't it?"

"You're a very smart girl," Tom said. "So I made a choice. Until I had more information, until I knew what was really going on, I decided to hide the evidence. I didn't know who gave your mom the gun and the drugs, but I took a lot of precautions to keep any trace evidence intact. I didn't want to destroy any fingerprints or damage the weapon. The gun was army issued, and I already had my suspicions about Lange. I knew that the MPs hadn't recovered his weapon.

"Your mother applied for a medical discharge from the army because she was pregnant. Lange was in a military prison, awaiting court-martial, and I had just committed a felony by hiding the drugs and the gun. At the time, I was thinking about you. My unborn baby girl. I was thinking about you being taken away from us, being raised by another family, never having a chance to be ours. I left the navy and bought this house in Shilo. Your mom got her discharge, and the next time we were together, it was here in this living room."

"What about the men who were after the drugs? Did they ever come?"

"You really are a smart girl," Tom said. "No. They never did, and your mom never gave me a good explanation as to why. But I found out soon enough. There were no men who had threatened her. Your mom confessed that she and Kip Lange were the only two people involved.

They had stolen the drugs from Stan Greeley, who was planning to smuggle them out of the country himself."

"Where did he get the drugs from?" asked Jill.

"We think they probably came from Afghanistan. I think he traded them for military secrets."

"So the gun belonged to Kip Lange?"

"That's right. The weapon that went missing was the one that I hid. Your mom's job was to keep Stan Greeley distracted. Lange knew that Greeley had the drugs hidden under some floorboards."

"How did he know that?" Jill said.

Here Tom paused. "I don't know," Tom said. "And your mom couldn't say. Lange just knew."

"How did Mom distract him?"

"Honey, I don't think you want to know."

"I'm not a child. I want to know."

"She seduced him. Went back with him to his house. Then she drugged him. Only it wasn't enough to knock Greeley out. He heard Lange looking for the drugs. That's when the shooting began."

Jill got a faraway look in her eyes.

"I'm sorry you have to hear all this."

"But why did Mom hate you? You helped her. You kept her out of prison."

"Kip Lange was in prison, and he wasn't going to be getting out anytime soon. Your mother wanted me to retrieve the drugs so we could sell them. We're talking millions of dollars. But I told her no. I told her I was going to destroy them. She started sobbing. She begged me not to do that. We both knew Lange would get out one day. If the drugs were destroyed, we'd have no leverage if he ever came after her—or you. And you were our lives!"

"What did you do?" asked Jill.

"I agreed. For the sake of our family, I agreed. But

even though I wouldn't destroy the drugs, I told your mom that I'd never reveal where they were hidden. And I hid them in a place where they'd never be found."

"So Mom wanted you to sell the drugs and you wouldn't? That's why she hated you?"

"That's why. She kept pressuring me to get the drugs. When our finances were in shambles, she'd say I could fix it. She became single-minded. Lange got his sentence. Twenty-five years to life. He was going to be locked up for a long time. That only made your mom more determined. Eventually, she gave up hope and asked for a divorce. Then she used the only weapon she had left to get what she wanted. She used you to hurt me."

Jill sucked in a breath.

"It's all my fault," she said repeatedly.

"No, honey. None of this is your fault. It was a bad situation to begin with, and we made it worse. But I don't regret it. I can't. Because if I didn't, you wouldn't have had those years with Mom."

"So it was Lange in the woods that night," Jill said.

"I'm pretty sure it was, yeah. He got out early on a technicality. We didn't know."

"You think he was the one who broke into the house?"

Tom nodded. "My guess is he came here looking for the drugs. Your mom saw him and panicked. There was a struggle. She ran. You know what happened next. Until I find Lange, I can't be sure of anything I just told you. But I have to think Kip Lange is somehow connected to the charges against me. I just don't know how, or even why."

Jill was quiet for a long while.

"Do you believe me?"

Jill shrugged. "I don't know what to think right now."

"I understand. I really do," Tom said. "But I didn't make all this up just to keep you from seeing Mitchell

Boyd. I told you the truth because I need you to trust me on this one. Will you do that, at least for now? Things aren't safe here. Roland Boyd is dangerous, and Kip Lange is still out there, somewhere. You need to keep away from the Boyds, and never go anywhere alone. You go to school, and you come home. That's it."

"I'm not ready to move back here, if that's what you're asking."

Tom looked away to hide his disappointment. "I can drive you back to Vern's, if that's what you want. But no more sneaking out. Understood?"

"I don't get it. Why would Kip Lange want to make it look like you're sleeping with Lindsey?"

"I don't know," Tom admitted. "I thought maybe Lange was going to blackmail me, but that didn't happen."

"Because maybe it's true."

"It's not."

Jill kept her interlocked hands between her knees and held her father's gaze. "This is a lot for me to process," she said.

"Now you know why I kept this a secret from you."

"I think I do," Jill said.

"Jill, I'm so very sorry," Tom said.

"For what?"

"Because now it's your secret to keep, too."

CHAPTER 39

Shilo High School's 250-seat auditorium was almost filled to capacity. Rainy peered out at the settling crowd through a part in the heavy auditorium stage curtain. The sound of students' voices was overpowering in the high-ceilinged room. Rainy wondered how the outnumbered teachers would ever quiet these kids down. Waiting with her backstage were the other speakers for the mandatory student assembly: Shilo High School principal Lester Osborne and police sergeant Brendan Murphy. Murphy apparently had learned his lesson and kept his hands appropriately to himself. Angie Didomenico, who had put this assembly in motion, had a schedule conflict and had sent regrets.

Rainy checked her watch. In five minutes, Lester Osborne would step onto the stage to make his introductory remarks. Shortly after, he'd bring out Sergeant Murphy to say a few words before commencing with the afternoon's main event—a cyber safety seminar presented by FBI special agent Loraine Miles.

Earlier in the day from his office in Boston, Walt Tomlinson had sent Rainy an email commending her initiative and praising her willingness to sacrifice a much-needed off day. This sort of community outreach, she knew, improved public perception of the FBI, and the positive public relations helped bolster Tomlinson's budgeting requests. In that same email he also issued a terse reminder about her role in the Hawkins investigation, which was none.

Tomlinson had begrudgingly allowed her to use Carter's time and expertise in assisting the Shilo PD with its investigation, but her request to take over the Hawkins case or, at the minimum, establish a federal nexus to it was denied. With the FBI, it was always a matter of resource allocation, and Tomlinson guarded his resources like precious gems.

The State of New Hampshire was going to prosecute Tom Hawkins, and that was that. It was a politically motivated move, something Rainy knew even before she'd been told. Such occurrences happened occasionally with high-profile cases. By controlling the pretrial press and media coverage, the New Hampshire D.A. could demonstrate to the voters his tough stance on sex crimes between teachers and students. It would go a long way to help with the D.A.'s reelection efforts.

The FBI preferred to not behave like bullies by taking over cases that the states wanted to prosecute themselves, and did so only when such action was legally necessary or beneficial to the FBI. Rainy didn't let go of the Hawkins case easily. During a closed door meeting in Tomlinson's office, she tried again to change his mind.

"The line connecting the state's case against Hawkins to my case against Mann is becoming increasingly clear," she had said to Tomlinson.

"By clear, you mean . . . ?"

"Tom Hawkins is the one who supplied Mann with the text images of Shilo girls and others."

"Did you check with the deputy U.S. attorney prosecuting Mann?"

"I did."

"And?"

"And she agrees with you. The state can prosecute Hawkins without impacting her case against James Mann. We've already given her most of what she'll need for trial."

"So why do you want to take on the Hawkins case as well?"

"Because I'm worried that a lack of continuity between the state and Feds could damage both investigations," Rainy said.

Tomlinson flipped through the Hawkins case report Rainy had provided. "Can you prove the interstate nexus in the Hawkins case?"

"Not with that Leterg program masking the IP addresses, we can't. We have no idea where those images were sent, no. But we've got enough circumstantial evidence to prove that he was Mann's supplier. He had the exact same images that Mann had. And we know that Mann was a receiver, not a distributor."

"I appreciate all you're doing, Agent Miles. I really do. But trust me on this one. The state will do a fine job, and he'll spend just as much time in state prison as he would in a federal," Tomlinson had said. "This is a big deal case for New Hampshire, and the D.A. wants to prosecute it. Unless you give me something better, I'm going to let him."

Rainy knew when to walk away from a battle she couldn't win. She still had one task to complete before her work on the Mann investigation could conclude. She needed to make an official ID of as many of the forty girls in the Text Image Collection as possible.

Rainy hoped her seminar would impart more than just wisdom to these developing minds. She wanted to inspire some of the girls photographed in the Text Image Collection to come to her without her having to go find them. There'd be fewer questions asked that way. The added discretion might help address Didomenico's concerns that a highly visible FBI investigation in a small town would stir up unwanted media attention.

Rainy also wondered if Lindsey Wells might change her mind and come clean with her. It was obvious the girl had lied about her images—of course she'd sent them to somebody. Maybe this seminar would convince Lindsey to stop protecting whoever had betrayed her. And she believed the betrayer to be either Tom Hawkins or a boy Hawkins had recruited to help him build up his merchandise inventory.

Principal Osborne kicked off the assembly, and he sounded sincere and concerned. Murphy, who spoke next, came across in a predictably intimidating way. Murphy remained less touchy with her while they waited backstage, which was good, but he was still a wild card that Rainy wanted to hold on to. She was glad he made it unnecessary to come down on him.

It was Rainy's turn to speak. Applause following her introduction was polite, but tepid. Rainy had given this talk dozens of times to dozens of different fresh-faced high school kids. She could recite most of what she'd say from memory. And while she'd be addressing everybody in attendance, Rainy would secretly direct her message to Lindsey Wells.

"Melanie Smyth texted naked pictures of herself to her boyfriend. He posted them on Facebook," Rainy began. "A few days later, she killed herself. Melanie was only fifteen years old." A picture of Melanie's bright, youthful face, projected from Rainy's PowerPoint slide deck, filled the screen behind her. Murmurs followed. Rainy's shocking opener achieved its objective. She had everyone's full attention.

Rainy made brief eye contact with Lindsey, who sat ten rows from the front. "Melanie killed herself because naked pictures of her were circulating around school." Rainy paused. She especially wanted to give Lindsey time to let those words sink in.

Rainy went on to explain her role with the FBI's cyber crime squad and, more specifically, the Innocent Images National Initiative. She pointed out the dangers of trusting people teens might meet in chat rooms. She told the story of the fifteen-year-old girl whose supposed sixteen-year-old soul mate turned out to be her fifty-five-year-old neighbor. Police recovered the girl's body two weeks after she went missing. The statistics Rainy shared were sobering and were meant to intimidate.

"Did you know that one in four teenage girls reported having met in person strangers they met online?" Rainy asked the group. Rainy got back only blank stares from the rows of students listening, but she knew that her words had sunk in and were taking some sort of meaningful shape in their minds. "One out of five teens has been solicited sexually online, and only three percent told an adult about the encounter."

When Rainy touched upon sexting, she could almost feel the teens' ears perk up. Their attentiveness did not surprise her. Statistically, nearly 40 percent of her audience had sent nude pictures of themselves via their cell phones.

"Did you know sexting a picture of yourself is considered child pornography?" No heads nodded. Not a hand rose. The students sat still, quiet, and Rainy could tell most were riveted to their seats. "You could go to prison for sending a naked picture of yourself or receiving a picture of your boyfriend or your girlfriend. I, for one, hope those laws will change. Your state legislators are becoming more savvy about the emotional scars public humiliation can cause. Scars that might lead to suicide."

Again, Melanie's beaming face filled the screen behind Rainy. From somewhere in the back, Rainy heard soft snickering, followed by a burst of laughter. Her fierce eyes locked on a pack of boys who'd begun fidgeting in their seats. One boy punched another in the arm. A teacher descended on the rowdy crew and ushered the two most obvious offenders out of the auditorium.

"This is nothing to laugh at," Rainy scolded the crowd. That comment only inspired more spurts of laughter from the increasingly fidgety teens. "Maybe you think it doesn't apply to you, or you're uncomfortable talking about it. But I assure you, this isn't a joke. Sexting might just be the stupidest thing you can do with a cell phone. Maybe you think it's funny to virtually flash your friends, but I assure you it's not seen that way by the law. You can end up on a sex offender watch list. That means you couldn't go to school here anymore, because you wouldn't be permitted near minors. You wouldn't be allowed inside a library. Your driver's license would carry a sex offender label on it. Go try to build a life from there. Try to get a job and overcome that stigma. You can't."

Rainy paused. This time, nobody laughed.

"These images don't just stay between you and your boyfriend or girlfriend. Trust me when I tell you that. In a second they can be distributed to hundreds, even thousands, of strangers. What you do online has no shelf life. Your behavior doesn't come with an expiration date."

Rainy flashed on her memories of James Mann's grieving family. She could pinpoint where on the lawn they stood when the SUV with Mann inside drove away.

"So what can you do if you've already sent sexually explicit images to somebody you trust?" Rainy asked.

Not a single hand went up. Expected.

"First, you could ask the person who received your picture to delete it. It's in your best interest to make certain your image wasn't posted to any Web sites or forwarded to somebody else. Ask to see their phone. If you trust them and they trust you, that shouldn't be a problem. I have some other suggestions, which I've included in your handouts. But I'm out of time, so I can't go through all of them here. I hope you found this seminar informative. Before I go, are there any questions?" No hands went up.

Rainy continued. "Mr. Osborne has graciously made his office available for me to use for an hour following this assembly. I'd be happy to answer any questions you'd feel more comfortable asking in private. Thank you again for your time."

Some kids applauded. Some just bolted out of their seats. The overpowering din of student chatter revved up in an instant. Rainy made her way to Lester Osborne's office with a quick and cordial good-bye to Sergeant Murphy.

Rainy watched Lindsey Wells walk away.

It's the state's case now, Miles, she said to herself. *Go ID the other girls and get the hell out of Shilo.*

But something told Rainy she was going to be hanging around this sleepy New England town for many more days to come.

CHAPTER 40

Lindsey Wells followed closely behind Jill Hawkins as the students left the auditorium. Jill, who hadn't returned a single text from the more than forty that Lindsey had sent, appeared committed to ending their friendship.

Empty.

Lindsey had never felt more empty and alone in all her life. She missed Jill's friendship each and every day. She missed it so much that it physically hurt. But thanks to Fidelius Charm, everyone at school now believed that it was Lindsey who wrote the blog posts detailing an affair with Jill's father. Some people even believed Jill was the mysterious Fidelius Charm, ratting out her dad by breaking the scandalous news. Rumors about Lindsey spread around Shilo as fast as it took someone to type The secret is out. Coach Hawkins is sleeping with Lindsey Wells, and hit SEND.

School had once been Lindsey's oasis, and soccer her favorite escape. But school no longer felt safe to her, either.

No place did.

Jill disappeared around a corner, and Lindsey followed

close behind. But the next moment Lindsey saw Jill, her friend was no longer alone.

Three senior girls surrounded her. Gretchen Stiller, Mandy Jensen, and Clair Hubert, known to some around school as the witches, kept pace with Jill stride for stride as they walked a long corridor lined on both sides with metal lockers.

The witches were considered the popular girls. They intimidated others. They seemed more worldly than most (not everybody went to Europe for the summer). They weren't athletes. Too messy. Nor were they honor students. Too hard. The witches were nothing more than rich girls with the right bodies to attract the boys and the right attitudes to act above it all. They went to college parties. They could make you feel inches tall with just a glance. One did coke. None of them were virgins.

Jill was trying to walk faster than the witches. But the three girls, dressed in their skinny jeans and empire-waist shirts, weren't making it easy for her to get away.

"Hey, Jilly. How's your daddy doing?" Lindsey overheard Gretchen say.

"Did Lindsey sleep over last night?" Mandy asked. "Does she stay in your room or your dad's?"

"No, she sleeps in Jill's room but then sneaks out to sleep with her dad," Clair said.

"Oh, that's so cute," Mandy said. "Is Lindsey going to be your new mom?"

Lindsey's heart sank. How could they be so cruel?

Jill glanced over her shoulder and saw that Lindsey was coming to intervene. Jill made a subtle shake of her head. "Shut up," Jill said softly, but loud enough for Lindsey to still hear. Jill started walking again.

Of course the witches followed, as did Lindsey. Lindsey stayed back, though; that was what Jill wanted. Her friend's inner strength amazed her.

"You don't tell us to shut up, bitch," Gretchen said. "You know what I think? I think Jill here owes each of us an hour of service. I mean, we had to sit through that stupid seminar because of what her daddy did."

Clair nodded. "I could use somebody to do my French homework. Are you good at French, Jill?"

Jill stopped walking and looked Gretchen in the eye. "I have an idea, Gretchen," Jill said in a calm voice. "Why don't you go fuck yourself?"

Lindsey put her hand to her mouth to suppress a surprised but delighted laugh.

Gretchen turned her head and looked in Lindsey's direction. "Oh, check it out," Gretchen said. "It's Daddy's little girlfriend coming to the rescue. How poetic."

Jill shoved her hands against Gretchen's shoulders. The taller girl stumbled backward, several staggered steps. Jill turned to walk away, but before she could make it very far, Clair reached out and grabbed hold of Jill's ponytail. Clair yanked on Jill's hair as though she were pulling a rope attached to a bell. Jill's head snapped back, and she let out a painful yelp. Mandy entered into the fracas and pushed Jill hard in her back. Jill fell into a row of lockers and tumbled to the floor. She let out another painful groan as soon as she landed.

Lindsey saw Clair pull her leg back, as if readying to kick Jill in her side. That was when Lindsey knew it was time to step in and help. She charged at Clair and pushed the already off-balance girl to the floor. Clair landed on the floor, not far from where Jill lay.

Jill scampered back to her feet and made fists with her hands. "Just leave us alone!" she screamed.

"Is Coach going to be your prom date, Lindsey?" Mandy asked.

"You don't know anything," Lindsey said.

"Your parents are divorced, isn't that right?" Clair addressed Lindsey. "So is the coach like a father figure to you? A daddy replacement?" Clair kept the tone of her voice overly empathetic, which only put more sting in her sarcasm.

"You don't even know what you're talking about," Lindsey retorted.

The witches formed a tight circle around the pair. Lindsey and Jill eyed each other and without words agreed that they would fight, not flee.

Thankfully, it didn't come to that. Merle Gornick, Lindsey's chemistry teacher, emerged from around the corner. "Don't you girls have someplace you're supposed to be?" she asked.

"Yes, Mrs. Gornick," the witches said in unison. Gretchen stopped and turned, mouthing the words, "Say hi to Daddy," as clearly as if she'd spoken them aloud. Merle must have guessed the other three were the aggressors, because she left Jill and Lindsey to gather up their things. She followed close behind the three girls, and when they reached the end of the hallway, they all disappeared around a corner.

Lindsey helped Jill put on her backpack. Both girls were breathing hard from the adrenaline rush.

"Can we talk?" Lindsey said to Jill.

Jill shrugged. "Sure. I guess."

"I didn't do this. I never had an affair with your dad. God, that's so gross to even think about."

This time, Jill seemed more open to listening. *A good sign,* Lindsey thought.

"Well then, why did the police confiscate your computer? Why did Fidelius Charm send out another batch of messages about you and my dad?"

"For the same reason that people think you're Fidelius Charm," Lindsey said.

"They what? That's ridiculous," Jill snapped.

"So is the idea of sleeping with your dad," Lindsey said. "You've got to believe me, Jill. I swear to you it's true. I've never done anything like that. I'd never."

Jill sighed. "Look, is that FBI lady still hanging around?"

Lindsey's insides went cold. It had been hard enough to sit through the mandatory assembly with Agent Lorraine Miles at the podium. She knew her pictures were probably the real reason the agent had come back to Shilo to address the students. Her mother had been in a rage ever since that embarrassing episode. And now with the police confiscating her computer, Facebook rumors escalating, she and her mother weren't even on speaking terms. Apparently, her mother, like the witches, believed that Lindsey and the coach were having an affair. Lindsey's stomach had been in knots for the entire hour of that assembly. She'd have skipped out if she could, but attendance was mandatory.

What could Jill want with Agent Miles? she wondered.

"I think so. Why?" Lindsey asked.

"You say you didn't write those blog posts. Well, she knows about computers. Maybe she can help explain who did."

"Would you believe me if she can?" Lindsey asked.

Again Jill shrugged. "Maybe. I think so," she said. "We used to be on the same team. Before all this, I mean."

"So?"

"So, maybe it's time we get on the same team again," said Jill.

CHAPTER 41

Rainy heard a knock on the open door of Principal Lester Osborne's office just as she was gathering up her things to leave. Two girls entered. Rainy was delighted to see that one of them was Lindsey Wells. She glanced over at the other girl and recognized her from a picture in Murphy's police report as Coach Hawkins's fifteen-year-old daughter, Jill.

Rainy's pulse jumped. She had wanted to dig deeper into the Coach Hawkins case, but aside from identifying other girls from Mann's unusual text image collection, she didn't have any jurisdiction, let alone reason to investigate. Perhaps Lindsey was going to change all that.

"Hi. Are you still talking to students? Answering questions, I mean," Lindsey said in an uncertain voice.

"Of course. Of course I am," Rainy replied, her pulse still hammering away.

Rainy didn't know what information, if any, Lindsey had shared with Jill about the sexting incident and its connection to Coach Hawkins. Rainy suspected that Lindsey had willingly shared her pictures with the coach, but, of course, that was only her theory and not yet an established fact.

"Let the evidence take you there," Tomlinson always said.

Whatever the truth, Rainy knew to keep her knowledge of Lindsey's naked pictures a secret between them. Lindsey didn't seem to be here to rehash that, anyway. She had a fresh urgency. "Do you girls want to sit down?" Rainy asked.

Lindsey gave her head a quick shake no. "If it's all right with you, we'd rather stand."

Both girls shuffled on their feet, and neither would make eye contact with Rainy.

"Okay. Then I'll stand with you," Rainy offered. "So, can you tell me your names?"

Rainy looked at Lindsey, her way of communicating that their secret was safe with her.

"Sure, I'm Lindsey Wells."

Rainy nodded, then looked to Jill. "And you are?" she asked.

"My name is Jill," the sweet-voiced girl answered. "Jill Hawkins."

Rainy moved out from behind Principal Osborne's steel desk. She wanted no barriers between herself and the girls.

The girls leaned their lithe bodies against the concrete wall, looking to Rainy like crookedly hung paintings. Their expressions simultaneously conveyed boredom, nervousness, indifference, and concern.

Teenagers.

"What is it you want to talk about?" Rainy asked.

The girls glanced at each other, then at Rainy, but neither replied.

Do you want to tell me why you sent Coach Hawkins your picture? she silently asked Lindsey. Rainy gripped the edge of the desk hard enough to make her fingers ache. "Girls, do you have something to ask me?" Rainy said again. Her investigator's mind swirled through the many possibilities and connections.

Lindsey broke free from her perch and took a cautious step forward. "Well, in that assembly you were talking about things not being like they seem on the Internet. That story you told about chatting with a boy, but it's not really a boy. It's a man."

"That's right."

"Well, I'm just wondering, um . . . How does somebody make it look like you were doing something on the Internet that you weren't doing?"

Rainy bit her lower lip. She could guess what Lindsey might be getting at.

"Well, that depends. Can you be more specific?" *Easy, Rainy. Easy.*

Jill let out an exasperated sigh, as though anticipating how long this was going to take without her intervention. Unlike Lindsey, Jill kept her shoulders rooted against the wall and her arms folded tightly against her chest. "Look, the police think Lindsey wrote these blog posts on Tumblr. com about my dad," Jill said. "They confiscated her computer."

"And that's what you wanted to talk to me about?" Rainy asked. Her heartbeat shifted into fifth gear from fourth.

"I want to know if you can do that," Jill said. "Lindsey says she didn't write any blog posts, she doesn't even have a Tumblr.com account, but the police are saying they can trace the posts back to her home computer. How is that even possible?"

"Well, they'd do it through IP addresses," Rainy explained. "There are logs that your Internet service provider keeps. We can match those logs up and use it to pinpoint an address."

Jill's expression contorted in a way suggestive of someone having eaten something unpleasant. Rainy glanced to Lindsey. "Lindsey is a minor," Rainy said, "and her identity is legally protected."

"Yeah, right," Jill muttered. "Protected."

"Do you mind telling me how people linked Lindsey with your father's case?" Rainy asked.

Rainy knew the link was there but couldn't believe that connection had leaked out to the rest of the Shilo community. Some safeguards.

"Because of Facebook," Lindsey said. "Somebody created this bogus Facebook profile, and they've been using it to spread rumors about me and Coach Hawkins online."

I'm not so sure they're rumors, Rainy thought.

"People have been writing really disgusting things about me on my Facebook page," Jill said. "I had to delete my profile. And forget about the text messages I'm getting."

"We're wondering if maybe somebody is trying to get at both of us," Lindsey suggested. "But it's nobody on the soccer team. We're sure of that."

"How can you be sure?" Rainy said.

It was Lindsey who made a face this time and probably would have said, "Duh! Because we know," if she and Rainy had been peers.

"So let me get this straight," Rainy said. "You didn't make any of those Tumblr blog posts?"

"No."

"But the police must have good reason to think you did."

"So you're saying they have proof?" Lindsey asked, the dismay evident in her voice.

"I'm saying if they think you're involved, they've traced the posts to your home address using an IP address."

"But I don't even have a Tumblr.com account. Can somebody make an account and make it look like it's me?" Lindsey asked.

"That's a pretty tricky thing to do, Lindsey," Rainy said. "But if they intercepted your wireless account, they could essentially create content online and the IP trace would lead right back to you. Do you know if your home network is secure?"

Lindsey just shrugged. "I don't know. My dad got it working ages ago. I know that we use wireless. I can get on the Internet from, like, my kitchen without a cable or anything."

Rainy just nodded. Home networks were often the most vulnerable to hackers. Without proper security in place, it was relatively easy to hijack those signals. It would explain why Lindsey was unaware of the Tumblr account. Somebody could have been parked on the street using the Wellses' Wi-Fi signal to make those pages and exchange messages. Probably the same person who created the bogus Facebook profile to accelerate the spread of the rumor.

Lindsey shook her head in disbelief. "So maybe somebody snuck into my house and wrote it," Lindsey said. "Isn't that possible?"

"Well, it's possible," Rainy said. "Same as somebody hijacking your Wi-Fi signal."

"Hang on a second." Lindsey took out her cell phone and dialed. She held the phone to her head and waited for the other party to answer.

"Daddy, it's me," Lindsey said into the phone. "Did you ever put a password or anything on our wireless network?"

Rainy watched Lindsey with intent focus. Lindsey pulled the phone away from her mouth.

"He doesn't think so. He said it was confusing enough just getting it to work. Besides, he says he forgets passwords all the time. Thanks, Daddy. I love you. Bye." Lindsey ended the call.

Jill looked saddened by the brief exchange. Rainy felt deep sympathy for both girls, but for different reasons.

"So it's possible somebody did what you said and pretended to be Lindsey?" Jill asked.

"If what your dad said is true, and your Wi-Fi isn't secure, it's definitely a possibility." Rainy confirmed that for the girls as much as she was convincing herself of that fact.

"Jilly, now will you believe me?" Lindsey asked.

"What can we do?" Jill said, throwing up her hands in exasperation. "It's like I want to drop out of school. It's hell around here for me."

"For both of us," Lindsey said.

"I mean, we just got jumped by these three girls," Jill added. "But I'm convinced of one thing now."

"What's that?" Rainy asked.

"Lindsey and my father aren't having a relationship. I don't care what the stupid Internet says. My dad thinks that somebody is framing him. Lindsey is saying the same thing. I'm not saying my dad is perfect or anything, but I don't think he's, y'know, *that* kind of person."

Rainy flashed on James Mann. According to him, he wasn't that sort of person, either. But according to his computer, his claim was a lie. Maybe, just maybe, Rainy thought, both men were telling the truth.

Rainy took two business cards from her cardholder. She set the cards facedown on Osborne's desk and wrote her home number on the back of each. She handed each girl a card. "Let me look into this for you, okay? Lindsey, I'll check out your home network. At least confirm if you have any security set up. So don't touch anything. Okay?"

"Sure," Lindsey said.

"But if you need someone to talk to in the interim, you call me, okay?"

The girls nodded. They moved out from behind Osborne's desk and returned to their prior perch up against the wall. Their expressions shifted from engaged to indifferent. Arms slipped back into tight folds across their chests, like two armadillos curling up into protective balls.

"Focus on school and I'm sure things will work out. I'll touch base with Sergeant Murphy, too. If he tells me anything about the investigation that I can share with you, I promise I will. Okay?"

"Okay," they both said.

Jill looked at her watch. "I'm going to be late for English."

"Lindsey, could you stay a moment so we can make arrangements for me to check out your home network for that security issue?"

"Sure," Lindsey said.

When they were alone, Rainy said to Lindsey, "Do you really want me to help you?"

"Of course."

"Then tell me who you sent your pictures to."

"I told you, I don't know."

"Then I don't think I can help."

Lindsey looked as though Rainy had just punched her in the stomach. Her color drained. "That's not fair," she eventually said.

"No, it's probably not," Rainy agreed. "But I'm only going to help you if you come clean with me, Lindsey. Did you send your pictures to Coach Hawkins?"

Lindsey made that sour-milk expression again. "God, no. No!"

"Then who? Talk to me. You're not in trouble. You're the victim here. Remember that. You're the victim. All I want to do is help you."

Lindsey bore holes into the floor with her eyes. She looked anywhere but at Rainy. In a whispered voice, she said, "Tanner."

"What?"

"You asked me who I sent those pictures to. I texted them to Tanner Farnsworth."

"Who's that?" Rainy asked.

"My boyfriend," said Lindsey. "My soon-to-be ex-boyfriend, I mean."

"Thank you for being honest with me, Lindsey."

Lindsey paused for a beat, then asked, "Remember when you wanted to see my cell phone, and I said no?"

"I do."

"Well, here," Lindsey said as she handed Rainy her cell phone. "I deleted the messages. But maybe your computer people can still recover who I sent the pictures to. It'll prove that Tanner got them."

Rainy took the phone and glanced at the display. "Don't you need your phone?" she asked.

"I'm getting a new one," Lindsey said. "New number, too."

"Mind if I ask you why?"

Lindsey made a pained expression. "When the entire school thinks you're sleeping with a teacher," she said, "the only way to survive is to disappear."

CHAPTER 42

Tom exited his Ford Taurus and walked around to the front of his car. He locked the car doors using the remote and listened for the troubling engine pings to fade. The Taurus had been acting up quite a bit lately. It was slow to accelerate, and he heard that constant pinging every time he shut off the engine. Probably just needed a tune-up. But Tom kept checking each time he turned the engine off to see if the noise was getting any worse. It seemed the case, like a mirror to his own circumstances.

Tom had wanted to be well rested for this important meeting with Marvin, but he had slept fitfully since making his confession. The statute of limitations for Class A felonies in New Hampshire was six years, and Jill couldn't be considered an accomplice to his crimes. Tom could justify it to himself all he wanted, Roland had left him no alternative, but it still didn't make it any easier to burden Jill with his terrible secret.

At least they were speaking by phone now. She sounded happy to hear from him when he called. They kept their text message safety checks going, and with Vern's help, they added a GPS tracking feature to her cell phone. Tom could monitor where Jill was at all times, but choked up when she told him that soon she'd be tracked back on Oak Street. She was thinking it was time to come home.

He'd also been thinking about Adriana. Tom had kept his distance to keep her—and himself—safe from Roland's wrath. He hoped she didn't think he was ignoring her or didn't appreciate what she had done. It was up to Marvin to get Adriana her money back. Tom had faith that his attorney would do just that.

Tom followed the familiar route to Marvin's office, pausing briefly to say a polite hello to his receptionist.

"Attorney Pressman is expecting you," his receptionist said, motioning for Tom to go right in. She didn't appear as nervous around Tom this time. Perhaps that was Marvin's doing, Tom thought.

Tom entered Marvin's office but couldn't see his attorney anywhere. From behind Marvin's desk, Tom heard a grunt, then Marvin's labored counting.

"Eighteen . . . nineteen . . . twenty . . ."

"Marvin?" Tom called out.

"One hundred ten . . . one hundred eleven . . ."

Marvin popped up from behind his desk. He wore a tracksuit, not his usual attorney garb. His face was dotted with sweat, which he dabbed away with a white towel. "Tom," he said with a bright smile on his face, "good to see you."

Marvin came around his desk to shake Tom's hand.

"You lost another pound," Tom said.

"Two!" Marvin announced proudly. "But who's counting? Okay, take a seat. We've much to discuss."

Marvin walked over to his desk, where he proceeded to study a tall stack of folders like a Jenga master contemplating a move. His hand reached into the middle of a stack, and almost without looking, he extracted the folder that he'd sought.

Taking a seat at the conference table across from Tom, Marvin said, "The game plan is to go over the discovery with you. But first, how is Jill holding up?"

Tom nodded and tried to show Marvin his appreciation. "She's fine," he said. "We've been taking things day by day but talking at least once a night. She's been staying with Vern and Sylvia Kalinowski. They have twin girls who are Jill's age."

"Good. That's good to know."

"How's the salt intake?" Tom asked.

"Lower."

"And you're taking a protein with every workout?"

"That nut mix you gave me is a good one."

"Soybeans, sunflower seeds, and almond slices. My favorite. We're hitting that goal weight, Marvin."

"First your case—"

"And I'm getting you a date with Rebecca Bartholomew."

"I might write off half of my fee if you make that happen, buddy."

"It's a done deal. Just say the word."

"I'll say it in another fifteen pounds."

"Ten," Tom said.

"Ten it is."

Marvin flipped through the pages of the open folder and scanned the documents within. "So, as we discussed, I waived your right to have a probable cause hearing in exchange for the D.A. speeding up my access to their discovery materials."

"Is it unusual they'd agree to that?" Tom asked.

"No, not really. It's sort of a 'you scratch my back, I'll scratch yours' protocol that we use a lot. But it does tell me they're eager to make a case and not at all worried about tipping their hand early."

"Why do you say that?" Tom asked.

"The D.A. has a mountain of evidence," Marvin said as he again sifted through the pages of an alarmingly thick set of papers. "They've got tons of computer forensic reports here, too. They even got the FBI involved."

Tom nodded. "I told you about the agent who questioned me after my arrest," he said.

"Right," Marvin said. "I know that the D.A. had promised to crack down on teacher-student relationships, and I think they're out to make a pretty big example out of you."

"Well, what do we do now?" Tom asked.

Marvin picked up a pencil on his desk and twirled it between his fingers like a baton. "Tom, we need to think about a plea bargain before this goes to trial," he said.

Tom shot Marvin a surprised look. "Doesn't that mean pleading guilty?"

Marvin nodded. "That it does. But it also means keeping you out of prison for ten-plus years."

"We haven't even started to prepare for the trial," Tom objected. "What the hell is in those discovery materials?"

"We're going to try and prove to the jury the evidence against you was planted."

"Right," Tom said, acknowledging the defense strategy that he believed was not only the best, but also the truth.

"Well, the D.A. is going to try and prove, via your alleged relationship with Lindsey Wells, that you're a sexual offender."

"That's insane," Tom snapped, his eyes growing narrow. "Of course I'm not. In all my years as a teacher and coach, not once has anybody ever suspected me of that sort of thing."

"Which is precisely why your involvement with Lindsey Wells is so critical to the prosecutor's case. Lindsey will be proof to the jury that the evidence on the laptop wasn't planted there. Once they think you're having sex with a minor, a jury can be convinced of just about anything."

"And why will they think I had a relationship with Lindsey in the first place?" Tom wanted to know.

"Well, according to the preliminary computer forensic audit, you've exchanged e-mails with Lindsey Wells. Graphic ones, at that."

"E-mails?" Tom stammered. "What are you talking about?"

"I'm talking about both of the state's computer forensic specialists matching up IP addresses that link you and your laptop to Lindsey Wells's home address."

"That's crazy. Lindsey's just a kid. She's my daughter's best friend, for goodness' sake!"

"And then there is this Leterg thing."

"Yeah, you mentioned something about that to me. Explain that again," Tom said.

"I had to research that myself. Leterg is 'Gretel' spelled backward. Every click on the Internet, every file sent or Web site accessed, is composed of broken-up data packets that originate from the sender and get reassembled by the receiver. IP addresses are what tell these broken-up data packets where to reassemble. Instead of leaving a single bread-crumb trail showing the actual route that the raw packets of data travel from point A to point B, Leterg manufactures bogus data routes, making it impossible for a computer forensic specialist to determine the exact path these data packets took."

"And the state believes I know how to use this Leterg thing?"

"They were able to crack part of the Leterg encryption algorithm. Because of that . . . call it a 'breakthrough' . . . the state now believes you've been collecting images of naked teenaged girls. The FBI has been cooperating with the Shilo and state police investigation. According to this affidavit," Marvin said, holding up a piece of paper, "the FBI believes these multimedia format images were sent originally as text messages."

"That's ridiculous. The only text messages I send are to Jill!"

Marvin continued, "With the help of the FBI, the state has been able to ID ten of the forty girls whose images they found on your laptop. In their opinion, thanks to the Leterg program, the part of the encryption they couldn't crack, you were able to conceal the identities of the people to whom you sent the images."

"But I wouldn't even know how to install a Leterg program, let alone use one," Tom said.

"It would appear that isn't the case," said Marvin. "But that's not all."

"What do you mean?"

"Money, Tom. According to the indictment, you were being paid for these images. And it's been going on for quite some time. Three years or so. The timing links you to all the girls from Shilo. The D.A. is going to ask for your help in identifying the girls they can't."

"I'm assuming one of those girls is the one who sent me her picture," Tom said.

"That's right. They were able to pull the deleted image from your cell phone provider's network. It hadn't been purged yet. Her image was there. They didn't find any others."

"This is insane, Marvin. Please tell me you believe that I'm innocent of all this."

"Remember what I said about professing your innocence to me?"

Tom nodded dully.

"The state looked into your finances, Tom. They've attached the records here. Did you know you have a bank account with over a hundred twenty thousand dollars in it?"

Tom's mouth fell open. "I what?"

"It'll take some time to untangle where the money came in from. But it looks like a lot of offshore accounts and shell businesses. It would appear you were very good at hiding the money trail."

"A hundred twenty thousand dollars?" Tom buried his head in his hands. "Oh, Marvin. This sounds bad."

"Well, like I said, that's the evidence detailed in these discovery documents," Marvin said, holding up the packet. "I mean, you don't usually see this many pages for a capital murder case."

"Do they have any sworn testimony?" Tom asked. "Has anybody questioned Lindsey yet?"

Marvin scanned through the pages, but his expression suggested that he already knew the answer. "They have," he said, " and she's denied, in sworn testimony, ever having any sort of sexual relationship with you, or having made wanted or unwanted *sexual* advances toward you, and she denies claims that you made wanted or unwanted *sexual* advances toward her."

"Well, so that's good. We've got a case. If Lindsey denies it all under oath, it could throw the rest of the charges against me into a tailspin. That Leterg thing, those images, this money that I didn't even know I had."

Marvin frowned. He set down the indictment, picked

up his pencil, and twirled it even faster. "I'm not sure a jury is going to care about a fifteen-year-old girl's testimony," Marvin said. "They're going to see computer logs and other forensic archives that the D.A. will insist prove your guilt. I don't know a single superior court judge who won't give you the maximum sentence allowed if you're convicted. Prison for sex offenders is an ugly place. Uglier still for child pornographers. That's why I'm suggesting we plead. Maybe do a couple years, tops."

"And live my life as a convicted sex offender? No thank you," Tom said. "I can't believe what you're even suggesting. You're my lawyer, Marvin. I'm innocent of all these charges!" Tom slammed his hand against Marvin's conference table for emphasis.

Marvin didn't flinch. "What is it you want me to do, Tom?" he asked.

Tom gave a pitiable laugh and threw his hands up in the air in a show of defeat. "You're my *lawyer*, Marvin. What is it I want you to do? I want you to prove that I'm innocent, that's what."

"And if we lose? Are you ready to face that possibility?"

"We're not going to lose," Tom said. "Because you're going to fight for me and we're going to win. If it's not Lange setting me up, then we need to figure out who else it could be. When I was a SEAL, I never went on a mission believing I was going to fail. I went knowing with every fiber in my being I was going to succeed. This is a battle I can't lose, Marvin. I need to know that you're going to fight for me. I need to know that you'll take this all the way."

Tom's eyes narrowed on Marvin. The pencil spinning about Marvin's fingers fell to the floor. Marvin held Tom's hard-edged stare with his own unblinking eyes. Then he smiled.

"I was hoping you'd say that," Marvin said.

Tom let go of the breath he'd been holding. "So what's our next move?"

"Well, police brought the FBI into this case," Marvin said.

"So?"

"So, I suggest that we do the same."

CHAPTER 43

The Shilo Wildcats won the Thursday night football game against Cumberland by a score of 37 to 17. Rainy Miles hadn't come to watch football, though. She'd come to talk with Tanner Farnsworth.

After the game, she spotted Tanner in the parking lot, hanging out by a red Mustang.

Nice car, she thought.

Tanner was out of shoulder pads and into his street clothes. He was also surrounded by a group of a dozen or so other teenagers. As a collective, the group seemed to be competing with each other for top prize in the Most Uninterested Teen contest.

Dressed in dark jeans and a suede jacket, Tanner radiated the sort of magnetism that drew the girls' glances and kept the boys hovering nearby. He was tall, well built, and handsome, coolly detached in a way that suggested he was the leader of this pack. Through her investigative work, Rainy had seen her fair share of boys like Tanner Farnsworth. One of them had passed around a naked picture of Melanie Smyth.

Rainy stepped out from the shadows and approached the group. Their expressions all said, "You're not thinking of talking to us, lady." But as she neared, that hostility dimmed as one by one they stopped paying attention to her. It was as if by tuning out this stranger, they had somehow become invisible to her. Of course they hadn't. They just wanted to be.

"Are you Tanner Farnsworth?" Rainy asked. She tried to sound friendly, but years spent arresting people tainted most everything she said with a hint of menace. The other boys took a few cautious steps in retreat, leaving an island of space around her and Tanner. He was tall, and Rainy had to crane her neck to make eye contact.

"Who are you?" Tanner asked.

"Agent Loraine Miles. I'm with the FBI."

Rainy flashed her badge and studied Tanner's expression for any sign of a tell. Rapid blinking. Head turning. Eyes averting her gaze. A hand to the face, throat, or mouth, some reflexive gesture to scratch away the invisible itch of guilt. Tanner did none of those things. Even so, Rainy's internal radar blinked out the word *creep* like a neon sign.

"Weren't you at our school?" Tanner said.

Tanner produced a cocky smile that Rainy disliked intensely. It suggested that he recognized her as an adversary, and that awareness brought him a degree of pleasure.

"Yes, I was," Rainy said. "I'd like to talk with you about Lindsey Wells."

Tanner's cocky armor began to crack. "What about her?" he asked.

Rainy had already sent a preservation request to Tanner's cell phone provider. Any evidence against him would remain on the servers.

"Are you two dating?"

"We were," Tanner said. "She dumped me. I guess she prefers older men."

"When did she dump you?" Rainy asked.

"A couple days ago. Are you here to investigate why we broke up?" He smiled a wry, unpleasant grin. The boy's arrogance was as repulsive to her as what she now believed he'd done with Lindsey's pictures.

"Did Lindsey Wells send you any pictures of herself?" Rainy asked.

"What sort of pictures?"

"You know what sort of pictures, Tanner. Ones she'd want only her boyfriend to see."

"No," he said.

"Would you be willing to submit to a consent search?"

"What's that?"

"Something that would let me check your phone. See what information and communication you've got stored there."

"I don't think I would."

"No. I didn't think you would, either. Did you encourage her to take pictures of herself and send them to you?"

"Nope."

"Do you know that constitutes a crime in the federal system? You could go to jail. Or were you one of those boys who weren't listening at my talk?"

"I was listening," Tanner said.

Rainy could see that she'd punched another small hole through his defenses. She was within her legal rights to question Tanner, a minor, without his parents present. But she wondered how much more she could press him before he figured out he was under attack and asked for a parent or attorney to be present. In truth, she'd love for that to happen. It became harder to hide the truth once a suspect officially entered the system. *Go ahead and lawyer up,* Rainy thought as she decided to push ahead with the informal interview.

"So if you were at my talk and listening, you'd remember how much hard time you'll do. Fifteen years. Maybe more. And that you'll be registered as a sex offender."

"What is it you want from me?" Tanner asked.

"The truth. Any idea why Lindsey thinks that you did something with those pictures?"

"You're the cop."

"FBI."

"Whatever."

"So, any ideas?"

"I told you, I don't have a clue. She dumped me, remember? If she said anything to you about any pictures, it was probably just to get back at me. Don't ask me for what. I'm not the one getting Tom-a-Hawked."

Rainy grimaced. "I'm assuming that's your crude euphemism for sex," Rainy said.

"Euphe-what?"

"Never mind," Rainy said with a dismissive wave.

Two people approached Rainy and Tanner from the right. One was an older man, tall and handsome, the way an ex-athlete might look years after the glory days. The other was a boy near to Tanner's age. They looked too much alike for them not to be father and son.

"What's going on?" asked the man.

"Hey, Mitchell, Mr. Boyd," Tanner said. "This is an agent from the FBI. She's asking me about Lindsey."

The older Boyd's unflinching expression would have befit a statue. The younger one's appearance was much edgier than Tanner's: short hair with gelled spikes, a silver cross earring in his right ear.

"What's up with Lindsey?" Mitchell asked. The boy's

expression darkened the way threatening clouds dim a sunny day.

"This is a private matter between myself and Tanner. It doesn't concern anybody else."

"Well, did he tell you what you wanted to know?" The older Boyd placed a hand on Tanner's shoulder. "Tanner's like family to us. If he's in any trouble, I'd like to know."

"Tanner's a big boy," Rainy said. "He knows what trouble he's in."

Roland stayed quiet for a long second. The kids circled around them again. Anyone watching from a distance would have expected to hear shouts of "Fight! Fight!" coming from the circle's perimeter.

Roland unexpectedly extended his hand. "Forgive my manners," he said. "My name is Roland Boyd. This is my son Mitchell."

Rainy shook Roland's hand. His grip was strong; the handshake professional.

"Well, if there is anything we can do to help with your efforts, you just let us know."

"I sure will," Rainy answered.

Something about the conversation struck Rainy as peculiar. Tanner didn't come across as someone with a great deal of respect for Coach Hawkins. He sure as heck didn't sound like an underling talking about the boss who allegedly paid him good money for naked pictures of Lindsey Wells.

CHAPTER 44

For several tense moments, nothing was said. Rainy had to get her audio recording equipment running. This session would be taped. She got approval from the front office to record it because the AUSA assigned to the James Mann case wasn't available to hear it first hand. Marvin had to agree to let Rainy record the session before she even considered the drive north. In exchange, Marvin promised no legal maneuverings that might delay the federal deposition of Tom Hawkins in connection to their case against James Mann.

"We both have something to gain," Marvin had told Tom when explaining why Agent Miles was willing to participate in the discussion.

"Just a reminder that we're on the record here," Rainy said after she positioned the microphone closest to Tom. The digital recorder's red light blinked in front of Tom in a threatening way.

She still wants to intimidate me, Tom thought.

"I've got nothing to hide," Tom said.

"You understand that everything you say here could be admissible in a court of law?"

"Understood," Tom and Marvin answered together.

Rainy nodded subtly. "What is it you're looking for from the FBI?" she asked Marvin. She rolled the sleeves of her jacket up to her elbows. Tom noticed that she wasn't wearing any rings.

"You suspect my client has somehow supplied material to a person or persons being brought up on federal child pornography charges."

"I'm not here to discuss my caseload," Rainy said. Tom saw the patience and interest drain from her eyes. "You said you had information for me," she reminded Marvin.

"Have you done a time line of the two cases?" Marvin asked her.

"Not sure what you're getting at."

"I've reviewed a lot of the D.A.'s discovery materials," continued Marvin. "Forty girls, ten from Shilo. Tom personally knows some of those girls, but not all of them. How did he get these girls to give him their pictures?"

"No evidence exists to prove that he couldn't have procured the images in question," Rainy said. "There is plenty of evidence to suggest that your client is in violation of numerous federal laws specific to child pornography material. Now, if your client is interested in working with the federal government, perhaps we can help to broker a deal with the state."

"Deal?" Tom said.

Rainy ignored Tom, directing her attack toward Marvin. "You know we haven't ruled out federal charges against your client, either—"

"But isn't that double jeopardy?" Tom interrupted. "You can't be tried for the same crime twice. Can you?"

"Double jeopardy has a separate sovereigns exception," Marvin explained. "In the American federal system, states and the federal government are considered separate sovereign powers."

"At this time," Rainy continued, "the quantity and nature of material found in your client's possession haven't generated enough federal interest to pursue the matter independent of the state's case against Mr. Hawkins. But that could change—quickly, too. Like the direction of the wind."

Marvin smiled at Rainy, who was seated directly across from him. Tom disliked the feeling that he wasn't even a presence in the room, but he was even more curious about where Marvin was taking this conversation. Instead of objecting, he remained a silent observer.

"I'm not here to get my client into any trouble with the federal government," Marvin said. "You're free to depose him for your case. I already promised you no legal tap dancing there. But when you do depose him, he'll tell you what he's been telling me from the get-go."

"Which is?"

"That he's being framed for something he didn't do," Marvin said.

"What are you asking me to do here?" asked Rainy.

"All I'm asking is that you look at this case through different eyes."

"Such as?"

"For starters, don't you think it's a little too convenient that you bust James Mann, and a few days after you come to Shilo, you bust his supplier? I would think that would give a seasoned investigator such as yourself a moment's pause."

"Is that what you think?" Rainy said.

"Do you know what the longest hitting streak is in baseball, Agent Miles?"

"Joe DiMaggio," Rainy said without hesitating. "Fifty-six games." She looked at both men, who seemed genuinely surprised by the quickness of her answer. "My mom got me into baseball," she explained.

"Well, the probability of that streak happening again has been mathematically proven. Guess how many years, statistically speaking, it will take before a streak like that happens again?"

"Fifty?" Rainy said.

"Try five hundred," Marvin replied.

"And your point is?"

"The probability of your coming to a small town like Shilo to make an ID of a girl and days later uncovering the supplier is more remote than that streak being broken in our lifetimes. That's what I think."

Rainy shrugged her shoulders. "I don't see how base-ball and the case against Mr. Hawkins—"

"Tom, please," Tom interrupted. He wanted Rainy to use his first name so she'd be more inclined to view him as a person, not just a case. Rainy, in response, flashed Tom a look as if to say he'd always be Mr. Hawkins to her.

"I don't see how baseball and the case are related," Rainy finished.

"I've done some digging of my own into James Mann," Marvin said. "The guy was about to become president of a major pharmaceutical company. Seems as unlikely a person to be procuring these images as my client is to be distributing them. That just makes it even more bizarre. Three times more unlikely to happen than the next DiMag-gio, I'm willing to bet."

"There is no typecasting for these crimes. You know that."

"No, but there is instinct. And I'm asking you to keep an open mind here. These men don't even know each other."

"The Internet makes friends out of strangers all the time," said Rainy. "Look, I appreciate what you're trying to do, Mr. Pressman. I realize that it's your job to believe in your client's innocence. But we've looked at the evidence against Mr. Hawkins. One of the top computer analysts in my squad even helped your computer forensic guys crack the encryption code."

"What about Tom's home computer?"

"That came back clean," Rainy said.

"Because his work computer is easier to access. Somebody would have to trick him into downloading a virus or break into his home to tamper with his home PC."

"It's true," Tom said. "I don't always lock my office. People are in and out of the building all the time. There aren't any security cameras, and people know when I'm at practice and won't be showing up unexpectedly."

Rainy fell silent. "What I strongly suggest," she eventually said, with an increasingly severe expression, "is that you think about cutting a deal."

Marvin leaned over the conference table, closer to Rainy. Tom could see the determination in his face. "Why would my client go through such extreme measures to launder the money he allegedly earned while engaged in this criminal activity, and then suddenly become reckless?" he asked.

"I'd say we'd need Tom to answer that question," replied Rainy.

Marvin appeared unmoved by her response. He continued. "Then he risks his carefully controlled enterprise, which he'd allegedly run in secret for years, by having an affair with one of the girls?"

"Attraction can make you do stupid things," said Rainy.

"And nobody in Shilo sees Tom coming and going,"

Marvin said. "No one notices him getting close to their kids. Nobody ever raised an alarm. No police reports filed. No request to investigate. Does that really make sense to you, Agent Miles? Do you really believe that to be true?"

"I believe in following the evidence," answered Rainy. "Not forming conclusions."

Marvin said, "And you think Lindsey could have kept this from her mother? All the other girls?"

"Kids keep secrets from their parents all the time," Rainy said. "Secrets are an essential part of growing up. We all have them. We all keep them. Teenagers, especially girls, are highly impressionable. They could have been convinced to stay quiet. Tom could have made these girls feel special, important, and different from the others. And they'd keep on feeling that way. They'd feel that way for as long as what they were doing stayed secret. That's what I believe."

"Agent Miles," Tom said, "do you have any kids?"

Marvin shot Tom a disapproving glance. Tom held up his hand to urge patience from his attorney.

"I don't see how that's relevant," Rainy replied.

"It's relevant because you'd think differently about me if you knew what it felt like to be a parent."

"I still don't see—"

"I'm not saying you'd think I was innocent," Tom continued, "but I do think a part of you would wonder if I was like most parents. If I spent my every waking moment thinking about my kid's well-being. If I'd sacrifice my own life for hers. If I'd do everything in my power to make sure my child had every possible advantage in life. You'd wonder that about me. I believe that's true. And then you'd wonder how in the hell I could do what I've been accused of doing."

"What is it you want from me, Mr. Hawkins?"

"Tom, please," he said. He looked Rainy in the eyes. Something about her expression had shifted. Where before he'd seen judgment, now he saw a trace of doubt.

"What is it you want from me, Tom?"

"What I want is for you to look at the evidence again," Tom said. "But this time, instead of hoping that you've miraculously found your missing link, try using a different approach."

"What approach would that be?" asked Rainy.

"This time, try to think of me as an innocent man." Tom held Rainy's gaze for a moment. He felt something pass between them. It wasn't that she suddenly believed him to be innocent. But he could see now that she wanted him to be innocent.

It was a start.

CHAPTER 45

Tom went out to get the mail a few hours before night-fall. He sifted through a stack of bills on his walk back up the driveway (those would have to wait), saw a promotional flyer from the Plenty Market (he'd canceled his customer loyalty card), and noticed one surprising item in the mix. It was a letter, addressed to him, from Adriana Boyd.

With his back against the kitchen counter, Tom opened the letter using a butter knife. Inside, he found a slender, hand-bordered card, monogrammed with Adriana's name. Her handwritten note, written in purple pen and elegantly scripted, wasn't dated.

> *Dear Tom,*
> *I hope this note finds you as well as can be. I be-lieve in you and know that you'll soon be cleared of any wrongdoing. I also wanted to apologize for Roland's recent behavior. I know that he's told you to keep away from me. He's asked that I do the same with you. I'm respecting my husband's wishes only in part, as I'm keeping you in my thoughts and*

prayers each day. It is important to me that you
know you haven't been forgotten.
I believe in you.
With care and concern,
Adriana

Tom reread Adriana's card before slipping it back in its
envelope. He tucked the card and envelope inside the
kitchen junk drawer, buried underneath a couple rolls of
Scotch tape, pens, pencils, an address book, and one partially used disposable camera.

The phone rang. He answered it and smiled before the
caller could finish her greeting.

"Hi, Dad," Jill said. "I just wanted to let you know that
I'm over at Lindsey's house. We're studying for a chem
test tomorrow."

"Hey!" Tom said. "I was just about to text you, but it's
a lot nicer hearing your voice."

The conversation that followed wasn't anything more
extraordinary than a parent and child playing catch-up:
"How are you? What's new at school? What have you
been up to?" After about ten minutes of back-and-forth
chitchat, Tom got the sense his daughter wanted to end
the call. It was just one of the many ways that he'd come
to know Jill's personality better.

"I hope you've been eating well," Jill said to him.

"Hey, who's the parent here?" Tom replied. "Anyway,
I'm eating fine."

"Dad, you can't cook."

"I'm not that bad."

"Whatever. I should probably get back to studying
with Lindsey."

Tom glanced over at the kitchen table, where he'd been
doing some studying of his own. On that table were six

large legal tomes, each splayed open, plus a bunch of printed-out documents and spiral-bound notebooks filled with Tom's research on child pornography and legal defenses. He'd drawn only one conclusion based on the cases he'd studied: Marvin really had his work cut out for him.

"I'm so glad you and Lindsey have reconciled," said Tom.

"Me too," Jill said.

"You know you can come home anytime," Tom said to her. "You don't have to stay at the Kalinowskis' if you don't want to."

Jill went quiet, and Tom allowed her to process without interruption.

"Maybe I will," she eventually said.

"Your room is waiting."

"Okay. Well, I really should keep cramming . . . unless you happen to know anything about the photoelectric effect."

"Does it have anything to do with taking pictures?"

"Good night, Dad," Jill said with a groan.

"Good night."

Tom set the cordless phone back in its cradle. He hadn't made it back over to the kitchen table when the phone rang again. Tom answered it on the second ring, assuming it was Jill calling him back.

"Whatcha forget?" he asked.

"Nothing," a man said in a raspy, monotonous tone. Tom's pulse kicked up a notch or two.

"Who is this?" asked Tom.

"You don't know my voice, but I'm pretty sure you'd recognize my face."

Tom's muscles tightened like a coil spring poised to unleash. He gripped the edge of the kitchen counter hard enough to make his fingers hurt.

"Lange? Is that you?"

"The one and only. We need to talk."

"I'd say. Come on over. I'll make us some tea."

Lange laughed lightly into the phone. "Can't do that, compadre," he said.

"Well then, why don't you start by telling me why you broke into Kelly's house?"

"You think you know what's happening here, Tom, but I'm calling to tell you that you're wrong. I'm not the enemy. Not even close."

"Funny, my friends don't spy on me from the woods."

"It wasn't me who broke into Kelly's house," Lange said. "And I'm not the one who chased her into the woods and down that ravine, either. But I know who did, why they did it, and why you're being set up to look like a kid-die porn collector."

Tom took a sharp breath, then let it out slowly. "Who is setting me up, Lange?" he asked. "What does this have to do with what happened to Kelly?"

"I can't tell you that over the phone, Tom. When you see what I have to show you, then you'll understand. And it's not what you think. You don't have the slightest clue why they think you're so dangerous."

"Who is 'they'?" Tom shouted into the phone.

"Meet me at Johnny Rockets in one hour," Lange said. "And come alone, or this time I'll vanish for good."

"Why should I trust you?"

Tom thought he heard Lange sigh into the phone. "I know you've been looking for me," Lange said. "You. Roland. That nosy attorney of yours. I stayed hidden because I was afraid of getting caught."

"Why show yourself now?"

"Because you need to see what I have," Lange said. "And I need you to protect me from them."

CHAPTER 46

Rainy and Carter ordered dinner from Monument Market. It was a credit to Monument's sandwiches, because hours earlier they'd ordered lunch there, too.

Sergeant Brendan Murphy had set them up in the Shilo Police Department's only interrogation room. From there they were able to conduct a second forensic audit on Hawkins's laptop computer. Murphy had no objection to granting the FBI access to Tom Hawkins's confiscated laptop. His only request, which had actually been relayed to the agents from the D.A. herself, was that the state be able to use whatever new evidence the FBI dug up. Rainy assured Murphy that the FBI would disclose anything new that they found. She didn't reveal that she had a secret agenda in returning to Shilo: she needed to settle her growing doubts about Tom Hawkins's guilt.

The facts of the Hawkins case more than just puzzled Rainy. She found them downright troubling. First, Lindsey Wells admitted to sending pictures of herself to Tanner Farnsworth, but not to Tom Hawkins. Why not to the man she was allegedly having an affair with? How did Hawkins end up with her pictures? She had a hard time believing Tanner Farnsworth worked for Tom Hawkins, not the way he talked about the coach—dismissively, and with evident disdain.

Lindsey wasn't the only girl from Shilo who had lied about her sexts, either. So far Rainy had interviewed six of the ten girls from Shilo's text image collection (the other four were away at college). Rainy got the girls to sign and date the back of the verification images while their parents looked on with disappointment. Though the girls admitted that the images were of them (hard to deny), none confessed to having text messaged them to anybody. Not to Tanner Farnsworth. Not to Coach Hawkins. Same as Lindsey, the girls claimed to have no idea how James Mann ended up with their naked pictures.

Something that Marvin Pressman had said stuck with Rainy as well. It was the *convenience* of it all. Here she was, hunting for James Mann's supplier, and Tom Hawkins literally fell into her lap. The chances that that was just a lucky break were about the same as someone breaking Joe DiMaggio's hitting streak.

But how would the jury see it?

Guilty, that's how. Rainy knew it and Carter did, too.

Carter spent a few hours re-creating a mirror image of Hawkins's laptop on a machine he'd brought with him, then returned the laptop to Murphy. Mindful of maintaining the integrity of the evidence, he used techniques similar to those CART employed to safeguard the machine. Carter had run through several series of advanced computer forensic tests on the mirror image. He kept searching for that single bit of exculpatory evidence that Rainy had come to believe he'd find. So far, though, they hadn't found a byte of evidence that suggested Tom Hawkins was an innocent man.

"So we've found archival evidence that shows illegal transactions going back several years," Rainy said.

"Which says to me he's been running this enterprise primarily from this machine," Carter replied.

"But why use his work computer?" Rainy said, recalling how Marvin drew her attention to that unusual choice. "That doesn't make any sense."

"I don't know, Rainy," Carter said. The tone of his voice held a tinge of exasperation.

He thinks I'm chasing shadows, Rainy thought.

"All I can tell you is that there is a lot of computer evidence to say Tom Hawkins was running a business selling images that appear to be teenage girls sexting, to interested parties all over the Internet. He used Leterg to mask the IP and MAC addresses of his clients. But we've got transaction logs that show the dates and times during which illegal images were sent out."

"And?"

"And we've matched those dates to when Mann downloaded images. The image batch Mann acquired equaled the cumulative file size of the entire Shilo text image collection found on Hawkins's computer. The exact same byte size. If it looks like a duck, quacks like a duck . . ."

"But we can't ID any other of Tom's alleged customers," Rainy said.

"Oh, it's 'alleged' now? How interesting."

"He hasn't been convicted," Rainy said defensively.

Carter gave a knowing smile, which Rainy didn't at all appreciate.

"There's not a direct IP link," Carter said. "We wouldn't have been able to link Hawkins to Mann if it wasn't for your work with Clarence Stern. But the circumstantial evidence is more than enough to prove our case. From log analysis we know that Hawkins is the distributor here. And his text image collection of forty different girls matches what we recovered off James Mann's machine. The exact same. Down to the image."

"What about the money trail? Can we trace it back to another buyer?"

Carter shook his head. "Nope. The way he moved money through his network of shell companies makes it impossible for us to get to a source. Hawkins was clever with his use of virtual servers and ghost machines. The way he cleaned his money would make any mobster jealous. He's that good."

"But think back to what Tom's lawyer said. Why would Hawkins be so reckless now if he's kept a low profile for so long?"

"Maybe he wanted to get caught," Carter offered. "Maybe he was tired. Maybe sleeping with the girl made him lazy. There are a thousand reasons to explain why he got sloppy. What's important is that there is enough evidence on this laptop to get the D.A. a conviction. A jury isn't going to care why he suddenly screwed up and turned reckless."

"But I care," Rainy said, more to herself than to Carter.

Carter was right. It didn't matter that Tom Hawkins got lazy about covering his tracks. What mattered was what the evidence against him said. This evidence screamed that Tom Hawkins was a guilty man, just as it did about James Mann.

"So what now?" Carter asked after he'd run through his final series of tests.

"I want to see that laptop," Rainy said.

"You like him, don't you?" Carter said.

"I do not."

"You do. I can tell."

"Take it back."

"Whatever," Carter said. "I take it back."

Rainy gave Carter a stern look. He didn't really mean it. That was fine. She didn't mean it, either.

Sergeant Brendan Murphy returned to the too-hot, too-small interrogation room, carrying with him the evidence against Tom Hawkins. The laptop was tucked neatly into a clear plastic evidence bag.

"You need to wear gloves," he said to Rainy.

It was out of the ordinary for any agent to work with the original evidence. Rainy would document her every move very carefully.

After donning a pair of gloves, Rainy powered up the machine. She watched the familiar Windows OS graphic go through its equally familiar boot-up sequence. She logged into the machine using the ID and password that Hawkins had used. She scanned through the folders and files. She saw where he kept the Leterg program. She opened the images of the girls that she'd first seen on James Mann's machine. She kept looking but wasn't seeing anything new or helpful.

"Rainy," Carter said, breaking a long period of silence, "I really want to go home now."

Rainy nodded slowly. She was closing the laptop screen when she suddenly and quickly pulled it open again.

"Carter," she said in barely a whisper, "our mirror image re-creates the software and operating system, right?"

"That's right," he said.

"But you can't re-create the hardware. You can't make the mirror image replicate any hardware defects, can you?"

"No. I can't do that," Carter agreed.

"Then what do you make of this?"

Rainy pointed to the computer's date and time display. Carter's eyes went wide.

The date on the computer display read January 1, 1970.

"Why is the computer's date nineteen seventy, Carter?" Rainy asked.

"It's probably an issue with the CMOS battery," Carter explained. "The complementary metal-oxide semiconductor battery located on the computer's motherboard is cheap, but when it goes bad, which they often do, it can bring even the mightiest PC to its knees."

Rainy recalled something similar happening to her machine. Several months ago her computer simply wouldn't boot up. She had brought it to Carter for help. As she later learned, the battery that acted as the controller between the computer's BIOS (Basic Input/ Output System) had failed. That failure prevented the CPU from communicating with the computer's motherboard. The result was an unsuccessful OS boot-up sequence. She was ready to junk a two-thousand-dollar machine, when all it needed was a cheap battery replacement.

"Carter, according to the logs, how long has Coach Hawkins been in the illegal image distribution business?"

"Two and half years . . . thereabout," Carter said.

"But if this battery is dead or dying, and the date of the machine is January first, nineteen seventy, shouldn't some of his transactions show a date in the nineteen seventies?"

"They should," Carter replied.

"But they don't."

Carter opened a scripting window, typed in some code, and executed the program.

"No. It looks like they don't," Carter agreed. "There are lots of files with a nineteen seventy date. I'm guessing the battery went bad almost ten months ago."

"How can you explain that, Cart?"

"You'd have to run a script to change the dates in the

transaction logs to whatever date you wanted them to read."

"Why would Tom Hawkins run a script that changes the dates of his transaction logs?"

"He wouldn't," Carter said.

"Then who would?" Rainy asked. She had been leading him along this thought trail and could see the awareness ignite in his eyes.

"Who would run that script?" Carter repeated the question. "Whoever was trying to frame Tom Hawkins, that's who."

CHAPTER 47

Tom ordered another cup of coffee from the bubbly waitress at Johnny Rockets. She poured and smiled. Tom wondered just how friendly she'd be if he took off his hat and sunglasses. Maybe she'd recognize him from the news. Probably wouldn't be so smiley if she did. The jukebox kept playing fifties-era tunes, none of which Tom recognized. He figured there was a good chance the song now playing was by a Platter or a Coaster or a Lad, but didn't bother to ask.

Tom checked his watch for the tenth time in as many minutes. Lange should have shown up by now. Tom felt a twinge of anxiety, but he had the place scoped out and his escape options planned if needed.

Tom's seat at the counter wasn't chosen at random. From his perch atop the shiny chrome stool with its red vinyl covering, Tom could see both to his left and right without any obstruction. He also could see behind him through the reflection of the stainless steel vent mounted to the ceiling and backsplash behind the open grill.

The other customers seemed harmless. He had stopped by a booth with three older gentlemen enjoying a leisurely late-night dinner. They chatted, and Tom didn't believe they posed any danger. His waitress confirmed that they were regulars. The staff didn't concern Tom, either. The two cooks and his waitress were young, fresh-faced, and fully focused on cleaning up their respective work areas to lock up for the night. The bathrooms, both for men and women, checked out fine as well. He had inspected the waste-baskets and paper towel dispensers, and lifted the toilet tanks.

The Godfather was one of Tom's all-time favorite movies.

Tom had surveyed the back of the restaurant as well, had seen the Dumpster there and a tall galvanized fence bordering the back-lot perimeter, but nothing had appeared out of the ordinary. The six cars parked out front matched the six people Tom had counted inside.

Tom sipped his black coffee and waited for Lange. It actually felt nice to get out of the house. He didn't let his thoughts sink into speculation, aware such thinking could quickly turn into a distraction. Tom needed to stay in the moment, clear-minded and hyperaware of his surround-ings. He could wait for Lange to show himself, wait to know who Lange feared, and what he believed "they" wanted.

He texted Jill and she texted back: Green.

Good luck on your test, he wrote.

Thanks! Gonna ace it! :)

Tom was ready weapons-wise as well. Still no gun, but Tom did have the knife he'd brought to the James Mann hoedown. Even though the blade was small, Tom thought it big enough to get him out of any trouble Lange might bring his way.

Tom was well aware that Lange might be using psy-chological operation tactics on him. If that was his game, he'd done it well. Lange offered only the vaguest explanation for events and hadn't provided any real information to back it up. He implied the exchange would be mutually beneficial. He insisted Tom come alone.

Deceive to achieve the objective.

These were tactics Tom knew so well, because he'd used them himself on many occasions. His involvement with Operation Imminent Thunder during The first Gulf War was now the stuff of psyops warfare legend. Imminent Thunder had been designed to deceive the Iraqi command as to the direction of the coalition's ground attack. Tom led a six-man demolition team, which had set off a series of explosive charges between the Saudi border and Ra's al Qulay'ah on the Kuwaiti coast. Six Navy SEALS and some aerial bombing were convincing enough to send several Iraqi divisions south to protect the beaches while coalition forces moved north into Kuwait.

Distract to evade the enemy.

The bell above the restaurant's front door chimed twice. Tom swiveled in his seat and saw a man enter. The face was the same one he'd seen that night in the woods.

Unmistakable.

Kip Lange.

Lange had on a pair of blue jeans and wore a black T-shirt underneath a dark blazer. Tom kept his eyes locked on Lange. He watched Lange approach, saw him take off his blazer. He carried no gun that Tom could see. Lange did a 360-spin move, presumably to show Tom that he didn't have a weapon tucked into the waistband of his jeans. Didn't mean he didn't have a weapon tucked someplace else.

Tom kept his gaze fixed firmly on Lange. Any slight move would put Lange on the defensive. Tom was ready to strike. Lange kept his hands where Tom could see them—

smart move—and sat down on the empty stool to Tom's left. Tom slipped the knife back into his boot.

"You can search me," Lange said. "I'm unarmed."

Tom checked Lange's ankles and turned the stool to see his back again. Clean enough for now.

The waitress came right over. "Sorry, sweetie," she said, "but we're closing for the night."

"No problem," Lange said. "We're heading out, anyway."

"Oh? Where are we going?" asked Tom.

Lange slapped his right hand onto the counter, palm facing down. He lifted his hand slowly, revealing to Tom a small plastic flash drive, the kind that stored digital computer files.

"What's that?" asked Tom.

"That's what they're after," Lange said. "And it's what you need to see."

"Tell me about it."

Lange shook his head and pushed the flash drive over to Tom. "Not here. We need to move."

Tom scooped up the flash drive and dropped it into his jacket pocket. He waited for Lange to stand. Lange motioned with his head for Tom to lead the way.

"After you," Tom said, pointing his outstretched arm toward the front door.

Tom dropped a ten on the counter. He followed Lange to the door, keeping a safe distance behind. Tom took a glance outside the restaurant's front windows. He saw no detectable threats in the parking lot. Still, Tom maintained his careful watch over Lange.

Lange reached the parking lot and headed straight for a beige four-door Chevy Impala with New Hampshire plates. That car hadn't been parked there before. Tom descended the restaurant's concrete front steps at a relaxed pace. The night air blew a cool, refreshing breeze, but for some reason Tom couldn't stop sweating.

Funny, I'm not nervous.

Lange climbed into his Impala and reached across to open the passenger-side door. He motioned for Tom to get in as well. Tom knew he shouldn't have let Lange put his hands where he couldn't see them. *Why didn't I react sooner?* he wondered. Tom took a few cautious steps but stopped several feet shy of Lange's vehicle. He was thinking it might be time to get his knife out again. "I'm not going anywhere with you," he said. "We talk here and now."

Lange got out of his car and approached Tom with his hands showing, fingers spread wide, and no weapons to be seen. Lange stopped within Tom's striking distance. "Okay," he said.

"What's on the flash drive you gave me?" Tom asked.

"Nothing," Lange said.

"What?" Tom put his hands to his temples. He felt light-headed.

"I said there's nothing on that flash drive. I bought it at Staples right before I came over here. I can show you the receipt."

Tom felt a buzzing in his head. The humlike vibration covered his entire scalp and seemed to seep underneath his skin. The tingling intensified. His vision didn't seem all that clear, either.

"How are you feeling, Tom?"

Tom's knees buckled beneath him, and Lange moved in quickly to keep him upright. Tom's limbs felt loose and rubbery. Lange, with his arm draped around Tom, walked him over to the Impala. Tom felt too weak to resist. His tongue swelled inside his mouth, choking off the airway.

"What did you do to me?" Tom demanded to know.

Only, his speech came out thick, garbled, and barely intelligible to himself.

Lange shoved Tom into his car. "I haven't done anything to you," he said. "Yet."

Tom heard the car door slam. His vision continued to blur and kept on blurring, too, until it went completely dark.

CHAPTER 48

Lindsey sat cross-legged on her bed and glared at her new cell phone. She pushed some buttons on the phone's keyboard, heard some beeps, but frowned at the display. Jill sat on the bed behind Lindsey and laughed when her friend shook the phone.

"It's not an Etch A Sketch," Jill said.

"I don't want to have to learn military time," Lindsey snarled. "I want this stupid thing to display hours and minutes like a normal phone."

Jill giggled at her friend's frustration.

"Don't just laugh at me," Lindsey said. "Help me fix the stupid thing."

"And then can we get back to studying for our test?"

Jill pushed a few keys and seconds later had the phone's display the way Lindsey had wanted it. Jill showed Lindsey her repair job.

"You always were a smart one," Lindsey said. She took the phone from Jill and, with a flick of her wrist, launched it into the air. The phone traveled across the room and landed harmlessly on top of a jumbled pile of clothes that Lindsey had left on the floor. Lindsey flopped down on her bed, and Jill did the same. The girls looked up at a poster of Dartmouth College, which Lindsey had tacked to her bedroom ceiling.

"Do you think you'll go there?" Jill asked.

Lindsey kept her eyes fixed on the poster and didn't turn her head to look at Jill. "I don't know," Lindsey said. "I'd like to. Remember that guy who came to speak to our class about colleges? He had tape on his glasses."

Jill laughed and pulled herself up to a seated position. She turned her head to look down at Lindsey, who was still lying on her back. "Yeah. Like from eighth grade. So?"

"So, that's the reason I've had this poster hanging here for—oh, I don't know. Since then, I guess. That guy said that something like eighty percent of the kids who hang up the poster of where they want to go college end up going to that school."

Jill nodded. "Yeah, I think I remember hearing him saying that."

"My father wants me to go there," Lindsey said. "Doubt I can get a soccer scholarship now. I doubt I'll be able to get in anyplace with this nightmare following me around."

Jill had been gazing up at the poster with a look of hope on her face. In a second, that hopeful look turned into one of despair.

"Want to see what one of the witches texted me?" Jill asked.

Lindsey nodded. Jill handed Lindsey her cell phone. Lindsey read the messages and covered her mouth to show her disgust.

"Did you let Principal Osborne read these? They could get expelled for that."

"Are you kidding? No. Best way to handle the witches is to ignore them. It'll blow over."

"Well, why do you think I got a new cell phone?" Lindsey said. "Too many nasty text messages. No more Facebook for me, either. People were posting the most horrible things."

"They're all just a bunch of bitches," Jill said.

"Big, bitchy witches," Lindsey agreed.

The girls shared a laugh. Then the mood turned serious again.

"Jill, I'm glad that you believe me," Lindsey said. "I'm glad you don't think I did what they're saying."

"That FBI lady convinced me. Now I know that it's possible to make it look like you had," said Jill.

"Who do you think sent around those Facebook friend requests?"

"You mean, Fidelius Charm? Who knows. But I bet it's the same person who wrote the blog posts."

"Has it been weird not living at home?" Lindsey asked.

Jill shrugged. "It's been fun living with Flo and Irena, I guess. They've been cool to me. But I miss my home. I miss my bed. I'm thinking about going back there. I mean, what if my dad's been set up, too? I know I've told you, like, a million times all the things my mom said about him, but I never got creepy, evil vibes from him. I mean, child pornography? That's so sick."

"But why are they setting me up?" Lindsey asked. "Who are they trying to ruin—me or him?"

Jill glanced down at her fingernails and began to nervously chip away at the red polish there. "You know how I've been hanging around with Mitchell Boyd?" Jill said. Lindsey shot Jill a look that said, "I'm your best friend, stupid," as she pushed herself up and off the bed. "I'm wondering if Mitchell is somehow involved."

Lindsey whirled around to look at Jill. "Why would you think that?"

"I don't know," Jill said. "He started acting nice to me right after my dad got in trouble. And then my dad had that major freak-out at the Spot. He told me that he and Mr. Boyd had some sort of falling-out and that I wasn't allowed to see Mitchell anymore."

"What do you think it could be?" said Lindsey.

"I dunno," Jill said.

"You think Mitchell is somehow helping out his father?"

Jill thought a moment and nodded. "I mean, Mitchell's dad is unbelievably rich, but Mitchell is always complaining his father won't give him anything. He says he has to earn it, because that's what his dad did. Maybe Mitchell's dad is paying him, and that's how Mitchell got that Mustang. Everybody's been wondering where he came up with the cash for the car."

"Mitchell's not that smart with computers. Is he?"

"I've been to his computer room before," Jill said. "He's got, like, three computers in there. A bunch of monitors, too. He definitely knows something."

Lindsey curled her upper lip in a snarl. "You think Mitchell got paid by his dad to set up your father?" Lindsey said. Jill thought about it and nodded again. Lindsey said, "Why would he pick me? He hardly knows me."

"I don't know, Lin. I'm just thinking, that's all." Jill noticed Lindsey's expression darken. "What? What is it?" she asked.

"I haven't been completely honest with you," Lindsey said.

Jill's body tensed, and Lindsey sat back down on the bed beside her.

Lindsey told Jill about how she'd met Agent Rainy Miles before the student assembly. How the FBI had come to her house with pictures that Lindsey had taken with her cell phone camera. Naked pictures of herself that she'd sent to Tanner Farnsworth.

When Lindsey finished, Jill threw her hands into the air and shouted, "Why are you telling me this now?"

"Because I was embarrassed," Lindsey said.

Jill looked at Lindsey in a way that reassured her. She more than understood.

"I didn't want anybody to know," Lindsey added, then shook her head, disgusted with herself. "After you left Principal Osborne's office, I told the FBI agent the truth. I told her that I'd sent the pictures to Tanner. Maybe Tanner showed them to Mitchell. They've been friends since grade school. Maybe . . . I don't know, maybe, somehow that's why Mitchell picked me."

Jill got up from the bed, crossed the room, and sat herself down on the corner of Lindsey's desk. Jill looked her friend in the eyes. "Mitchell texted me. He said he's bummed we're not hanging out anymore. He invited me to come over to his house tomorrow night," Jill said.

"So?"

"So, if I'm alone in Mitchell's bedroom, where Mitchell keeps his computers, maybe there's a way I can find out."

CHAPTER 49

Tom could feel the ground beneath him. His fingers dug at the dirt. Grass tickled his face. Jagged rocks pressed uncomfortably against his legs and arms. Tom thought he'd opened his eyes, but still couldn't see. That was when he knew he'd been blindfolded. He listened for any recognizable sounds. But the only noise was a steady buzz that could have been insects or just his own drugged mind.

The ground beneath him seemed to be spinning. Each revolution came faster, turned tighter. He tried to swallow but gagged instead. His mouth had gone completely dry, beyond anything he imagined possible, as if every drop of moisture was being sucked up by an invisible sponge.

Someone pulled on his shirt. He felt himself dragged across the rocky ground and slammed up against the side of a car. He sat slumped on the ground, the car keeping him upright.

"Where are my drugs?"

Tom recognized the voice. His monotonous speech and raspy tenor were unmistakable.

Lange.

Tom labored to work his jaw, mouth, and swollen

tongue to form his words. "What . . . drugs?" he managed to say.

"Not the ones I gave you, dumb ass," Lange said to him. "You know what drugs I'm talking about. Look, Tom, you're helpless out here. Don't make this harder than it needs to be."

Tom heard a car approach and could tell by the sound of its tires that it had pulled to a stop close by.

Someone else is here.

Tom heard a car door open, then slam shut. He heard heavy footsteps crunching across the ground. He struggled to stand, but rough hands pushed him back down.

"Is he talking yet?" Tom heard a man say. He thought he knew that voice. Deeper than Lange's. Gruff. But from where?

"Not yet," Lange said.

"Tie his hands," said the other man.

"Why? This guy is drugged out of his gourd."

"No unnecessary chances. Remember?"

"Well, I can't really see out here."

"I'll turn on his headlights."

Moments later, Tom felt himself being thrown to the ground. He was again facedown in the dirt. Somebody wrenched his arms behind his back. The drugs made it impossible to resist. The rope wrapped around his wrists several times. Tom could tell it was made from nylon. He pushed against the rope as it was being secured, enough to hold his wrists slightly apart. It wasn't a conscious act, so much as a reflex, his training kicking in, even though his thoughts were far from lucid. The spacing Tom created was slight, hardly enough for his captors to have noticed. They pushed him back up against the car.

"I'm going to ask you again," Lange said. "And then we're going to hurt you. Where. Are. My. Drugs?"

"What drugs?"

Tom couldn't see the punch coming. He made no move to avoid it. A nanosecond passed between the moment Tom knew he'd been hit in the face and the first eye-stabbing jolt of pain. He felt his skin tear and knew the wetness dripping down his cheek was blood.

"Douche bag, I asked you a question. Where are my drugs? Where did you hide them?"

"Destroyed them . . . burned them up."

"Bad answer," Lange said.

The second blow struck Tom on the face, in the exact same spot as before. The pain doubled in intensity. Oddly enough, it gave Tom a little spark of awareness. He felt a tick or two stronger. He worked discreetly to loosen the rope binding his wrists and tried to conceal his panic when it seemed the space he had created might not be large enough. Tom knew he needed to buy himself more time. Lange and Mr. Mighty Punch had no intention of letting Tom live, even if he gave up the drugs' hidden location.

"Can't talk," Tom croaked out. "Need water. Mouth too dry."

"That's a normal side effect of the drug," Tom heard Lange say. "Get him something to drink."

"He's got water in his car."

Tom heard footsteps crunching over dirt. Tom kept twisting his wrists, trying to work the rope free. He had more mobility than before.

"I can't kill you," Lange said to him. "I don't want to hurt you to the point where you can't talk, either. No use putting you in the hospital. So let me tell you what's about to happen. Are you listening?"

Tom turned his head in Lange's direction. "I'm sorry. . . . Were you talking to me?"

Lange laughed.

"Cute. Keep up the humor. You're going to need it when I tell you that I'm about to leave you with my friend here and go get your daughter. She's over at Lindsey's house. Right? Studying for a chem test in the morning."

Tom struggled again to free himself. He felt the rope starting to give. The buzzing in his head grew louder, like static from the radio blasting in both his ears.

"I'll tell you. . . . I'll tell you. . . ."

"Good."

"Just need water."

Tom heard footsteps returning. Strong fingers pressed against his skull and pulled his head backward. Tom could smell the sour breath of whoever bent down to give him a drink. A plastic bottle touched against his mouth. Tom's tongue slid out from between his cracked lips. Tom pushed his head away.

"What is it?" asked Tom.

"Water. Drink up," the gruff-sounding man said.

Tom had wanted him to speak. Unable to see his target, Tom needed a sound cue to pinpoint his strike area. The man's displeasing breath helped him lock on a target even more. With his wrists now free from the restraints, Tom swung his arms out from behind his back, hoping that he guessed the right level to grab hold of the man's head.

Tom felt his hands grip a thick, round head.

Pay dirt.

Tom didn't hesitate. *The first rule of an attack is to keep on attacking.*

Tom squeezed the man's ears hard, as if they were a horse's reins. He snapped his head forward, using the hairline area of his forehead as the striking surface. He aimed where he envisioned the man's nose to be, heard a satisfying crunch, and felt the cartilage give way. The man didn't scream, but Tom heard him fall.

Next, Tom ripped the blindfold from his eyes. His vision blurred by drugs and not yet adjusted to the light, he could see only Lange's silhouette closing in fast. Maybe he was reaching for a gun, but Tom couldn't tell. Falling to the ground, Tom slithered his body underneath the car and emerged on the other side. He used the car's door handle for leverage to stand but still stumbled getting back to his feet. Tom noticed bright headlights to his right. They were shining on him.

He remembered they had used a car's headlamp to illuminate his wrists when they bound them. The driver-side door looked open. Tom staggered toward the car. A gunshot rang out, but Tom didn't turn to see what direction it came from. Instead, he jumped into the car, fumbled for the ignition, found the key, and fired up the engine.

Tom pressed down on the gas, and the car lunged forward, wheels bouncing into potholes and over rocks. He made four quick observations. First, they'd brought him to a clearing in the woods. He could see trees all around him. Second, there didn't appear to be any other roads around, so the way in must also be the way out. Third, he'd actually taken his own car in the escape. He was driving the Taurus. Lange must have brought him to the clearing in the Impala, and the other guy had driven his car to the rendezvous spot. Maybe they were going to ditch the Taurus after Tom told them what they wanted to know.

The fourth observation was the only one that really mattered.

Lange was driving right behind him.

Glaring white lights from Lange's Impala made it difficult for Tom to see the road ahead. A powerful jolt jarred his whole body. Lange had slammed Tom's car from behind.

Here we go. Ford versus Chevy, thought Tom.

His heart raced and sputtered. His skin felt afire, but scratching didn't abate the sensation. He wondered how long the drug would stay in his system. Lange bumped his car again. Tom kept driving, decelerating when he thought he saw traffic moving up ahead. He glanced down at the speedometer. Couldn't read a single number.

The dirt road seemed to be ending. Tom jerked the steering wheel hard right and skidded onto a paved road. He heard Lange's tires screech against the same asphalt not more than a hundred feet behind him.

The red taillights from the cars up ahead blurred together to form a single long and wavy neon light that danced before Tom's eyes. Tom found his way into the center lane of a wide three-lane road. Cars were on every side of him. He could no longer see the road's white-painted dividing lines. He didn't know Lange was behind him until he felt another bump, this one hard enough to snap his head forward. The Taurus fishtailed several times, but Tom managed to straighten it out.

Tom pulled his car hard to the right. Glass broke and metal crunched as he plowed into the side of a car he didn't see traveling beside him at the same rate of speed. The Taurus's side mirror snapped free with a loud crack. Tom's body shook violently from side to side, and he heard tires screeching and car horns blasting at him from all directions. He looked left and saw that Lange had pulled parallel to him in the adjacent lane. Tom jerked the steering wheel hard to the left and applied just enough brake to keep the Taurus from spinning 180 degrees around.

Sweat poured out his body and soaked his loose-fitting

T-shirt. It stung at his eyes, making his already impaired vision even worse.

"Are you buckled?" Tom said aloud. He kept the pressure on the accelerator at a constant, while his hands held the steering wheel on a straight-ahead course. What little vision he had left went completely dark. Tom felt his eyelids begin to descend, as if lead weights were pulling them closed. His mouth had gone even drier, if that were possible. He didn't know if he could hold his head up any longer. He just needed to sleep . . . to close his eyes . . . for just a moment.

Wake up! Wake up!

Tom came to. His internal voice had been screaming at him. His vision returned slightly, just enough for him to see a ball of red light coming toward him. As it neared, the ball grew from a barely visible speck to a blinding red glow. He could see other balls of red. *Cars,* Tom managed to think. *Stopped at a traffic light. No time to brake.*

Tom turned the wheel and punched the gas pedal to the floor. The car lurched forward with a force that made his stomach drop and his body go tense. He felt a violent jolt, and his whole body shook when Lange's car slammed into the side of the Taurus. Their cars locked together.

Tom bit his tongue until blood began to seep into his mouth. The shock was just enough to counter the drugs. His vision cleared slightly. He was in the center lane, with Lange's car pressed up against his door.

Tom saw the opening he needed.

He saw a light post, too.

His escape.

He jerked the wheel and broke away from Lange's car. He pushed against the gas pedal as far as it would go. He kept the car on a diagonal trajectory as it rocketed forward. Lange pursued Tom from behind.

Tom threaded the Taurus between two cars and, having seen the light post through the gap, spun the wheel to avoid a direct hit. He counted on Lange not having seen what he maneuvered to avoid. The side of Tom's car scraped against a light post cemented into the sidewalk. He glanced over his left shoulder, just in time to see Lange's vehicle slam into that very same post without slowing. Lange's car folded in on itself as the stone post crushed metal and glass.

Tom's car hadn't stopped moving, as he hoped it would. Instead, it listed hard to its side, two wheels lifting off the ground. Then it flipped over onto its roof. The car began to slide down an embankment. Tom was knocked unconscious. Otherwise, he would have been screaming.

CHAPTER 50

"Tom . . . Tom, can you hear me?"

Tom blinked. The darkness receded. In its place came a flood of light so intense that it forced his eyes shut again.

"Tom . . . try one more time. Try to open your eyes."

Tom blinked again and kept blinking, because each flash of light hurt too much to keep the lids open.

"Good. You're doing great," the voice said.

Tom continued to blink until he opened his eyes wide. The first thing he saw was a face staring down at him. His vision was blurry, but the face was clearly a man's, though Tom didn't recognize him. He tried to lift his head, but the pain exploding from someplace behind his eyes was nothing short of extraordinary. He grunted and fell back onto a soft pillow.

"Don't try to do too much at once," the man said. "I'm Dr. Paul Prince. You've been in a bad accident. You're in the hospital. Do you remember anything about that?"

Tom let his mind relax so that he could process the man's words.

A doctor. An accident. A hospital.

Tom's throat felt parched, but he wanted to speak. "No. I don't."

"Well, that's not uncommon from a patient coming out of a coma," the doctor said.

He tried to move his right hand to scratch his cheek. His hand moved only two inches toward his face. He heard the sound of metal scraping against metal, and his hand jerked to a sudden stop. He looked down and saw a handcuff secured around his right wrist. The other end was locked around the bed railing.

"What the hell? What's going on?" Tom's strength returned with an intense rush of anger. He managed to work himself into a seated position, though it took some maneuvering of the handcuff and a little help from Dr. Prince. "I demand an explanation," Tom said, though he was breathless because it hurt that much to move.

Before Dr. Prince could answer, the door to Tom's hospital room flew open and Marvin Pressman came storming in. He clutched a piece of paper in his left hand.

"Get the police in here right now, and get this man unlocked," Marvin barked at the doctor. Prince didn't budge or respond. Marvin didn't back down. "Do it now, or I swear I'll have the Joint Commission here tomorrow for a surprise hospital inspection, and trust me when I say you won't like what they'll find."

Dr. Prince gave Marvin an angry look. "It's my understanding that this man is in violation of his bail and that he poses a flight risk. That's what the police told us."

"And exactly what violation are you referring to, Doctor?" Marvin growled back.

"Driving under the influence."

Marvin fluttered the piece of paper in front of Prince's face in a taunting way. "Well, I have a medical power of attorney for Mr. Hawkins. His toxicology report from your lab just came in. Guess what it showed?"

"I haven't a clue," Dr. Prince replied in a calm, low voice.

"Marvin, where's Jill? Is she here?" Tom asked.

Marvin placed a hand on Tom's shoulder. He looked down at his client and said, "Yes, but hang on a second, Tom. Let me get this straightened out first. The toxicology report shows enough scopolamine in his system to knock out an elephant, that's what."

Tom shook his head, because he'd never heard of the drug before. "What the hell is scopol—whatever you said?"

"It's a colorless, odorless, tasteless drug used to treat motion sickness and Parkinson's disease."

"Why would I be given that?" asked Tom.

"It's also used by criminals to commit robbery and date rape, not to mention prisoner interrogations. It zaps your memory, along with a lot of other functions," Marvin explained. "If you think my client intentionally ingested this narcotic, get ready for that inspection I promised you."

Prince was visibly flustered. Red splotches on his face showed his anger. "The officer in charge of Mr. Hawkins's case told me to call him the moment he awoke. I'll do so right now. Though we do have a key, in case of a medical emergency."

"Then I suggest that you go and get it. Now, Doctor." Marvin's smile to Prince was really just a reminder of his threat.

Prince, in turn, called for a nurse to come check Tom's vitals. He left the room with a snort of disgust.

"I'm guessing the last name of that officer in charge is Murphy," Tom said.

"And you'd be right," Marvin said. He added, "I can get Murphy's badge for what he did to you here. But it's not worth the fight right now. We need to keep our focus on your trial."

"What the hell happened to me?"

"Well, I'm not a doctor," Marvin said as he flipped through a series of charts and reports attached to a clipboard at the foot of Tom's bed. "From what I'm reading here, I'd say you've suffered a grade-three concussion and apparently came within inches of never walking again. Just a little something."

Marvin grabbed a chair and came around to the side of the bed. He sat down and got himself eye level with Tom. The concern shown on Marvin's face told Tom that his lawyer considered him a friend, too.

"You think I was drugged?"

"I think that somebody couldn't wait for your trial to punish you," Marvin said matter-of-factly. Marvin glanced at the toxicology report in his hand. He turned on a floor lamp to help him read the file. Tom winced in pain and groaned as soon as the light came on.

"Sorry, buddy," Marvin said. He switched off the lamp. "I'm not up on all the concussion symptoms. I guess that sensitivity to light is one of them." Marvin pushed himself up and out of his chair with a grunt. He crossed the room and stepped over to a window that was letting in a good deal of sunlight.

Tom followed Marvin with his eyes. He noticed a cup with a straw on a nearby tray. He leaned over, desperate to quench a desertlike thirst, but his handcuffs kept the drink just out of reach. Marvin lowered the window shade and handed Tom the cup.

"Thanks for the drink," Tom said after a long sip. "How long have I been in the hospital?" he asked.

Marvin glanced at his watch. "The accident happened last night. It's noon now. A bit shy of twelve hours, I'd say."

"Look, Marvin . . . I don't remember anything," Tom said, as if it were a secret.

Marvin returned a telling look. "Two cars were involved in the accident. Witnesses are saying it was road rage on the part of the other driver. That driver died of his injuries. Tom, it was Kip Lange."

CHAPTER 51

Tom let out a long, deep breath. "Lange's dead," he said in a voice that didn't disguise his relief.

"What happened to you out there, Tom?"

Tom told Marvin all he could remember—about the phone call from Lange, about scouting Johnny Rockets for a possible ambush, about meeting Lange—but after that, his memories vanished.

"How do you think you got drugged?" asked Marvin.

"I don't know," Tom said. "The coffee, maybe. That's all I drank."

"But you didn't see Lange slip anything into your drink."

"No," Tom said. "I doubt it was any of the waitstaff. But I can't be sure. Maybe there was a manager on duty, someone I didn't see."

Marvin leaned in close and seemed to study Tom's face. "That's a nasty injury you've got there," he said. "Have you seen it?"

"What? No beauty pageants in my future?"

Marvin scrutinized the injury even more intently. "Doesn't look like it could have come from a car accident," he said, with his eye inches from Tom's face. "There's a pattern to it, too. It looks like . . . like a star. Do you remember being hit in the face? Punched?"

Tom couldn't easily shake his head to tell Marvin no.

"Something about it . . . Do you mind if I snap a picture?"

Tom forced a weak smile. "Don't post it to Facebook," he said.

Marvin chuckled and snapped a few pictures with his cell phone. He put his phone away, then picked up Tom's, which had been resting atop the dresser by the hospital bed.

"I've got most of the stuff police recovered from your car in a cardboard box at my office. But I figured you'd want to have your phone by the bed."

"Yeah, Lange might be calling to cut a deal," said Tom.

"Not unless you believe in ghosts. They found more of Lange on the light post than they did inside his car."

"Is it going to be harder to prove Lange was the one framing me now that he's dead?" asked Tom.

"We don't know for sure that it even was Lange," Marvin said. "For all we know, it could have been Murphy working outside the law to make his case against you, or a disgruntled player, a parent even."

"You don't really believe that. Do you?" Tom said. "The motive just isn't there. Lange's the only one with a real reason to frame me. He wanted what he thought I had. It's obvious."

"We're going to go after any and all witnesses connected to Lange," Marvin said, trying to sound reassuring. "I'm turning my investigators loose as we speak. Rest assured, I won't leave a single stone unturned."

"That's the way we're going to beat this rap," Tom said. "I'm sure of it."

"Hope you're right, buddy," Marvin said. "But something isn't adding up for me."

"What isn't?"

"Lange never made one real extortion attempt. And whoever did this frame job knows his computer chops. I mean, really knows what he's doing. Computer skills classes in prison are good, but they're not that good."

"What are you thinking?"

"I'm thinking we might not be out of the woods yet. Not by a long shot."

Tom took another long sip of water and was about to respond to what Marvin had said when his hospital room door opened slowly. A head poked into the room. It took Tom a moment to realize that it was Jill. His face brightened.

"Is it okay to come in?" Jill asked Marvin.

Marvin nodded his head in Tom's direction. "He looks happy to see you," the lawyer replied.

"I am happy," Tom said. "Come give your old man a hug." Tom lifted his arms to accept an embrace but forgot about his handcuffed wrist. The metal scraped loudly against the bed frame. Jill took a few steps backward, as if she'd been pushed.

"Get that doctor in here, and get these handcuffs off me. Will you, Marvin?" Tom asked. He managed to keep his voice calm despite his embarrassment.

"On it. Excuse me, Jill." Marvin shot Tom an apologetic look and left the room to go find Prince.

Tom shrugged and hoisted his chained wrist again. "I'm sorry you have to see me like this, Jill," Tom said. "I'm just glad that you're here." Jill kept her distance, but Tom managed to coax her forward a few feet with his unencumbered arm. When he pointed to the chair by his bedside, Jill sat down.

"You look okay," Jill said. "I mean, considering what could have happened."

Tom smiled at her. "Yeah, I'm tough. But I'm worried about you. Are you okay?"

Jill broke away from her father's gaze and began to search for anything else that she could focus on. "I'm fine," she said in a quiet voice.

Tom couldn't help but marvel at his daughter. She looked so beautiful to him, grown up and capable. He wanted to tell her that he loved her. He wanted her to know that he'd always be there for her. He didn't want her to leave the room, however, so he kept those thoughts to himself. They were together, and though neither spoke for several minutes, for Tom it was the best medicine he could receive.

Jill took a quick visual inventory of all the equipment connected to her father: heart monitors, IV drips, and such. "When do you get out of here?" she asked.

"I don't know. I feel okay. Hopefully soon. How'd that chem test go?"

"My teacher is going to let me take it tomorrow, because of what happened to you and all. In truth I could use the extra study time."

"Happy to help," Tom said.

Though it hurt Tom to laugh, he couldn't resist a chuckle, and neither could Jill.

"Hey, I forgot to ask you about Manadnock. How'd the team do?"

"We beat 'em two–zip. So that was cool."

"Yeah? Did you play well?"

"I dunno. I did all right, I guess."

"Come on. Don't be modest. Did you rock the pitch or not?"

Jill smiled. "Yeah, I rocked it pretty good," she admitted.

Tom balled his left hand into a fist and raised it up. Jill gave him a fist bump without his having to ask.

"I knew you would."

"Does it hurt bad?" Jill asked. "It looks like it hurts."

"It's not too bad," he said. "I guess I was pretty lucky."

"Yeah . . . well, you're a lot luckier than Mom."

"I'm so sorry, Jill," Tom said. "I wasn't thinking about the memories this would bring up for you."

Jill let out a sigh of exasperation as she stood up from her chair. "I don't think of Mom as a memory. They can't be memories when I think about her all the time."

Tom took hold of Jill's hand, but she recoiled from his touch. "Jill, wait. What I mean—"

"I know what you mean. It's fine. Honest. Look, I gotta run. We have a game this afternoon. The team already left. Lindsey's mom is waiting downstairs to drive me there."

"I'm really glad you two are talking again."

"Yeah," Jill said.

"Does that mean you're willing to believe me?"

"I think so. Look, I had to change my cell phone number." Jill took out a piece of paper and wrote down the number. Tom gave Jill a skeptical look. "I knew the code the wireless company needed to make changes to our family plan," Jill explained, unprompted. "If you need me for anything while I'm at the game, just call or text."

She put the paper on Tom's nightstand.

"Why don't you call me right now?" Tom suggested. "That way I'll have the number in my phone. We still have to do our check-ins, you know. Just because I'm hand-cuffed to a hospital bed doesn't mean the same safety rules don't apply."

Tom didn't mention that a giant weight had been lifted

from his shoulders with Lange's death. He didn't want his daughter relaxing her vigilance.

Jill dialed, and Tom heard his phone chirp.

"I'm glad you're going to be okay," Jill said. "I'm going to study after the game. But I'll come early, before school, so we can hang out longer. Okay?"

Tom nodded and squinted his eyes to hide his tears. "Okay. Thanks for being here, Jill."

"No problem."

Jill made it halfway to the door but stopped when Tom called her name. Jill turned.

"Will you come home when I get out of here?" Tom asked her. "This is going to turn out to be a big misunderstanding. You'll see. I promise you that."

Jill looked down at her feet, and her hands slipped defensively into the pockets of her blue hooded Shilo Wildcats sweatshirt. "Yeah, I think so," Jill said.

Tom nodded and smiled at her. He could tell that she had more to say about his situation and their future as a family. He couldn't blame her for avoiding the conflict.

"Bye, baby," Tom said in whispered voice. Jill smiled back at him weakly and waved. Marvin entered the room just as Jill was leaving. The two exchanged a pleasant good-bye, and Marvin crossed to Tom's bedside.

"I told Prince to give you two a few minutes alone. That's why you're still locked up and nobody's been in to check on your vitals. In case you were wondering."

"Thanks, Marvin."

"I'm all about client satisfaction. Mine's a referral business, you know."

Tom grinned, but his expression darkened. "Marvin, I need you to do me a favor."

"Ask and ye shall receive."

"Can you have the PI pals of yours keep an eye on Jill until I'm out of here? Just to make sure she keeps safe. You can add it to my tab."

"Consider it done and gratis. These guys owe me some hours for all the business I've sent their way. I'll write off what they don't cover."

"Nice. Never thought I'd be somebody's charitable contribution."

"You're in very good company—American Red Cross, Save the Children . . ."

Marvin stopped talking, and his expression changed abruptly, making Tom just a little bit concerned. Again, Marvin leaned in close to get a better look at Tom's face.

"Ten cc's of morphine for your thoughts," Tom said.

"It's that injury to your face," Marvin said. "It's still bugging me."

"Why?"

"It looks like you were hit by somebody wearing a ring," Marvin said.

"So?"

"So, the imprint looks familiar to me. I can't figure out why. So while Jill was here, I snuck down to the ER to see if I could make nice with any of the EMTs who were on the scene of the accident. Found one, too. He was pretty sure Lange wasn't wearing any rings when they pried him off that post."

"What are you getting at, Marvin?"

"What I'm getting at is that maybe, just maybe, Lange wasn't working alone."

CHAPTER 52

Mitchell held Jill's hand. He led her through an open doorway and into an immaculate kitchen with granite counters, a wide tiled floor, and gleaming stainless steel appliances. There wasn't a speck of dirt to be seen, and Jill wondered if any meals had ever been prepared there.

Mitchell went straight for the refrigerator. He leaned down low and inserted enough of his body inside the appliance that Jill thought he might disappear entirely. He emerged holding two cans of Coke. He tossed one of the cans over to Jill.

"Surprised you're not offering Jill a beer," Roland said with a devilish grin.

Mitchell shrugged. "Do you want one?" he asked her.

Jill shook her head but couldn't relax enough to respond verbally.

Mitchell popped the top of his soda can and took a long drink. "Where's Mom?" he asked.

"Out with friends. And I have work to do, so I'd appreciate it if you two keep the music below jet engine decibels."

The three exited the kitchen together and passed into a

long hallway so richly decorated that Jill felt nervous she'd soil the plush oriental carpeting or bump into some priceless artifact displayed on the many antique tables. They emerged into a majestic foyer dominated by a corkscrew staircase with pearly white banisters. Roland passed by Jill and stopped at the foot of the staircase, where he called out Mitchell's name. Mitchell turned to face his father.

"Mitchell, remember you said you were going to help me get the wireless printer working," Roland said. "I need to print out something for work."

"Can't it wait?" said Mitchell.

"Not really," Roland said.

Mitchell, ignoring his father's request, called for Jill, who bounded up the stairs after him. Jill's stomach remained knotted. The evening stress began when she snuck out the back of Lindsey's house to ditch the private investigators who were staked out front. She knew they worked for Marvin. Lindsey and Jill brought them home-baked cookies.

Mitchell had his mobile phone out and was texting as he walked. Jill followed him down a long corridor. They passed by several closed doors on each side. The hallway felt like a gallery, with paintings on both walls. She noticed the one and only family portrait, a large photograph set in an ornate gilded frame. She found it disturbing that nobody in that portrait was smiling. Next to the portrait, Jill knew, was a photograph of Mitchell's dead brother, Stephen.

They never talked about Stephen.

The hallway ended at the door to Mitchell's room. He opened his door with his head down and eyes fixed on his texting. He expected Jill to follow him into his room, which she did.

Mitchell slipped his phone back into his pants pocket and turned on the overhead light. With the shades pulled low and the room's navy-painted walls and gray carpeting, his was easily the darkest room in the house. The room featured all the trappings Jill expected in a boy's room. The first time she'd set foot in his room, Jill felt a tinge of envy that his sleeping quarters were easily triple the size of her own. Posters of popular TV shows, rappers, and various pop culture paraphernalia were affixed to the walls in a haphazard manner. Clothes were more out than in his dresser drawers. Piles of pants, shirts, and shoes kept a closet door from shutting closed.

"Hey, did you see that YouTube video of the baby dancing to Gaga?" Jill asked. "It's hilarious!"

"No. Show me," Mitchell said while crossing the room.

He opened another door, which led into an oversized alcove. There were six computer monitors and three computers crammed into the tiny space. It looked more like an office than a high school student's study area. The desk, papers, printers, fax machine, and filing cabinet were all lit by the monitors' eerie glow.

Jill felt a surge of excitement. She'd made it this far—inside Mitchell's computer room. But just as quickly, her spirits sank. If there was a connection between Mitchell, Lindsey, and her father, finding it amid so much machinery would be like scoring a goal blindfolded.

She thought hard about what to do next and absent-mindedly crushed the aluminum sides of her Coke can. Hearing the metallic crinkling sound, Mitchell glanced over his shoulder—and Jill got an idea.

Jill set the now wobbly, lopsided can on a table, near Mitchell's laptop computers. He didn't seem to notice. Instead, he flicked his mouse and activated a bunch of computer screens. He began to check different things on different screens. Something was interesting enough that he opened an e-mail message and typed a quick reply. When he returned his attention to Jill, he left his computers unlocked and available for her to use.

"Why do you have so many computers?" Jill asked. She had her hand perched near the wobbly can of soda.

"Work. Stuff," Mitchell said. "Anyway, that baby rap thing can wait, but this can't."

Mitchell grabbed hold of Jill's waist and pulled her toward him. He kissed her on the lips as he ground into her.

Jill could feel him becoming aroused, and she didn't want things between them to progress. With a flick of her fingers she sent the Coke can tumbling over. Brown liquid spilled out from the open top and pooled dangerously close to Mitchell's electronics.

"Shit," he breathed. He bent down and picked a rumpled shirt off the floor to use as a towel. "Mom will get the stain out," he said.

"Oh, I kind of wanted that Coke. Could you grab me another one?" Jill kissed him, hoping that would seal the deal.

Mitchell shrugged. "Yeah, back in a minute. Might as well help my dad with the wireless printer while I'm down there. Won't take long." He used the shirt as a dam and left the can where it had toppled over.

"Can I check my Facebook while you're gone?"

"Sure."

Mitchell fired up a Web browser for Jill to use. Jill followed Mitchell to the entrance to his computer room.

"Back in a bit," Mitchell said.

As soon as he left the room, Jill was back inside his computer room. She figured she had five, ten minutes at best to make a quick search. Perhaps she'd get a lucky strike, but that was doubtful. Still, she had gone this far and couldn't back out now. If nothing came of it, Jill would be fine with making out with Mitchell for a while, but nothing more. She'd ask him to drive her home, and she'd never come back here again.

Jill knew how to search a computer for files. Thirty seconds after Mitchell departed, she typed the word "Lindsey" into the file system search field and ran the query. She didn't know how else to go about looking for evidence; since Lindsey was at the center of this, her name seemed a perfectly good place to start.

No results.

She tried a couple variations of Lindsey's name.

Still nothing.

On a whim, she typed in the number twenty-seven, which was Lindsey's jersey number.

Seconds later a group of files returned. Jill was somewhat taken aback, having fully expected to get nothing from that effort as well. She clicked on one of the files in the returned result set. It opened an image program. When the image appeared on the screen, her breathing momentarily stopped.

Jill gazed wide-eyed at a picture of Lindsey lying naked on her bed. Apart from Lindsey being naked, the composition of the image looked similar to other pictures her friends had taken of themselves and posted to Facebook. Jill clicked on another of the images from the batch that her quick search had returned and saw more pictures of Lindsey.

Jill ran another search, this time for the number thirty-four—*her* jersey number. At least fifty pictures came back. Jill clicked and opened the first image in the set. She thought she might get sick. It was a picture of herself, lying on a bed, with her shirt unbuttoned and her breasts exposed. She knew when the picture had been taken, too.

It was at a party she had attended in June to celebrate the end of school. A senior boy had invited her, one she really liked. She'd gotten drunk on vodka punch and passed out. The boy later told her that she had slept through most of the party. Was he the one who had unbuttoned her top? Did he dress her again?

A new thought sent a shiver rippling through her.

Wasn't Tanner Farnsworth at that party that night?

Jill looked around Mitchell's computer and noticed a flash drive lodged in the USB slot. She dragged a bunch of the images onto the desktop icon for that storage key.

As it copied, she opened the folder where all the images seemed to be stored. Hundreds of pictures were listed within. She opened one and saw a naked picture of Gretchen Stiller—one of the witches. Like Lindsey, Gretchen looked proud to be taking her own picture. Unlike Jill, Gretchen was wide awake and smiling at the camera. Jill dragged a bunch of those images onto the flash drive as well.

She took the storage key from the key slot and put it in the pocket of her jeans. She took out her cell phone, thinking she'd text Lindsey to ask what she should do next. Her hand brushed up against the rippled metal of the toppled Coke can. The contact summoned her back into the moment. God, how had she lost track of the time!

Jill was in the process of shutting down the image application when Mitchell entered the room.

His mouth fell open when he saw what she was looking at. "What are you doing?" he asked.

Jill's heart pounded so fast that she felt it might burst. She set her cell down on the table. She wanted to look as innocent as possible. But she felt the flash drive in her pants pocket, with all the images that she copied to it, like a hot coal searing the skin of her leg. "I was just trying to check my e-mail," she managed to say.

"Don't lie to me," Mitchell said, closing in. "I can check the recent activity, you know."

"I didn't see anything," Jill said, though her voice wavered the way it did just before she cried.

Mitchell, undeterred and unconvinced, stepped even closer. Before she could slip past him, he had his hands wrapped around her neck. Jill's eyes bulged in their sockets as he began to squeeze.

"What did you see?" he growled in her ear. "You were just supposed to be using the Web browser, not snooping around my files."

With one hand Jill tried without success to push Mitchell away from her. She stretched the fingers of her other hand and hoped beyond hope to find her phone still in reach.

Mitchell tightened his grip around Jill's neck. He didn't seem to notice her hand, and she found her phone. She tried to relax as she brought the phone to her side and out of Mitchell's view. Mitchell wasn't squeezing her neck anymore. But he kept his hands there, holding her immobilized.

Jill felt the ridges of the phone. By touch and memory she pushed the right button to redial the last number called. Jill almost never used her phone to make phone calls. Texting had become her communication method of choice. But she remembered whom she last dialed. The phone began to ring in her hand, but Mitchell didn't hear it, because he was yelling at her again.

"Did you see anything? Answer me?"

"No."

The phone rang and rang.

Mitchell let go of her throat. "I need to think . . . need to think. . . ." Mitchell let out a heavy breath. He was still blocking her way out of the alcove.

The phone kept ringing. Jill covered the speaker with her hand. Mitchell was still pacing. He didn't hear the rings.

"Just take me home, okay?" Jill said.

"I can't do that yet. I gotta think. That was really stupid of you, Jill."

Mitchell turned around and put his hand to his head. He walked out of the alcove and back into his bedroom.

Jill faked a move to her left and went right, emulating her best soccer technique for getting by an aggressive defender. Mitchell wasn't fooled and positioned his body in such a way that he effectively blocked the door—her only exit out. Jill knew there was no way she'd get by him.

She heard a click and a voice, which gave her a pulse of hope that she'd escape from this alive.

"Jill? Honey, is that you?"

She didn't answer her father, though, because Mitchell had turned around. He was coming toward her again.

CHAPTER 53

Tom tensed and gripped his cell phone tighter. He pressed the phone hard to his ear because he couldn't hear the caller otherwise. The ringing had awoken him from a deep, drugged-induced slumber, and it took him a moment to convince himself he wasn't dreaming now.

It took less time, though, to realize that the voice he'd just heard belonged to his daughter. He called her name again, but something in the few words he picked up made him stop speaking so he could listen.

"Mitchell . . . don't worry . . . saw nothing . . . Don't be angry. . . ."

Tom sat upright in his hospital bed, quicker than he should have moved. Blood rushed to his head. An intense pain exploded from behind his eyes, painting his vision white. He sat still until the pain receded into something he could breathe through again.

"Jill, honey, is that you?" Tom asked into the phone. "Are you okay? Where are you?"

Tom's voice sounded weak. His throat was parched. Worse than the thirst was the constricting fear wrapped tight around his chest, telling him something was horribly wrong.

A nurse making her nightly room checks glanced at Tom with concern. Tom pointed frantically to the phone pressed to his ear and motioned her back into the hall.

This could be nothing, he thought. What did Jill once call it—*ass dialing*—when you accidentally called somebody because you sat on the cell phone in your back pocket? Maybe that was all this was. But what had caused the urgency in what few bits of conversation he actually could hear?

No, he had instincts for this sort of thing, and a growing certainty that this was a call for help. The next four words that he picked up, spoken in his daughter's stricken voice, confirmed those suspicions in the gravest of ways.

"Please . . . don't hurt me. . . ."

Tom slid his feet off of the bed. He stood on shaky legs. Had he heard her right? God, where was she? He wanted to scream to her to talk to him but didn't say a word. What if the person she was talking to didn't know she'd called him? The situation could escalate if her assailant became aware that she'd dialed for help. But he needed to know her location before he could take action.

Tom took his first few steps in hours and stumbled. He nearly toppled over the food tray by his bed. His IV was still attached. He turned and frantically pressed the call button, summoning the nurse he'd just shooed away.

"Get this IV off me," he demanded. "Please, do it now. It's important."

The nurse looked at him in confusion but failed to take a single step. Tom put the phone tight against his lips and whispered, "Jilly-bean, give me something. Say something. Tell me where you are. Come on. Tell me."

He held his breath, willing himself to become calm so that he could focus all his energy on listening. Compartmentalizing fear was a battlefield requirement Tom could access in a way similar to muscle memory.

He removed the tape that secured the plastic IV tube to his arm, oblivious to the painful pull against his skin as it lifted. There was tape on his wrist, too, which he unsecured with the same haste. Tom had dressed war wounds before, so he knew to shut off the flow of medicine before extracting the needle stuck into the back of his hand. Blood flowed, but less than Tom had expected. Now he needed to find his clothes.

"Sir . . . Mr. Hawkins . . . you haven't been discharged."

Tom covered the phone's receiver before he spoke. "Where are my clothes?"

"Mr. Hawkins, Dr. Prince wanted you here overnight for observation."

"Yeah, well, that's not happening anymore. Get me my clothes."

Tom's expression communicated his intended threat: "Your way, or the easy way." The nurse responded by handing Tom his street clothes, which were folded inside a pinewood wardrobe.

Though his legs were wobbly and his balance dramatically compromised, Tom managed to keep the phone close to his ear while he dressed. The pain wasn't too bad. It was hardest to ignore when he looked down to pull on his jeans and put on his shoes. The room spun as though everything in it were water in a bathtub going down a drain. He shook his head to refocus his thoughts, but that only ignited embers of pain into a flash point.

Gritting through the agony, Tom managed to catch something Jill said.

"Mitchell, take me home . . . please. . . ."

Take me home. Where could they be?

When Tom was fully dressed, the duty nurse objected once again. "Mr. Hawkins, we can't authorize your leaving."

Tom staggered toward her, pushing his way by the woman, who blocked the door. "You don't have to authorize it," he said. "Just don't try to stop it."

He would have taken the elevator down from the third floor but didn't want to risk dropping the connection. He could call Jill back, but he worried that the phone's ringing might put her in deeper peril. So he took the stairs, though his steps were shaky and each footstep felt just the way he expected it would after surviving a major car accident.

Horrible.

"Jilly, come on. Give me something, and I'll come get you," Tom whispered into the phone.

The more he moved, the stronger he felt and the faster he moved. He exited through the stairwell door and into the deserted parking lot of Catholic Memorial Hospital.

Tom stood statue still, with his eyes closed and the phone to his ear. He waited for something that would inspire his next move. Some tidbit of information he could act upon. He remembered the GPS location app installed on Jill's phone. Tom accessed the FamilyWhere app on his Android-powered smartphone, and when he got what he wanted, Tom felt a thousand miles away, though at best he was only a short cab ride's distance from her.

"You're scaring me. . . . I'll scream. . . ."

Tom heard Mitchell Boyd speak for the first time, and the boy's words pierced him with fear.

"My dad's in his office. He can't hear you scream."

Tom saw a cab pulled to a stop by the emergency room entrance, some fifty yards from where he stood. He raced over to the cab, careless of the pain that exploded inside him with every stride.

The cabdriver acted surprised that it was Tom who had jumped into his cab.

"Hey, I'm here for a Mrs. Wilcox. You her?" He let out a mocking laugh; obviously, the answer was no.

"Yeah, I'm her," Tom said. He gave the driver Roland Boyd's home address. The driver appeared ready to protest, but one look at Tom in the cab's rearview mirror must have convinced him that Mrs. Wilcox could find herself another ride. Once the cab got moving, Tom closed his eyes tight and cupped the phone to his ear with both hands. "I'm coming, baby girl," he whispered. "You hang on, and I'll be there soon."

"Can you drive faster?" Tom asked the cabdriver.

"If you pay the speeding ticket."

Tom thought better of it. "No. Don't get pulled over," Tom said. "Get me there as fast as you can."

Tom leaned back against the cab's hard vinyl seat and closed his eyes. His headache was worsening.

His mind sped through different scenarios. He needed to formulate a plan with the best odds for success. Sergeant Brendan Murphy had single-handedly made it a no-go to contact the Shilo PD.

Tom called Roland's home number. Roland answered on the third ring.

"Roland, it's Tom."

"What do you want, Tom?"

"Is my daughter there?"

"She's here."

"Is she all right?"

"She's with my son. They're in his room, hanging out. How are you feeling?"

"Roland, I need you to forget about our issues. I need you to just think of me as a father. Forget anything else you suspect, or believe. Now, Jill called me. She sounded like she was in trouble. Can you please go check on her?"

"What are you talking about?"

"Roland! Please. Just check on her."

Roland sighed into the phone. "Hang on," he said.

One minute passed . . . then two.

Roland got back on the phone. "They're fine," he said.

"Did you speak to my daughter?"

"She said she was fine," said Roland.

"Did you see her?"

Roland sighed again. "No. The door to Mitchell's room was closed. But they said they were fine."

"Roland, I need you to check again. I need you to open the door to the room and make sure she's all right."

"You know what, Tom? I've got other things to do with my time than listen to your paranoid delusions about my son. I think whatever pain meds they gave you have gone to your head. You have a good night. Glad you're all right. Now, get some rest."

Tom didn't say anything more. Roland had hung up on him.

CHAPTER 54

Tom decided his course of action well before the driver turned his cab onto Route 101A. The cab took the right-hand exit for south Shilo. Tom had no plans to try and reestablish contact with Jill. But when he got to Roland's home, he'd attack the way an unconventional warrior was trained to wage a war.

The three characteristics of Navy SEAL mission planning were bottom up, extremely flexible, and short fused. By the time conventional forces finished developing their preliminary course of action briefs, a SEAL could be geared up, out the door, and engaging the enemy. Tom had been trained to think fluidly, to respond to information that could lead him from a dry target to one of high value.

Roland's mistake was failing to establish visual confirmation of Jill's well-being. Tom knew something was wrong. He'd heard the panic in her voice. He had no choice but to assume Jill was under duress when she claimed to be fine. That meant she needed to be extracted from the threat.

That was his one and only mission.

Tom kept his plan simple. He would enter through the

front door with force, address any threats encountered, and exit with his daughter the way he came in. If there was time, he'd devise a backup plan before engagement. He'd learned that almost no plan survived first contact with the enemy. One of the SEALs many mottos evoked their ruthless determination. "The only easy day was yesterday!" His daughter was the objective. Anybody who stood in his way would be met with violence of action.

From what Roland had relayed, Tom believed his daughter was in Mitchell's bedroom. He suspected the two were alone. Mitchell wouldn't have risked attacking Jill otherwise. But if anybody became an obstacle, Tom would act decisively to ensure that the objective was safely extricated from the premises. *No, not the objective,* Tom reminded himself. *His daughter.*

Tom could drain himself of most emotion.

Just not all of it.

Tom mentally constructed a probable sequence leading up to his daughter's phone call. Jill had gone to Mitchell Boyd's house.

Why?

They were still seeing each other. Still involved. She knew that Tom disapproved. That was why she kept the relationship a secret from him.

Why didn't they go to Jill's house? he asked himself. He was in the hospital, and her house was empty.

Mitchell was a known womanizer, that was why. He wanted to show off in his domain. He wanted to impress her. To seduce her.

So, they were alone in his bedroom. Mitchell got aggressive. His daughter rejected him. Mitchell became angry. Simple as that.

"How far now?" Tom asked the driver.

"Three minutes. Four at the most," the driver said. Tom

had figured on that answer. He'd been keeping mental track of the time.

"What's the big rush?" the driver asked. "Is there a fire where you're going?"

"Not yet," Tom answered him.

The cab turned onto Roland Boyd's street.

"Shut off your lights," Tom instructed. "Pull the cab to a stop fifty feet before the driveway on your right."

"Shut off my—"

"Do it," Tom commanded.

The cabdriver did as he was told.

"Do you have any duct tape in the trunk?"

The man stuttered before he could respond. "I think so," he managed to say.

"Pop the trunk." Tom heard a click as the trunk latch released. "How much money do you need to guarantee you'll wait for me here?" Tom asked.

"Are you breaking the law?" the man asked.

"Give me a number."

"Five hundred?" the driver said, though he made it sound like a question and not a demand.

"Done. I'll be right back."

Tom flicked a switch to shut off the cab's interior light so he could exit the vehicle in darkness. He walked to the back of the cab and opened the trunk. He moved quickly to cover the trunk light with his cupped hand. Inside the trunk he found a roll of duct tape and, even better, a box of spark plugs.

Tom closed the trunk and fished around on the ground for a suitable rock. He took a single spark plug out from the box and, using the rock's edge, knocked off a piece of the ceramic insulator. He slipped the ceramic piece into his pocket, grabbed the duct tape, and closed the trunk.

Tom cut a zigzagged path across the well-kept,

chemical-green lawn. He avoided the lighted walkway and kept mostly to the shadows. He crouched low when he reached the front of the house. It was mostly windows, with more lights on in the home than he expected to see. But a long, trimmed row of evergreen shrubs kept him hidden from view. He was glad the Boyds didn't have a dog, but was angry with himself for not having secured a weapon of some sort before he left the hospital.

Tom's first objective was to enter the house silently. Cutting power to the home was one option, but he worried Mitchell might panic if the house went dark. Jill might try to escape and could get hurt in the process. A loud shattering window could result in the same. So Tom needed to break the window without making a sound.

The steps to the front landing were lit as well. Tom hid behind a large ceramic planter perched at the top of the landing. Somebody would have to open the front door to see him crouched there.

He confirmed that the front door was locked before pulling off the first strip of duct tape. He secured several strips of tape in an X-shaped pattern to the opaque, rectangular sidelight window nearest to the brass handle of the mahogany front door.

With the tape in place, Tom retrieved the ceramic spark-plug chip from his pants pocket. He moved out from the shadows and stood about five feet from the taped window. He threw the ceramic chip at the center of the X with a dart player's grace. There was a quiet, near imperceptible popping sound when the chip hit the window. Veins of breaking glass danced an erratic pattern across the cracked window. But the combination of ceramic and duct tape made the break no louder than a drop of water landing in an empty bucket.

Tom popped the glass pane free from the door's raised

molding and removed it as silently as it had broken. He reached his hand through that opening and unlocked the door from the inside.

He stood in the same foyer where weeks ago he'd come to ask Roland about Kip Lange. He listened for any sounds that might direct him. He heard nothing useful. Tom's footsteps fell silently as he ascended the winding staircase in front of him. He assumed Mitchell's bedroom was located on the second level. If his daughter was still in the house, that was where he would find her.

At the top of the stairs, Tom came to a long east-west-running corridor. Light seeped from a closed door at one end of the hallway.

Tom moved toward that door. He kept his breathing quiet. When he couldn't pad his footsteps on the plush carpeting, he stayed close to the wall, where the floors typically creaked less.

Tom continued noiselessly down the hall. He moved the way he'd been trained. He set his heel down first and rolled his foot slowly and gently toward his toes. He bent low at the knees to improve his balance. He tightened the muscle on the inside of his pelvis.

At the end of the hallway, Tom pressed his body against the wall and leaned his head toward the door to get a better listen. No sound. Nothing at all.

He heard a cry. It was a soft, plaintive, scared-sounding cry. It was Jill. Close as he was to rescuing her, Tom managed to remain calm. He took a few breaths to center himself. He reached for the doorknob.

With a gentle nudge, Tom pushed the door open. Only part of his body was exposed to the room. He peeked inside.

Mitchell Boyd was standing with his back to the door. Jill was seated on his bed. The boy's position kept him from getting a clear visual of his daughter. Jill's sobbing was louder now. There was no way for Tom to tell if she was hurt or not. Tom needed to ascertain if Mitchell carried a weapon.

Tom pressed his body against the wall. Through the slot between the door and the doorjamb, he had Mitchell directly in his line of sight. He knocked on the open door.

Mitchell whirled around. Nobody was standing in the doorway. Mitchell appeared to be confused.

Tom determined the boy was unarmed. That was all the information he needed. Mitchell took a single step toward the open door. Tom pushed himself clear of the wall.

"Dad!" Jill cried out. He could hear the relief in her voice.

Tom charged at Mitchell. There were hundreds of ways Tom could incapacitate him. What he needed was one that wouldn't permanently injure or kill the boy.

In hand-to-hand combat, the body got divided into three sections—high, middle, and low. Each section was rife with vital targets, key nerves and arteries that, when struck, caused debilitating pain, unconsciousness, or even death. Tom knew every target and could attack them at will with bold precision. A strong blow to the side of the neck—specifically, below and slightly in front of the ear—shocked the carotid artery, jugular vein, and vagus nerve. Such a strike would render his opponent instantly unconscious. A lesser blow would result in intense, but incapacitating pain.

Tom opted not to hit Mitchell at all. Rather, he applied pressure to the strike area. Mitchell shrieked at Tom's touch and fell helplessly to the floor. Jill leapt up from the bed as soon as Mitchell went down, and grabbed hold of her father. Tom felt her body shake with sobs.

"Are you okay?" Tom asked. "Are you hurt, Jill?"

She was hyperventilating. Her hot tears wet his shirt. Mitchell was still groaning on the floor beside them.

"Slow your breathing. Are you hurt? Did he rape you?"

Jill shook her head. Tom let out a huge relieved breath.

"Can you walk out of here with me?"

"Yes. . . . Please . . . take . . . me . . . home. . . ." Each word she spoke was punctuated by a fast breath that was also part cry.

They turned to leave.

But Roland Boyd was blocking the doorway. "What the hell is going on here!" Roland shouted.

Tom let go of Jill and rushed at Roland. Before Roland could even put his hands up in defense, Tom secured a grip around his neck and had him pinned against the door frame.

"You wouldn't open the door! You wouldn't check in on my daughter!"

"What . . . what did Mitchell do?" Roland said. Roland's face turned red from the constricted blood flow. His words came out weak because of the grip Tom held around his throat.

"By the looks of it, he assaulted her," Tom said to him. "We're leaving. Now."

"You can't just break into my home and attack my family," Roland managed to say.

"I'm leaving with my daughter now, and you can't stop me," Tom shot back.

Mitchell was still writhing on the floor in pain. He was holding his neck and whimpering.

"You can go back to jail for this," Roland said.

"Cool. Mitchell and I can become prison pals."

Tom eased his grip around Roland's neck. Roland slumped to the floor and began rubbing at the spot where Tom's hand had been.

"Let's be rational here," Roland said, still breathing hard. Mitchell had managed to get himself onto his knees. He wasn't going to be standing anytime soon.

"Okay, let's," Tom said. "I need five hundred dollars for my cab ride home."

"Are you buying what I think you are?" said Roland.

Tom got low to the floor. He leaned in close to Roland so that Jill couldn't overhear him. "I'm not buying my daughter's silence, if that's what you're asking. If she wants to press charges against Mitchell, that'll be her decision."

Roland took out his wallet. He stayed slumped on the floor. He fished out five crisply pressed hundred-dollar bills.

"I hope it doesn't come to that," Roland said.

Tom plucked another hundred from the billfold. "For the tip," he said.

Tom stood and took hold of Jill's hand. They walked the length of the hallway together. He helped his daughter navigate the majestic staircase, because her footing was uncertain. They emerged into a star-drenched night, bathed by a warm southerly breeze, and followed the walkway to the driveway's edge.

Tom signaled for the waiting cab. The driver kept his headlights turned off. He pulled over to pick them up. Tom eased Jill into the backseat of the cab. He came around the other side and slipped in beside her.

"Where to?" the driver asked.

"Home," Tom said.

Jill rested her head on his shoulder as she wept.

CHAPTER 55

Tom eased Jill onto the sofa. Her skin was pale and clammy to the touch. Her breathing was shallow. He covered her with a thick fleece blanket and left the living room, to return holding a blood pressure cuff and gauge. Over the years coaching soccer, Tom had amassed enough medical equipment to open his own ambulatory service. To his relief, the blood pressure reading was normal, so while Jill exhibited some of the symptoms of shock, he didn't need to rush her to a hospital.

Tom sat on the faded yellow armchair across from Jill. His head continued to pound. Adding to his discomfort, Tom's knee had ballooned to the size of a youth soccer ball, and the IV puncture hole had begun to bleed.

Jill pointed to the red river of blood that snaked across the back of Tom's hand and ended up as drips on the armchair.

"You're bleeding, Dad," she said. Those were the first words she'd spoken since the cab ride home. "I'll get you a bandage."

Jill came back with a Hello Kitty Band-Aid. The two shared a quick laugh after she secured it in place.

"Are you ready to talk?" Tom asked.

Jill retreated to the sofa and rested her head on a makeshift platform of her interlocking fingers. She kept her eyes fixed to a spot on the floor, and her expression remained grave.

"I'm not going to judge you, honey," Tom added, "but I'd like to know the truth. What did Mitchell Boyd do to you?"

Jill stared up at her father through a glaze of tears. Her bottom lip trembled, and Tom knew it meant a flood was imminent. "I can't tell you," she sobbed into her hands.

Just thinking about Mitchell Boyd made him want to return to that house and inflict further misery on the boy.

"Jill, this is really important," Tom said. "I need you to trust me. Did he hurt you? Did he touch you in a threatening way?"

Jill's gaze again retreated to that spot on the floor, and she shook her head. It was a tentative no at best.

"Tell me exactly what he did that got you so scared," he said.

"I guess I thought he was going to hurt me," Jill responded. The timbre of her voice came at him weak and rueful. "I didn't know who else to call," she continued. "I'm sorry I caused so much trouble. Maybe . . . I just overreacted."

Tom stood up and plopped down on the sofa beside her. He pulled Jill close to him. Something inside of her must have let go when he did. Tom felt her whole body begin to relax. He brushed away a tear that lingered near her eye. Jill crinkled her nose and smiled at him after he smoothed it away.

"Jill," Tom said in a more somber tone, "I need you to open up to me about Mitchell. I need to know everything."

Jill shook her head. Her posture changed. She seemed

more closed off again. "I don't want to talk about what happened."

Tom glanced over at the whiteboard, and that big, obtrusive square with the word *trust* in the center. Jill leaned over and gently kissed her father on the cheek.

"Will you come back home?" Tom said.

"I am home," Jill said. She inhaled a sob, then let her own tears fall freely. She fell into her father's open arms, and he wrapped her warmer than any fleece blanket ever could.

"Please trust me," Tom said. "Please give me a chance. I told you my greatest secret. Please don't burden yourself by keeping secrets from me."

Jill nodded.

Tom stood up and walked over to the whiteboard. With the palm of his hand he erased the square blocking the goal. Tom turned around to look at Jill.

"What really happened at Mitchell's?" asked Tom.

Jill took in a heavy breath and breathed it out slowly. "We were hanging out in his room. But we weren't doing *anything*—"

"I know," Tom said, nodding so that she could skip over the uncomfortable details. "Go on."

"Well, he wanted to do things that I wasn't comfortable doing. He started to push me into it, and I got scared. I didn't know who else to call. So I called you."

"Did he rape you, Jill?"

Jill shook her head. "No. I think maybe he might have if you hadn't come. I don't know."

Tom bit his lip. The furious impulse to inflict permanent damage to Mitchell Boyd had returned. "Okay. Is that everything? Are you sure you're telling me everything, Jill? No more secrets."

Jill nodded emphatically. "That's everything. I swear."

CHAPTER 56

R ainy was back at work in Boston. She was getting ready to leave for the day. Her report on the James Mann investigation for the USAO was nearly complete. It was detailed and heinous, a report on the darkest of hearts. She would be glad to be done with it. But she had more reports like this to write, and more investigations to conclude.

This was the job in the cyber crimes squad. It never got easier.

Rainy's work in Shilo was basically over. She'd interviewed all ten girls from Shilo High School whose pictures were found on computers belonging to James Mann and Tom Hawkins. The four new girls she'd interviewed lied to her as well. They'd sent their pictures to somebody, but Rainy couldn't prove it. From the subpoenaed phone records all Rainy could ascertain was that they didn't text or call Tom Hawkins. Several had texted and called Tanner Farnsworth, as they had lots of different boys from Shilo High School.

Rainy even got three of the girls to agree to consent to searches of their phones. But she found nothing useful. The sent messages were mostly texts. The pictures attached were of friends and parties. Nothing lewd. Nothing lascivious.

Nothing illegal.

The girls had probably deleted those images long ago. Rainy had already put in preservation requests with their cell phone carriers. A search of those servers was a dead end, too. The girls had sent thousands of text messages since her request went into effect. They'd sent hundreds of pictures as well, but the only alarms in those images were underage drinking, some pot smoking, and lots of cigarettes. It was the business of their parents, not the FBI.

Tanner Farnsworth remained uncooperative throughout her investigation. Meanwhile, Tom Hawkins and James Mann were both going to be found guilty of crimes by a jury of their peers.

A small failed battery was enough to convince both Rainy and Carter that Hawkins was probably innocent. They'd brought their finding to the D.A. and Shilo PD, who had thanked them for the information. Rainy could tell they weren't going to drop the charges against Hawkins. But at least Marvin Pressman had some new ammunition to use for Hawkins's defense.

Rainy wished she could stop thinking about Tom Hawkins, but he'd wormed his way into her consciousness, where he seemed destined to remain.

"Any plans tonight, Miles?" Carter asked.

"Does attempting to revive my spider plants count as a plan?"

"A certain-to-fail one, but yes, it counts."

Rainy's desk phone rang. She answered it. "Hello. This is Agent Miles. How can I help you?"

"Rainy Miles, my name is James Mann. I believe you arrested me."

Rainy cupped the phone's receiver and mouthed the

words "James Mann" to Carter. Carter naturally took interest.

Were your ears ringing? she thought.

"Mr. Mann," Rainy said. "I can't speak with you unless I have permission from your defense counsel. I'm afraid we have to end this communication immediately until that permission is granted."

Rainy hung up the phone after Mann gave her a number where he could be reached. In State court, prosecuting attorneys were barred from speaking with a defendent without prior approval. The McDade Act subjected Rainy to the same professional standards.

Hours later, Rainy called James Mann.

"We're able to speak freely," Rainy said, having procured the necessary permissions. "So tell me, what can I do for you?"

"I'd like you to come over to my apartment," Mann said.

"Why would you like me to do that?" asked Rainy.

"I have something I want to show you."

"And what would that be?" Rainy asked.

"Evidence that's going to prove I'm not guilty of any crimes."

CHAPTER 57

Rainy made Carter go with her to Mann's apartment. She carried a firearm and knew how to use it, but she wasn't stupid, either. She'd be happy to look at the evidence James Mann claimed to have, but only with armed backup at her side.

Mann's new residence was a far cry from his former home. Rainy knew that Mann and his wife had separated, and that Mann had spent a week or so at a Motel 6 after he posted bail. Other than that, she didn't know much about his life after his arrest. She didn't know he had found this place to live. Mann's apartment building was in deplorable condition and was located in a rather sketchy section of Brighton, a neighborhood of Boston.

Rainy pushed her finger against the apartment's grimy buzzer. The door unlocked, and they entered a dark foyer. They climbed two flights of paint-chipped wooden stairs.

James Mann opened his apartment door when they reached the second landing. Mann looked tired. His skin color looked gray; his eyes were sunken and marred by dark rings. Rainy gave Mann and his rail-thin body three months to survive in prison. Four at the outside.

The floor to Mann's dingy apartment was littered with

file folders stuffed with papers. She saw pictures of his wife and kids scattered about the room, in dull or dusty frames. It looked like a haphazard attempt to restore order to a disordered life.

Furniture in the poorly lit studio apartment was bleak at best. Mann had laid a mattress askew on the varnished wood floor. A patchwork fabric couch and orange velvet armchair took up one corner of the room. The armchair had enough holes to make it look spotted. The whole apartment smelled like an animal.

"Thanks for coming over," Mann said. He gestured over to the couch, inviting Rainy and Carter to sit.

"We're fine to stand," Rainy said. "Let's get to the point. What evidence did you want to show us?"

Mann walked over to his laptop computer and took out a flash drive. He handed the storage key to Rainy.

"I used to be a real person," Mann said. "With a wife I loved. Children I cherished. A job I was a passionate about—"

"You were arrested for a crime against children, Mr. Mann," said Carter.

"Let me finish," Mann said. "I have a rather extensive network of people I've met along the way. People from my career who still believe in me. Who believe, despite my current situation."

"And what's your point?" Carter asked.

"I've spent every minute since I posted bail trying to figure out how I can prove to you that I didn't do this."

Carter just scoffed. "And . . ."

"I've got a lot of enemies. I climbed the ladder. I'm sure I stepped on plenty of toes along the way. A friend of mine, somebody I'd rather not name, encouraged me to take a different approach."

"What approach would that be?" Rainy asked. She had to admit that he'd managed to get her interest. She could hear the conviction in his voice. She understood now that his apparent disregard for himself was the result of an intense and focused effort. This was a man who was possessed with getting to the truth. A man who reminded her, in some ways, of Tom Hawkins.

"He told me to try to clear my name the same way you were going to try and prove my guilt. I took his advice to heart. I learned all about your methods. I know about the Child Victim Identification Program. The clearinghouse, if you will, for child pornography cases, like mine."

"Okay. Good for you." Carter looked and sounded frustrated. Rainy touched his arm to urge him to stay patient.

"CVIP analysts use the Child Recognition and Identification System to help them identify children and then coordinate a response. Rescue efforts. Evidence for trials."

"You've done your homework," Rainy said.

"I know that the software generates a digital fingerprint for each image—a hash value, I believe it's called. It's that identifier which helps to match images to a known series, or if there is no digital fingerprint match, then it is used to designate a new one."

"Where is this going?" asked Rainy. "What's on the flash drive?"

"My friend gave me some names to look up. Girls whose images I supposedly bought from someone. The plan was simple. By figuring out where I could buy the real images, I'd be able to find the real source. Hopefully, I'd be able to get us both out of trouble."

"You did what?" Rainy said.

"Yeah, I have no idea how to procure that type of

garbage. But I took the money I could have used for a nicer apartment and paid a computer professional to help me figure it out."

"What did you reel in?" asked Carter.

"A lot of pictures."

"So you re-created our case against you? And you're confessing to another crime in the process. Do you know that?" said Rainy.

"I was in a learning mode," Mann said. "I wanted to know who distributes these images. Who buys them. Who sells them. How they do it. How they keep from getting caught."

"So?" Now it was Rainy's turn to sound frustrated.

"When I say I wanted to learn about it, I mean I treated it like a job. I found out how these predators hide in a web of virtual servers. I learned the questions they ask to get the police to reveal themselves. I know how money gets secretly exchanged. My computer guy made me a database of everything he found and where he found it."

"You want to give us a bunch of new sources of child pornography in exchange for our dropping the case against you?" Rainy asked.

"No. I'll give you that, anyway," said Mann. "But in the process we found something unusual that I thought you should know about."

"And that would be?" Rainy inquired.

"My own Lisbeth Salander generated digital finger-prints, those hash values, for all the images he found, just like you guys do. He did it to keep all the images organized. We could tell by looking at the digital fingerprint of each image how many different sources were distributing the identical image."

"We're not hiring, if that's what you're after," Carter said.

Mann returned a weak smile. "There are images on this flash drive, dozens of them, that look to be the exact same to me. Same composition. Same background. Same subject. But these here are not like the other duplicates we found," Mann said.

"And why is that?" asked Rainy.

"Even though these images appear to be exact duplicates of one another, their digital fingerprints, the hash values each image generated, were all different. All the other duplicates my guy sourced generated identical hash values. These didn't."

"That's your proof?" Rainy wondered.

"These pictures appear to be identical in every way. So, logically, they should produce an identical fingerprint."

"Like I said, that's your proof of innocence?" said Rainy.

Mann's expression revealed an infinite sorrow. "My friend told me not to ignore any outliers."

Rainy felt the flesh on the back of her neck begin to rise.

That sounds like something Tom's lawyer would have said.

"I don't know if this will in fact prove my innocence. I needed something to lure you into coming over here and taking a look. But I do know that these images are outliers. They're the only duplicates that don't generate the same hash values. I need to understand why. No stone left uncovered. This is my life on the line, Agent Miles."

"Okay, we'll do that for you," said Rainy. "But you and this jock of yours are going to turn over all the evidence you've gathered."

"I've got it ready to send to you," Mann said. "But first you'll have to promise that there will be no charges against him, or new ones against me."

"I'm sure that can be arranged," Rainy said.

"And there's one other thing," Mann said. "The images with the hash values that don't match but should—they look similar to me."

"Yeah? In what way?" asked Carter.

"They all look like they were taken with a cell phone camera."

CHAPTER 58

Prospect Park was once a weed-infested lot of broken bottles, crumpled beer cans, and cigarette butts. It was just down the road from Lindsey's house, but all the years she could have played there (before it became uncool to play), the park was essentially unusable. Apart from all the litter, the playground itself was in shambles. The swings were broken. The slide could cut your leg if you hugged too close to the right going down. There were relics of a zip line, which the town selectmen had ordered taken down after some kid broke his arm. The only apparatus that wasn't broken, rusted, or falling apart was the tire bridge, and that was never much fun to play on.

Some years earlier, a group of concerned parents, Lindsey's mother among them, had rallied the town for funds to clean up Prospect Park. Bake sales were followed by a town appropriations vote, and the park had been reborn.

The park's renaissance, however, came too late for Lindsey to enjoy the benefits fully. Yet even though she was well beyond the monkey-bar years, she still liked coming here. Her quick jaunts to Prospect Park began around the time of her parents' divorce.

She sat awhile on the wide hard-plastic swing just to think. Over time, what had been an occasional desire had turned into something of a habit. She'd come to the park whenever she needed an escape, which, sadly, was more and more often. That was why she came here mostly at night—when the little kids were all in bed, and her mother was passed out on the sofa with half a bottle of Chardonnay. At least her mother's drinking problem made it easy for Lindsey to sneak unnoticed out of the house.

Normal parents would know if their kid had walked out the front door at midnight. But getting her mother's attention would require Lindsey to scream in the poor woman's ear. Come morning, Lindsey doubted her mother would even remember the conversation. When Lindsey slipped on her light blue cotton jacket and slipped out the front door minutes before the grandfather clock chimed twelve, she did so without leaving a note as to her whereabouts. She'd be home in an hour.

The moon was just a sliver in the sky, and it was late enough that even the crickets, normally deafening, seemed to have retired for the night. Lindsey rocked herself backward and forward, pumping her legs just enough to keep her momentum, but not so much that the swing hinges creaked out her presence. She wanted only Tanner Farnsworth to know that she was there, and judging by her cell phone's clock, the boy who had betrayed her trust wouldn't show for another ten minutes. That is, if he dared to come at all.

Lindsey let her thoughts drift back to the events that preceded this planned rendezvous. It had all begun with a frantic phone call from Jill.

"Slow down, Jill," Lindsey had to shout into her phone. "I can't understand you."

But once Lindsey finally grasped what Jill had been

saying, she couldn't believe what she heard. Their plan had been simply to figure out whether Mitchell was involved in the computer attacks. But in a single sentence, the life that Lindsey believed couldn't get worse had done just that.

"Mitchell had what on his computer?"

"Your pictures," Jill said. "The ones you told me you sent to Tanner. And that's not all. He had pictures of me, too, and a bunch of other girls as well."

"Oh my God."

They went back and forth for a few minutes, with Lindsey punctuating each new revelation with another "Oh. My. God."

"You've got to promise, swear to me, Lindsey, that you're not going to do anything about this. I didn't even tell my dad."

"Your dad came and rescued you. Don't you think you can trust him?"

"Yeah, a lot more now," Jill agreed. "But that doesn't mean I want him to know that I passed out at a party, or that somebody took pictures of me with my clothes off. You can't tell anyone I told you this. Mitchell swore to me that he'd put my pictures everywhere if you did. Yours, too. I mean, we'll be totally destroyed."

"We went after one thing and found another."

"What do you mean?" asked Jill.

"The police found child porn on your dad's computers. But this isn't the same thing. Mitchell can't be the one who framed him."

"That doesn't mean I want my dad to know about these pictures!" Jill cried.

Lindsey tried to calm her crying friend, but it wasn't easy to do over the phone. Eventually, Jill managed to calm herself.

"We can't just let this go," Lindsey said. "How many other girls' pictures did Mitchell have?"

"A bunch," Jill said. "Like I said, I didn't look long. I copied them, though. I still have the storage key. When Mitchell found me looking, I swear I thought I was going to die. I can't tell you how freaked out I was."

"Okay. Let me think about it. We'll figure out what to do. I'll call you back soon."

Lindsey didn't call back. She biked over to Jill's house and text messaged her friend to meet her in the backyard and bring the flash drive. Jill snuck downstairs without her father noticing and met Lindsey outside.

"Why do you want this?" Jill had asked.

"I just need to check it out for myself," Lindsey had said. "I'll give it back to you tomorrow. And don't worry. I won't do anything stupid."

"Text me after you look at them," Jill said.

"I will."

Lindsey never did text Jill. She rode home and looked at those pictures. Jill had tried to call her every ten minutes since, it seemed. Sent a bunch of texts, too. But Lindsey couldn't talk to her friend until after she did what had to be done.

Tanner gave Mitchell the pictures that she'd sent to him. That was all Lindsey could think about. Did Tanner do this to other girls? He'd certainly had enough girlfriends. Maybe he'd done it to some, if not all. But Jill had said there were lots of girls and lots of pictures.

Lindsey didn't care about the other girls. There was only one possible route her pictures could have traveled to get to Mitchell Boyd's computer.

Tanner Farnsworth.

Lindsey didn't even know she had a temper until Tanner Farnsworth answered her call. She didn't cry once during their twenty-minute conversation. Her voice never lacked confidence. She liked standing up for herself. Powerful when enraged. Combative when wronged. Perhaps one day she'd be a lawyer, as her father often predicted.

"You tell Mitchell Boyd that the only life that's going to be ruined is his! You tell him to leave Jill alone!" she shouted into the phone.

"Lindsey, you sound hysterical," Tanner said.

"I swear, I'm so done with people picking on me. I don't care if you plaster my picture on every Web site in the world. Go ahead! But I'm bringing you down with me. Do you hear me, Tanner? I have the images. Jill copied them, and I have them."

That outburst met only silence.

"I don't know what you're talking about," Tanner said.

"Oh, that's bullshit, and you know it. You can do better than that, Tanner," Lindsey said.

"Or what?"

"Or I'll call that FBI lady and get her to arrest you."

"I didn't do anything," Tanner protested. "You're acting all hysterical, and I don't know what you're talking about, Lin. I never sent your pictures to anybody. I swear."

"Then figure out how Mitchell Boyd got my pictures, because if you don't come back with something that makes sense, you know where this goes from here." Lindsey hung up without giving Tanner a chance to respond. For months she had been studying for the SAT; the word *virile* came to mind when she reflected on how surprisingly strong she'd sounded. Jill didn't have to worry about Mitchell Boyd's threats anymore, she assured herself. Tanner would make certain of that.

Lindsey texted Jill that everything was cool, and Jill quickly replied with an all-cap THANK YOU. They agreed to talk in the morning.

Lindsey knew Jill had understood "cool" to mean that she wouldn't say or do anything about Mitchell Boyd. She felt bad for being deceitful, but hadn't Jill been through enough?

Tanner called Lindsey a few hours later.

"I know what happened," he said. "Mitchell took the pictures off my phone without my knowing. Can we meet?"

"Why?"

"Because I love you and I want to fix things between us."

Lindsey closed her eyes tight and tried to wish away what he'd just said, but couldn't. *I love you.*

"Okay. Where?"

"The park by your house. Two hours. You've got to bring the pictures. I'll bring my laptop. I'll show you how Mitchell was able to steal them."

"Mom, I'm going out," Lindsey said on her way out the door, knowing her mother was passed out on the sofa. Her mother's drunken snores completed Lindsey's private joke.

Lindsey continued to swing. She checked the time on her cell phone. Tanner was late. Maybe he'd bailed. She wasn't about to call, begging him to come. *Forget that.* She thought about Mitchell Boyd getting off to pictures of her and Jill, and it churned her stomach.

Whatever Tanner's explanation was would have to wait. She wasn't going to stick around to hear it. She felt angry at herself for even agreeing to meet him.

"I love you," she said aloud, mocking the words' now apparent stupidity.

Lindsey was about to leave when she heard rustling in the bushes behind her. Her heart leapt into her throat. She remembered a path to the park through the woods, which Tanner must have taken.

She looked toward the road and didn't see any headlights. Tanner must have parked on the dead-end street and used the back path to get to her. Maybe he was trying to sneak up and scare her. *He's too stupid to even do that right,* she thought.

She leapt off the swing and spun around in the direction of the noise.

"Very funny, Tanner. Don't be a jerk."

The bushes concealing the path parted, but nobody emerged from the dark.

"Tanner, don't be an ass," Lindsey said. "I know it's just you trying to scare me. It's not going to work."

Lindsey took a tentative step onto the path. She didn't cry out when someone stepped out from the bushes and onto the path. She'd been expecting it. A tingle of panic ran through her when she realized it wasn't Tanner standing in front of her. Her panic quickly escalated as the shadowy figure lunged at her, and grew into terror when she felt hands wrap around her neck.

She didn't know she was going to die. Not then, anyway. That came soon enough, when she realized that despite the humid night, her attacker wore leather gloves. He felt around her legs and pulled the flash drive from the front pocket of her jeans. She felt his hands squeeze tighter around her neck.

Lindsey closed her eyes. She wanted this to be a nightmare. She wanted to wake up. At that moment, what she wanted most of all was her mother.

CHAPTER 59

Tom struggled through his headache and bum knee to finish his morning workout, which consisted of 150 push-ups, 500 sit-ups, a six-mile run, followed by thirty minutes of strength and flexibility exercises. He showered and made breakfast. He set the table for two. He covered Jill's plate with another plate so that the food beneath could remain hot. He also wanted Jill to be surprised when she saw what he had prepared. He poured two glasses of fresh-squeezed orange juice and decorated each with a drink umbrella.

Long past the hour he predicted Jill would rise, his daughter ambled into the kitchen. She moved about sleepily. She was dressed and ready for school, with her hair pulled back into a tight ponytail. She carried a blue nylon backpack, which was slung across one shoulder. Earbuds were planted in both ears, and without concentrating Tom could hear the drone of whatever music blasted from her iPod.

She marched by the kitchen table, unaware that the table was set for breakfast, and headed straight to the refrigerator, where she extracted a yogurt container from the recently replenished supplies. She grabbed a spoon from the nearby drawer, peeled back the yogurt top, and began to eat.

It was only then that she looked up and saw Tom standing before the mountain of dirty dishes that overflowed the kitchen sink. She popped out her earbuds, muted the iPod, and smiled at her father.

"Mornin', Dad," she said.

"Morning," Tom replied. He tilted his head in the direction of the kitchen table, encouraging Jill to look.

"Oh, Dad," Jill said once she saw the spread. "What are you doing?"

"Well, I thought we should kick off our new start with a special father-daughter breakfast before school. Check it out."

Jill lifted the plate covering the food and couldn't resist a smile. Tom had made his famous Mickey Mouse pancakes for her. He blended three pancakes together to form the head and ears. He used whipped cream for the whites of the eyes, and three black raspberries, two for the pupils and one for the nose. The mouth was made of whipped cream, too, and he used a strawberry for the tongue.

"Oh, Dad, you shouldn't have done that," Jill said. But Tom could see that his daughter was touched by the effort, as well as the memory.

"I think you were six the last time I made this for you."

"Every Sunday," Jill said, remembering.

"Come. Sit. Eat." Tom sauntered over to the table and pulled out her chair from underneath.

Jill smiled and bounded over to him. She brushed his cheek with one quick peck.

"Wow, this is so . . . sweet," Jill said. "But I'm late for the bus. And I don't really have time for breakfast . . . pretty much, ever."

She handed him the empty yogurt container and descended the front stairs, seemingly without stepping on any of them.

"I'm going to make rosemary chicken for dinner tonight," Tom called after her.

"Going over to Lindsey's after practice," Jill yelled back. "We have a math test already. Her mom will drive me home after dinner. Bye."

"Well, call and let me know what time you're coming home," Tom said, though he knew his words had bounced, unheard, off the front door.

The phone rang moments after Jill departed. Tom answered it without checking caller ID and was glad to hear Marvin's voice on the other end of the line.

"Hey! Called the hospital and heard you checked yourself out," Marvin said.

"Yeah, long story. What's up, Marvin?"

"What are you doing?"

"Ah, let's see . . . recovering from a concussion, cleaning up from a reconciliation breakfast that nobody ate, and waiting for my lawyer to call with news that all charges against me have been dropped."

Marvin made a slight chuckle. "Well, no can do on the last item on your list. But I do have something. Pretty interesting stuff, too. When can you get over here?"

"Not many people want to hang with an alleged sex offender. I'd say my calendar is wide open today, tomorrow . . . and, well, for the foreseeable future."

"Well, get over here right away," Marvin said. "You really need to see this for yourself."

CHAPTER 60

Marvin didn't pick up his head when Tom entered his office. The lawyer remained hunched over his conference table, where he appeared to be reading from a baseball almanac. A coffee mug and a hefty law journal kept the thick tome pried open. Stacks of papers set upon the floor created a mini obstacle course for Tom to navigate.

"Have I inspired you into a new career as a private investigator?" Tom asked in a voice loud enough to get Marvin's attention. "Hope you do better than the guys you hired to watch Jill."

Marvin looked up and impatiently waved Tom over. "I was going to call back and see if you're even allowed to drive with your head all banged up," Marvin said, "but I figured a guy who leaves the hospital against medical advice isn't going to follow any prescribed driving restrictions, either."

"I'm fine to drive. My head hurts pretty much all the time, so it's become sort of normal now."

"Well, that's one way to cure a headache. Make it the norm. Okay, I'm going to tell you a story."

"Oh, good," Tom said. "For a second there I thought

you had something really important and useful to show me."

"Patience, my good man. Patience."

Tom worked his way over to the conference table. Marvin flipped his dangling tie over his shoulder so that Tom had a clear view of the page in the almanac he'd been reading.

"What do you know about the nineteen eighty-eight Los Angeles Dodgers?" asked Marvin.

"They played baseball," Tom said. "And got paid a lot of money to do it."

"Kirk Gibson signed a three-year four-point-five-million-dollar free agent contract to play for the team," Marvin said. "You couldn't afford a utility player for that kind of cash today."

"I wouldn't sneeze at it," Tom said.

"Before Gibson signed with the team, the Dodgers typically finished around the middle of their division. Fred Claire, the team GM at the time, brought in Gibson because he knew the guy was a game changer. Real workhorse-type player."

"So Kirk Gibson framed me?" Tom said.

"Cute. No. He didn't. But he did impart the fear of failure to his teammates and got them into first place at the end of May."

"Go, Kirk," Tom said.

"Well, nobody picked them to win at the start of the season. And nobody thought they were going to beat the Mets, but that's just what they did to win the NLCS. Next up, the World Series against the Oakland A's—Canseco, McGwire, and Henderson, the big bad three. Don Baylor went and made the egregious mistake of expressing his disappointment that the A's wouldn't be facing the best

team in the National League. The Dodgers, huge under-
dogs, were more than a little fired up. Gibson was pretty
much tapped out, though. He'd strained his knee and torn
a hamstring in the NLCS."

Tom had been training to become a SEAL that year,
but even he saw the most memorable moment from that
Series.

"Gibson smacked a home run, then hobbled around the
bases," Tom said.

"Game one, bottom of the ninth, the crowd went crazy
when Gibson took the field. Eckersley was on the mound.
Three-two count. Gibson's swing looked to be one-handed,
but he made enough contact to win the game with a home
run to right. Dodgers went on to win the series in five
games."

Tom gave Marvin his best "I'm still waiting for the
punch line" look.

"A lot of people say that home run was the greatest in
World Series history. I'm one of them."

"Marvin, this is all very interesting, but what does any
of this have to do with my case?" Tom tried to keep his
frustration from showing.

"Take a look at this."

Tom followed Marvin over to his computer, where he
had a Web page open with a picture of the Los Angeles
Dodgers 1988 World Series championship ring on display. Marvin held up his cell phone to show Tom the
image he'd taken of the injury to his cheek. Tom didn't
need long to see a matching pattern.

"I knew I'd seen that shape before," Marvin said. "It's
a baseball diamond, of course. But when I first saw
your injury, I thought, if it is a World Series ring, those
other markings could be the bottom part of the letters

D,O,D,G,E,R,S. I remembered that their ring had the team name on it. I got kind of obsessed over that team after their big underdog win."

"Outliers," Tom said.

"But I didn't want to say anything until I checked it out. So I put on my investigator's hat and cross-referenced the employees of the restaurant where somebody slipped you a Mickey with people on the Dodger team payroll."

Tom looked dubious.

"I was assaulted by a former major league baseball player?" he asked.

"Players aren't the only ones to get rings," Marvin said. "Anybody on the Dodgers' payroll that year would have gotten a ring—personal trainers, batting practice pitchers, and such."

Tom's face lit up. "Marvin, you are a beautiful, beautiful man," Tom said. "What did you find?"

Marvin couldn't keep from smiling. "A ring from eighty-eight could have been pawned or sold on eBay. It was a long shot I knew, but I got a hit."

"Who?"

"A former equipment manager named Frank T. Delacroix. Know him?"

Tom tried to link the name but shook his head. "Should I?"

"He lives in southern New Hampshire and was in heavy rotation on the local news a while back. That's why I'm asking," Marvin said. Reaching for the floor, Marvin hauled up a stack of papers with a glossy black-and-white photograph on top. He handed the photograph to Tom.

Tom examined the picture and nodded as soon as he connected the dots. "Wait, I do know this guy," Tom said. "He was at the country club shindig Boyd invited me to."

Marvin returned a puzzled look. "Forgive the judgment pass, but you just don't strike me as the country club type," Marvin said.

"I'm not. Believe me, Boyd won't be inviting me back anytime soon. He's convinced I'm sleeping with his wife. But before all that, he introduced me to this guy as Frank Dee, not Delacroix."

Tom flashed on a memory of Frank Dee from the club that night. He remembered wondering whether Dee had recently divorced. Apparently, it wasn't a wedding ring he typically wore on that hand.

"Frank Dee is his new name," Marvin said. "He changed it after he was released from prison."

"Prison? What for?"

"Guess."

"Betting on baseball?"

"Guess again."

"Okay. Scopolamine smuggling."

"Close," Marvin said, smiling. "Try crystal meth. Seems like this guy was a master cooker. But as you now know, that's not all he can cook. Mr. My-Name-Once-Was-Delacroix got into the restaurant business after he got out of the meth cooking business. He's now the franchise owner for a bunch of restaurants throughout the state, including that Johnny Rockets on one-forty."

"But why wasn't this guy in jail? Isn't crystal meth a pretty serious offense?"

"Case never went to trial," Marvin said. "A few weeks before the trial a wee little procedural no-no came up. A technicality with the search warrant, which renders all the crucial evidence against Delacroix inadmissible in court."

"D.A. dropped the charges after that, I suppose," Tom said.

Marvin pantomimed the ringing of an imaginary bell. "And guess who Mr. Delacroix-Dee is related to? First cousin related."

"Kip Lange," Tom said.

Again, Marvin pantomimed that ringing bell.

"So Lange must have brought Dee into the deal," Tom said. "Probably promised him a cut. But how does a guy like Dee run a family business? With the Web being what it is, you'd think somebody would have picked up on his past and made a big stink about it."

"Well, Mr. Delacroix went through a pretty extensive life makeover. New ID. New Social Security number. Essentially, he became a whole new person. You search the Web and it's clean of any link between the old Delacroix and the new Dee. Then I came across this *New York Times* investigative report about how the Internet is making it easier for people to live a double life. One article in the series focused on the Delacroix to Dee transformation. Apparently, the new Dee hired a company that specializes in online reputation management."

"What's online reputation management?" asked Tom.

"Basically, you can pay these specialists and they'll keep you looking good on the Web. Its like a twenty-four-hour-a-day Internet watchdog to stamp out slander, lies, and malicious rumors about their clients. I wanted to know if Dee's online reputation was still being scrubbed clean by somebody, so I posted a bunch of pretty inflammatory comments on the *New York Times* Web site that I figured would get picked up in a search engine and broadcast to anybody monitoring for such things."

"And what happened?" Tom asked.

"Within twelve hours, my comments were removed. Then I got an e-mail from somebody at Cortland & Associates, warning me to refrain from any further attempts at slander or face legal action."

"Who's that?"

"Cortland & Associates is a large PR firm headquartered in Boston, but with offices all around the world. They do a lot of standard corporate PR work, but it seems they have a subspecialty in online reputation management."

"But what you posted about Dee wasn't a rumor. It was the truth."

"The Internet is fast replacing television as the disseminator of the truth," Marvin said. "What's available online for people to find and read is what the people now believe."

Tom moved the keyboard to Marvin's computer over to where he could type.

"You look like you've lost another liter of blood," Marvin said.

"No, it's the name of that PR firm," Tom said. "I met a guy at the club the night Boyd introduced me to Frank Dee. His name was Simon Cortland."

"Interesting."

"But you just made me think of something even more interesting than that. After I got out on bail, I paid a little visit to James Mann."

"You did what?"

"I knew you wouldn't approve."

"I wouldn't and I don't."

"I suggested Mann conduct a little bit of research. He took the risk. I just supplied him with some names. Anyway, we were talking about who would have framed him and why. He thought it had something to do with an upcoming promotion, but only a few people in the company even knew about that, or so he believed. But they did have the press releases ready to go."

"Press releases," Marvin said. "Are you thinking . . ."

Tom brought up the Web site for Cortland & Associates. He showed Marvin the page listing all of Cortland's many clients. Using Marvin's computer mouse, Tom highlighted one name in particular.

PrimaMed Corporation.

Tom and Marvin regrouped at the conference table.

"So Frank Dee is connected to Kip Lange," Marvin said. "And we've got Cortland & Associates connected to PrimaMed Corporation, which is also connected to Mr. James Mann."

"Lange is connected to me," Tom said. "And so is James Mann."

"But from what you told me, the only real connection we've established between Dee and Cortland is Roland Boyd."

"So how is Boyd connected to Lange?"

"Well, he knew Lange," Marvin said. "Weren't you guys all on the same military base in Germany at the same time?"

"But he wasn't involved with what happened to Greeley or with the heroin I took out of the country. Kelly was only worried about one person—the guy who orchestrated the heist and recruited her into his plan. Kip Lange. I can tell you after my run-ins with Roland Boyd that he's just as dangerous as Lange. Kelly would have been terrified of him if she felt she had any reason."

"What about Cortland and PrimaMed?" Marvin asked. "Do you think they have any links back to Boyd?"

"I don't know," Tom said. "But it sure seems worth finding out."

Marvin fixed Tom with a cold, unblinking stare. "I need

you to come clean with me, Tom. Not that I don't trust you after you kept your James Mann rendezvous a secret from me, but is there any other reason for Boyd to have you penned on his permanent shit list?"

"No," Tom said. "We were friends right up until he thought I was sleeping with his wife."

Tom told Marvin about his having to break in and rescue Jill from inside Roland's house.

"Are you and Adriana having an affair?" Marvin asked afterward. "Answer me honestly, Tom. Please."

"No. God, no. Marvin, you can ask Adriana yourself if you don't believe me."

"Yes. Ask me."

Tom and Marvin looked up and saw Adriana Boyd. Their jaws fell open simultaneously. Her truculent stance matched the coldness in her eyes. Tom's face lit up at the sight of her.

Adriana crossed the room in four long strides. She maneuvered over to where Tom stood, dodging the paper piles with graceful steps.

"Adriana," he said. "What are you doing here?"

Adriana raised her arm. If Tom hadn't been so surprised, he would have reflexively shifted into a defensive posture. She swung her open palm in an arc toward Tom's face. The blow landed hard against his cheek, making a thunderclap sound. Tom felt pulses of pain where her hand had been.

"Don't you dare touch my son again," she said. Her voice was low and menacing.

"Adriana . . . you don't understand. . . ." Tom could only stammer out the words.

"I understand that you laid your hands on my son Mitchell. Roland, of all people, convinced me not to press charges against you. He said it was all some big misunderstanding. You're lucky I waited outside in my car as long as I did, or I might not be in control of myself."

"You followed me here?" Tom said, incredulous.

"I came to your house just as you were pulling out of your driveway," Adriana said. "Believe me when I tell you that I'm much calmer now."

"Adriana, look, I understand that you're upset. But something happened between my daughter and Mitchell that you should know about."

"I don't want to know anything about anything, Tom. Stay away from my family. I mean it."

With that, Adriana Boyd turned on her heels and left.

Minutes passed before either man spoke. Marvin broke the silence first.

"Tom, why didn't Roland Boyd go to the police after you broke into his house? You told him Jill would probably report the incident. This is a guy who locked you in a cooler because he thinks you were sleeping with his wife. Don't you think it's a little bit curious that he didn't want to press any charges?"

"More than a little," Tom said.

CHAPTER 61

Tom drove Kelly's eight-year-old Honda home from Marvin's on autopilot. He was lost in a fog. Only when he neared the house could he vaguely recall having driven there.

Marvin had made Tom swear, with his right hand pressed on his case file, that he'd keep his distance from Roland Boyd and Frank Dee.

"Let me do some more digging before you go charging at them," his lawyer pleaded. "I'm not convinced this doesn't have something to do with your trial. I need to learn everything I can about Frank Dee and how he operates. Last thing we need is an incendiary like you blowing things up before I can even piece it together."

"Agreed," Tom said.

The first call he made was to Adriana. He dialed her cell phone from the landline in the kitchen. As he expected, the call went to voice mail.

"I'm not looking for redemption here, Adriana," Tom said in his message. "I value our friendship, and I'm forever grateful for your generosity. But my child was in danger, and you may be as well. Please give me a chance to explain. Call me."

Tom set the wireless phone back in its cradle. He felt a sudden craving for a cup of tea. He selected a packet Kelly had kept in the cupboard. His head still wasn't right, and Marvin's findings, though provocative, cluttered his thoughts and overwhelmed him. Perhaps a cup of raspberry green tea and an afternoon nap would do him some good. Concussions, after all, weren't overcome by the sheer desire to overcome them. He didn't need a medical degree to know that a bit of rest was good medicine. He could clean up the kitchen after a quick nap.

Still sensitive to light, Tom lowered the shades in the living room. Teacup in hand, he settled himself onto the couch. Two sips and already his eyelids were shutting. He set the cup and saucer carefully on the floor and laid his body lengthwise on the couch. The quiet was blissful. There was a distinct smell that the late morning sun had baked into the cushions—an odor of sleepiness.

And so the darkness came to him.

"Dad!"

Tom stirred.

"Dad!" Jill's voice cried again.

Tom opened his eyes and saw his daughter's tear-streaked face staring down at him. He sat upright and knocked over the teacup with a loud clank when his feet found the floor.

"Jill . . . what are you doing home?" he asked, while his hands vigorously rubbed his face awake. "What time is it?" Tom peeked at the gap between the window and shade and saw bright light seeping through.

"Lindsey is missing," Jill managed to say before her tears said the rest.

"Missing? What are you talking about?" Tom stood and gripped his daughter by the shoulder.

Jill regained some composure after taking a few deep breaths. "She wasn't at school. Hasn't been answering her cell phone, either. I figured she was home sick. Then her mother called me. She wanted to know if I'd seen Lindsey at school."

"Didn't her mother know if she went to school?"

Jill shook her head no. "She says she was asleep and didn't hear Lin leave. But I know that means she was passed out in the living room. Lindsey could be missing for hours. What are we going to do? Her mom is totally freaking out, and so am I."

Tom encouraged Jill to take a seat on the couch. "Wait here," he said to her. He gathered up the teacup and saucer, then returned them to the kitchen. He came back holding a tall glass of water. "Drink this slowly," he instructed. Jill did as she was told, and it seemed to help. "Now, tell me why you think she's missing and didn't run away or something. She's under a lot of pressure."

"No. Lindsey wouldn't do that. I know her. She'd have called me."

"How can you be so sure of that?" Tom asked. "You don't always know what your friends will do."

"No, there's more. I didn't tell you the truth about that night at Mitchell's. I think something's happened to Lindsey because of it, and it's my fault."

Tom felt his chest tightening. "What did you hide from me, Jill?" Tom said as he braced himself to hear the word *rape*.

"Mitchell didn't try to have sex with me," Jill confessed. "I found images on his computer. Naked pictures of me. There were pictures of Lindsey, too. And other girls from school. Girls I didn't even know."

Tom gave his daughter a fractured look. He could not have misheard her, but what she said didn't make any sense. "Pictures? What do you mean?"

Again Jill took in a breath. She told her father about the party she'd attended last June. About getting drunk and passing out. She confessed to having no memory of her top coming off—whether she'd done it herself or someone had done it for her. Then she told him why she'd gone to Mitchell's in the first place.

"Lindsey and I wanted to know if Mr. Boyd was paying Mitchell to get you in trouble."

"Jill, this is very serious," Tom said. "The police found pictures of Lindsey on my computer. Other girls from Shilo High School, too. They might be the same images you found on Mitchell's computer."

"You didn't tell me what they found," Jill said. "All I knew was that they were illegal. I couldn't think about what that really meant."

Tom nodded. He'd shielded Jill from those pictures. He couldn't face telling her that one set of images was of her best friend naked.

"Why would you think Roland Boyd was involved?" Tom asked, more forcefully than he intended.

"You were so freaked out about my hanging around with Mitchell," Jill said somewhat sheepishly. "You told me that Roland Boyd was dangerous, and I'd seen Mitchell's computer room."

Tom grimaced, but at least it explained her thinking. "Okay, so you go to Mitchell's house to spy on him and you find these pictures."

Jill nodded.

"How many pictures are we talking about here?"

Jill shrugged. "I took what I could get. Mitchell found me looking at them."

"You took them?"

"I copied the images to a storage key he had."

"And then he attacked you?"

Jill nodded. "He didn't see me call you. Then, for the longest time, he just paced around in his bedroom with me there on his bed. He kept saying, 'What am I going to do?' over and over again. He didn't hit me or anything. He just kept walking back and forth. Making me swear that I wouldn't say anything, and whenever I thought he was going to let me go, he'd make me sit back down on the bed and swear to him again."

"Did he hurt you?" asked Tom.

Jill touched her neck. "He put his hands on me," she said. "I swear, I thought he was going to kill me. He looked totally insane. But then he'd calm down. I think I had him convinced I'd stay quiet. That's when you showed up."

"So he wanted you to stay quiet about the pictures. Is that it?"

"He said if I didn't, he'd ruin me," Jill explained. "He threatened to publish the pictures all over the Internet and send them to everybody in school."

"You could have told me. Why didn't you tell me?"

"I didn't want you to be ashamed of me," she said in a low voice.

"Jilly, I'm your father. I'll never be ashamed of you. But I can't promise I'll always be proud of your decisions, either. What you did at that party was a stupid mistake. Dangerous, too, and you know it."

Jill frowned. "I told Lindsey about it," said Jill. "And I gave her the images I copied."

"Do you think Lindsey confronted Mitchell?"

Jill shrugged. "I don't know. She might have. We need to call the police," Jill said. "Something bad has happened. I can feel it."

The police, Tom thought. *Oh . . . no.* "Jill, think about this for a second. Why did I get arrested?"

"But none of that's true. We talked about that."

"Sergeant Murphy isn't going to see it that way. I've got a feeling, if Lindsey really is missing, I'm about to become a prime suspect in her disappearance."

"No. I was here with you all last night. I'm an alibi."

"That's not how it works. Did you fall asleep?"

Jill nodded weakly.

"There goes your alibi. I better let Marvin know what's going on. I've got a feeling I might not be out on bail much longer."

Tom moved to get the phone in the kitchen, but Jill caught him by the arm and turned him around. "If the police focus on you, they won't be looking for Lindsey," Jill said. "They'll just keep asking you what happened to her."

"Honey, that's their job. You've got to trust that they know how to do it."

"But you just said they won't do it right."

Tom fixed Jill with the look he typically reserved for her best plays on the soccer field. Jill was always quick thinking, but her logic impressed him nonetheless. Tom studied Jill's pained expression. She was smart enough to know they had no easy way out of the conundrum. "You'll need to tell the police about Mitchell and the pictures. If something happened to Lindsey, it would give them another motive to explore."

Jill seemed to disappear into thought, and when she returned, she did so with a worried look on her face. "The evidence is gone. I'm sure of it," Jill said. "Mitchell wouldn't leave stuff lying around. It'll be my word against his."

"And being that you're the daughter of the guy with a motive, your word isn't going to be all that credible."

"Not very credible at all," Jill agreed.

"I'll call Marvin and brace him. Lindsey's mother should call the police."

"What about Mitchell?" Jill protested. "If they keep looking at you, they're going to miss something that will lead them to Lin. I just know it."

"I don't know anything about computers, Jill. I can work high-tech weapons blindfolded, but I can't even get on the Internet without your help."

"Wait here," Jill said.

Tom watched her storm down the hallway and disappear into her bedroom. She emerged holding something white in her hand. Only when she got closer could Tom see that it was a business card.

Jill handed the card to Tom, then took a step back to wait for a reaction.

"The FBI?" Tom said. "I know this lady. How do you know her?"

"She gave a talk at our school about sexting and stuff."

"Why'd she give you a card?"

"Lindsey and I went to see her after. We wanted to find out how somebody could have made it look like Lindsey was the one who wrote those blog posts."

"And?"

Jill gave a quick, nearly imperceptible shrug. "She's just really smart about this stuff. If there's anybody who'd know how to recover evidence that Mitchell destroyed, it's Special Agent Loraine Miles."

CHAPTER 62

The room smelled of wet earth.

Lindsey cowered in the corner of a square, windowless space, twelve by twelve, if her measurements were right, with walls made of concrete bricks. She could stand if she wanted; only her wrists were bound. But she preferred to keep huddled in her makeshift nest. The smooth concrete floor slanted toward a drain in her corner of the room. Lindsey sat on top of that drain, imagining it could suck her through its tiny holes and spit her back outside. She could hear the trickle of a fast-moving stream beyond her prison walls, but only from that corner of the room. The darkness around her, enveloping and impenetrable, clung to her body and weighed her down with fear. The only door in, she knew, stayed locked from the outside.

She'd tried opening it with her feet but ended up scraping her back.

The cold earth seeped through the thin fabric of her clothes and chilled her skin. To keep warm, Lindsey sat on a nappy gray wool blanket that strangely reeked of fried grease.

She felt better now than before. She no longer believed

her heart would keep beating faster and faster until it
burst. She could breathe without hyperventilating. But
she couldn't speak or scream, not with the thick cloth gag
in her mouth. Her throat still ached where she'd been
choked. Her hips and knees were sore now, too, probably
because she'd slept with her body all folded up. Her headache, throbbing and persistent before, had finally subsided some. But she could feel it starting to return. Her
stomach rumbled, and the first pang of real hunger forced
her onto her side.

Sounds came from outside the room, or was that her
ears playing tricks?

Lindsey worked herself into a kneeling position, using
her lateral muscles to lift herself off the floor. She listened, wondering now if the sound had just been her racing heart. She became disoriented, no longer sure of the
location of the door. In the dark, the room became a seam-
less black void.

She heard the distinct sound of a padlock's shackle
being released. She shivered and turned her head in that
direction, flinching when the latch was lifted.

A crack of sunlight soon appeared, painting the outline of a door. She stood, though worried her shaky legs
would give out beneath her, and took a few steps toward
the open door. In her mind this was a rescue. Her father
would be standing in the doorway, arms outstretched,
feeling about the darkness for his missing daughter. A
lump formed in her throat. But the door opened slowly,
without any urgency, allowing the rusted hinges to creak
and groan. A fresh grip of fear kept Lindsey frozen to her
spot on the floor.

The door opened some more.

Please be Daddy . . . please. . . .

Bright light flooded the room and shone on Lindsey's

face, blinding her completely. She heard the door slam shut and the fast shuffle of footsteps come toward her. Rough hands (a man's, Lindsey thought) grabbed her by the shoulders and pushed her back to the floor. She felt a cloth being wrapped around her head, covering her eyes, secured in place by a tight knot tied by capable hands.

Something sharp, pointed, pressed against her neck.

A knife.

Instinctively, she knew the blindfold was a good sign. It meant her captor didn't want to be seen. Maybe because he planned to let her live.

"If you scream, I'll cut your throat," said a man. He spoke in a deep voice that would have been threatening even without the knife. She didn't recognize his voice. The man undid her gag.

Lindsey sucked down her fear, working it into her stomach like something unpleasant she'd been forced to swallow. She managed to speak despite her quivering lips and fast-fluttering heart. "Please . . . please just let me go. . . . I won't say anything about the pictures. . . . Please . . ."

"Are you hungry?"

Lindsey's empty stomach grumbled and churned, as though answering for her. "How long have I been here? Why are you doing this to me?"

"I brought you some food."

"Please, I just want to go home."

"Do you have to use the bathroom?"

"What?"

"Do you have to use the bathroom?" the man repeated.

Lindsey realized that she did, the intense pressure building up. It would only get worse, until eventually she'd soil herself. "Yes," Lindsey said in a shaky voice.

She heard the man set something down beside her. He

grabbed her bound wrists and pulled her down, forcing her fingers to feel around the edges of the object he placed by her feet. Lindsey could tell by touch alone that it was a plastic bucket, the kind she once used to make sand castles at the beach.

"You can pee in this bucket. I'll help you."

Lindsey's mind started to race. In a panic, she tried to back away, but the man grabbed hold and pressed the knife harder to her throat.

"Please. My parents will pay you money. They'll pay to have me back. Please, mister, I just want to go home."

Lindsey sensed something pulling on the front of her denim jeans, a single hand working to free the button from its hole. She shook with fear, hearing every single tooth of her zipper as they pulled apart. She felt the man's hand exploring the contours of her slender waist. He maneuvered himself behind her. That same hand pulled the fabric down, moving from one side of her waist to the other, until he shimmied her jeans down around her ankles.

"Don't worry," said the man. "I won't look."

CHAPTER 63

For the past few hours Rainy and Carter had tried without success to make sense of the disparate hash values of the images Mann had given them. They were examining four of Mann's pictures. The girl Rainy had officially ID'd was Gretchen Stiller.

"Same composition," Rainy said to Carter.

"Exact same."

"So why don't these images generate the same hash value?"

"The pixels aren't the exact same, that's why."

"How so?" Rainy asked.

"Take a look at the color composition of the images when compared side to side. I've arranged them on my monitor screen to run from lightest to darkest."

Rainy could see that each image was progressively darker than the previous one.

"So the colors aren't the same. What do you know about color depth in computer graphics?" asked Carter.

"About as much as I know about caring for houseplants," Rainy said. Her spider plants were almost ready for their last rites.

"Maybe if you used your home for something more

than a glorified storage locker, they might be thriving," Carter said.

"Back to the color depth," Rainy said.

"The job is never going to end, Rainy. There's always going to be bad guys out there. We can't get them all."

"As you were saying—"

"These images are moments in time that'll last forever. You can't say the same thing about your life."

"The color depth, please, Cart," Rainy said, more irritated this time.

"Right. Color depth in computer graphics describes the number of bits used to create the color of a single pixel. The higher the color depth, the greater the range of distinct colors that can be used."

"And the connection to these four?"

"The precision to which color can be represented gets pretty technical. At the pixel level there are slight variations to color that aren't visible to the naked eye, but that would change the hash values."

"Where did Mann get these images?"

"Four different sources," Carter said.

"So each source altered the pixel colors slightly?"

"It looks that way to me," Carter said.

"Why would somebody do that?" Rainy asked.

"That's the question we need to answer."

Rainy's cell phone rang. She answered it.

"It's the coach," Rainy said, covering the phone. Rainy felt a little pulse of excitement, which took her by surprise. She couldn't believe how happy she was to hear from him.

What is wrong with you, Miles? Rainy scolded herself. *He's good looking and probably innocent, that's what's wrong. Bad combination.*

Rainy listened to Tom talk for several minutes without saying a word. "Of course I will," she eventually said into the phone. She ended the call and turned to Carter. "Lindsey Wells is missing," she said.

"Missing? As of when?"

"Sometime between last night and this morning."

"Why is Hawkins calling you?" asked Carter.

"His daughter, Jill, may have found the sext image collection on Mitchell Boyd's computer."

"What now?" Carter asked.

"You're going to try to figure out why people would make slight alterations to the same image composition."

"And you?"

"I'm going to check out a new lead for our James Mann investigation," Rainy answered him. "And maybe, just maybe, help find a missing girl in the process."

CHAPTER 64

On the drive to Shilo, Rainy thought about Lindsey Wells. Her mind painted the gruesome image of a dead girl in the woods, and so she tried to think of something, anything else. Then she'd think about Tom Hawkins.

Rainy parked her sedan on the side of the road. She exited the car and followed a brick walkway to the front door. She rang the bell and waited. Through the sidelight window, Rainy watched Tom Hawkins descend the staircase. He extended his hand to her as he opened the door.

"Thanks for taking the time to come all the way up here," Tom said.

Again Rainy felt that flash of attraction. Was she not seeing the case right? Was that attraction clouding her judgment? She pushed those thoughts aside. She needed to reestablish the divide between the law and the rest. "Are you sure it's okay for me to come inside?" she asked.

That's what I'd say to a suspect, Rainy thought. What was Tom really to her? Suspect? Victim? Or something else? Rainy wanted to trust him. To believe in his innocence. But the girl linked to him had gone missing. Trust was something she wasn't fully ready to give.

"Of course," Tom said. "We're glad you're here."

"We?"

"Marvin, my attorney. And Jill."

Rainy followed Tom into the home. Jill was waiting for them at the top of the stairs. She waved as soon as she saw Rainy. When Rainy reached the top of the landing, the two shook hands. Rainy glanced into the living room and next down the hallway but saw nothing out of the ordinary.

"Jill, I'm so sorry we're meeting again under these circumstances," Rainy said.

Jill nodded quickly, several times, which Rainy took to mean "Thanks, but I can't talk about it yet."

Marvin, who was dressed in a tracksuit, shook Rainy's hand as well. "Sorry about the attire," Marvin said. "Tom's got me on a new workout program. Five pounds in two weeks. Not bad."

"No. Very impressive," said Rainy.

"I really appreciate the tip you gave me about the computer battery," Marvin said. "It's going to make a difference."

"D.A. isn't going to drop the charges," Rainy said. "They told me that several times."

"Me as well," Marvin said. "But the jury is going to see it as a huge hole. Big enough to dump in truckloads of reasonable doubt."

"As long as we're on the same page," Rainy heard herself say. She sounded cold. Detached. Was she just being protective of herself? Was she afraid of getting close to them—to Tom and Jill? He was going to be tried for the very crimes she'd dedicated her life to preventing. She worried it was a trial they couldn't win. Unless she could prove otherwise, Tom Hawkins might be going to jail for a very long time.

"Agent Miles, this case is not what it seems," Marvin said. "I'm glad you're here to help."

I don't know what to believe, Rainy thought.

"Why don't we sit at the kitchen table," Tom suggested.

"Sounds good," Rainy said. She followed Tom into the spacious, bright kitchen and took a seat at the rectangular table. Her seat faced the windows, and she could see out into the backyard, with its spacious, well-kept lawn. There were no tents or tarps out back that could conceal a hostage or a body. No storage shed, either, at least from what she could see.

The battery. James Mann. A collection of sexts. Different pixel colors used for the same image composition. A missing girl. Rainy wanted the delineation between guilt and innocence to be as clear as the bright and cloudless Shilo sky.

"Can I get you something to drink, Agent Miles?" Tom asked.

"No, thank you," Rainy said. She would never accept a drink from a suspect, but of course, she wouldn't tell him that.

Tom sat across from Rainy, Jill in the seat to her right, and Marvin next to Jill.

"Are you sure you want to talk to me?" Rainy asked.

Tom nodded, though he now appeared confused. "Of course we want to talk to you. We invited you here."

"Of course," Rainy said. She knew to overdo the questions, to plug any holes Marvin might use to try to demonstrate entrapment. Marvin and Tom seemed to think Rainy was on their side, but she wasn't sure whose side she was on.

"Let's start with Lindsey," Rainy continued. "You said

on the phone that she's missing. Have there been any new developments?"

Tom took hold of Jill's hand. Jill didn't pull away. Did she no longer believe Lindsey and her father were having an affair? Rainy wondered if she was partly responsible for that turnaround.

"Nothing has changed," Tom said. "Lindsey's mother has filed a missing persons report. I guess notices have been sent to all the New England and New York police departments. If she doesn't turn up in twenty-four hours, they'll organize a search."

"Have the police questioned you in connection to Lindsey's disappearance?" Rainy asked.

"Not yet," Marvin answered. "But I'm sure they will."

"At this point, people usually tell me they didn't have anything to do with a disappearance," Rainy replied.

"I didn't think I had to," Tom replied.

"Why don't you tell me how you think this is connected to sexting."

It took Jill several minutes to tell Rainy everything she knew.

"So, Lindsey told you that she sent pictures of herself to Tanner Farnsworth?"

Jill nodded.

"You found topless pictures of yourself on Mitchell Boyd's computer?"

Again, Jill nodded. "There were other girls on Mitchell's computer, too," Jill added. "Some I knew. Some I didn't."

Marvin brought Rainy up to date on Tom's car accident, careful not to reveal too much privileged information. Tom recounted how he rescued his daughter from Mitchell's bedroom.

"I'm worried the police are going to focus on my dad," Jill said. "What if Mitchell Boyd had something to do with Lindsey's disappearance?"

"Well, I can speak with the Shilo PD and make sure they have all this information," Rainy said.

"That would be a big help," said Marvin. "I don't think anything we have to say will carry much weight with them."

"Did you tell the police what you told me?" asked Rainy.

"No," Tom said. "But when you talk to them, you can't mention that I broke into the house. They can't know."

"Why?"

"Because Roland Boyd could use that to press charges against me. If he starts to feel any heat on Mitchell, he could say that he wasn't aware I'd broken into his home. It would get my bail revoked. Jill would be left vulnerable."

"I see," Rainy said. "Well, I can tell them Jill's side of the story. They need to know where to start looking."

"I think that's a good idea," said Tom.

Marvin appeared satisfied, but Jill looked worried.

"Mitchell won't do anything with your pictures, Jill," Tom said. "Not with people watching him now."

"After I talk to the Shilo PD, I think I'll take a trip over to Roland Boyd's house myself," said Rainy.

"Why?" Tom asked.

"I'd like to see just how cooperative Roland Boyd and his son feel like being with me."

"That sounds great," Marvin said. "I've got a trip planned for the afternoon myself."

Tom shot Marvin a surprised look. "Where are you going? I thought you said you had witness depositions for my case this afternoon."

"I moved them," Marvin said. "I managed to get a meeting at Cortland & Associates this afternoon."

"Cortland? What for?" Tom asked.

"Can't say just yet, but I think these guys do a lot more than help creeps like Frank Dee erase their digital past."

CHAPTER 65

Marvin Pressman used the power of intention to create the perfect parking space. As he cruised the one-way streets and maddening intersections of downtown Boston in his pre-owned Subaru Impreza, he softly recited his foolproof space-making mantra. "There'll be a space in front of the building. . . . There'll be a space in front of the building." Sure enough, as Marvin neared the twelve-story office tower where Cortland & Associates was headquartered, the taillights of a gray sedan flashed, and soon after, the car vacated a metered space five steps from his destination.

Marvin fished two hours' worth of quarters from an ashtray that had never been blemished by a single ash. He exited the car, fed the meter, and paused to study his reflection in the building's tall ground-level window.

You're getting there. . . . Five more pounds . . .

Hugging his briefcase close to his side, Marvin spun through the revolving glass door and emerged into an air-conditioned marble foyer that spoke of success. He signed in at the security desk, stuck his peel-away name badge to his suit's breast pocket, and took the elevator to the tenth floor.

Gold-plated letters spelling out CORTLAND & ASSOCI-ATES filled one black marble wall of the tenth-floor lobby. The double glass doors to Cortland's offices were locked, and they opened only after Marvin pushed a button on the intercom.

Marvin approached the reception desk. "I have a meeting with Simon Cortland," he announced to the receptionist.

"Yes, Mr. Pressman. Please have a seat. Mr. Cortland will be with you shortly."

Marvin sat on one of the stylish black leather chairs in the waiting area. He felt uncomfortably low to the ground.

Simon Cortland soon appeared. He was tall, accentuating Marvin's low position. Marvin wondered if that was the furniture's intended purpose. Cortland was dressed splendidly in a dark blue suit, pink shirt, and rich burgundy tie. He looked young, handsome, and rich. Marvin disliked him for those offenses alone.

"Marvin Pressman?"

"Yes," Marvin said. "Simon Cortland, I presume."

"Correct. Pleasure to meet you," Cortland said.

Cortland's handshake was firm. The man's cuff links were gold, and his shoes Italian. Marvin felt woefully underdressed, despite having worn the best suit in his arsenal.

"I'm glad our schedules worked out for this meeting," Marvin said.

Cortland nodded and said, "Me too. We're incredibly busy, and I'm with clients more than I'm in the office. You caught a lucky break. A client meeting was canceled. My colleague, Aaron Donovan, is waiting for us in the conference room. Please, follow me."

Marvin took in what he could of the office layout as he trailed Cortland to the conference room.

The floor layout was the typical division of the haves and have-nots. The closed door offices had views of the city skyline. The gray-walled cubicles in the interior space offered views of the neighboring cube.

Cortland held open the conference room door. Marvin entered first. A man, whom Marvin assumed to be Aaron Donovan, rose from his high-back leather chair to greet him. They exchanged business cards after shaking hands. Donovan was essentially a Cortland clone, dressed in equal splendor. The man hid his confidence with all the subtlety of a floodlight. Marvin took a seat at the expansive conference table, across from the two.

"All I've shared with Aaron is that you have a high-net-worth client in need of our services," Cortland began, "but I don't have the specifics."

Marvin took out a yellow legal pad from his briefcase and set a ballpoint pen atop a blank page. "My client is a resident of Shilo, New Hampshire," Marvin began. "He's been charged with a felony. I'm his attorney of record. However, we're also friends. He's looking to rebuild his life and salvage his reputation once this unfortunate incident is behind him."

"And how is it you came to Cortland & Associates?" Donovan asked. "The majority of our public relations work is done for corporations."

"Well, reputations spread—both the good and the bad. Isn't that your business?"

Cortland cleared his throat and made a slight hand gesture, indicating to Donovan that he take the lead.

"Our business services encompass a broad spectrum of capabilities," Donovan said. "Strategic planning, crisis communication, media relations, and even investor training."

"Reputation management is a core competency as well,

is it not?" Marvin asked. "At least it says so on your Web site."

Cortland nodded. "Yes. We have a business unit dedicated to reputation management. With the explosion of the social Web in recent years, we believe this will become an increasingly important component of our business."

"Which is exactly why I came to you," Marvin said. "My client is quite well off, as I've told you. So funding his reemergence, if you will, won't be a problem. My interest lies with the approach. How is it you go about salvaging corporate reputations under attack?"

Cortland passed Donovan a look that encouraged the man to answer and signaled to Marvin that he was the technical brains behind the operation.

"It's really all about measurement and trust," Donovan began.

Marvin shrugged his shoulders to show he wasn't following. "Feel free to consider me an ignorant lawyer who knows nothing about your business processes, because, in fact, that is what I am."

Cortland smiled at Marvin. "Your friend is lucky to have you take such an interest in his life outside the trial," he said.

"He's been a good friend to me over the years. I consider us both lucky."

Donovan continued with his explanation. "We have tremendous technology talent on staff," he said.

"Aaron being among the best," Cortland interjected. "Carnegie Mellon undergrad. CalTech for a PhD in computer science."

"Believe me," Aaron said, "I'm not even the best on staff."

"Impressive," Marvin said. "It surprises me that you

tech types went into PR. I'd have thought you'd be building some whiz-bang dot-com business or something."

"Well, this business is whiz-bang, Mr. Pressman,"
Donovan said. "Our mission is to protect the brand. To do
that, we've developed highly sophisticated real-time search
engines that scour every corner of the Internet for mention of our clients. From there, we have tools that can
weigh the importance of the messages based on a propri-
etary social scale we've developed."

"Social scale?"

"We first understand who communicated the message,
then quantify and rank their influence using a set of custom algorithms."

"Impressive," Marvin said. "You can tell if a reputation attack is something that can be ignored or something
to be addressed based on this rating?"

Donovan nodded. "Precisely."

"How does all this measuring and monitoring translate
into results for your clients?"

"Do you recall the Baby Natural crisis?" Cortland
asked.

Marvin nodded. "Sure. A disgruntled employee started
spreading rumors online that the food was contaminated.
He made up fictitious stories about babies getting sick.
Created a bunch of online personas that weren't real to
make it look like the issue was serious and widespread."

"Well said," Donovan commended. "And, of course, all
lies. Thanks to our technology, we knew the scam was
happening before anybody at Baby Natural did. But the
public isn't always willing to believe a company, even if
the claims against it are false."

"So I don't get it. How did you help? The damage was
done. Word got out, and I'm sure sales were lost."

"Actually, the opposite happened. Sales jumped from

the publicity that the story generated. The only reason you heard about the incident is because we wanted you to hear about it. We tracked down the scammer before too many people had a chance to read his posts. Then we controlled all communication about the incident to the general public. Baby Natural came across as the victim. They had the full support of the FDA. The post-incident PR campaign projected a company that was transparent to the consumers and highly responsive."

"And got a whole lot of publicity," Marvin concurred. "Well done."

"This is the future, Marvin," Cortland broke in. "And we believe reputation management cuts across all businesses and all borders. And you're also correct in assuming that in some cases, we treat individuals of certain wealth and prominence as business entities unto themselves."

"And also men like Frank Delacroix, for instance," Marvin said in response. "Or is it Frank Dee?"

Cortland and Donavan returned Marvin's friendly smile with stony expressions.

"Let's do this," Cortland said as he rose from his chair. "I have a conference call in a few minutes. I suggest we set up an in-person meeting between Aaron and your client. I'm sure after your client learns of all our capabilities, he'll be quite pleased with our services."

"Would Mr. Delacroix be willing to give you a reference?" Marvin asked Cortland. "You said yourself that the public often is reticent to trust the word of a company."

This time Cortland smiled, though Marvin could see that his congeniality was forced. "If we had a client by that name," Cortland said in a humorless voice, "I'm certain that he would." Cortland headed for the conference room door but stopped after Marvin called his name.

"I did a little homework before our meeting," Marvin said. "After all, my reputation reflects every recommendation that I make."

"Oh?"

"Do you know Roland Boyd? He's an investor and venture capitalist type. Lives up my way. In the sticks, as you city folk like to call it."

Cortland took two steps toward Marvin and stopped. His expression turned grim. "What's your point, Mr. Pressman?"

"Well, he appears to have taken advantage of your failure. I mean, you're the reputation guardians. Just thought you guys were good at it, is all."

"We are good," Cortland said.

"But your client, PrimaMed, suffered a terrible PR setback from the recent arrest of James Mann on child pornography, did they not?"

"You've obviously read the stories," Cortland said.

"Yeah, I read them. A lot of the stories I read were posted before the guy got arrested. There was talk on a bunch of pretty influential blogs and message boards about Mann's pending doom. Some anonymous poster claimed he had inside information that Mann was going down. Can you imagine that?"

"Well, rumors are what make the Web go round."

"And rumors also affect company stock price. Early news of his arrest sent the PrimaMed stock into a bit of a tailspin."

"I don't know the specifics," Cortland said.

"I bet someone made some money off that," Marvin continued.

"How do you mean?"

"Well, if someone shorted a bunch of shares of Prima-Med stock, they'd be pretty darn lucky. The stock dropped to twenty on those reports alone, went down to eleven after Mann's arrest."

"Well, someone was lucky, if that's the case."

"Or someone—maybe your pal Roland Boyd, even—knew to short the stock because he knew James Mann was going to be attacked."

"If that were the case," Cortland said, "perhaps this Mr. Boyd had some association with the employee charged. You seem quite the investigative sort. Have you explored that connection?"

"To be honest, Simon, I have a hard time looking anywhere but at you."

"Are you suggesting that we attacked the reputation of a client who entrusted us to guard it?"

"Just asking the question."

"That would be insider trading, and it would put us out of business."

"Well," Marvin said with a conciliatory nod of his head, "I guess when you put it that way, it does sound pretty outlandish."

CHAPTER 66

Somebody was home at the Boyds' house. It was six o'clock in the evening. Lights were on inside the home, and that cherry red Mustang was parked in the driveway.

Rainy had left an earlier message for Sergeant Brendan Murphy, explaining her intentions. This was his jurisdiction and his case to run. But Rainy had done enough of the courtesy protocol to begin investigating on her own. This interview would be FBI exclusive. Rainy rang the doorbell. Carter kept to one side of the landing. Twice now, Rainy had brought Carter into the field with her. She needed his expertise to gather potential evidence from Mitchell Boyd's computers. Carter seemed to welcome the break from life inside the Lair.

Mitchell Boyd opened the door. He gave Rainy the same arrogant smile as Tanner Farnsworth had.

Rainy showed Mitchell her ID. "Do you have a few minutes to chat?" she asked.

"What about?" said Mitchell.

"Lindsey Wells, for starters."

"She's missing," Mitchell said.

"Yes, I know that."

"Then what's there to talk about?"

"Do you know where she is?"

"No. Do you?"

"When did you see her last?"

Mitchell shrugged. "I don't really hang with her. I don't know. School, I guess."

"Is Tanner around?"

"Tanner who?"

"Your friend Tanner Farnsworth."

"Haven't seen him."

"Would you tell me if you had?"

"Sure. Why not? Am I a suspect or something?"

"You tell me."

"No."

"Okay, then. Any idea what happened to Lindsey?"

"You're the cop."

"FBI."

"Whatever."

"So, any ideas?"

"Maybe she ran away. That's what people are saying."

"Why would they say that?"

"Because she was sleeping with the coach."

Roland Boyd approached from down the hall.

"Hey, Dad," Mitchell said. "This is that agent from the FBI. We met at the parking lot before. Remember?"

Roland said that he did.

"She's asking me about Lindsey Wells."

"Why are you asking my son about that?" Roland said.

"I'm assisting with the investigation into Lindsey's disappearance."

"Under whose authority?" Roland asked.

"My own," Rainy said.

"Do our police know about this?"

"I've left a message with Sergeant Brendan Murphy, so yes."

"He doesn't have to talk to you." Roland placed his hand on Mitchell's shoulder.

"No, he doesn't," Rainy agreed.

Roland stayed quiet for a long second. "Forgive me for being so discourteous. The whole town is praying for Lindsey's safe return," Roland continued. "You can imagine why we're all so on edge, as parents."

"I can imagine," Rainy said.

"Well, if there is anything we can do to help, you just let us know."

"Well, actually, there is," said Rainy.

"Oh?"

"I'd like to have a look at your son's computers. I've brought one of our computer analysts from Boston with me. If you wouldn't mind, we'd like to create mirror copies of the machines to conduct our own forensic analysis. I've brought some paperwork to sign that would authorize the search."

"We don't have to permit that, you know," Roland said.

"Of course not."

Mitchell looked at the older Boyd, then back to Rainy.

"Have at it," he said. "But I've had to rebuild all the machines."

"Rebuild?"

"Got hit with a virus," Mitchell explained. "Nearly ruined my machines. Salvaged some stuff, but lost a bunch, too. Basically, every computer I've got is a new install. Not sure how it'll help."

"Just so we're clear, you don't mind if we search your computers? You'll sign the consent search forms?"

Mitchell nodded. "If you think it'll help find Lindsey, I'll do whatever you need me to do," he said.

Again that smile.

Rainy felt like she was playing a game. A losing one at that. Rainy and Carter followed Mitchell upstairs. Roland Boyd followed. Mitchell showed them the alcove where he kept what he called his computer lab.

"Why all the machines?" Carter asked him.

"Got to stay on top of technology if you want to stay ahead," Mitchell said.

Roland Boyd stepped closer to his son. "Mitchell's got a great head for business and technology. Those are the skills of tomorrow. He'll do quite well."

Carter connected his equipment to the first of Mitchell's three computers. The screen flickered on. The computer was locked. The background image on the screen was a skull colored to look like the yin and yang symbol.

"What's that?" Carter asked.

"Oh, I have them on all my computers," Mitchell said. The boy turned around, pulled down his shirt collar, and showed them his tattoo. "Got the same design in ink," he said with his back turned. "I think it's the ultimate symbol of life. The yin. The yang. And death."

"The skills of tomorrow," Rainy muttered into Carter's ear.

"This will take a little while," Carter said. "We appreciate your being so cooperative."

"No problem," Mitchell replied. "I'll be downstairs if you need me."

Mitchell left the alcove. Roland followed him out. Rainy sat down on a chair.

"What do you think?" Carter asked when they were alone.

"I think a yin and yang skull makes for one macabre calling card," she said.

CHAPTER 67

Tom drove past a dozen hand-painted signs on his way to Marvin's office. WE LOVE YOU LINDSEY, one of them read. COME HOME SOON, read another. They'd painted Lindsey's jersey number on many of them.

The first volunteer search effort to look for Lindsay was getting underway. She'd been missing for almost twenty-four hours. Jill's name was on the volunteer list, along with the names of hundreds of other town residents.

Marvin spoke before Tom had a chance to sit down. "Cortland is fishy," he said. "And Boyd is caught up in something big."

"Big in what way?" Tom asked.

"I can't put all the pieces together yet," Marvin said.

"Well, what pieces do you have?"

"I think Boyd is somehow profiting off Cortland's clients."

Tom looked mystified. "How so?" he asked.

"What do you know about short selling stocks?"

Tom formed the shape of a zero with his fingers. "Zip," he said.

"It's a common investing practice," Marvin explained. "Basically, the investor is making a bet a stock price will drop. But here's the tricky part. When you short a stock, you're essentially selling something you don't own."

"Oh, that clears it up," Tom said.

"Think about an agreement between you and a broker. You sell a stock you don't own, but you have to buy it back. You hope that when you buy it back the price went down, not up."

"Illustrate please," Tom said.

"Okay, hypothetically, you think a stock is going to take a dumper. Say it's trading at a hundred bucks a share, and you think it's overvalued and going to drop. In this hypothetical example, you short the stock and sell a thousand shares that you don't own at a hundred bucks a share."

"Who buys stock that I don't own?"

"A broker. But they do it with a promise you'll buy those shares back. So step one, the broker has to give you cash for the stocks you sold but didn't own. Bang! They put a hundred grand into your account."

"So it's like a loan," Tom said.

Marvin nodded emphatically. "Exactly," he said. "It's like a loan. The broker essentially adds the fake shares that you sold to their books. But you're legally obligated to buy back the thousand shares at some point in time. Either when you want to cover the buy or the broker requests that you cover. You follow?"

Tom gestured yes with a quick head nod and motioned for Marvin to continue.

"Now, let's say that stock tanks by fifty percent. You decide it's time to cover that thousand shares. How much do those shares cost you?"

"Fifty grand," Tom said. "Fifty bucks a share for a thousand shares."

"How much did the broker dump in your account?"

"A hundred grand."

"Forgetting the commission and fees you'd owe, what'd you clear?"

"Fifty grand," Tom said.

"That's a nice payday," Marvin added.

"But what if the stock goes up and you have to cover?"

"Then if you're asked to cover, you'd buy the shares at a loss."

"And you think Boyd is doing this with Cortland's help?" Tom asked.

"Well, that I don't know," Marvin said. "But I think Boyd may have somehow profited off the misfortune of Cortland's clients."

"What makes you think that?"

"It all comes back to my fascination with outliers," Marvin said.

"Right. In a world of patterns, the evidence that deviates the most from the norm is often the most interesting," Tom said, paraphrasing what Marvin had once said.

Marvin nodded. "Cause and effect. Rafael Nadal uses a lighter racket with a thinner grip than most men on tour. The result? He generates more spin than Bjorn Borg. Even with outliers like Nadal, there's always an explanation."

"And you think you found an outlier with Cortland?"

"I do. That's why I arranged the meeting. I lied and said I had a rich client who needed reputation management services. But my real intent was to gauge their reaction when I brought up PrimaMed."

"And?"

"And I started with Boyd. I checked, but he's not on PrimaMed's board of directors."

"Helpful?"

"No, not really," Marvin said. "Then I asked myself,

does he invest in PrimaMed? I mean, that is his primary business. Well, turns out public information about mutual fund investing is pretty limited. But Boyd's own marketing material shows that one of his funds does in fact invest in PrimaMed."

"So?"

"So, I looked to see how the fund performed. Is PrimaMed a winning stock? Mostly I'm curious about a specific quarter—when the unfortunate James Mann incident occurred."

"What did you find?"

"Not much. Hedge fund managers guard their investment strategies with religious zeal. But Lorne Cuthbert does not."

"Who's Lorne Cuthbert?" asked Tom.

"He works for Boyd. Bottom-rung guy. I figured he'd give up some information if I gave him the right motivation."

"And?"

"And I followed him to a bar. Sat on the stool next to his. Pretended that I knew him from an investment seminar, then asked if he cleaned up on PrimaMed like I did."

"You lied?"

"I deceived," Marvin said.

"To achieve the objective," added Tom. "So?"

"We got to talking. He didn't like that my payday eclipsed his paltry bonus. He was told it was a closed deal. Boyd shorted a lot of PrimaMed stock. Cuthbert, all drunk and fuming mad, recited the numbers off the top of his head."

"So you think Boyd shorted the stock knowing Mann was going to be arrested and made a profit?"

Marvin nodded. "I checked the stock price for that

time period," Marvin said. "It was flat all quarter, except for a big dip when James Mann got arrested."

"But how did Boyd know the arrest was going to go down?"

"I'm guessing our friends at Cortland turned Mr. Mann into a child pornographer. And then they tipped off the FBI. But I don't think that's Cortland's only scam. I think they're inventing online reputation attacks of their own, framing innocent people in the process, and then profiting on the big bucks these corporations pay to clean up the mess Cortland intentionally made."

"You think Boyd and Cortland did the same thing to me?"

"I do," Marvin said.

"Why?" asked Tom.

"That, my friend, is the next question to answer."

CHAPTER 68

Marvin Pressman cleared his checkpoint, two metal posts marking a wide, well-maintained path in the Willards Woods complex of running trails. He glanced down at his watch and couldn't believe what he saw. Unless there was some mechanical failure, Marvin was on pace to complete his thrice weekly five-K run in under forty minutes.

Under forty!

His first attempt at running lasted about five minutes and ended in much wheezing. But he stuck with it, kept pushing himself past the wall. He still had another lap to go, but by his calculations, this was shaping up to be a record-setting effort for the eight-pounds-lighter attorney.

Apple Race, here I come, thought Marvin, who now believed Tom's prediction that he could enter the Shilo road race in October and actually finish. Marvin kicked off his third and final lap with a self-congratulatory pump of his fist. He preferred running through the woods. The trails in Willards Woods were extensive, clearly marked, and less painful on his joints than pavement. He especially enjoyed running in the late afternoon, when he was typically the only runner on the trails. He hated being passed by faster runners. He tended to push himself harder to keep pace, finding that little spurt of adrenaline short-lived and costly in terms of finishing.

He never listened to music when he ran, preferring to enjoy the natural sound track instead. His runs were sacred time, not to be squandered. Here, among the tall trees and chirping birds, Marvin freed himself from e-mail, phone calls, and yes, even those outdated faxes.

And Marvin had much on his mind of late.

The Tom Hawkins case had gone from being just another job to a borderline obsession. He'd defended innocent clients before, but Tom was something else entirely. Someone was out to destroy the reputation of an innocent man, and Marvin wanted to know why. If it was an extortion plot by Kip Lange, why make no demands? Coincidently, Marvin's investigators discovered that Frank Dee had gone on vacation. *Interesting timing for a trip away,* Marvin thought.

Marvin sensed himself closing in on an answer but was still fumbling in the dark for the light switch. If it was a player Tom coached, how could the computer sabotage have been so sophisticated? If it was Cortland, who seemed capable of such feats, what was the motive? Murphy? He would have framed Tom for Kelly's murder, if anything. And how did Boyd fit into all this? Marvin wondered. He had uncovered Roland's connection to Cortland, but the motivation for destroying Tom just wasn't there. Roland's troubles with Tom stemmed from his jealousy over Adriana. But according to Tom, Roland didn't become hostile until after Tom's arrest.

Marvin reached the halfway point of his final lap, but instead of running ahead, he stopped and looked down another path. Something caught his eye. About fifty yards down another trail, Marvin noticed a man stretching.

Even from a distance, Marvin could tell that man was Frank Dee.

Dee wore a black workout suit and had headphones cupping both ears. Dee picked up a pair of small hand-held weights and began walking away from Marvin. Marvin didn't have his cell phone with him, or he'd have called Tom. Marvin took several cautious glances about but saw nobody else in the vicinity. He followed Dee, walking down a trail he didn't know and never took. He kept enough distance so that Dee wouldn't notice the tail.

Dee walked at a slow pace, but his swinging weights obviously intensified the workout. Dee turned off one trail and onto another after covering about half a mile's distance. Marvin followed, maintaining the same safe distance between them. Dee should be in California, visiting family, according to the waitress Marvin's investigator had interviewed.

What was he doing here in the woods? Where was he headed?

Marvin didn't worry about journeying deeper into the forest. There were plenty of posted trail maps to help him find his way out. Marvin used tree cover to keep himself hidden whenever he felt particularly exposed. Dee's head-phones stayed on the entire time.

Marvin felt confident he couldn't be heard.

Dee changed trails again; this one followed a narrow, winding stream with slow-moving water only a few inches deep. Marvin checked a posted trail map and confirmed his suspicions.

They were now in south Shilo.

Damn, how he wished he could call Tom.

Dee followed the water. The wooded trail ended at a wide-open meadow, alive with colorful wildflowers and swaying grasses. Marvin lashed himself to a tall pine tree at the meadow's edge and watched Dee mash down the tall meadow grasses as he made his way toward a hillside. Here the stream fed a much larger body of water.

Marvin now knew where they were: the Willard Pond Icehouse.

The old icehouse was built into the hillside where Dee was now headed. A farmhouse had once stood there, but it had been abandoned long ago and was now broken and dilapidated. Before refrigeration, farmers used icehouses, typically built near water, to keep food perishables fresh. The Shilo historical society had funded a restoration project a few years back that kept the Willard Pond Icehouse from crumbling, but they couldn't afford to save the farmhouse.

What was Dee doing at the icehouse?

Marvin kept clear of the meadow. He saw Dee go into the icehouse. Five minutes passed before Dee emerged from within the hillside bunker. Dee still had his headphones on. Marvin watched him walk up the hill and vanish once again into the woods. Marvin let several minutes pass with no sign of Dee before it felt safe to reveal himself. It took Marvin a minute to cross the meadow, about a football field worth of tall grass, and reach the icehouse door. A wooden fence, three posts long, stood to one side of the icehouse entrance. The icehouse door was built into the hillside. Light-colored grass grew everywhere. Bright green moss clung to the crumbling concrete of the icehouse's outer wall. The wooden door was latched, but not locked. Marvin lifted the latch and pushed the door open. A shaft of light cut a triangular shape that widened with the opening door. Marvin stooped low to clear the door frame and stepped inside.

The room was both dark and dank. He looked to his left, saw nothing. He looked right. For a moment, Marvin couldn't breathe. He couldn't take in what he was seeing. Arms. Legs. A body. A girl's body. She looked like a crumpled ball somebody had tossed aside. It had to be her—Lindsey Wells. Marvin's heart sank.

Then she moved.

"Lindsey! Lindsey Wells! God, I've found you!" he cried out.

Lindsey let out a muffled sob.

Marvin rushed to Lindsey's side, falling hard and slamming his knees painfully against the concrete floor when he reached her. He touched her shoulders. She fell against his chest. Marvin's eyes adjusted to the minimal light. He could see Lindsey's restraints for the first time: wrists bound, feet tied, she'd been blindfolded and gagged, too.

Marvin undid her blindfold first. He wanted her to see that she was safe.

Lindsey's eyes were wide and filled with fear. Her head shook violently from side to side. Her screams, suppressed and unintelligible because of the gag, communicated a profound terror.

"It's okay," Marvin said, clutching her shoulders. "You're safe now, Lindsey. You're safe."

Lindsey kept shaking her head violently, screaming through her gag, thrashing her body wildly about.

Marvin flashed on a thought. Why was the door left unlocked?

"Lindsey, I'm not going to hurt you," Marvin said.

A voice behind Marvin answered. "But *I'm* going to hurt *you*."

Fear swept through Marvin's body, inducing a momentary paralysis. Marvin tried to turn around, but a thick arm wrapped around his neck and began to squeeze. Hard. The man holding him stood, pulling Marvin off the floor. The only thing Marvin could see was Lindsey, those wide eyes, frozen in terror. Marvin felt something sharp press against his side; he flinched in pain. He flailed his body about, making every effort to get free, but to no avail. Marvin felt the knife pressing harder.

"Close your eyes, Lindsey!" he shouted. "Close them tight and keep them closed!"

The tip of the knife pressed hard against Marvin's skin. He felt it puncture, then tear, followed by an agony without equal in his memory. Marvin screamed. The sharp point of the knife ripped through his clothes and dug deep into Marvin's belly without much resistance.

Marvin saw that Lindsey's eyes were shut tight.

Then, blessedly, his pain was gone.

CHAPTER 69

As was customary in the Jewish faith, Marvin Pressman's funeral took place as soon as possible. He'd been dead for less than forty-eight hours. In a few hours more, he'd be laid to permanent rest in the ground. His parents lived in Connecticut, but they were too distraught to drive themselves north. Tom arranged for a car service to bring them to the funeral home. Hundreds attended—colleagues, judges, and clients—joining Marvin's extensive family in a heartbreaking celebration of his life.

Tom sat next to Rainy in the back row of the packed funeral home. The service was brief and dignified, befitting a life lived the same way. Rabbi Toby Hurwitz delivered a thoughtful eulogy, but Tom's tears came at the end of the service, when Marvin's mother spoke. Afterward, people in the front rows began to file out.

Rainy turned to Tom as she pulled a tissue from her purse, and whispered in his ear, "Are you all right?"

Tom nodded. "It's just so senseless," he said. "So sad and wrong. It was an honor to call him my friend. But hearing his mother speak tore me up inside. It made me think about my mother. It made me miss her. No parent should bury a child. It just isn't right."

"I agree, it isn't," said Rainy.

Tom wished Jill were beside him. He wanted to hug her close and keep her safe.

Tom had rarely let Jill out of his sight since Lindsey's disappearance. But he couldn't make her come to Marvin's funeral. Not with the memory of her own mother's service still fresh in her mind.

Tom recalled the phone call from Marvin's assistant that had shattered his world.

Marvin's dead, she had said. *Marvin's gone.*

Police had found his bloodied body on a running trail in Willards Woods. Later that day, on an anonymous tip, they arrested a serial felon in Millis and found in his possession Marvin's wallet and the murder weapon.

A bloodstained knife.

Tom had jumped into action, planning the funeral. It was all he could do to help. Marvin's sister, Amanda, the other lawyer in the family, and a few relatives lived in or near Shilo, but they were distraught and welcomed his help.

The planning was over. Now Tom could ponder the magnitude of what had occurred. Now he could allow himself to grieve.

The crowd soon thinned out, and he and Rainy stood to leave. Outside the morning sun gave way to clouds, and a chill fought its way into the air.

They stopped in front of a missing persons poster tacked to a telephone pole. Lindsey Wells's cheerful face seemed to be watching them. Instructions on the poster detailed where to meet for the afternoon search.

"Is Jill going?" Rainy asked.

"No. I can't let her. Believe me, she wants to."

"Because you think Lindsey's disappearance might be connected to what Jill found on Mitchell's computer?"

"Exactly for that reason. Until I know what's going on, she's either with Vern and his kids or at home with me. She's never alone."

"I see."

"I wish I could go on the search," Tom said. "I'm trained, and with a phone call I can get a dozen military-trained search-and-rescue experts here in a blink."

"Did you offer?"

"I did."

"And?"

"Lindsey's father wouldn't even look me in the eyes when he said no."

"Why?"

"Because he's thinking what everybody around here is thinking."

"What's that?"

"That I had something to do with Lindsey's disappearance. That I did something to her to keep her from testifying against me."

"You told me you didn't. Should I still believe you?"

Tom glared at Rainy but softened the angry look that flashed across his face.

"Yes, you should believe me," he said. "Why do you even ask?"

"Because in my profession, I deal with liars all the time. Do you know anything about antisocial personality disorder?"

"You mean a sociopath? Some, I suppose."

"These people make a lifestyle out of their criminal behavior. They lie without remorse. But they're not delusional. They don't believe their lies. They're just unbelievably good at lying."

"The navy trained me in kinesics. I got pretty good at telling when people were lying."

"Well, I've come across sociopaths who are so good at lying, they can fool a lie detector."

"Not a hard thing to do."

"These people can fool seasoned FBI investigators, spouses, children, parents . . . kinesics experts, too."

"And you think I'm a sociopath and a liar?"

"No," Rainy said. "I just asked if you were."

"Well, if I'm that good a liar, why would you ever believe me?"

"Because I want to believe you," Rainy said.

Tom made sure to look Rainy in the eyes. He knew all the tells of a liar—rapid blinking, excessive face touching, smiling with just the mouth, even a defensive posture.

"I had nothing to do with the disappearance of Lindsey Wells," Tom repeated. Tom didn't say anything more. Rainy would know liars often overexplained themselves, offering more details than requested.

"What's the real reason you asked me to come to Marvin's funeral, Tom?"

"Let's go to your car, and I'll tell you on the way to the cemetery."

Rainy's sedan brought up the rear of a forty-vehicle-long procession. Tom sat in the passenger seat. He had not forgotten that his last trip with a law enforcement officer was spent handcuffed in the backseat.

Rainy spoke first. "Are you ready to talk?" she asked.

"I wanted you to see how much Marvin was loved. I wanted you to get a feel for who he was as a person. Because I wanted you to care about his death."

"Care in what way?"

"You don't really believe Marvin died the way they said he did, do you?"

"What am I supposed to believe?" Rainy answered. "They caught the guy who did it."

"But he's denying having anything to do with it. He says the evidence was planted in his apartment. It's a frame job. I told you what Marvin found out."

"About Boyd's stock-trading scheme?"

"You know this wasn't a random attack. You know to look for connections."

"Possible. But how do you prove it?"

"Look, we've got to come down hard on Cortland," Tom said. "If you don't want vigilante justice, than that's what you've got to do."

Rainy sighed and gave Tom a disapproving look. "I could talk to some people," she offered. "There might be something we can do to investigate Cortland. But it'll take a lot of paperwork, a lot of meetings, and I'm not promising anything. Okay?"

"I reserve my judgment until I see how much you do," he said.

"Tom, no joke. You can't go after these guys yourself, just because you think they did this to Marvin."

"I know they did it to him," he said. "Just promise me that you'll do your best."

"I promise," Rainy said.

At the cemetery Marvin's pallbearers stopped seven times while carrying the casket to the grave. Mourners followed behind as a show of respect. A misty rain fell as Marvin's casket was lowered into the ground. Mourners used the back of a spade to shovel dirt into the hole, a symbolic gesture of their unwillingness to part with the departed.

Tom expressed his condolences to the parents and relatives waiting in two rows to receive them. Tears prickled his eyes again. He promised to pay a condolence call during shivah, the customary seven-day period of deep mourning.

The rain fell harder on their walk out of the cemetery. Tom held a black umbrella high enough to let Rainy stay dry, too. As they passed underneath the cemetery's iron gates, Tom turned and looked behind him. He could still see mourners clustered around Marvin's grave.

A sour taste washed the back of his throat. *It's my fault you're dead,* Tom thought to himself. Marvin was trying to help him, and it cost him his life.

Back inside her car, Rainy turned the ignition and put the vehicle into drive. It was a quiet ride back to the funeral home parking lot. Rainy pulled up next to Tom's car.

"I'm so sorry about Marvin," Rainy said, with the sedan's engine still idling.

"Rainy, I'm glad you came. I know you'll do whatever you can to help. I'm going to get some of my military friends involved, too."

Tom broke from her gaze. Rainy touched his arm and brought him back to her.

"Tom, do you need me to stay longer?"

The moment she asked, Tom realized that he did. He needed her to stay more than anything. He had wanted Rainy to come to Marvin's funeral so she could see the man Marvin had been, but just as strongly, Tom had wanted to be near Rainy again.

"You'd do that?"

"I'm not seeing this case the same way I did when I first came to Shilo."

"What's changed?"

"Now I'm seeing a father who loves his daughter more than anything in the world. And then I've got a laptop computer that was obviously tampered with to make the log file dates sync up. I've got a plausible reason for somebody to frame James Mann, evidence your daughter found on Mitchell Boyd's computer that could link Boyd to Prima-

Med, and then, suddenly, Lindsey Wells goes missing? Marvin was right. The evidence against you fell into my lap. It was too neat and pat. And you're right, too. I know better than to overlook a coincidence."

"Marvin died because he got too close to the truth."

"Speaking of truth, if I find out you're lying to me, I swear to you, Tom Hawkins, I'll put you down so hard, you'll never get back up."

Tom smiled. He found the fierceness in her voice irresistible.

"I'm supposed to bring pizza home for dinner."

"I love pizza," Rainy said.

CHAPTER 70

Tom cleared the dinner dishes from the table and put the pizza boxes in the trash. He returned to the kitchen, carrying with him two glasses of wine, a merlot from a California vineyard that he'd grown fond of. For Jill he brought a Diet Coke.

Tom raised his glass and looked up at the ceiling. "To Marvin," he said, hoisting his glass skyward. "You fought for me. Now I'm going to fight for you."

Tom and Rainy each took a sip of wine. Jill drank some Coke, then went back to texting.

"They didn't find her," Jill said, looking up from her phone with a longing in her eyes.

"Do you want to talk about it?" Rainy asked.

Jill shrugged. "Maybe you can convince my dad to let me go on the search."

"I can't do that," she said. "I think your father is right to keep a close watch over you. Whatever happened to Lindsey could be connected to Mitchell Boyd. Until we know more, it's better if you stay close by."

"The whole team is planning two shifts, starting at six in the morning and another at four in the afternoon," Jill said. "How much safer can I be? I'm like a prisoner. It's not fair."

"I agree, it's not," said Tom. "But it is safest. Once we know what's going on, we can reassess. For now, it's the way it's got to be. What if something really bad happened to Lindsey? What if you're the next target, Jill? I can't let anything happen to you. I won't."

"If something happened to her, it would be because of me," Jill said.

And to Marvin because of me, thought Tom.

"She's going to be found," Tom said, trying to reassure her.

"I know she is," Jill said softly. She looked a bit sheepish, uncomfortable even. Tom could tell she wanted to say something else but wasn't sure how to say it. "Are you guys dating, or something?" she blurted.

Tom hadn't known what Jill was going to say, but he certainly didn't expect that. He suppressed most of an embarrassed cough, while Rainy's cheeks flushed.

"No," Tom said. "Rainy's going to help investigate what happened to Marvin."

Jill turned to Rainy, seeming satisfied with that answer. "What about Mitchell Boyd? The pictures I saw on his computer? Are they connected to Lindsey's disappearance?"

"We looked at his computers. His phone, too. Everything came back clean."

"I knew it would," Jill replied. Her voice was downtrodden and weighty.

"But I'm not done looking," said Rainy. "I think there is something there. With Tanner Farnsworth. Mitchell Boyd. Something, but I don't know what. Not yet, at least."

"I understand," Jill said. "I'm just glad you believe

me." Jill took another sip of Coke and stood up from the table. "I've got a lot of homework to do. I'm going to go to my room. Thanks for dinner, Dad. Good night, Rainy."

"Good night, Jill."

Tom watched Jill and Rainy shake hands good-bye. He caught a glimmer of sadness in his daughter's eyes. He wondered if it was over Lindsey Wells, or something else. Did Rainy's presence make her miss her mother? he wondered.

Rainy sat down across from Tom. Her face, naturally beautiful, looked angelic in the flickering glow of two low-burning candles. Tom waited for the expected music to blast out of Jill's room before he spoke. He didn't want his daughter to overhear the conversation to come.

"Tell me more about what you found at Boyd's house," Tom said. "You think he's the link?"

Rainy kept her gaze fixed on Tom as she took in a deep breath. *She could look at me like that for hours,* he thought.

"I think we need to figure out who set you up."

"Well, Mitchell Boyd had these images, too. Isn't that what Jill found on his computer?"

"Allegedly, yes."

"So, we go after him."

"It's not that easy. He says he had a virus. He rebuilt all his computers from scratch."

"He's a liar," Tom said.

"Tom, why didn't Roland Boyd go to the police after you broke into his house?"

"Maybe he was worried about the police finding out what was on Mitchell's computers."

"Could be," Rainy said. "Murphy told me they questioned Tanner Farnsworth. According to phone records, Lindsey called him last."

"And?"

"And he's got an airtight alibi. Mitchell Boyd does as well."

"Let me guess," said Tom. "Both kids were with Roland Boyd."

"You read the report."

"In this town, I know where the questions stop. I get framed for something I didn't do. Jill finds pictures of herself and Lindsey on Mitchell Boyd's computer. Lindsey goes missing. Mitchell's computers get a virus. Marvin is murdered. Connect the dots and it draws a picture of Roland and Mitchell Boyd."

"You can't prove that."

"What does proof have to do with justice?" Tom said, too loudly. "Can you prove that I'm innocent?"

"No. I can't prove it," Rainy said. "But I can still believe it."

Tom shook his head in disgust. "So you can't prove I'm innocent. Only believe it. And you can't prove the Boyds are guilty."

"No, but I can work on getting search warrants and wiretaps to find out the truth. The courts and lawyers are the ones to prove it."

"You've got a lot of faith in the system."

"I have to. Otherwise, I couldn't do my job."

"Marvin had faith, too. Look where that got him."

"You've got to be patient. It's just not going to happen overnight." Rainy took a sip of wine and glanced down at her watch. "It's getting late," she said. "I better go."

"I'm glad you came."

"Me too," Rainy said.

"I'll walk you out."

The clouds had cleared, and the night sky was a canvas of stars. Rainy pulled her car keys out of her purse but didn't immediately open the car door.

"You really are on my side, aren't you?" he said.

Rainy smiled from the corner of her mouth, in a way that Tom had never seen before. It made her look even more attractive. He didn't know what made him reach out and take hold of her hand. He was just glad that she let him.

"So what was this really?" Rainy asked, still holding Tom's hand.

"Dinner," Tom said.

"But was it . . . a date?"

"I wouldn't lie to my daughter."

Rainy laughed. "No, you wouldn't."

"But this could be a date."

"What? Here? Outside your house, by my car?"

Tom nodded. "Not the best of locations, I agree. Not the best circumstances, by any stretch. But it's all about intention." Tom took hold of Rainy's other hand and tingled as their fingers interlocked.

"Is our date over?" Rainy asked.

Tom nodded again. "Yeah, busy day tomorrow."

"Well, I had a nice time."

"Do you kiss on the first date?"

"I don't know."

"You don't know?"

"I haven't been on a date in so long, it's hard to remember."

"So you might be willing to kiss, is that what you're implying?"

Rainy cocked her head in a coy, playful gesture. "Jury's out on that one," she said.

Tom let go of Rainy's hands. He cupped her cheeks with his hands. Her eyes grew wide and seemed to draw him to her. There was a brief hesitation when their lips first touched. She leaned into him, and they kissed harder.

They each pulled away at the same instant. Again, he held Rainy's hands.

"The jury may be out," Rainy said, "but the verdict is in."

She gave Tom a last quick kiss, then climbed into her car. Tom stood at the edge of the driveway and watched her drive away. He waited until her car's taillights faded from his view.

He had made it halfway back up the driveway when he heard a loud crash. He recognized the sound instantly. It was the noise glass made when it shattered. The next sound he recognized, too, but it was one he'd never heard before.

It was the sound of his daughter screaming.

When Tom got to Jill's bedroom, his daughter was still screaming. He saw shattered glass and the rock someone had thrown through her bedroom window. He picked up the rock and saw a note attached with rubber bands. The note read:

Your father is a rapist and a kidnapper. He's probably got Lindsey in your basement. You should kill yourself so you don't have to live with him. If you don't, somebody will do it for you.

CHAPTER 71

When Rainy showed up to work the next morning, she thought everybody was looking at her strangely. Other agents. Receptionists. Security. *Could it be because of Tom?* She decided it was just her imagination running away with her. If Tomlinson knew what she'd done, he wouldn't be his usual terse, grouchy self. He'd be downright furious.

"You *kissed* a guy you were investigating?" he'd probably scream.

But Tomlinson didn't know. Nobody did. Only Tom and Rainy knew what had happened between them. It might never happen again. It was a downright stupid thing to have done. Inexcusable and indefensible, really. Perhaps, with enough persuasion, what she'd done could be rationalized: the emotions of the funeral, the missing girl, and the failed computer battery proving his innocence to her. But engaging in debatable behavior wasn't a wise career strategy at the FBI. In a world of black and white, rights and wrongs, the stuff in the middle typically did not sit well with management.

For a brief moment, while they were kissing, Rainy felt happy. She felt truly happy. She'd allowed herself to be lost in that moment. To feel like she was finally thinking of herself.

Rainy had slept only a few restless hours. She kept thinking about him. She had woken up thinking about him. She had showered thinking about him. She had tried not thinking about him, which in itself was thinking about him. Rainy knew only one way she'd be able to kiss Tom Hawkins again. Kiss him and feel truly free to do it again.

She had to get Tom Hawkins out of the middle. She had to convince the D.A. prosecuting his case to drop the charges. And to do that, Rainy needed something more powerful than belief in his innocence.

She needed proof.

The only avenue left for Rainy to explore was those images James Mann had given to her. Mann was right to be perplexed about those disparate hash values. The oddity wasn't limited to an isolated image or two. Every duplicate image James Mann sourced from what she had officially logged as the Shilo NH Sext Image Collection generated a different hash value. It didn't make sense.

Why were the pixel colors changed, but the image composition left untouched? she wondered.

Carter wondered if opening an image in a photo-editing software program, such as Photoshop, could have altered the pixels in some way. They tested Carter's theory, but without success. This was shaping up to be the sort of outlier Marvin Pressman would have jumped all over. It was the sort of curiosity that demanded an explanation.

Rainy and Carter worked late in the Lair trying to solve what was shaping up to be an unsolvable puzzle.

Tomlinson showed up an hour later. "Agent Miles, I need you to do a PowerPoint presentation for me," he said.

Rainy groaned. Years ago she had made the tragic mistake of demonstrating to Tomlinson her mastery of PowerPoint. The ability to make effective slides was a skill management coveted.

"When do you need it, sir?" Rainy asked.

"Yesterday."

"What about this evening? By eight?"

"Why? What do you got going on here?"

"We're trying to figure out why the images don't generate identical hash values. And we're not having much luck."

"Is it important?"

"Yes, I believe it is, sir."

"In that case, eight will be fine."

Tomlinson left. Rainy and Carter returned to their work.

"Can you magnify this one?" she said. She pointed to a copy of Lindsey Wells's picture, one of the many copies that had begun populating the Web soon after she'd texted it to Tanner.

Carter magnified the image three hundred times. Rainy kept staring at the screen.

"What are you looking for?" asked Carter.

"Something I noticed when Clarence Stern was helping me ID the Lindsey Wells photograph."

"And that something would be?"

"He saw things at a high magnification level. Just by looking at the color gradation, he was able to add missing pixels to form a complete image. You can see it only when the image is magnified."

"It just looks like a bunch of colored squares," Carter said.

"But there's a smoothness to how those squares are stacked together. That smoothness is the logical next color variant to complete the picture. It's how Clarence was able to guess which pixels were missing."

"Are you looking for that same smoothness on this image?" asked Carter. He'd magnified the image so that all Rainy could see were rows and columns of colored blocks no more than an inch tall and wide.

"I'm looking for the out of the ordinary," said Rainy. "Something that shouldn't be there. Something we can't easily see with our eyes. Look. There." Rainy pointed to a section of the image. "The squares here go from light to dark without any gradation," she said. "It's jarring. It happens almost too quickly. Can you show me the same section, same magnification, but for a different image? I want to compare them."

Carter did, and Rainy saw it right away. "We've got the same jarring transition in the same section of both images," she said.

"The unusual shading pattern looks similar, but they're not identical," Carter said. "The pixel colors are different, too."

"But it's something," Rainy said. She was feeling breathless. "Each image looks identical. Only at magnification can we see the actual location of pixel color variation. Why?"

"It's probably a watermark," said a voice from behind them.

Rainy turned, and her eyes went wide with delight. Clarence Stern had just entered the Lair.

"Tomlinson said he'll need that PowerPoint deck by six," Stern announced. "Now, move over, Carter. Let me figure this out."

CHAPTER 72

"You think it's an invisible watermark?"

"Seems like it to me," Stern said to Rainy. "Watermarks are nothing more than embedding information into a digital media. Could be audio. Could be a picture."

"Could be spinning the Beatles' 'I'm So Tired' backward and hearing Paul is dead," Carter said.

"Well, that's a watermark of sorts, I guess," Stern said. "It's used a lot in copyright protection. It's also used in source tracing."

Rainy nodded. "Of course. The movie industry has been using source trace watermarks for ages. They can identify who downloads their intellectual property and then create a map of the distribution network. We've been exploring applications for them as well."

Carter nodded enthusiastically. "If each of the images Mann gave us has a unique watermark, it would explain why they weren't generating the same hash value. The watermark is what makes each image unique from the other. But it's hidden, so we can't easily see the difference with our eyes."

"The question now is," Stern said, "how do we reveal the watermark?"

Stern picked one image to work with. He spent a half an hour bumping up the contrast and adjusting the image levels.

"I've got the contrast here set to one hundred percent."

Rainy looked. "See anything?"

"I've got to run the contrast filter a bunch of times over before I can say."

Stern was back to his Stern ways. Grunting. Sighing. Pouting. He picked up a pencil and prepared to throw it at the monitor.

"That's my monitor, Clarence," Carter said. "I trust you. But not that much."

Stern set down the pencil. He looked over at Rainy. "Do you have an original?" he asked.

"What do you mean?"

"An original source. One that hasn't been moved from a point A to a point B. One that wouldn't have a watermark applied."

Rainy thought a moment. "Lindsey Wells," she said. "After my seminar she gave me her cell phone. She deleted the sent messages, but not the pictures. She thought they might somehow be helpful."

"Well, she just might be right," said Stern. "Let me have it."

Rainy returned to the workstation with Lindsey's cell phone. It took only a few minutes for Stern to download the pictures to Carter's machine.

"What are you going to do?" Rainy asked.

"I'm going to run a difference filter," Stern said.

"I'm not familiar with that," Rainy said.

"The difference filter compares the original to a copy. Look, I'll compare the original to itself."

Stern did just that, and all Rainy saw afterward was a black square on the screen.

"A black square means the images are identical," Stern explained. "All pixels turned a pure black color. Now let's run the difference filter on the original and one of the matching images."

Rainy examined the completed output. "It still looks like a black square to me," she said.

"But some of the pixels are not quite pure black," Stern said. "When I change the color levels to brighten all the very dark colors, I suspect our hidden watermark will become visible."

Stern adjusted the levels. The dark colors transformed to bright, almost neon shades. Rainy's hand went to her mouth when she saw what appeared. Most of the image square was still black. But not all of it. At the bottom of the square, Rainy saw a series of numbers. Stern's level adjustment had turned the color of those numbers a bright yellow.

"I bet those numbers are an IP address," Stern said. "Whoever embedded this watermark wanted to track the distribution of their copies, that's for sure. But what the heck is that?"

Stern was pointing to another newly revealed part of the watermark. Rainy knew exactly what it was. Even with the colors being off, she could see it clearly. A yin and yang symbol designed to look like a human skull.

"That right there is more than just a watermark," Rainy said. "That is a calling card."

CHAPTER 73

The spray paint was not going to come off. That was Tom's final conclusion after hours of effort. He'd tried Goop-Off and GoneIt, and two heavy-duty cleaners that the hardware store salesman had recommended. No luck. The paint had set, and he'd have to replace the siding, or paint over it, to get rid of the disgusting words. HEY RAPIST—BRING LINDSEY HOME. That was the message somebody had spray painted three times, in three different colors.

Jill didn't want to go to school the next day, and Tom wouldn't have let her go. It wasn't safe for her in Shilo anymore. She kept to her room for most of the day. She didn't even come out to eat.

Tom was on the ladder, trying one more application of GoneIt, when Jill shuffled into the backyard through the basement door.

"Hey, honey," he said, climbing down. "You hungry yet?"

"No."

Tom checked his watch. "It's quarter to seven. You haven't eaten anything all day."

Jill looked up at the house and recoiled at the sight.

"Who would do this?" she asked. "Why won't they just leave us alone?"

"I'm so sorry about all of this," Tom said. "But it'll be all right. You'll see. Everything is going to turn out just fine."

"Did you go to the police?" Jill asked.

Tom made a conciliatory expression. "You know I can't do that," he said. "Pretty much the whole town is against me at this point. The police most of all."

"Rainy's on our side," said Jill. "Can't she fix this?" Tom's face formed a grimace, which Jill noticed right away. "What is it?" she asked.

"Rainy," Tom said with a sigh. "I should have called her hours ago, but I got so caught up in this vandalism that I forgot." Tom put his arm around Jill. "I'll give her a call in a few. Maybe she'll have some good news to share."

Tom's cell phone buzzed in his pocket. He took it out and showed Jill that it was Rainy calling him.

"I guess she beat you to it," Jill said.

"Hey there," Tom said into the phone. "I was just about to call you. I'm planning to see Marvin's parents tonight. They're sitting shivah at his sister's house. I was hoping you'd come with me."

"Tom! Tom! I think we've got it."

"Got what?" he asked.

"Evidence that'll prove Mitchell Boyd is the distribution source of the images on your laptop. I'm not saying you're in the clear. But when we put the pressure on him, I bet he's going to start talking."

"Rainy, that's great news. Just great. Where are you now?"

"I'm with Carter. We're on our way to Shilo to have a little chat with Mitchell Boyd."

Tom's phone buzzed again. He was getting another call. He glanced at the number but didn't recognize the caller. "Rainy, let me call you right back," he said.

Tom clicked over to the incoming call. "Hello. This is Tom."

"Tom Hawkins," said a much-younger sounding voice. "It's Tanner Farnsworth."

Tom's jaw muscles tightened, and he squeezed his phone harder. "What do you want, Tanner?" said Tom.

"Look, I know I've done some pretty bad things. But I also know you didn't have anything to do with what happened to Lindsey."

"And how do you know that?" asked Tom.

"Because I know who did it," Tanner said. "It was Mitchell Boyd."

"What?"

"I was just over at Mitchell's house. We were eavesdropping on his dad. He was talking with Brendan Murphy from the police department. Mr. Boyd gets all the inside scoop. I overheard him say that they found Lindsey's body."

Tom's heart sank. Jill looked over at her father. Her expression revealed a growing alarm.

Tom turned his back so that Jill couldn't see him. He took a few steps away so that she couldn't hear him, either. "Where?" Tom whispered.

"In the woods near the Pine Hill Pond. They found your knife nearby, too."

"My knife?"

"Small knife, about the size of my palm," Tanner said. "It's yours. Don't ask me how Mitchell got it, but he took it from your house. The police pulled your prints off the knife. They're coming to arrest you. Not just the Shilo PD, either. State police, too. And soon."

"Hang on." Tom raced back into the house. He looked for his knife. It was gone. "Tanner, listen to me. You've got to call the police yourself. Right now. Tell them what you just told me."

"I can't do that," Tanner said. "I can't turn myself in. Can't turn on my best friend, either. I won't do it. But that doesn't mean I can't do something right."

"Do something right? What right thing are you doing here?" Tom shouted into the phone.

"I'm telling you to run."

CHAPTER 74

Tom turned to Jill. "Get inside the house," he said. "Stay out of your room. Stay in the basement. Don't move until I come for you."

"Dad, what is it? What's going on?"

Tom kept his voice calm and controlled. "Just do as I say," he ordered.

Jill fled into the house.

Tom didn't know what he should tell Jill. Was Tanner lying? Could Lindsey really be dead? Were the police coming to arrest him? Tom didn't have time to think through the possibilities. He only had time to ready an escape. He'd been arrested for a crime that he hadn't committed once before. He wasn't about to let it happen again.

Distract and evade.

If it came to it, that was what he would do.

Distract and evade.

Tom needed to survey his best exit points. He crouched low and kept to the side of the house. Where possible, he used trees and shrubs to keep himself hidden. Oak Street was clear. But if Tanner was telling the truth, the street would soon be active with police. He picked this as the place where he'd set the distraction.

Next, Tom crossed to the back of the house. The ravine where Kelly fell and died had an 8 percent grade. He'd have to descend into the ravine and climb back up the other side to get to Pine Street. Beyond Pine Street lay hundreds of acres of conservation land. Tom knew the Shilo topography better than most. He knew he could get away.

Tom returned to the house, where he slipped inside through the basement back door. He saw Jill standing there, waiting for him. She was pale and looked frightened.

"First thing I need you to do is relax," Tom said. He put his hands on his daughter's shoulders. "Take some deep breaths. I need you with me."

Jill nodded.

"Some people are coming for me," Tom said. He remained calm, which helped Jill. "I'm pretty sure they're coming to arrest me."

"Why?"

"I don't know." *She'll never forgive you for lying to her,* he thought.

Jill nodded again, but more slowly. "You're not leaving without me?" she cried. "You can't leave me alone."

"No. Never. But listen to me. We need to separate for a short while. Do as I say and we'll be together again soon."

"Why do we have to separate?"

"You'll slow me down if we stick together. It's me they're after, not you. But you're not safe on your own, either. I'm not going to leave you alone for long. I promise."

"Okay."

"Now I'm going to tell you exactly what to do. I'm

going to give you very specific instructions. You're going to follow my instructions exactly as I give them to you. Do you understand?"

"I think so."

"Don't think, Jill. Be decisive. Do you understand?"

"Yes," Jill said.

"Okay, we'll need to do some things first."

"What things?"

"Go upstairs. Hurry. Grab all the hair gel you have. There's hydrogen peroxide under the sink in the upstairs bathroom. Grab that too. Then get the rubbing alcohol from the first aid kit. Bring it all back downstairs to me, along with every Ziploc bag we have."

"What are you going to do?" asked Jill.

"While you're doing that," Tom said, "I'm going to build the detonator."

CHAPTER 75

Tom watched Jill drag the forty-gallon plastic trash barrel to the curb. She completed her mission with calm efficiency. Tomorrow was trash day. Oak Street was dotted with lots of green plastic barrels set out in front of lots of curbs. Their barrel looked full of trash. But the bags within it were stuffed full of newspaper. They looked puffy and full. Tom made certain nothing heavy was lodged inside those bags. Nothing that could become a projectile when he triggered the device.

Jill returned unhurriedly to the house. For the next several minutes she would be out of Tom's sight. But he wasn't worried. Jill knew what needed to be done. Tom looked out the window again. The street was still quiet.

Was the storm even coming?

Better to be prepared than to be a sitting target, he thought.

Tom called Rainy and told her that he'd call her back later. Something had come up, he said. It was a brief exchange, but it had to be done. Nobody else would be calling him. That was important, too. His phone was now part of the trigger mechanism.

Jill reappeared in the driveway. She was wheeling her red Schwinn World S bike alongside her. She leaned the bike up against the stone wall that abutted the driveway and disappeared from his view again. That was her signal to Tom that everything was in place.

Tom snatched the cordless phone from the kitchen. Next, he grabbed Jill's nylon backpack, which he'd stuffed with needed supplies. He descended the basement stairs, slipped out the back door, and worked his way around to the side of the house. Jill was waiting for him there.

The mountain bike was there, leaning up against the house. Jill had retrieved it from the shed after she grabbed her Schwinn.

Tom looked the bike over. It appeared to be in decent condition. The bike had belonged to Kelly's boyfriend, Alfonso. The same Alfonso who had used Kelly's house as a storage locker and got arrested for DWI.

The mountain bike had more gears than most riders had the skill to use. Hydroformed aluminum frame. Cold-forged dropouts. The front shock was an open bath damper type, which was fine by him so long as the oil levels in each leg were adequate to lube the other sliding parts. The tires were Bontrager, and the wheels Shimano. Quality parts as well. He inspected the shifters and derailleur. Those were fine, too.

Jill came over and stood beside her father.

"You're going to stay on the move for fifteen minutes." Tom said it as an instruction, but Jill understood that it was also a question.

"Yes."

"You know where we're going to meet."

"I do."

"You'll do exactly what I told you to do."

Jill nodded. "I will."

Tom raised his head like a bloodhound catching a fresh scent. "Okay, then. Ride."

"What if nothing happens? What if they don't come?" she asked.

"Then we'll go get ourselves a bite to eat," Tom said.

Jill nodded. She got on her bike and coasted down to the end of the driveway. Tom inched himself to the edge of the house. He needed to have a clear view of the street. Jill turned left and began to pedal away from the house. The street was quiet. No cars. No noise.

It didn't stay quiet for long. Tom heard the police car sirens well before he saw the flashing strobe lights. Five police cars turned onto Oak Street. Three state police cruisers were in the mix as well. All the police cars had their lights flashing and sirens blaring.

And they were headed straight for Jill.

"Hurry, baby. Pedal faster."

Tom noticed Jill pick up her pace and pedal faster. Her legs were pumping. He had wanted her to be a good hundred yards away from the house before he made the call. The police cars didn't slow as they passed Jill. They kept right on driving.

"Keep going. That's it, Jilly-bean," Tom whispered to himself.

Next, Tom checked in both directions on Oak Street for any pedestrians or coming motorists. All was clear. Jill was at a safe distance. The line of approaching police cars was some fifty yards from the house.

Tom knew he was about to commit a crime. Several of them, in fact. But the situation had left him no alternative. If the police arrested him, he'd be charged and convicted for Lindsey's murder. He'd spend the rest of his life in jail for a crime he didn't commit. Jill would be vulnerable. Perhaps the next victim of Lindsey's killer.

Tom's other option was to evade capture. Take Jill to a safe house. His military contacts and network could keep close watch over her. And while she was secure, he'd be free to track down Lindsey's real killer and bring him to justice. Tom had no intention of running forever. Once Jill was safe and Lindsey's killer behind bars, he'd gladly pay for the crimes he committed. All of them. Including his role in the drugs he'd smuggled out of Germany.

Using the portable house phone, Tom dialed his cell phone number. His cell phone was buried at the bottom of the trash barrel, but the call went through with no problem. Electricity passed through the wires of his cell phone's ringer mechanism, which Tom had rigged earlier to the flash trigger of a disposable camera. The electric circuit of the camera's flash detonated the bomb.

A jet of fire erupted two hundred feet into the air, streaking skyward in a thick column of flames approximately the diameter of the trash barrel. The explosion rattled windows in some houses. Shattered them in others. Car alarms made an orchestral shriek that rose above the siren noise. A powerful shock wave lifted the wheels of the approaching police cars off the ground, before gravity resettled them with an unforgiving crunch.

The police cars swerved off the road. Their wheels skidded against the pavement as they gripped for traction. They came to a stop in odd angles on sidewalks and lawns. The street was completely clear of traffic. But Tom wasn't headed for the street. He was headed for the woods.

Distract and evade.

It was time for him to leave.

CHAPTER 76

Tom shouldered the mountain bike down the steep ravine behind the house, then up the other side. He rode across Pine Street and vanished into the dense, root-covered forest that lay just beyond. He knew without instruments that he was riding his target cadence of eighty-five rpm's. His right hand effortlessly worked the lever controlling the rear gears, while his left operated the front mechanism, shifting the chain from one chainwheel to another depending on the terrain or obstacle in his path.

The SEALs could evade with whatever was at their disposal. Tom could fly a plane, steal a car, ride a motorcycle, or sail a boat if it meant avoiding capture. A long-standing joke in the navy was that the SEALs were the only outfit capable of escape by unicycle. Tom did with the mountain bike precisely what the navy had prepared him to do. He grabbed the best available option and pedaled as though he'd been preparing for this race all his life.

The conservation land behind Pine Street was especially hilly, so Tom kept the chain mostly to the inner chainwheels. He remembered to ease off the pedal pressure some just before shifting gears. He sped up, didn't brake, while going over obstacles. On the downhill, he leaned back to apply more grip to the rear tire. Uphill he leaned forward to accomplish the same on the front. The biggest problem was the clipless pedals, for which he didn't have the proper cleats. His feet slipped, but not often.

Tom kept clear of the paths, which meant more obstacles to overcome. The unbalanced weight of Jill's nylon backpack somewhat hampered his ability to maneuver the bike. Still, he managed to bunny hop a fallen moss-covered maple tree without having to dead stop. On a couple of steep run-ups, Tom had to dismount and shoulder the bike to the top. He used the densest parts of the woods to his advantage, turning the tall, leafy trees into a natural canopy that concealed his location from air surveillance.

Tom was glad he kept up a disciplined exercise schedule. Even with the injuries he had sustained in the car accident, his breathing was unlabored as he pedaled through a river swollen from a recent rain. Trained athletes would have been sucking air at his pace. Weekend warriors would have been hyperventilating, probably injured by now. He saw obstacles—roots and rocks—that normal riders would have missed. His heartbeat stayed steady.

As he rode, he visualized the response to his escape. The Shilo police weren't a significant concern, even though they would call in reinforcements from the state police. They'd organize a containment strategy of sorts. Patrol cars and motorcycles at the major access roads bordering the section of woodland directly behind his house. They'd figure on covering about a ten-mile radius. But Tom was riding fast enough that they'd need to double that acreage to have any hope of spotting him.

But SWAT was a legitimate concern.

Some of those guys had his level of training. They

could mobilize fast, too. It was what they were organized to do. The state police would call for SWAT. They'd come at him from the air. But they'd also come by land.

Tom had a map of Shilo in his backpack, but he didn't need to refer to it. He knew exactly where he was riding. If he could slip by SWAT, he was gone. Nobody would find him then. Not unless he wanted them to.

Of all the concerns clouding his thoughts, his biggest worry was Jill. Would she be all right? Would she do exactly as he had instructed? He recalled how she had screamed into the dark woods, daring the vandals who desecrated her house to show their cowardly faces. He saw a fight in his daughter she'd shown only on the soccer field. It was reassuring. It gave him confidence that she'd be fine. Soon, they'd be together.

The terrain flattened out for several hundred yards but then began a steady incline. Tom rode in a zigzag pattern, with his body over the rear wheel to establish a greater center of gravity. His outside foot leaned forward into each turn, granting him added mobility so that he could swivel at a much greater angle. He moved toward each turn, looking nine feet ahead in anticipation of the next.

The forest here was composed mostly of hemlock, white pine, beech, and oak trees. The composition of the terrain seemed to vary every few feet. In parts the soil was rocky, but it soon became a coarse washed till and just as quickly turned sandy and fine. The riding was challenging, but not impossible. He knew where he could lose any pursuer, and didn't have that far to go.

Tom was beginning to think the chase would be easier than he'd anticipated. Then he heard the sound of a helicopter's rotors slicing the air.

SWAT had arrived.

Tom craned his neck skyward. The land in front of him

dipped. He nearly lost his balance trying to pinpoint the chopper's exact position. There was a quick break in the tree cover. The helicopter was almost directly overhead. The forest thickened again, but the damage was already done. The helicopter pilots had seen him. Same as he'd seen them.

For ten minutes the helicopter kept pace with Tom. He knew what was coming next. He heard the sound in his mind before he heard it in his ears. The whining engines of ATVs barked out their warning from the dark wood behind him. As he expected, SWAT had mobilized a task force to hunt him down. The helicopter worked as a spotter. Now it was up to the ATV riders to bring him in.

Good luck, Tom thought.

The ATVs sounded at most five hundred yards to his back. He knew not to be confident in that assessment. The forest made pinpointing location by sound a misleading endeavor.

He accelerated to ninety-five rpm's. His destination was nearing. It would be a race to see who got there first. Diffused light from the late-day sky flattened out the shadows and blended dangerous obstacles in with the harmless terrain. Tom's night vision acuity couldn't reveal everything, and when Tom hit the rock, a small boulder buried beneath a lump of decaying forest rot, his only option was to take the fall.

The wheel of his bike connected with the rock's jagged side at full speed and sent Tom lurching forward. He catapulted over the handlebars like a projectile launched from a slingshot. With a grunt, Tom landed on the hard-packed ground, feeling the impact like a thunderclap rolling about his head.

He staggered to his feet and retrieved the crumpled bike, which had landed some twenty feet from where he rose. The bike's front wheel was bent slightly; a few spokes had become dislodged on impact. He checked it quickly; it could still be ridden. The noise of ATV engines grew louder with every passing second. They buzzed, seemingly from all directions.

As Tom remounted his bike, headlights appeared at the top of the hilly rise several hundred feet behind him. The headlights, like a swarm of gnats with glowing eyes, six sets in total, lit Tom's face and cast threatening beams that danced over the rocks and trees of the darkening wood.

Tom began to pedal again. It wasn't far now. He'd studied the maps before he'd left the house. He knew how the terrain changed beyond the creek. Where the land rose again stood a forest of densely packed, smaller trees. Skiers in the Northeast might refer to the tree line up ahead as glades. But Tom had a different name for it.

Escape.

A voice from a megaphone overhead cut through the noise of the ATV engines and whirling rotors.

"This is the police. We've got you surrounded. Dismount your bicycle. We have orders to shoot. Dismount and get down on the ground."

Tom pushed harder against the pedals. He was sweating. The muscles in his calves and thighs burned as fibers broke down and lactic acid built up.

"Last warning. Dismount now," boomed the voice from above.

Tom risked a glance behind him and saw that five of the ATVs were still in pursuit. He estimated the distance at fifty yards back, but closing in quick. The sixth rider had stopped to ready a weapon.

Fifty yards to the glades. . . . now forty . . .

The crack of a rifle shot exploded in the distance. The bullet slapped into a tree not far to Tom's right. It splintered the wood with an alarming snap. Another shot, this one passing close enough for Tom to hear the bullet whiz by.

Twenty yards to go . . .

The riders were close enough now for Tom to feel the heat of their headlamps. All forest sounds gave way to the noise of their engines revving in pursuit.

Ten . . .

Another shot rang out. The bullet was way off target. Even so, the lead ATV had managed to pull alongside Tom. The ATV rider slowed to keep pace. He wore a black helmet and had on leather protective gear.

Good for him. He'll need both, Tom thought.

The rider released one hand from the ATV handlebars and motioned wildly for Tom to stop.

Tom released his hand from the handlebar. He used that free hand to point to something up ahead.

The rider turned to look to where Tom pointed. Tom could see the rider try to brake. But he braked too late. The spacing between the trees was twenty inches, twenty-five at most. Tom needed only eighteen to clear the obstacle. The ATV required more than seventy. The impact when the ATV threaded two trees was ferocious.

Traveling at over thirty miles per hour, the front of the ATV collided against two trees with only a tap of the brakes to decelerate. Metal crunched against wood, and the ATV's engine made a desperate whirring sound, as though taking its final breath. The vehicle flipped over onto its front, but the trees held it in an inverted position, which kept it from toppling over. The rider flew into the air, arms outstretched, and landed, miraculously, between two other trees. The force of his fall buried his head beneath a dense pack of ground cover. The other ATVs stopped inches before hitting the glades.

Tom's bike, however, wove in and out of the trees, tracing a zigzag path between the obstacles like a seamstress's stitch. The forest canopy thickened again.

Above, Tom heard the helicopter circling, but he could no longer see it overhead.

Behind, Tom listened to the angry idling of five waiting ATV engines.

Ahead, Tom saw only trees. Densely packed and narrow.

The final passage to his escape.

CHAPTER 77

Tom rode the bike in a wide circle. The police would assume he'd continued on his northerly course. He doubted anybody would suspect that he'd backtracked toward home. But that was the direction he had to ride if he wanted to make it to the Plenty Market—and to Jill.

The sun had set, and the late summer song of crickets and other woodland critters punctuated the evening's calm. In this part of town, there was nothing unusual to draw the people's attention. No all-points-bulletins had been issued to locals, warning them that Tom Hawkins was a fugitive from justice. Sure, news spread fast in Shilo. But Tom was confident it didn't spread that fast. Whatever was happening on Oak Street was taking place a world away from where he was now. Here, there were only food shoppers.

Tom entered the market. He wore a baseball cap he'd packed in the backpack and kept his head low. The high-powered air conditioners chilled his skin. He intentionally proceeded down an aisle without any other shoppers. He headed straight to the back of the supermarket without slowing. Once there, he pushed open the swinging double doors that led into the back storeroom.

Gill Sullivan was sitting at his desk in the little office with the big plate-glass front window. If Sullivan hadn't been there, Tom had plan B ready to roll, but he was glad to see the bastard hard at work. Sullivan looked up, frowned at Tom, rose from his seat, and was quick to leave his office.

Puzzled, Sullivan took hurried steps toward Tom, slowing as he neared. "What are you doing back here, Hawkins?" he asked.

Tom lunged at Sullivan with a burst of acceleration that took Sullivan by surprise. Sullivan's eyes went wide with fright. A panicked look replaced his earlier confidence.

Tom sliced the side of his hand through the air as though he were brandishing a sword. The blow connected against Sullivan's windpipe with enough force to drop the man to his knees, but not quite enough to crush the organ.

Sullivan clutched at his throat, gagging for breath. He dropped to the floor and lay flat on his stomach. Tom straddled Sullivan's back, seized a clump of greasy hair, and pulled his head back.

"Where are your car keys?" Tom asked in a calm voice.

Sullivan grabbed at his throat and struggled to speak. Tom pushed Sullivan's face to the floor. He pressed the knuckles of his fist into the back of Sullivan's head. His other fist dug deep into the man's spine. Sullivan gasped and coughed up a glob of green phlegm mixed with strawberry-colored blood.

"Car keys," Tom said, repeating the demand.

Sullivan patted the side of his pants, and Tom fished out the keys.

"Make and model," he said.

"Chevy Equinox," Sullivan squeaked out. His voice was raspy and weak.

"Where is it parked?"

"Out back," Sullivan said. "Loading dock."

"Okay. Thanks."

"What do you want?" Sullivan asked.

"Well, first, I wanted a car. Thanks for that. Now I want information. Who killed Lindsey Wells? Was it Mitchell? Did Roland say?"

Sullivan tried to shake his head but couldn't move it much with his face still to the floor. Tom turned Sullivan over so he could study the man's body language.

"I don't know what you're talking about," Sullivan said. "I didn't even know she was dead."

No tell. Nothing to suggest that Sullivan was lying.

"What about Marvin? Was Boyd involved? Did Roland Boyd have anything to do with Marvin's death?"

"I don't know. You'd have to ask him."

Tom noticed something this time. A twitch at the corner of Sullivan's mouth. It was slight. But it was there. Maybe, what Sullivan needed was some added motivation to talk. Tom turned Sullivan over and hoisted him up by his belt loop. He saw the man's massive belly swinging below his compressed waist like the pendulum of a grandfather clock. Tom pulled Sullivan to his feet.

"I'm going to put you on a new diet, Gilly," Tom said, patting the man's sizable midsection and purposefully using Roland's nickname for him. "It's called the Frozen Feast Diet. Ever hear of it?"

Sullivan's expression shifted from a look of concern to one of panic. He began to shake, and his knees went slack. Tom kept him propped up, though.

"Unlike South Beach, you actually won't be able to

eat anything," Tom went on, "because all the food is frozen. Get it? Frozen Feast. Works wonders."

Sullivan tried to resist, but he lacked the strength. Tom opened the cooler door and tossed Sullivan inside. He noticed the automatic light was working again. Sullivan crashed into a shelving unit at the back of the freezer. Frozen meat and other provisions toppled on top of him.

"You fixed that shelf I had to break, I see," Tom said. "I'll give you one more chance. Did Roland Boyd have anything to do with Marvin's murder?"

"Screw you, Hawkins," Sullivan said.

Tom knew Sullivan was going to waste his time. The man might be hiding something, but he wasn't going to reveal it without a good deal of effort, which Tom didn't have the time to expend. For now, at least, he was done with Gilly Sullivan. What he was going to do next was purely for revenge. Tom used a frozen sausage to shatter the lightbulb, hitting it like a bat connecting with a ball. The space descended into darkness.

"I noticed you fixed the safety latch, too," Tom said. He pushed against the well-oiled mechanism and saw how it easily disengaged the latch. "I wouldn't want you to break your diet by sneaking out," Tom continued. With one hand he bent the release rod back and forth, using the hole for leverage. He twisted the metal until it snapped off. Tom made sure it couldn't be opened from the inside.

"One more part of the diet I forgot to mention," Tom said before he left the cooler.

Sullivan cast Tom a doleful expression. He was still rubbing at his throat and looked to be on the verge of tears.

"The best way to ignore hunger pangs is to have something more painful to focus on." Tom took a step forward and unleashed two quick jabs. The first connected just below Sullivan's right orbital socket. The second punch tracked the position of Sullivan's head as he rolled away from the initial blow. That punch caught Sullivan in the jaw, strong enough to push the heavy man up off of his feet. Sullivan went sprawling backward. His body fell into an open carton of swordfish steaks that were frozen hard as bricks. The steaks cracked against Sullivan's skull as they fell.

Sullivan lay at the back of the cooler, groaning and massaging his tender face. A large red swath coated much of Sullivan's injured throat like a rash.

"If I find out you were involved in Marvin's death," Tom said to him, "consider this the warm-up act. Speaking of warm-up, make sure to cover your head with something. That's where you'll lose most of your body heat."

Tom closed the door and waited. Sullivan was probably banging against the insulation and was probably screaming for help, too. Good thing the thick walls blocked out all sound from within.

He left through the back door, with Sullivan's car keys dangling in his hand. Tom found the Equinox parked where Sullivan said it would be. Maybe Sullivan would be found in twenty minutes. Maybe sooner. Probably longer. Either way, he'd ditch the car long before the police knew to look for it.

Tom drove unnoticed past several police cars on his way to the meeting spot. The location he'd picked was a development under construction. No residents. And at this hour, no workers, either.

Tom pulled up to the first house on the right. He could see Jill's bike parked in what would eventually become the garage. He honked the car horn. Jill didn't come out of hiding. He honked again. Still no Jill.

Tom got out of the car and walked over to the bike. He looked at the ground. He saw Jill's cell phone.

Tom picked up the phone. He looked at the text message someone had earlier composed. His stomach sank the moment he read it. The two-word instruction made Tom's whole body go weak.

Turn around.

Tom turned and looked behind. Roland Boyd was standing there. Roland held a gun leveled at Tom's chest. It was a Smith & Wesson 22LR, not the best handgun, but at this range the best didn't much matter.

"Hi, Tom," Roland said.

"Where's Jill? What have you done with her, Roland?"

"I've got to search you. Don't get cute."

Roland searched but didn't find any weapons. He checked Tom's backpack, too. He found the kitchen knife Tom had packed.

"My car is parked at the end of the street," Roland said afterward. "Walk with me."

"And you'll shoot me if I don't?"

"No, Tom," said Roland. "But somebody will shoot your daughter."

"What do you want?"

"Simple," Roland said. "I want to know where you hid ten million dollars' worth of my heroin."

CHAPTER 78

Rainy couldn't wait to have her little chat with Mitchell Boyd. Depending on his reaction to her questions, she'd decide the next best move. The federal magistrate might already have enough probable cause to issue an arrest with the watermark evidence alone, but Rainy didn't want to burn through the opportunity. She'd present Mitchell with her findings, ask for another consent search, and fully expected him to become much less cooperative. That little turnaround should be more than enough to guarantee Mitchell's federal arrest warrant on child pornography charges.

Rainy rang the front door bell and waited. Seconds passed. She rang the bell again. Mitchell opened the door, but only a crack. Rainy flashed him her badge.

"Hi, Mitchell," she said. "Mind if I come in and have a word with you?"

"Why?"

"Are your parents at home?"

"My mom's here."

"Good. Can we come in and talk?"

Mitchell pulled the door open wider. Rainy and Carter stepped into the high-ceilinged foyer of the Boyds' grand residence, with the majestic corkscrew staircase at its center. Rainy looked up to see Adriana descending the stairs.

"Who's the daytime soap star?" Carter whispered into Rainy's ear.

"That's Mama," said Rainy.

"Mamma mia!" Carter whispered back.

"Hello. Can I help you?" Adriana asked the agents as soon as she reached the landing.

Rainy and Carter inadvertently synchronized the flashing of their badges.

"We met at Cathleen Wells's house a few weeks ago," Rainy said. "My name is Special Agent Loraine Miles, and this is Special Agent Carter Dumas. We're with the FBI's Innocent Images National Initiative. We'd like to have a few words with your son, if that's all right with you."

"What's this all about?" Adriana asked, her face long with worry.

"We'd like him to explain something we've discovered as part of an ongoing investigation."

From within a manila envelope, Carter extracted a color printout of the once hidden digital watermark. He handed the glossy paper, ink still fresh, over to Adriana. The three huddled close.

"What is this?" Adriana asked.

"It's a watermark," Rainy said. "We believe the creator of this watermark is also a distributor of illegal images. We also think the same distributor automatically applied Internet addresses to these watermarked images to keep track of who was downloading the content and from where."

"And you think Mitchell had something to do with this, because the watermark matches his tattoo?"

"We'd sure like to ask him a few questions."

"Mitchell, do you have anything to say about this?" Adriana asked in a harsh tone, turning around to address her son.

To Rainy's surprise, Mitchell didn't answer her back. Alarmed, she realized why.

Mitchell Boyd wasn't with them in the foyer anymore.

CHAPTER 79

Tom told Roland where he'd hidden the drugs. Roland, in response, communicated his threat to Tom quite clearly. Jill would be shot if they didn't arrive at that destination by a certain time. Tom didn't know who was holding Jill. So he let Roland drive and he kept silent.

He held Jill's cell phone, praying that she'd call him. Each second the phone didn't ring was agony to him. He decided to keep pressing Roland for more information.

"How did you know where Jill would be?" Tom asked.

"I didn't," said Roland. "But I knew I could follow her. And I knew she wasn't going to be with you."

"How'd you know that?"

"I'm the one who told Tanner to call you," said Roland. "I scripted him on exactly what to say. I knew you'd believe it and try and run. I knew Jill would slow you down when you did. You SEALs are consistent with your training, if anything. Your only option was to separate."

"Did you kill Lindsey!" Tom shouted.

"Easy, Tom," Roland said. "I told you, I don't hurt people."

"No. You have people do that for you. I forgot."

Roland turned his head, with a smile on his face that made Tom's insides shiver.

"Is Frank Dee one of your cronies?"

"Maybe."

"How do you do it?" Tom asked. "Gilly. Dee. How do you get these guys to work for you?"

"For Gilly, let's just say the return on investments with Boyd Investments is well above the industry average. I pride myself on building customer loyalty. Dee I took care of as a favor to his cousin. I think you know who I mean. You're a smart man."

"No, Marvin was a smart man, and you killed him."

"Don't jump to any conclusions," Roland said.

"How'd you know about the drugs?"

"Considering I'm the one who told Lange about Greeley trading military secrets for heroin, I'd say I was in the know from the start."

"Kelly never told me you were involved."

"That's because Kelly didn't know," Roland said. "It was just me and Lange. I was the one who told Lange to bring Kelly into the deal. I knew she'd play the perfect little vixen. She was so sexy, hard for any man to resist."

"You planned to be off the base. Didn't you?"

"As smart as you are, Tom, I was a bit surprised you never checked my records. I transferred out from Greeley's command three months before the heist."

"Guess I didn't think of everything," Tom said.

"Lange could keep his mouth shut. But you and I both know that Kelly was a talker, so we kept her in the dark. We didn't have any idea what happened to the drugs. Lange told Kelly to ditch 'em, and that was the last he knew. I kept close watch over Kelly when I got back to Shilo. She didn't change her spending habits any. She married you.

She divorced you. She kept her job at the bar. This wasn't a woman with millions of dollars at her disposal."

"You didn't know Kelly gave me the drugs," Tom said, more to himself than to Roland.

"I figured she tossed them," Roland said. "I had to let it go. Imagine that. Meanwhile, I kept my word to Lange that I'd help get him out of prison. Got his cousin a new life. As my business started to take off, I had the funds to keep my promise."

Roland made several turns without having to ask Tom for directions. He knew how to get where they were going.

"I don't get it. Why did Lange break into the house if he knew the drugs were gone?"

"Because Lange couldn't let it go," Roland said. "He was convinced you had something to do with it. I told him he was wrong. He didn't know Tom the way I knew Tom. I figured even a Boy Scout like yourself couldn't pass up on that kind of money. But Lange, he didn't listen to me.

"First thing he did when he got out of prison was go see Kelly. He broke into the house, hit her, spooked her, and she ran out the back door. She died the way the police say she did, falling down that ravine. But even after all that, Lange couldn't let it go. He started spying on you. He thought you were going to try and move the stuff. Guess he didn't know who he was messing with."

"Guess he didn't," Tom said.

"But then, out of the freakin' blue, you came over to my house, asking about Kip Lange. Well, that's when I knew. I knew Lange had been right all along. You did know about the drugs. But I didn't know if you had them, hid them, or destroyed them. So I bugged your house."

"You what?"

"The alarm company," Roland said. "The owner also is a major investor in my funds, if you know what I mean."

"So you listened in on my conversation with Jill. That's how you knew I hid the drugs."

"Not every word. I had keywords programmed. Got snippets with any mention of heroin. And that's when I told Lange to come out of hiding and make a strike. Dee arranged to have your coffee drugged. As you know, that plan didn't go very well, either. But good news, I'm the project manager for this one. And I promise you, it's going to go just as planned."

Tom had more questions for Roland, specifically about why he framed him for child pornography, his connection to Cortland, but those would have to wait.

They'd arrived at their destination.

Roland parked his car in the lot used to access the most popular trail into Willards Woods. The lot was empty. Weeknights the place should be deserted.

Tom and Roland got out of the car at the same time. Roland kept a few paces behind Tom as they marched ahead. Night had fallen and moonlight made the trail easy to walk without flashlights, but Roland used his nonetheless. Even in the darkness, Tom couldn't see any way of disarming Roland. Not without risk. He'd never gamble with Jill's life.

Tom reached the clearing in the woods and stopped walking.

"Haven't been back here since we were kids," Roland said.

"The Spot hasn't changed any," Tom said.

Tom's back was to a tree. Roland was facing him.

"Where is Jill?"

"With a friend."

"I want to see her. Nothing happens until I do."

"Then we wait."

Roland's phone rang while they were waiting. Tom watched Roland check the number, then answer the call.

"Don't do anything stupid," Tom heard Roland say. "Just get out of there. . . . I don't care how. . . . The Spot . . . I'll wait for you here. Be safe."

Roland put his phone away just as Frank Dee came lumbering down the only path to the Spot. Roland trained his flashlight on Dee. Jill was wrapped in Dee's massive arms. She was blindfolded and gagged with a bandanna. Her wrists were bound, too.

Tom rushed toward her. But Roland waved his gun, which made Tom stop. He motioned for Dee to take Jill into the woods.

"You buried my drugs in the dirt?" Roland said to Tom.

"Not the dirt," Tom said, pointing to the quarry.

"My drugs have been underwater for fifteen years? You ruined ten million dollars of heroin?"

"I made sure the packages stayed protected," Tom said. "I wanted to preserve the drugs and any fingerprint evidence in case I needed some leverage."

"Good thinking. You ready to go swimming?"

"And if I do this, you'll let Jill go."

"I will."

"But she's got you for kidnapping, Boyd. Why should I believe she'll be safe after?"

"Somebody kidnapped her," said Roland. "She didn't see who it was. She can't prove I was involved. I'm not worried."

"And what if I refuse?"

"Then my heroin won't be the only thing buried in that quarry."

CHAPTER 80

R ainy and Carter each drew their weapons. Adriana screamed Mitchell's name. Meanwhile, Rainy searched the living room. Nothing. She ran down the long hallway that opened into the kitchen. Empty as well.

"Is there another way to get upstairs?" Rainy called to Adriana, who'd been trailing close behind her.

"No. But there's a door to the basement from the mudroom."

"Is there a basement door to the outside?"

"Only the bulkhead," Adriana said, her voice shaking like her hands. "The basement is below ground. But the bulkhead's locked from the outside."

"Carter, cover me."

Rainy pressed her back up against the wall and used the door as a shield when she flung it open. She popped off the wall, spun around, and sank down into a crouching position. She trained her weapon into the dark stairwell.

"Mitchell Boyd," Rainy called into the black. "If you're in the basement, I need you to show yourself now. Keep your hands where I can see them."

"Mitchell," Adriana echoed from behind Rainy. "Do

what she says. Please, just come up and let's talk about this."

Rainy whirled around. She hadn't realized Adriana stood so close behind. "You've got to get out of here," Rainy said.

"I'm not leaving my son," Adriana snapped.

Rainy refocused on the stairwell. She stood, took a single step down into this vast darkness, feeling the walls for a light switch. She flicked the switch on. The stairwell remained dark. She flicked it again. Still no light.

"Do you have a fuse box down there?" Rainy asked Adriana.

"Yes," Adriana said.

"Carter, go get a flashlight from Mrs. Boyd."

Rainy took another step down, her body halfway between the light and dark.

"Mitchell, you're not in any trouble," Rainy said. "But you're creating a threatening situation for federal agents. This is not a smart choice. You need to show yourself right now."

Rainy stopped to listen. She heard a soft creak, knew the sound well. *Footsteps. But coming up or going down?* Rainy felt a gentle tap on her shoulder. She didn't turn around. Keeping her eyes forward, hoping they'd adjust to the lack of light, Rainy held up her hand. Carter pressed a metal flashlight into the palm. Rainy took another step down. Again, she stopped to listen. She heard a stair groan, louder this time than last, and higher up, she thought. *He's definitely coming up the stairs*.

Rainy turned on the flashlight. She shone the beam down the stairs. The beam cut through the darkness and illuminated Mitchell Boyd, standing on a stair landing many steps beneath her.

Rainy thought the boy looked exceptionally frightened. She took a cautious step backward. As she did, Rainy focused her flashlight beam on Mitchell's hands and found the reason he looked so afraid.

"Gun!" Rainy shouted. "He's got a gun!"

A burst of flame erupted from the barrel of Mitchell's weapon. Rainy fell, smashing her lower back hard against the unforgiving sill. The bullet whizzed over her head. Her nostrils filled with the acrid stench of gunpowder. The fall and blow to her back took Rainy's breath away.

Stunned, Rainy couldn't control her slide down the stairs. She bounced down each step, slamming her back against one stair's edge, sliding to another, and repeating the painful pattern a dozen times over on her way down. Even with her ears still ringing from the gunshot, she could hear the flashlight clattering as it tumbled into the darkness.

The dark of the stairwell turned bright again, but only for brief flashes. Rainy heard two quick pops. The bullets fired from Mitchell's gun slammed into the stairs where Rainy's sliding body had just been. Splintered wood peppered her face and hair. Rainy aimed her weapon at the flashes of light and pulled the trigger. Her unsteady hand jumped with the gun's recoil. She heard a grunt, followed by the sound of a body falling. Rainy finished her slide down. She expected to slam into the stairwell wall, but Mitchell's body cushioned her impact.

Rainy felt around in the inky darkness for his weapon. Soon her fingers brushed against something steel. Rainy pushed the weapon down the remaining stairs. Still fumbling in the dark, Rainy felt something wet and sticky to the touch. A flashlight beam lit Rainy from above. Behind her, Rainy heard a woman's scream. She turned to see Adriana hurrying down the stairs, her flashlight beam jostled wildly with each unsteady step. The light danced back and forth, creating a miniature strobe.

Rainy could see what had made Adriana scream. Mitchell lay slumped on the landing with his back pressed up against the wall. Blood pooled around him.

Adriana reached the landing and fell to her knees. She caressed Mitchell's cheek, shining her flashlight on his face.

"Baby! Mitchell! Can you hear me?" Adriana put her ear to Mitchell's chest. "He's breathing! Call an ambulance. Hurry!" she shouted.

"I'm on it," Carter yelled from above.

"Give me your flashlight," Rainy said. "I'm going to check the fuse box. We need light."

Adriana handed Rainy her light. Rainy used the flashlight to look around. She could see the distraught mother stroking her son's face with blood-covered hands. She checked Mitchell, making sure he wasn't still armed. She also could see where she'd shot him in the shoulder. Another few inches to the right and he'd probably have been paralyzed, more likely killed.

The kid was hurt, but he'd live.

"Where did he get a weapon?" Rainy called to Adriana as soon as she reached the basement.

"It's probably Roland's gun," Adriana shouted back. "Mitchell knows where he keeps the key to the gun safe."

Rainy needed only a couple minutes to locate the fuse box. She flicked the breaker, and the basement was engulfed in light. Rainy stood in place, waiting for her eyes to adjust. She walked back up the stairs to the landing where Mitchell lay groaning. Adriana knelt by his side.

"He's not going to die," Adriana said, her voice desperate.

"No," Rainy said. "He's not."

"You'll make sure he's taken care of?"

"Of course," Rainy said. "The ambulance is probably on its way."

Adriana walked back up the stairs. To Rainy, it looked as if she were in some sort of trance, almost floating.

"Good," Rainy heard her say. "My boy will be all right."

Rainy checked Mitchell's pulse, pleased it felt so strong. Carter raced down the stairs, carrying a first aid kit.

"Found this in the kitchen," Carter said.

"Can you hear me, Mitchell?" Rainy asked.

Mitchell just groaned.

"You've been shot twice. I'm going to administer first aid. You're going to be all right. Stay with me, okay? You stay with me now."

Rainy cut away Mitchell's bloody shirt with scissors she found inside the kit. She protected her hands with latex gloves, then used a wad of gauze to apply pressure to the wounds. Rainy and Carter both looked up the stairs as soon as they heard a door slam.

"Go check it out," Rainy said to Carter.

Carter bounded back up the stairs, returning moments later. He called down to Rainy. From Rainy's vantage point, the outline of Carter's figure standing in the doorway's threshold looked aglow.

"It's Adriana," Carter said breathlessly. "She's gone."

CHAPTER 81

Moonlight danced across the rippling quarry water. Roland was somewhere in the dark woods. Jill was nearby, too. A waterproof duffel bag rested on the quarry bottom, some sixty feet beneath the water. Roland had given Tom his flashlight. Even with the moonlight, Tom needed that light to locate the bag.

"I'm going to have to come up another way," Tom said. He could hear Roland but didn't know where he was standing. "The cliff is too steep for me to get back up here. I'm going to have to take the longer way out."

"That's fine, Tom," Roland said. "I'll watch your light. You just get the job done and come back to the Spot."

Oh, you bet I will, Tom thought. *With a big surprise, too.*

Tom looked out over the water. He raised his arms high above his head and took in a deep breath. He kept his clothes on, opting to sacrifice some mobility for the extra layer of warmth. He breathed in four sharp, quick breaths. To build up his final oxygen supply, he gulped the air like a fish breathes on land. With his legs bent, Tom propelled himself off the quarry's ledge and into the air.

He went into his dive, confident he'd gone out far enough to avoid hitting the railroad ties below.

Tom's body pierced the water's surface with barely a back splash. The air was cold, but the water was freezing. At first, Tom was too stunned to swim. The cold felt as if it had stopped his heart. But he was already ten feet deep, and his body had angled to let him dive even deeper. Tom used dolphin kicks to descend. The flashlight's beam cut through the darkness and offered only a pinhole-sized glimpse into the infinite. He kept close to the quarry's smooth rock wall as he sank.

In the navy, he could hold his breath longer than most other SEALs. Five minutes was his record. But out of practice he had three, maybe four minutes of surplus oxygen in him at best. To conserve oxygen, his body would soon begin shutting down nonessential functions. Eventually, the essential ones would stop working as well.

Tom's skin went numb and blood pounded in his ears as the pressure in his head built up. It was coming, Tom thought. That irresistible, desperate need to breathe. It was coming, and a lot sooner than he expected.

Keep pushing. . . . Don't give in. . . . Don't try to breathe.

Tom kept his body inverted as he sank. His chest was on fire. The tightness in his throat held down the most intense pressure building up in his lungs. He might have given up and surfaced had he not reached the point in the dive where the cliff face jutted out.

Tom guessed that he'd traveled forty feet down. Perhaps as deep as fifty. Ten or so to go. Tom's mouth began to open. Water seeped inside. Stale tasting. Frozen. Terrifying to take in. He tried to close his mouth tight. But he couldn't control his own muscles. He was losing consciousness, too. He couldn't resist the urge to open his mouth even more. It was ready to take in water for air.

Tom tried to find the belief in himself. The will to complete the mission. The belief he needed to survive. But the pain in his chest, his throat—that constricting, all-consuming agony—only intensified. Water continued to penetrate his mouth. Water that he lacked the strength to expel.

Just a few more kicks . . .

He reached with his hand. His vision went dark. But he could still feel the flashlight in his grip. More important, his other hand felt the ledge. He'd discovered the little underwater alcove as a high school kid who loved to challenge anybody to try and dive deeper than he could.

I'm blacking out. . . . Hurry. . . .

Tom maneuvered his body under the ledge and felt about the alcove in the darkness. He touched something made of fabric. It brought him back. He gripped the slick duffel bag. The bag bunched up enough so that Tom could grab hold. He pulled, but the bag was stuck on something and wouldn't budge. He pulled again.

Breathe. That was all his brain wanted him to do. *Breathe.*

Tom opened his mouth wider. Water began to fill his lungs. He pulled once more. The duffel bag, which he'd last seen fifteen years ago, slid out from underneath the ledge. But the bag was heavy with the extra weights Tom had added. It dragged Tom deeper into the abyss. He kicked. He kicked with every bit of his remaining strength.

Tom imagined himself as a young man again. Going up, this time with the drugs. Not headed down. Doing what he should have done years ago. Kicking against the past. Using the power of his youthful muscles and strong lungs to make things right again. And he kept on kicking. Even though he knew he wasn't going to make it back to the surface.

Tom had no idea how deep under he was when the darkness about him turned to light. His eyes fell upon the most beautiful bright white light he'd ever seen. So intense and spectral that he thought it truly divine. Spiritual. It was warming, too. It pleaded for him. The light summoned him to it like a calling.

And Tom went. He sped toward that light, weightless and swift. He felt full of breath and life. He couldn't tell if he was going up or down. He couldn't feel anything but desire and peace.

His head broke the water's surface. Tom felt cold air hit his face like a thousand tiny needles puncturing his skin. Water jetted from his lungs. He took in a deep, life-restoring breath. He felt the slimy slickness of the duffel bag still in his grasp. Tom gazed up at that beautiful white light.

He marveled at the moon.

CHAPTER 82

The zipper had rusted shut. Tom had to tear the fabric away to get the duffel bag open. He shone his flashlight into the bag. Inside were a dozen, thirty-ounce, green vinyl dry bags. The roll-top closure feature ensured the best watertight seal possible. Tom had wanted to preserve not only the narcotics stuffed inside those bags but any fingerprint evidence as well.

Tom waved the flashlight back and forth. It was a signal to Roland that he'd left the water. Tom cradled the duffel bag in his arms as if he were carrying a wounded solider away from battle. He followed the overgrown path back to the Spot. The wind had picked up, and Tom was freezing. His body shook to warm him. But Tom's shivering was becoming more intense. Each wind gust was agony. It made him long for the water. For a moment at least, he would feel warmer under the water than he did on dry land.

Tom arrived at the Spot. He gently set the duffel bag onto the ground. His teeth knocked together in a frozen rhythm. His shivering would not abate. His clothes stiffened as though they were icing over. He spun around in a tight circle and trained the flashlight's beam onto the dark trees that surrounded him. The trees formed a clearing and defined the borders of the Spot.

Roland stepped out from behind a tree. Tom saw the gun still in his hand.

"Let's get this over with," Tom said.

"Yes. Let's. Are my drugs in the bag?"

"Look for yourself," said Tom.

Roland came over to the duffel bag. He peered inside. He inspected the contents and seemed pleased with what he found.

For a second, Roland was vulnerable to attack. Tom could have disarmed him. But Jill was still somewhere in the woods. Still in the clutches of that monster. No, he'd wait to see how this was going to play out. Then he'd make his move. Only when Tom was certain would he strike with violence of action.

"You did real good, Tom," Roland said.

"Where's my daughter?" Tom's body was shaking violently.

"She's here."

"I want to see her."

Roland whistled. Dee came out of hiding. He dragged Jill alongside him. She still had her blindfold on. Her mouth was still gagged. Wrists bound. Tom could see that she was shivering, too. But more out of fear than cold.

"Jilly-bean, it's me, sweetheart. It's Daddy. You just stay calm, honey. You stay calm and they're going to let you go."

Jill shook and struggled to get free. Tom could feel her desperation to get away, her desire to run to the sound of her father's voice. But Dee held her tight. Her legs kicked at the air as though she were pedaling an invisible bicycle.

"I walk out of here with my daughter," Tom said. "You've got my word that I'll stay quiet about the drugs."

Roland looked over at Dee. "Take it off," he said.

Dee removed Jill's blindfold but still kept her gagged. He held Jill locked in his massive arm like a vise.

"What are you doing?" Tom said. "Now she knows it was you, Boyd. She knows you kidnapped her." But Tom had anticipated it would come to this. Roland had had another plan all along.

Roland distanced himself a few paces from Tom. The gun was steady in Roland's hand. Moonlight fell on Dee's bloated face. The man had one arm wrapped around Jill, and Tom could see the glint cast off by his massive ring. Dee's other hand held a gun pointed at Jill's head.

"Get on your knees, Tom," Roland said.

"What are you doing, Roland?"

"Get on your knees now, Tom. Or Frankie will shoot your daughter."

Jill let out a muffled cry. She struggled again to get free. Dee pressed the gun barrel against Jill's temple. Tom sank to his knees, as though praying to the duffel bag that lay in front of him.

"This is the scene of a double homicide. A murder-suicide, to be exact. You killed Lindsey Wells. You couldn't let Jill live, because the scars of what you've done will damage her forever. No, you decided she'd be better off dead. It'll be easier for her that way."

Tom heard Jill's muffled shriek again.

Roland circled out of Tom's direct line of sight. Tom kept his eyes focused forward and locked on Jill. He didn't turn his head to see where Roland had moved. Instead, he listened to Roland's footsteps. Roland was standing to his right. He assumed Roland was pointing his gun at Tom's head. It made sense. Murder-suicide. Roland would shoot Tom in the side of his head. Then he'd shoot Jill.

Tom kept his eyes locked forward. He focused only on

Jill. He looked into her eyes. Even in the dark he could see they were wide with fear, like two black moons against a pale white sky. Those eyes were filled with tears. She struggled again to get free. But Dee pressed the gun barrel to her head until she stopped fighting.

Jill went limp. Fainted, perhaps. Dee kept her propped up like a doll.

"Sorry it came down to this, Tom. But it's the cleanest way. You're a family man. You can understand. I have to do this for my family. I can't give up on my boy."

Tom heard the emotion in Roland's voice. A weakness in his resolve, perhaps.

"Did Mitchell kill Lindsey? You want to pin this on me, is that it?"

"Kids can make stupid mistakes," Roland said. "You and I both know that."

"Roland, you don't have to do this. There's another way. We can come up with something."

Silence.

Tom's heart pounded in his chest. Jill had come back to her senses and was struggling again. But Dee held her fast.

Roland spoke. "There's no other way, Tom. This cleans it all up. Nobody will investigate anything now. It'll all fall on you. You're the guy running the sexting ring. You killed Lindsey to silence a witness. You realized all the lives you ruined. You took decisive action."

"The angle of your shot won't be right," Tom said. "Forensics will pick up on that."

"Won't happen. I know where to hit you. But if it isn't, I've got the connections to make questions go away."

"What about the gun? Where'd I get it? Did you think of that?"

"You stole it. Stole it from me, in fact. When you broke into my house. The police report's already been filed."

"Why wouldn't I use my own gun?"

Roland laughed. "You know, I thought you'd have one, being a SEAL and all. But we looked. When you were at Marvin's funeral, Frank searched all through your house. He found the knife and put that where the police would find it. But no gun to be found."

"That's where you're wrong, Roland—"

"Good-bye, Tom. I really am sorry it came to this."

"I do have a gun." Tom fell sideways. In a single motion, he reached behind his back and pulled a gun from the waistband of his sodden jeans. The gun was remarkably well preserved, even though it had lain hidden beneath the water for fifteen years. For fifteen years, the gun had been sealed inside a waterproof dry bag. Its only companion was a stash of drugs that a young Tom Hawkins couldn't allow to get wet and ruined.

The gun was a Beretta M9. An army private named Kip Lange had used it during a robbery gone bad. It had been fired only twice. On his way back to the Spot, Tom had checked the gun over for corrosion, to see if it still had a chance of firing. The bullets, four in total, were dry and lodged inside the magazine. Tom believed the gun would fire. But he didn't have any proof. Just as Rainy believed in his innocence but lacked the proof. Just as Jill believed in her father enough to trust him again. Tom *believed* the gun would fire.

And so he pulled the trigger as he fell. There was a flash. An explosion and burst of light followed. The recoil from the thrust as the bullet dislodged from the barrel.

There was his proof.

The first bullet slammed into Roland's shoulder. The second shot hit him in the leg. Roland fell to the ground with a thud.

Frank Dee did exactly what Tom expected of him. He acted to remove the immediate threat. Dee pulled his gun away from Jill and pointed the weapon at Tom. Tom fired two quick shots before Dee got off one.

The first bullet hit Dee in his firing hand. Dee's gun fell to the ground as a splash of blood sprayed out from the fresh wound like a burst of red fireworks. Tom's second shot could have been a kill shot. He had the time and skill to take aim and hit the target. But killing was in his past. So the bullet that could have flattened Dee's skull instead tore through the man's abdomen. Blood spurted from that hole as well. Dee fell backward to the ground.

Jill sprinted to her father as Dee was falling. Dee landed on the ground, groaning and clutching at his wounds. Tom doubted he'd hit any vital organs. Dee would live. Roland would live, too.

Killing was in his past.

Jill stumbled as she ran. Tom got to his feet and wrapped his daughter in his frozen arms. He removed the gag covering her mouth and unbound her wrists. She was hyperventilating. Couldn't speak. She clutched Tom like a life preserver that she couldn't grip tightly enough.

Tom went over to Roland, who was still on the ground. He dropped the Beretta into the duffel bag, then retrieved Roland's gun, which had fallen nearby. He stared down at Roland, who was writhing in pain and covered in blood and dirt. He heard Dee groaning, too. Both threats were neutralized.

Jill kept clutched to her father's waist. She was shivering. But he was hot with adrenaline.

"If all you wanted were the drugs, why didn't you

make any demands?" Tom said to Roland. His speech came out rapid and breathless. "Why'd you frame me for having an affair with Lindsey? Why make it look like I was running a sexting ring, but never try to blackmail me into giving up where I hid them? It doesn't make sense. I need to know why you did it."

"Wouldn't you . . . like to know . . ." Roland's words came out in spurts. He licked at his shivering lips to wet them. His breathing, labored and heavy, accentuated the rise and fall of his heaving chest.

"Yeah, I get it. You've got people who do it for you," Tom said, kneeling beside Roland. "You've got Cortland. But my question is why?" Tom dug the barrel of the gun into the bloody mess he made of Roland's shoulder. Roland shrieked out in pain.

"It wasn't me!" he yelled. "I didn't do it."

"Bullshit," Tom said, using the barrel to poke around for the actual bullet hole.

"I swear . . . it wasn't me. . . . I didn't set you up. . . ."

Tom heard footsteps approach.

"Tom? Are you there? Tom?"

Tom looked in the direction of the voice. He saw a flashlight beam dance in the darkness. A figure emerged from the path that led to the Spot. Moonlight helped Tom to see the woman who had spoken. The voice that had come from the woods.

Adriana Boyd.

CHAPTER 83

"Adriana, what are you doing here?"

"Oh, Tom," Adriana said, racing over to him. She put a hand on his shoulder. "I found out everything. Mitchell told me everything. That's how I knew you were here."

Tom stood and pulled Jill up with him. "What's going on, Adriana?"

"Roland is the one who framed you," Adriana said. "Roland's been framing people for sex crimes for years. I didn't want to believe it. But the FBI came to arrest Mitchell. He confessed to everything."

Tom kept Jill close beside him. "Are the police on their way?"

"Yes," Adriana said. "They're coming."

Adriana circled the chaos about them with her flashlight beam. She shone her light on the opened duffel bag.

"What's going on?" Adriana said. "What's in the bag?"

"That's what Roland is after. It's millions of dollars worth of heroin that I smuggled out of Germany."

"You?"

"Kelly and Kip Lange stole the drugs. Kelly used me as a mule. Roland orchestrated the whole heist, but Kelly never knew Roland was the man behind the scenes."

"I see. . . ."

Adriana strolled over to Frank Dee. Dee writhed on the ground, clutching at his bleeding abdomen. Adriana picked up Dee's gun. She hefted it in her hands, pointed the gun at Dee's head, and pulled the trigger.

Dee's skull exploded in a spray of blood. Red droplets and fragments of bone lit by the moonlight fell to the ground like rain.

"Adriana!" Tom shouted. "What are you doing?"

Adriana turned and pointed Dee's gun at Tom.

"Put your gun down, Tom," she said, her voice calm and eerily detached. "This doesn't concern you. But it will if you don't toss me that gun."

Jill clung tightly to her father. Tom tossed his weapon at Adriana's feet. He didn't set the safety, hoping the gun might accidentally discharge and startle Adriana. It would be enough for him to gain the advantage. To Tom's displeasure, the gun landed with a wholly unsatisfying thud.

"Walk away. Stand over there." Adriana motioned for Tom and Jill to move toward the quarry's edge. She had the gun, so Tom followed her rules.

Adriana walked over to Roland as calmly as she had approached the now very dead Frank Dee. She stood over her injured husband. Tom and Jill huddled together only a few feet from where Roland lay. Adriana had smartly positioned herself so that Tom and Jill stood directly in front of her, with Roland in the middle. She'd be able to get off a shot quicker than Tom and Jill could get to the trees.

But the woods weren't their only escape option.

Tom took a small step backward.

"Roland," Adriana said, poking at Roland with her feet. "Are those drugs?"

"Adriana, help me. . . ."

"You're dealing drugs, too? On top of destroying innocent people's lives, you're also a drug dealer?"

"Please . . . Adriana . . . help. . . ."

"I didn't frame Tom because of greed. I did it to save our son," Adriana said, the tone of her voice pure venom.

"You framed me?" Tom said incredulously. "It wasn't Roland? It was you?"

Adriana seemed to forget about her husband for a moment. "Tom, dear Tom . . . I'm truly sorry. I can't tell you how sorry I am."

"Why?"

"To protect my family. To save my son. Someone had to take the fall. You."

Tom was shivering. He held Jill close to him for warmth. Tom wanted to keep Adriana talking, buy himself time. He made Jill take another small step backward.

"But why frame me?"

"You fit the suit," Adriana said. "You worked with girls. You've been the soccer coach for years. You're handsome. Girls are attracted to you. It was believable. Simple as that. I knew eventually the police would come after Mitchell. And eventually they did."

"You did this all just to protect your son? He's a criminal. You'd destroy my life to save his?"

"I already lost one son. I couldn't just stand idle and watch Mitchell throw his life away. But before you judge me," Adriana said, "ask yourself this. How far would you go to save your daughter?"

Putting all the pressure she could manage on the gas pedal, Rainy couldn't make her sedan go a mile faster. The lone red strobe light on the roof of her car warned what little traffic she encountered on the quiet streets of Shilo to stay out of her way. Carter made sure he had the GPS coordinates entered right. They didn't trust Mitchell Boyd to give them directions. But the closer they got, the more it seemed that Mitchell had told them the truth. Mitchell had insisted his mother would be at this place called the Spot, and his father, too. She had to believe that Tom and Jill would be there as well. If Mitchell told the truth about one thing, he was confessing to it all.

Rainy's police radio crackled. Carter replied to the state police inquiry with their current location.

"ETA is about five minutes," Carter said to Rainy.

"That might be five minutes too late," Rainy said.

Roland groaned.

"Secrets . . . ," Adriana said, looking down at him. "We kept so many secrets. I guess both Roland and I did what we believed was best to protect what we had. We knew the same horrible truth about our son but didn't tell each other. Instead, we tried to fix it." Adriana pointed Dee's gun at Roland's head.

"Adriana, what are you doing?" Tom cried.

"You disgust me," Adriana said to Roland. "I did everything I could to save our son. And you? You're dealing in the same crap that killed my Stephen. Were you just going to peddle this garbage to somebody else's kid? You're a callous, sick man, and the reason Stephen is dead."

"Adriana . . . help. . . ."

"Did my son murder Lindsey Wells? Is my Mitchell a killer?"

"No . . . no . . . Lindsey was alive when Mitchell

brought her to me," Roland said, struggling to speak. "But she had to die. You understand. To save our son, she had to die."

"You killed her?" Adriana asked.

"No. It was Dee. I had Dee kill her. Adriana, please . . . we can fix things."

"Nothing can be fixed," Adriana said. "But maybe I can start over." She knelt down, placing the barrel of Dee's gun inches from Roland's head.

"Good-bye, Roland," she said.

Adriana pulled the trigger.

CHAPTER 84

Adriana stood from her crouched position quicker than Tom anticipated. Even so, he was ready to act. He'd been whispering in Jill's ear while Adriana kept herself occupied with Roland. Jill assured him she was ready. She squeezed Tom's hand with a strength he didn't realize his daughter possessed.

Adriana raised her gun higher. Her face, savage with a gruesome covering of blood splatter, contorted into a vicious snarl.

"I'm sorry, Tom. I'm going to have to disappear. I don't see any other way." She aimed the weapon at Jill.

Tom shoved Jill backward, hard as he could, coiling and uncoiling his hips to enhance his leverage. Jill's feet lifted off the ground. Tom prayed they had taken enough backward steps that he could shove her far enough out to clear the railroad ties below. He dove to his right at the same instant Adriana fired her shot. Tom heard the bullet slice through the air, then a loud splash. Tom rolled twice, getting closer to Adriana with each revolution.

Please . . . please be all right, he thought.

Another shot rang out. Then another. *Pop! Pop!* Tom rolled again and, in a single motion, sprang back to his feet, within striking distance of his target. Tom didn't attack right away. He couldn't make his decisive move until he knew for certain Jill was safe.

The delay gave Adriana precious seconds to get herself reoriented. She aimed the gun point-blank at Tom's chest.

Finally, Tom heard what he'd been waiting for.

"Green! Green!"

Jill's songbird voice echoed off the quarry walls and filled Tom's heart. He lunged at Adriana, clutching her in his arms before she could get off a third shot. They grappled together, spinning around several times, as though in a frenzied dance. Tom lost his grip on Adriana's arm. He felt the gun barrel digging into his abdomen. Tom somehow maneuvered them close to the edge of the quarry. He kept hold of Adriana as he fell backward. They tumbled over the lip of the quarry's steep cliff with their arms wrapped tightly around each other.

Time slowed. Tom sensed himself floating above the water. The darkness below appeared infinite, and their bodies felt weightless. The fall shouldn't have taken Tom by surprise, but it did. A ripping wind howled in his ears as he plummeted downward, shattering the momentary stillness. As Tom fell, he heard Adriana's loud screams puncturing the night, and the explosion of a gun.

Rainy reached the path before the others. She sprinted ahead of Carter, who didn't have nearly enough leg strength to keep pace. Off in the distance, Rainy heard the sound of sirens, screeching as though the whole town of Shilo were on fire. She could hear cars pulling to a quick stop, doors opening, then slamming shut. She heard the sputter of radios crackling as more sirens arrived. She pushed ahead, sprinting at full speed with her gun drawn. She felt dizzy with adrenaline. Her thoughts were spinning.

Why had Adriana left Mitchell? Why did Roland bring Tom to the Spot? Where was Lindsey Wells?

Rainy broke free of the woods and stumbled into the clearing. It was just as Mitchell had described. She looked around and saw two bodies on the ground. She heard a gunshot, followed by a splash.

Still falling, Tom heard Jill cry out from somewhere in the water below, "Dad! No!"

The railroad ties, the ones Tom had prayed Jill would clear, emerged from the darkness like a predator about to strike. Tom struck the water and twisted his body to avoid a direct hit. He heard the sickening crack of bone, felt Adriana's skull crack against his own. Blood splatter sprayed his face like seawater called up from a fast-moving boat.

Tom floated in the water, clutching Adriana's limp body in his arms. It wasn't just the cold water making it hard for Tom to breathe. No, something else was wrong. A spot on his abdomen felt exquisitely sore to the touch.

Tom suddenly knew why he'd begun to sink. Water filled his nostrils. He gagged to clear his airway, but the pain felt worse than drowning.

Tom's body bobbed vertically in the water, as if he were climbing the rungs of an invisible ladder. His mouth angled for each struggling breath. He let the water fill him up and pull him under.

His muscles were tiring. *Any moment now.*

Drowning wasn't anything like the movies or TV portrayed it to be. It was far more terrifying, because no overt signals, like splashing or frantic hand waving, warned of any peril. Drowning, Tom knew, was a far more cerebral experience. But no matter how people imagined a drowning victim suffered, in the end everyone died the same way: the heart simply stopped beating.

Tom's limp body sank into a free fall. He made several hard kicks, fighting to surface against the decreased mobility of his denim jeans. His lungs were afire. His chest felt as if it were being squeezed by a bone-crunching weight.

He felt a sudden pull on his shirt. His whole body jerked upward. His body jerked again. Instead of sinking, Tom felt himself starting to rise. Tom broke the surface, the fire in his burning lungs extinguished with that first blessed breath of air. He began to tread water. He could feel the blood rushing out the bullet hole in his stomach. He saw Jill treading water beside to him. She was holding on to his shirt. A body, floating facedown nearby, had to be Adriana. He could see the depression where the railroad tie had crushed her skull.

Tom felt another tug on his shirt, followed by the sensation of being pulled. Jill was swimming for the shoreline. And she was dragging him with her.

Tom felt the rocks and sand of the shoreline pricking at his neck and arms. He could see the moon and the stars above him. The world was spinning. The last words Tom heard before he lost consciousness repeated in his fast-fading thoughts.

"Don't you die on me, Dad! Don't you dare die!"

CHAPTER 85

Tom struggled to open his eyes. When he did, he was looking up at Rainy's smiling face.

"Are you an angel?" he managed to croak.

"No. I'm not."

"Is this heaven?" he asked.

"No. It's St. Elizabeth's Hospital," Rainy said.

"I don't believe you. No, I'm sure this is heaven."

"Have you ever been kissed by an angel?" Rainy asked.

Tom felt the warmth of her lips pressing gently against his eyelids, then brushing over his mouth. "I think I can get used to heaven."

"Well, heaven can wait."

"Warren Beatty," Tom said.

"What?"

"That's my favorite Warren Beatty movie. *Heaven Can Wait.*"

"I see."

"We can watch it together."

Tom tried to sit up and felt a sharp pain in his gut.

"Not time for that just yet," Rainy said.

He lifted up his hands, expecting at least one of them to be handcuffed. "I'm still a free man?" he asked.

"You're a lucky man," Rainy said. "The bullet hit you in the side, not the stomach. But it was touch and go for a while there."

"Rainy . . . what happened . . . ?"

"What happened is the Boyd family is not going to make the cover of *Parents* magazine, that's for sure."

"How did Adriana frame me? Why?"

"A lot's happened since you've been out of pocket."

"How long?"

"Three days. Going on four."

"Jill?"

"She's fine. She's with Lindsey Wells."

Tom's expression went blank, and his jaw fell slack.

"But I thought Lindsey was dead. The police found her body in the woods. That's why they were coming to arrest me."

"They found her blood-soaked jacket in the woods and your knife nearby. Frank Dee was supposed to kill her but decided to keep her locked up in the icehouse. Apparently, he'd been . . . assaulting her. Instead of killing Lindsey, he cut her hand and soiled her jacket. I guess he planned on absconding with her, but Adriana didn't give him that choice. One of the Willards Woods employees noticed the lock on the icehouse door wasn't the one she put there. She called the police, and they found Lindsey alive. Traumatized, but at least she's alive."

"Thank God," Tom breathed. "What happened? Did Mitchell try to kill her?"

"He did," Rainy said. "Lindsey called Tanner and told him about the flash drive Jill gave her. Tanner called Mitchell. They hatched a plan to get the flash drive back.

Mitchell planned to kill Lindsey. Only he couldn't do it. He choked her until she passed out. He put her in the trunk of his car and drove her back to his house. Then he went to Daddy. He told Roland everything, about his illegal image business and what he did to Lindsey. Only, he didn't tell Dad that Mommy already knew about his sexting ring and told him to shut it down."

"Sexting ring?"

"This kid was pretty entrepreneurial. He contracted a bunch of his friends and strangers he met over the Internet. These kids coerced their girlfriends into taking naked pictures of themselves. Mitchell paid them for any pictures they got, then sold them on the Internet for a profit. He basically tapped into an underserviced, but highly desired fetish market. The kid was making a fortune."

"Tanner Farnsworth?"

"He was one of them. So was Gretchen Stiller."

"A girl was coercing her own girlfriends into taking these pictures?"

"Sexting is anybody's game."

"So Mitchell knew his mom was framing me?"

"He did. This family kept a lot of secrets from each other."

"I saw Adriana kill Dee and Roland. It's like she just snapped."

"Well, Adriana wasn't who she pretended to be," Rainy said, stroking Tom's hair. "This woman nearly destroyed your life."

"How? She's not a computer wizard."

"No," Rainy said. "But following your tip about Cortland, we made several arrests. One of the people we arrested, a guy named Aaron Donovan, turned state's witness. He told us everything."

"Everything?"

"Adriana seduced Simon Cortland. She knew about the stock scheme Cortland concocted with her husband. She knew he had the ability to destroy people's reputations. Apparently, Adriana was curious about Mitchell's growing wealth. She seduced Cortland and had him install spyware on Mitchell's computers. That's how she found out Mitchell had been running a sexting ring."

"So Adriana got Cortland to frame me for Mitchell's crimes."

"Simon Cortland hijacked Lindsey's wireless network and wrote the Tumblr blog posts about her supposed affair with you. He was 'Fidelius Charm' and sent you the text messages of one of Mitchell's many victims. Marvin was right."

"How so?"

"Adriana came up with the idea to make it look like you were sleeping with one of your players."

"Why?"

"She wanted to make you look like a sexual predator. A jury would be more willing to believe you were running a sophisticated sexting ring that way. According to Donovan, Adriana was paranoid about the plan falling apart. That's why she posted your bail. She wanted to keep the suspicion as far away from herself and Mitchell as possible. Who would think that the woman who bailed you out of jail was also the one who put you there?"

"So Cortland put that Leterg program on my computer? Faked those bank accounts, too?"

"He did," Rainy said. "Only Cortland couldn't easily get to your home computer, especially after you installed the alarm, which is why he used your work computer instead."

"Grateful for that."

"Me too. The failed battery was the turning point for me."

"And James Mann?" asked Tom. He kept his eyes closed, picturing Mitchell Boyd and this Aaron Donovan telling Rainy their stories.

"Simon was opportunistic," Rainy said. "He knew about PrimaMed's pending drug approval. His firm wrote the press releases. He already had his stock scheme going with Roland Boyd. 'Two for the price of one,' is how Donovan put it. He'd bring you down and make a mint with Boyd in the process."

"Then who killed Marvin?"

"Frank Dee," Rainy said. "Sadly, Lindsey Wells witnessed it all."

"Why?"

"Because Marvin figured out the connection between Cortland and Boyd. That's why Boyd had Marvin killed."

Tom closed his eyes tightly and tried to swallow his anger. "Boyd got what he deserved," he said. "Dee too."

"And so did you," Rainy said. "You're now an innocent man."

"In less than twenty-four hours I went from being a rapist, child pornographer, and drug smuggler to almost being in the clear," Tom said with some amazement.

"What do you mean, almost?"

"I did ignite a fireball in front of a bunch of police cars," Tom said.

"Well, the good news is I've had a chat with Sergeant Brendan Murphy. He's sorry about how he treated you. I think you might find you're in less hot water than you'd expect. My guess is you'll get off with probation. No jail time."

"But I'll still need a lawyer."

"I'd say that'd be a smart move."

"Do me a favor," Tom said.

"Anything."

"Call Amanda Pressman. She's the only attorney I'll ever use."

EPILOGUE

The Shilo High School parking lot was crowded with runners. There were a thousand registered participants, all of whom were stretching in preparation for the first annual Marvin Pressman 5k Memorial Run for Teen Safety. Organizing the event in such a compressed timeline would have been too massive an undertaking for Tom without Rainy's guidance and expertise. In fact, it was Rainy who had inspired Tom to organize Marvin's run. She participated in the Melanie Smyth Memorial Run, held each year in Newton, and had been more than happy to help Tom pull this race together.

Media coverage of the shocking events that had occurred in the sleepy hamlet of Shilo, New Hampshire not only helped to spread the word about Marvin's run, but also proved instrumental in securing numerous event sponsors. Donations flooded in to the scholarship fund established in Marvin's name.

Shilo's main road, equipped with a lone traffic light, couldn't accommodate the large crowds expected. School buses were brought in to shuttle runners from the parking lot at Silver Lake to the high school where the race would commence. Runners were asked to raise money through individual sponsorships, with a suggested minimum of one hundred dollars to enter the race. Most of the entrants doubled that.

One runner in particular raised more than anybody else—by a factor of ten. Accordingly, his picture was featured on a poster that hung on a telephone pole near the starting line. Out-of-towners who passed by that poster glanced at the top fundraiser's photograph, not recognizing his name. But everyone from Shilo knew Sergeant Brendan Murphy. Murphy took some responsibility for what happened to Tom, though his aggressive fundraising effort was the most he could manage by way of an apology.

Seven months had passed since Jill had dragged Tom's limp and bleeding body to the shoreline of the quarry. Although he was fully prepared to accept punishment for his crimes, Tom never anticipated how it would all play out.

He'd hired Marvin's sister, Amanda, to be his attorney. Amanda was more than happy to take on his case. It was, she said, what Marvin would have wanted. The statute of limitations for Tom's narcotics related crimes was long past. The firebomb he detonated, several counts of assault, grand theft auto for stealing Sullivan's car, and resisting arrest were not.

The media portrayed Tom as a folk hero. They viewed him as a man committed to protecting his family at all costs. It didn't hurt Tom's profile that in the process he had helped to bring down a child pornography ring, along with a financial scheme that had ruined hundreds of lives. But Tom didn't care how he was viewed by the media or by the masses. The threats against his daughter had been neutralized. That was most important to him. He was ready to pay the penalty for what he had done. However, the DA accepted Amanda's deal without reservation. Tom would plead guilty to criminal mischief, a Class A Misdemeanor, and in exchange he would get probation instead of jail time.

The spring sun was warm and bright in the perfect late morning sky. Tom noticed Lindsey Wells stretching to get ready for her run. She caught Tom's eye, gave him a slight wave and what he interpreted to be a sad smile. He knew she had a long road ahead of her, but there were signs of her continued improvement. She was seeing her friends now and started working out again in part to train for this race. According to Jill, there were some nights that Lindsey didn't cry herself to sleep.

A wave of high profile arrests followed the shooting at the Spot in Willards Woods. Simon Cortland, along with several of his associates, were charged with numerous felony crimes pertaining to their stock scheme and vicious online reputation attacks. In the process, a dozen innocent people framed by Cortland were cleared of their crimes. A dozen more cases were under active review. Gill Sullivan was in prison, awaiting trial on racketeering charges. Roland Boyd's financial empire crumbled upon his death.

Mitchell Boyd was in custody, charged with two counts of attempted murder, and numerous other charges pertaining to his sexting ring. All of Mitchell's suppliers were arrested and they too were awaiting trial. Mitchell was being tried as an adult. He didn't make bail, but from prison he did send Jill a letter. In it, he expressed real feelings for her. He didn't view her in the same way as the other girls in his operation, and went on to say he had never sold her pictures. Not once. Not to anybody.

"Maybe he didn't," Jill had said to Tom after she read the letter. "But I guess I can never know for certain if that's true."

Tom waded through the crowd of appreciative racers on his way to the makeshift stage that had been erected at the edge of the parking lot abutting the soccer field. Soon, from that stage, Tom would signal the start of the race. Rainy and Jill were waiting for Tom at the front of the stage. Tom choked up seeing them standing close together, talking freely, sharing several laughs. Rainy and Jill had formed their own bond and Tom couldn't have been happier.

"Dad!" Jill yelled, waving frantically as he neared. "This is amazing! Can you believe all the runners?"

"Amazing," Tom agreed, shouting to be heard above the din of the crowd, then giving Jill a warm embrace.

Rainy leaned in and gave Tom an affectionate kiss hello.

Jill smiled, winked and gave Tom the "thumbs up" sign. She was both teasing him and encouraging him at the same time, having already suggested that perhaps he should go ring shopping.

"Too soon," Tom had said, not admitting that he had already checked out a couple jewelry stores and was seriously contemplating making a purchase.

Tom knew that a relationship begun under such extreme circumstances had a low probability for success, but then again, there was nothing probable about how Tom and Rainy became a couple.

A light breeze filled the air with the scent of blooming flowers, and the freshness of a new day. Tom looked at Jill and smiled.

"What?"

"Have I told you how proud I am of you?" he asked.

"Just about everyday," Jill said.

"I guess I can't tell you enough," he said.

Jill held her father's affectionate gaze, and smiled broadly.

"I'm proud of you too, Dad," Jill said. "For everything." Here, she paused. "Say, is it true that they offered you your job back?" Jill asked him. "Lauren Grass said she heard that from her mom."

Tom nodded. "They did, but I declined."

Jill looked surprised. "Really? Why?"

"I keep getting offers to work as a private security contractor. It's more lucrative than coaching, even though I miss it and the kids. In the long run it'll be better for both of us. Trust me."

Jill looked at her father, emotion welling in her eyes. "I do trust you, Dad," she said. "More than anything."

Rainy answered a page she received from her handheld Motorola Talkabout. "We're ready to start the race," she said to Tom after clicking off. "The last bus has just finished unloading."

"Who is going to give the go signal?" Jill asked.

"I am," Tom said.

Tom got up on the stage and spoke into the microphone.

"Excuse me," he said. "Hello runners. May I have your attention please."

It was hard for them to hear Tom over the crowd noise. Runners continued to talk. Then, using just two fingers, Tom whistled loud enough to get everyone's attention.

In this chilling, brilliantly plotted new thriller, Daniel Palmer explores the terrifying aftermath of a good man's bad decision, the flip side of identity theft, and the lengths some will go to save a life—or destroy one . . .

The future has never looked brighter for Boston couple John Bodine and Ruby Dawes. John's online gaming business is growing, Ruby is pursuing her dream career, and they're talking about starting a family.

Then Ruby receives a life-changing diagnosis, and their cut-rate insurance won't cover the treatment she desperately needs. Faced with a ticking clock, John makes a risky move: he steals a customer's identity and files a false claim for Ruby's medication.

The plan works perfectly—until the customer in question contacts John with a startling proposition. If John an Ruby agree to play a little game he's devised, he won't report their fraud. The rules of 'Criminal' are simple: commit *real* crimes. Fail in your assigned tasks, and there will be deadly consequences.

John assumes it's a sick joke, until people start dying. With each round, the stakes are escalating, the crimes getting more twisted. John and Ruby can't disappear—and they can't go to the police. Their only option is to keep playing, all the while trying to outwit a psychopath who has no intention of letting them leave this game alive. . . .

Please turn the page for an exciting sneak peek of Daniel Palmer's

STOLEN

coming next month wherever hardcover books are sold!

L et me tell you how it feels to learn that your wife is going to die. It's like you've swallowed something bitter, something permanently stuck in your throat. In an instant, the future you've been planning together is gone. The sadness is all-consuming. Trust me, a heavy heart is more than an expression. You try to act strong, sound reassuring. You glom on to statistics, study the odds like a Vegas bookmaker. You say things like, "We can beat this thing. We're going to be the twenty-five percent who make it."

At night, darker thoughts sneak past your mental defenses. You imagine your life after the inevitable. You think about all the holidays and birthdays that will come and go without your beloved. You cry and hate yourself because you're not the one who is dying.

My name is John Bodine. I'm twenty-nine years old. I'm married to the love of my life. And no matter what it takes, or how far I have to go, I'm not going to let her die.

Eight weeks earlier . . .

I'm like a dog. Soon as I heard the sound of keys jangling in the front door lock, my heartbeat kicked into overdrive. I got all excited. Five years of marriage hadn't dulled my pleasure. The sound of keys meant Ruby was home. I glanced at the electric stove, the only working clock within eyesight. Twenty minutes until midnight. Poor Ruby. Poor sweet, tired—no, make that utterly exhausted—Ruby. God, I was glad she was home.

I greeted Ruby in the cramped entranceway of our one-bedroom apartment with a mug of mint tea at the ready. Ruby's strawberry blond hair, cut stylishly and kept shoulder length, glistened from a light nighttime rain. She shivered off the cold and inhaled the sweet mint smell emanating from the steaming mug.

"My hero to the rescue," Ruby said.

Ruby cupped the mug in both hands and let the aroma warm her bones. She kissed me sweetly on the lips. Her eyes, the color of wan sapphires, flashed her desire for a more prolonged kiss with a lot less clothing. But her shoulders, sagging from the weight of her backpack stuffed with textbooks, told me otherwise. For an acupuncture and herbal medicine school that taught the healing arts, Ruby's education took an extraordinary physical and mental toll.

"Hold this," Ruby said. She handed me back the mug of tea, slung her backpack from off her shoulder, and then knelt down to unzip it on the floor. From within she pulled out a brown paper bag. The second I saw it, my eyes went wide.

"You went to Sinful Squares?" I asked, feeling my mouth already watering.

"That's why I left so early this morning. I'm sure you forgot, but it's your mom's birthday on Thursday. I mailed her a dozen of her favorite brownies, and it just so happens that I knew they were your favorite, too. Don't eat them all at once."

She gave me a soft kiss on the lips.

"Ruby, Sinful Squares is way out of your way. You didn't have to do that."

"Well, I love you, and I love your mom. So, happy birthday to us all."

We shared a brownie. Heaven.

"Want to watch TV?" Ruby asked.

"You know it."

We didn't have cable, way too expensive on our limited budget. We had cut back on most all expenses now that we had tuition to pay. But I like to please Ruby, so I rigged Hulu up to our thirty-inch television. Now she could watch her favorite shows anytime she wanted. Ruby didn't have much time for TV, but after a late-night study session, it helped her clear the brain, decompress.

As I expected, Ruby wanted to watch her favorite HGTV show, *Designed to Sell*. She sank deeply into the soft sofa cushions, almost vanishing between them. I always watched with Ruby, even though I'm an ESPN sort of guy, and this episode, one we'd never seen, featured a three-million-dollar Beverly Hills mansion in desperate need of a makeover before going on the market. Ruby spread her long and beautifully toned legs across my lap.

"Wait," I said, after watching a minute of the show. "The challenge is to redesign an enormous mansion with a few-thousand-dollar budget?"

"Yeah. Cool, isn't it?" Ruby said. Her voice drifted off, as if she was already in a dream.

"Well, it seems a little bit odd," I said. "I mean, they live in a mansion. You'd think they could spend a bit more, is all."

"That's not the point of the show. The point is to teach people how to do more with less."

"So if our one-bedroom got featured, they'd redesign it for what? Fifty bucks?"

Ruby dug her toes between my ribs until I cried out in mock pain. Actually, it felt pretty darn good.

"The show doesn't use a sliding scale, darling. And besides, our place doesn't need to be redesigned. I like it just the way it is."

"Small," I said.

"I prefer to think of it as conducive to closeness."

"Oh, in that case . . ."

I changed position and kissed Ruby, long and deep. Ruby responded in kind as best she could, but tonight her romantic mood had the life span of a mayfly.

"Baby, I want to," Ruby said. Her voice sounded as sweet as the mint tea tasted on her lips.

"All right, then, let's go," I whispered between gentle kisses planted on her freckled cheeks.

"But I need you to quiz me."

I sat up.

"Quiz you?" I said. "Ruby, it's after midnight."

Ruby surprised me by breaking into song. "And we're gonna let it all hang out," she sang.

The melody was to the tune of one of our favorite Eric Clapton covers. Ruby held up a finger for me to see. That was her way of marking the musical reference as being worth one point in our long-standing game. A point could be earned if either of us completed a song lyric, tune required, from something the other had said. We didn't keep a running tally, because it was obvious Ruby possessed an insurmountable lead. Let's just say if *Jeopardy* devoted an entire board to trivia about music and bands, she'd clear it without giving the other contestants a chance to buzz.

Ruby got off the sofa to grab her schoolbooks.

As I waited, I ran my hands through my hair, half expecting to feel the long locks I had chopped off after the Labuche Kang tragedy. A lot about my appearance had changed in the aftermath of that day. My face still looked young but had weathered, with newly formed creases and crevices, which Ruby thought made me ruggedly handsome. My eyes had grown deeper set, too, and like mountain river streams, changed color with the day or my mood. Sometimes they were clear like a well-marked path, but at other times they'd cloud over, and Ruby would ask, "What are you thinking?" Ruby was the only person who could see through my haze, burrow into me, to get beyond the surface layers I allowed others see. After the shock, the therapy sessions, the black depression, it was Ruby who brought me back from the brink. She held the map to my soul.

Ruby returned with backpack in hand.

"You can't really be serious about wanting me to quiz you," I said. "How can your brain even function?"

"Remember when I said that I loved how small our place is?" Ruby asked.

"Yeah."

"I lied."

"Oh."

"Well, not entirely. I do like being close to you."

"We could be closer," I said with a wink.

"Come on, baby. Just a quick quiz tonight."

I pretended to have fallen asleep, and Ruby needled me again in the ribs, this time with her fingers.

"I'm up! I'm up!" I said, feigning alertness.

Ruby ruffled through her backpack, looking for her notes, but something else caught her eye. "Oh, I almost forgot," she said. "I went to the computer lab and made you something today."

"Moi?"

Ruby removed a single sheet of paper from a folder in her backpack. It was a logo for my online game, One World. I loved the overall design she made, but it was the *O* in the word *One* that literally took away my breath.

She had created three concentric circles. The outer circle she rendered to look like wood grain, the next circle was made to look like rock, another like water, and in the center was the earth. It was astoundingly beautiful. *Professional* didn't do it justice.

"Ruby, I'm speechless. I love it."

"I'm so glad. It took me a while, but I think it came out great. What's today's number?"

"One hundred twenty-three thousand registered players."

Ruby broke into a smile. "Forget acupuncture. You're taking us to Beverly Hills, baby!"

"Last I checked, mortgage companies aren't accepting future potential as a down payment on a mansion. I really need closer to a million registered players before I can start touting my rags-to-riches story."

"I believe in you, John. I know it's going to happen."

I made a "Who knows?" shrug.

With a hundred thousand registered players, I should be rolling in the dough. Only, I didn't charge people to play. I'd basically built FarmVille meets Minecraft. It's an eco-conscious game, which takes longer to build a loyal enough following to start charging a fee. Like a lot of game designers, I make my money selling virtual items that enhance the game play. After expenses, I cleared about fifty thousand dollars, most of which got reinvested back into the business. In addition to Ruby's tuition, we have other expenses to pay as well. Rent. Food. Bills. Insurance. All the usual suspects. Hence, no cable.

"I'm glad you like the logo," Ruby said.

"I don't just like it. I love it. It goes live tomorrow."

"Good. I'm going to get something to drink before we start. Want anything?"

"No," I said.

I watched her go. Hard not to. I felt like yelling out that I was the luckiest man alive, only Ruby didn't believe in luck.

A few years back, Ruby hung a vision board on our bedroom wall. The vision board was a three-foot-by-three-foot corkboard, covered with a purple silk cloth—for prosperity—and decorated with images and words that conveyed our shared desires. Ask and the universe will provide, at least that's what Ruby believed. I believe in relying on yourself to solve your own problems. The mountain has a cold and angry way of reinforcing that kind of thinking.

Still, Ruby pleaded with me to ask the universe to make One World a smash success. I thought it was silly at first, but I relented—Ruby's hard to refuse, especially when pleading—and so I tacked up the logo of a prominent gaming blog onto the vision board. A few weeks later, I got a five-star review. Did I think the universe had answered by wishes? No, not in the least. Coincidence? Sure. Now, that's something I can believe in. I have a degree in computer science from Boston University, so logic is the ruler of my world. Trusting in the universe is a heartwarming idea, but I'm a bigger believer in hard work, determination, and a sprinkle of talent.

A game designer needs to understand computers the way a general contractor must know all facets of building a house, which is why it took a team of people to put my game together, but now I manage the code and servers on my own. Anyway, the bloggers seemed to like the idea behind the game. Players are tasked with building the coolest, biggest, most awesome virtual world possible without pil-laging One World's limited resources. Oh, and you've got to do all this while battling marauding hordes of zombies, who come out only at night.

There was a time, not that long ago, I couldn't muster the energy to get out of bed. I just lay there, hearing Brooks's screams as he fell to his death. Dark years. Ruby plastered the vision board with every image of health and happiness she could find. Three weeks later, Ruby found a flyer for a local acupuncturist in the mail and urged me to give it a try. The results were so astounding that Ruby decided to quit her job as the in-house graphic designer for a finance company to concentrate on becoming an acupuncturist herself. I encouraged her to do it. We could squeak by on one income for a while. It's amazing how far a few judicious cuts can take you.

Ruby returned and got her study materials together, but I wasn't done trying to woo her into bed. I started rubbing the soles of her feet.

"Hmmmm," Ruby said. "That feels nice."

I removed Ruby's cotton socks and dug my thumbs gently against ten years of jogging calluses. Ruby cooed some more, and I kept on massaging. I thought about the number—one hundred twenty-three thousand registered players—and couldn't help but imagine how a million would alter our lives. I wondered if Ruby and I would start a family sooner than our current post-school thinking.

Brooks Hall would never have children, and I might. "Where's the fairness in that, dear universe?" I switched from the right foot to massage Ruby's left. My thumb traveled from the toes and finished at the heel. But my fingers brushed against something strange. A sensation that felt surprising to touch. I ran my thumb over the offending area again, and still again.

"Hey, the rest of my foot is getting jealous," Ruby said, shaking it.

I raised Ruby's leg and shifted position to get a better look at the underside of her foot.

"What is it?" Ruby asked. A touch of alarm seeped into her voice.

I went to the kitchen and grabbed the penlight flashlight I used to build or repair my computers. When I returned, Ruby was sitting on the floor cross-legged, examining the bottom of her foot. I got down on my knees and took a closer look with the penlight. Ruby's eyes were wide, dancing nervously. I knew she hated when I went silent on her.

"What's going on?" Ruby asked again.

"Have you seen this dark patchy area before?" I asked her. "Do you have any idea how long it's been there?"

"I'm not checking out the bottom of my foot every day, if that's what you're asking. John, you're scaring me."

"I don't like how this looks," I said.

I had reason to be concerned. Mountaineering exposed climbers like myself to a greater degree of ultraviolet radiation. I had studied up on the latest gear, lotions, and trends for delivering maximum sun protection. I had also learned to detect the signs and symptoms of skin cancer—asymmetrical growth, ragged edges, nonuniform coloration, and a large diameter. The oddly shaped mole on the underside of Ruby's foot, about the size of two pencil erasers, was far larger than the quarter-inch safety limit. What I didn't know, and what Ruby couldn't tell me, was if the area of concern had grown in size, and if so, how quickly it had evolved.

"John, you're really starting to freak me out," Ruby said, pulling her foot away from my lengthy and silent examination. "What are you thinking?"

I moved in close to Ruby, cupping her flushed cheek in my hands.

"I think we need to call a doctor, just to be safe," I said. I made sure my voice sounded soothing. "But I also think that everything is going to be just fine."

Ruby looked me in the eyes and strained to smile.

We've been married five years, and we dated for an equal amount of time.

She could always tell when I was lying.